My Lady Miriam and her entourage rushed back from the barred windows of the women's apartments on the second floor, squealing for effect. The tanks were so huge that the mirror-helmeted men watching from the turret hatches were nearly on a level with the upper story of the palace.

The Baron's soldiers had boasted that they were better men than the mercenaries if it ever came down to cases. The fear that the women had mimed from behind stone walls seemed real enough now to the soldiers whose bluster and assault rifles were insignificant against the iridium titans which entered the courtyard.

Even at idle speed, the tanks roared as their fans maintained the cushions of air that slid them over the ground. Three of the Baron's men dodged back through the palace doorway, their curses inaudible over the intake whine of the approaching vehicles.

They did not need to respect us. They were

THE TANK LORDS

BAEN BOOKS by DAVID DRAKE

Hammer's Slammers
The Tank Lords
Caught in the Crossfire (forthcoming)
The Butcher's Bill (forthcoming)

Independent Novels and Collections
Redliners
Starliner
Ranks of Bronze
Lacey and His Friends
Old Nathan
Mark II: The Military Dimension
All the Way to the Gallows

The General series:
(With S.M. Stirling)
The Forge
The Hammer
The Anvil
The Steel
The Sword
The Chosen

The Undesired Princess
and the Enchanted Bunny
(with L.Sprague de Camp)
Lest Darkness Fall and To Bring the Light
(with L. Sprague de Camp)
An Honorable Defense
(with Thomas T. Thomas
Enemy of My Enemy
(with Ben Ohlander)

THE TANK LORDS

DAVID DRAKE

BAEN

A Baen Books Original

Baen Publishing Enterprises
P.O. Box 1403
Riverdale, NY 10471

ISBN: 0-671-87794-1

Cover art by Larry Elmore

First printing, August 1997

Distributed by Simon & Schuster
1230 Avenue of the Americas
New York, NY 10020

Typeset by Windhaven Press, Auburn, NH
Printed in the United States of America

CONTENTS

Under the Hammer...1

Rolling Hot..25

Night March...257

Code-Name Feirefitz..279

The Tank Lords..317

Appendix...369

Afterword: We Happy Few.......................................387

Under the Hammer

"Think you're going to like killing, boy?" asked the old man on double crutches.

Rob Jenne turned from the streams of moving cargo to his unnoticed companion in the shade of the starship's hull. His own eyes were pale gray, suited like the dead-white skin to Burlage, whose ruddy sun could raise a blush but not a tan. When they adjusted, they took in the clerical collar which completed the other's costume. The smooth, black synthetic contrasted oddly with the coveralls and shirt of local weave. At that, the Curwinite's outfit was a cut above Rob's own, the same worksuit of Burlage sisal that he had worn as a quarryhand at home. Uniform issue would come soon.

At least, he hoped and prayed it would.

When the youth looked away after an embarrassed grin, the priest chuckled. "Another damned old fool, hey, boy? There were a few in your family, weren't there . . . the ones who'd quote the Book of the Way saying not to kill— and here you go off for a hired murderer. Right?" He laughed again, seeing he had the younger man's attention. "But that by itself wouldn't be so hard to take—you were

1

leaving your family anyways, weren't you, nobody really believes they'll keep close to their people after five years, ten years of star hopping. But your mates, though, the team you worked with . . . how did you explain to them why you were leaving a good job to go on contract? 'Via!'" the priest mimicked, his tones so close to those of Barney Larsen, the gang boss, that Rob started in surprise, "you get your coppy ass shot off, lad, and it'll serve you right for being a fool!"

"How do you know I signed for a mercenary?" Jenne asked, clenching his great, callused hands on the handle of his carry-all. It was everything he owned in the universe in which he no longer had a home. "And how'd you know about my Aunt Gudrun?"

"Haven't I seen a thousand of you?" the priest blazed back, his eyes like sparks glinting from the drill shaft as the sledge drove it deeper into the rock. "You're young and strong and bright enough to pass Alois Hammer's tests—you be proud of that, boy, few enough are fit for Hammer's Slammers. There you were, a man grown who'd read all the cop about mercenaries, believed most of it . . . more'n ever you did the Book of the Way, anyhow. Sure, I know. So you got some off-planet factor to send your papers in for you, for the sake of the bounty he'll get from the colonel if you make the grade—"

The priest caught Rob's blink of surprise. He chuckled again, a cruel, unpriestly sound, and said, "He told you it was for friendship? One a these days you'll learn what friendship counts, when you get an order that means the death of a friend—and you carry it out."

Rob stared at the priest in repulsion, the grizzled chin resting on interlaced fingers and the crutches under either armpit supporting most of his weight. "It's my life," the recruit said with sulky defiance. "Soon as they pick me up here, you can go back to living your own. 'Less you'd be willing to do that right now?"

"They'll come soon enough, boy," the older man said

in a milder voice. "Sure, you've been ridden by everybody you know . . . now that you're alone, here's a stranger riding you too. I don't mean it like I sound . . . wasn't born to the work, I guess. There's priests—and maybe the better ones—who'd say that signing on with mercenaries means so long a spiral down that maybe your soul won't come out of it in another life or another hundred. But I don't see it like that."

"Life's a forge, boy, and the purest metal comes from the hottest fire. When you've been under the hammer a few times, you'll find you've been beaten down to the real, no lies, no excuses. There'll be a time, then, when you got to look over the product . . . and if you don't like what you see, well, maybe there's time for change, too."

The priest turned his head to scan the half of the horizon not blocked by the bellied-down bulk of the starship. Ant columns of stevedores manhandled cargo from the ship's rollerway into horse and oxdrawn wagons in the foreground: like most frontier worlds, Burlage included, self-powered machinery was rare in the backcountry. Beyond the men and draft animals stretched the fields, studded frequently by orange-golden clumps of native vegetation.

"Nobody knows how little his life's worth till he's put it on the line a couple times," the old man said. "For nothing. Look at it here on Curwin—the seaboard taxed these uplands into revolt, then had to spend what they'd robbed and more to hire an armored regiment. So boys like you from—Scania? Felsen?—"

"Burlage, sir."

"Sure, a quarryman, should have known from your shoulders. You come in to shoot farmers for a gang of coastal moneymen you don't know and wouldn't like if you did." The priest paused, less for effect than to heave in a quick, angry breath that threatened his shirt buttons. "And maybe you'll die, too; if the Slammers were immortal, they wouldn't need recruits. But some that die will die like saints, boy, die martyrs of the Way, for no reason, for no reason . . ."

"Your ride's here, boy."

The suddenly emotionless words surprised Rob as much as a scream in a silent prayer would have. Hissing like a gun-studded dragon, a gray-metal combat car slid onto the landing field from the west. Light dust puffed from beneath it: although the flatbed trailer behind was supported on standard wheels, the armored vehicle itself hovered a hand's breadth above the surface at all points. A dozen powerful fans on the underside of the car kept it floating on an invisible bubble of air, despite the weight of the fusion power generator and the iridium-ceramic armor. Rob had seen combat cars on the entertainment cube occasionally, but those skittering miniatures gave no hint of the awesome power that emanated in reality from the machines. This one was seven meters long and three wide at the base, the armored sides curving up like a turtle's back to the open fighting compartment in the rear.

From the hatch in front of the powerplant stuck the driver's head, a black-mirrored ball in a helmet with full face shield down. Road dust drifted away from the man in a barely-visible haze, cleansed from the helmet's optics by a static charge. Faceless and terrible to the unfamiliar Burlager, the driver guided toward the starship a machine that appeared no more inhuman than did the man himself.

"Undercrewed," the priest murmured. "Two men on the back deck aren't enough for a car running single."

The older man's jargon was unfamiliar but Rob could follow his gist by looking at the vehicle. The two men standing above the waist-high armor of the rear compartment were clearly fewer than had been contemplated when the combat car was designed. Its visible armament comprised a heavy powergun forward to fire over the head of the driver, and similar weapons, also swivel-mounted, on either side to command the flanks and rear of the vehicle. But with only two men in the compartment there was a dangerous gap in the circle of fire the car could lay down if ambushed. Another vehicle for escort would have eased the danger, but this one was alone save for the trailer it pulled.

Though as the combat car drew closer, Rob began to wonder if the two soldiers present couldn't handle anything that occurred. Both were in full battle dress, wearing helmets and laminated back and breast armor over their khaki. Their faceplates were clipped open. The one at the forward gun, his eyes as deep-sunken and deadly as the three revolving barrels of his weapon, was in his forties and further aged by the dust sweated into black grime in the creases of his face. His head rotated in tiny jerks, taking in every nuance of the sullen crowd parting for his war-car. The other soldier was huge by comparison with the first and lounged across the back in feigned leisure: feigned, because either hand was within its breadth of a powergun's trigger, and his limbs were as controlled as spring steel.

With careless expertise, the driver backed his trailer up to the conveyor line. A delicate hand with the fans allowed him to angle them slightly, drifting the rear of the combat car to edge the trailer in the opposite direction. The larger soldier contemptuously thumbed a waiting horse and wagon out of its slot. The teamster's curse brought only a grin and a big hand rested on a powergun's receiver, less a threat than a promise. The combat car eased into the space.

"Wait for an old man," the priest said as Rob lifted his carry-all, "and I'll go with you." Glad even for that company, the recruit smiled nervously, fitting his stride to the other's surprisingly nimble swing-and-pause, swing-and-pause.

The driver dialed back minisculy on the power and allowed the big vehicle to settle on the ground without a skip or a tremor. One hand slid back the face shield to a high, narrow nose and eyes that alertly focused on the two men approaching. "The Lord and his martyrs!" the driver cried in amazement. "It's Blacky himself come in with our newbie!"

Both soldiers on the back deck slewed their eyes around at the cry. The smaller one took one glance, then leaped the two meters to the ground to clasp Rob's companion. "Hey!" he shouted, oblivious to the recruit shifting his weight uncertainly. "Via, it's good to see you! But what're you doing on Curwin?"

"I came back here afterwards," the older man answered with a smile. "Born here, I must've told you . . . though we didn't talk a lot. I'm a priest now, see?"

"And I'm a flirt like the load we're supposed to pick up," the driver said, dismounting with more care than his companion. Abreast of the first soldier, he too took in the round collar and halted gapemouthed. "Lord, I'll be a coppy rag if you ain't," he breathed. "Whoever heard of a blower chief taking the Way?"

"Shut up, Jake," the first soldier said without rancor. He stepped back from the priest to take a better look, then seemed to notice Rob. "Umm," he said, "you the recruit from Burlage?"

"Yessir. M—my name's Rob Jenne, sir."

"Not 'sir,' there's enough sirs around already," the veteran said. "I'm Cheer, except if there's lots of brass around, then make it Sergeant-Commander Worzer. Look, take your gear back to the trailer and give Leon a hand with the load."

"Hey, Blacky," he continued with concern, ignoring rob again, "what's wrong with your legs? We got the best there was."

"Oh, they're fine." Rob heard the old man reply, "but they need a weekly tuning. Out here we don't have the computers, you know; so I get the astrogation boys to sync me up on the ships' hardware whenever one docks in—just waiting for a chance now. But in six months the servos are far enough out of line that I have to shut off the power till the next ship arrives. You'd be surprised how well I get around on these pegs, though. . . ."

Leon, the huge third crew member, had loosed the top catches of his body armor for ventilation. From the look of it, the laminated casing should have been a size larger; but Rob wasn't sure anything larger was made. The gunner's skin where exposed was the dense black of a basalt outcropping. "They'll be a big crate to go on, so just set your gear down till we get it loaded," he said. Then he grinned at Rob, teeth square and slightly yellow against his face. "Think you can take me?"

That was a challenge the recruit could understand, the first he could meet fairly since boarding the starship with a one-way ticket to a planet he had never heard of. He took in the waiting veteran quickly but carefully, proud of his own rock-hardened muscles but certain the other man had been raised just as hard. "I give you best," the blond said. "Unless you feel you got to prove it?"

The grin broadened and a great black hand reached out to clasp Rob's. "Naw," the soldier said, "just like to clear the air at the start. Some of the big ones; Lord, testy ain't the word. All they can think about's what they want to prove with me . . . so they don't watch their side of the car, and then there's trouble for everybody."

"Hammer's Regiment?" called an unfamiliar voice. Both men looked up. Down the conveyor rode a blue-tunicked ship's man in front of what first appeared to be a huge crate. At second glance Rob saw that it was a cage of light alloy holding four . . . "Dear Lord!" the recruit gasped.

"Roger, Hammer's," Leon agreed, handing the crewman a plastic chit while the latter cut power to the rollers to halt the cage. The chit slipped into the computer linkage on the crewman's left wrist, lighting a green indicator when it proved itself a genuine bill of lading.

There were four female humanoids in the cage—stark naked except for a dusting of fine blue scales. Rob blinked. One of the near-women stood with a smile— Lord, she had no teeth!—and rubbed her groin deliberately against one of the vertical bars.

"First quality Genefran flirts," Leon chuckled. "Ain't human, boy, but the next best thing."

"Better," threw in Jake, who had swung himself into the fighting compartment as soon as the cage arrived. "I tell you, kid, you never had it till you had a flirt. Surgically modified and psychologically prepared. Rowf!"

"N-not human?" Rob stumbled, unable to take his eyes off the cage, "you mean like *monkeys?*"

Leon's grin lit his face again, and the driver cackled, "Well, don't know about monkeys, but they're a whole lot like sheep."

"You take the left side and we'll get this aboard," Leon directed. The trailer's bed was half a meter below the rollerway so that the cage, though heavy and awkward, could be slid without much lifting.

Rob gripped the bars numbly, turning his face down from the tittering beside him. "Amazing what they can do with implants and a wig," Jake was going on, "though a course there's a lot of cutting to do first, but those ain't the differences you see, if you follow. The scales, now— they have a way—"

"Lift!" Leon ordered, and Rob straightened at the knees. They took two steps backward with the cage wobbling above them as the girls—the flirts!—squealed and hopped about. "Down!" and cage clashed on trailer as the two big men moved in unison.

Rob stepped back, his mouth working in distaste, unaware of the black soldier's new look of respect. Quarry work left a man used to awkward weights. "This is foul," the recruit marveled. "Are those really going back with us for, for . . ."

"Rest'n relaxation," Leon agreed, snapping tiedowns around the bars.

"But how . . ." Rob began, looking again at the cage. When the red-wiggled flirt fondled her left breast upward, he could see the implant scars pale against the blue. The scales were more thinly spread where the skin had been stretched in molding it. "I'll *never* touch something like that. Look, maybe Burlage is pretty backward about . . . things, about sex, I don't know. But I don't see how anybody could . . . I mean—"

"Via, wait till you been here as long as we have," Jake gibed. He clenched his right hand and pumped it suggestively. "Field expedients, that's all."

"On this kinda contract," Leon explained, stepping around to get at the remaining tiedowns, "you can't trust the local girls. Least not in the field, like we are. The colonel likes to keep us patrol sections pretty much self-contained."

"Yeah," Jake broke in—would his cracked tenor never cease? "Why, some of these whores, they take a razor blade, see—in a cork you know?—and, well, never mind." He laughed, seeing Rob's face.

"Jake," Sergeant Worzer called, "Shut up and hop in."

The driver slipped instantly into his hatch. Disgusting as Rob found the little man, he recognized his ability. Jake moved with lethal certainty and a speed that belied the weight of his body armor.

"Ready to life, Chero?" he asked.

The priest was levering himself toward the starship again. Worzer watched him go for a moment, shook his head. "Just run us out to the edge of the field," he directed. "I got a few things to show our recruit before we head back; nobody rides in my car without knowing how to work the guns." With a sigh he hopped into the fighting compartment. Leon motioned Rob in front of him. Gingerly, the recruit stepped onto the trailer hitch, gripped the armored rim with both hands, lifted himself aboard. Leon followed. The trailer bonged as he pushed off from it, and his bulk cramped the littered compartment as soon as he grunted over the side.

"Put this on," Worzer ordered, handing Rob a dusty, bulbous helmet like the others wore. "Brought a battle suit for you, too," he said, kicking the jointed armor leaning against the back of the compartment, "but it'd no more fit you than it would Leon there."

The black laughed. "Gonna be tight back here till the kid or me gets zapped."

"Move 'er out," Worzer ordered. The words came through unsuspected earphones in Rob's helmet, although the sergeant had simply spoken, without visibly activating a pick up.

The car vibrated as the fans revved, then lifted with scarcely a jerk. From behind came the squeals and chirrups of the flirts as the trailer rocked over the irregularities in the field.

Worzer looked hard at the starship's open crew portal as they hissed past it. "Funny what folks go an' do," he said to no one in particular. "Via, wonder what I'll be in another ten years."

"Pet food, likely," joked the driver, taking part in the conversation although physically separated from the other crewmen.

"Shut up, Jake," repeated the blower captain. "And you can hold it up here, we're out far enough."

The combat car obediently settled on the edge of the stabilized area. The port itself had capacity for two ships at a time; the region it served did not. Though with the high cost of animal transport many manufactures could be star-hopped to Curwin's back country more cheaply than they could be carried from the planet's own more urbanized areas, the only available exchange was raw agricultural produce—again limited to the immediate locality by the archaic transport. Its fans purring below audibility, the armored vehicle rested on an empty area of no significance to the region—unless the central government should choose to land another regiment of mercenaries on it.

"Look," the sergeant said, his deep-set eyes catching Rob's, "we'll pass you on to the firebase when we take the other three flirts in next week. They got a training section there. We got six cars in this patrol, that's not enough margin to fool with training a newbie. But neither's it enough to keep somebody useless underfoot for a week, so we'll give you some basics. Not so you can wise-ass when you get to training section, just so you don't get somebody killed it if drops in the pot. Clear?"

"Yessir." Rob broke his eyes away, then realized how foolish he must look staring at his own clasped hands. He looked back at Worzer.

"Just so its understood," the sergeant said with a nod. "Leon, show him how the gun works."

The big black rotated his weapon so that the muzzle faced forward and the right side was toward Rob and the interior of the car. The mechanism itself was encased with knobs and levers of unguessable intent. The barrels were stubby iridium cylinders with smooth, 2 cm bores. Leon touched one of the buttons, then threw a lever back. The plate to which the barrels were attached rotated 120 degrees around their common axis, and a thick disk of plastic popped out into the gunner's hand.

"When the bottom barrel's ready to fire, the next one clockwise is loading one a these"—Leon held up the 2 cm disk—"and the other barrel, the one that's just fired, blows out the empty."

"There's a liquid nitrogen ejector," Worzer put in. "Cools the bore same time it kicks out the empty."

"She feeds up through the mount," the big soldier went on, his index finger tracing the path of the energized disks from the closed hopper bulging in the sidewall, through the ball joint and into the weapon's receiver. "If you try to fire and she don't, check this." The columnar finger indicated but did not move the stud it had first pressed on the side of the gun. "That's the safety. She still doesn't fire, pull this"—he clacked the lever, rotating the barrel cluster around one-third turn and catching the loaded round that flew out. "Maybe there was a dud round. She still don't go, just get down outa the way. We start telling you about second-order malfunctions and you won't remember where the trigger is?"

"Ah, where is the trigger?" Rob asked diffidently.

Jake's laughter rang through the earphones and Worzer himself smiled for the first time. The sergeant reached out and rotated the gun. "See the grips?" he asked, pointing to the double handles at the back of the receiver. Rob nodded.

"OK," Worzer continued, "you hold it there"—he demonstrated—"and to fire, you just press your thumbs against the trigger plate between 'em. Let up and it quits. Simple."

"You can clear this field as quick as you can spin this little honey," Leon said, patting the gun with affection. "The hicks out there"—his arm swept the woods and cultivated fields promiscuously—"got some rifles, they hunted before the trouble started, but no powerguns to mention. About all they do since we moved in is maybe pop a shot or two off, and hide in their holes."

"They've got some underground stockpiles," Worzer said, amplifying Leon's words, "explosives, maybe some factories to make rifle ammo. But the colonel set up a recce net—spy satellites, you know—as part of the contract. Any funny movement day or night, a signal goes down to whoever's patrolling there. A couple calls and we check out the area with ground sensors . . . anything funny then—vibration, hollows showing up on the echo sounder, magnetics—anything!—and bam! we call in the artillery."

"Won't take much of a jog on the way back," Leon suggested, "and we can check out that report from last night."

"Via, that was just a couple dogs," Jake objected.

"OK, so we prove it was a couple dogs," rumbled the gunner. "Or maybe the hicks got smart and they're shielding their infra-red now. Been too damn long since anything popped in this sector."

"Thing to remember, kid," Worzer summed up, "is never get buzzed at this job. Stay cool, you're fine. This car's got more firepower'n everything hostile in fifty klicks. One call to the firebase brings in our arty, anything from smoke shells to a nuke. The rest of our section can be here in twenty minutes, or a tank platoon from the firebase in two hours. Just stay cool."

Turning forward, the sergeant said, "OK, take her home Jake. We'll try that movement report on the way."

The combat car shuddered off the ground, the flirts shrieking. Rob eyed them, blushed, and turned back to his powergun, feeling conspicuous. He took the grips, liking the deliberate way the weapon swung. The safety button was glowing green, but he suddenly realized that he didn't know the color code. Green for safe? Or green for ready? He extended his index finger to the switch.

"Whoa, careful, kid!" Leon warned. "You cut fifty civvies in half your first day and the colonel won't like it one bit."

Sheepishly, Rob drew back his finger. His ears burned, mercifully hidden beneath the helmet.

They slid over the dusty road in a flat, white cloud at about forty kph. It seemed shockingly fast to the recruit, but he realized that the car could probably move much faster were it not for the live cargo behind. Even as it was, the trailer bounced dangerously from side to side.

The road led through a gullied scattering of grain plots, generally fenced with withers rather than imported metal. Houses were relatively uncommon. Apparently each farmer plowed several separate locations rather than trying to work the rugged or less productive areas. Occasionally they passed a rough-garbed local at work. The scowls thrown up at the smoothly running war-car were hostile, but there was nothing more overt.

"OK," Jake warned, "here's where it gets interesting. Sure you still want this half-assed check while we got the trailer hitched?"

"It won't be far," Worzer answered. "Go ahead." He turned to Rob, touching the recruit's shoulder and pointing to the lighted map panel beside the forward gun. "Look, Jenne," he said, keeping one eye on the countryside as Jake took the car off the road in a sweeping turn, "if you need to call in a location to the firebase, here's the trick. The red dot"—it was in the center of the display and remained there although the map itself seemed to be flowing kitty-corner across the screen as the combat car moved—"that's us. The black dot"—the veteran thumbed a small wheel beside the display and the map, red dot and all, shifted to the right on the panel, leaving a black dot in the center—"that's your pointer. The computer feeds out the grid coordinates here"—his finger touched the window above the map display. Six digits changing as the map moved under the centered black dot, winked brightly. "You just put the black dot on a bunker site, say, and read off the figures to Fire Central. The arty'll do all the rest."

"Ah," Rob murmured, "ah . . . Sergeant, how do you get the little dot off that and onto a bunker like you said?"

There was a moment's silence. "You know how to read a map, don't you kid?" Worzer finally asked.

"What's that, sir?"

The earphones boomed and cackled with raucous

laughter. "Oh my coppy ass!" the sergeant snarled. He snapped the little wheel back, re-centering the red dot. "Lord, I don't know how the training cadre takes it!"

Rob hid his flaming embarrassment by staring over his gunsights. He didn't really know how to use them, either. He didn't know why he'd left Conner's Stoneworks, where he was the cleanest, fastest driller on the whole coppy crew. His powerful hands squeezed at the grips as if they were the driver's throat through which bubbles of laughter still burst.

"Shut up, Jake," the sergeant finally ordered. "Most of us had to learn something new when we joined. Remember how the ol' man found you your first day, pissing up against the barracks?"

Jake quieted.

They had skirted a fence of cane palings, brushing in once without serious effect. Russet grass flanking the fence flattened under the combat car's downdraft, then sprang up unharmed as the vehicle moved past. Jake seemed to be following a farm track leading from the field to a rambling, substantially-constructed building on the rear hilltop. Instead of running with the ground's rise, however, the car cut through brush and down a half-meter bank into a broad-based arroyo. The bushes were too stiff to lie down under the fans. They crunched and howled in the blades, making the car buck, and ricocheted wildly from under the skirts. The bottom of the arroyo was sand, clean-swept by recent run-off. It boiled fiercely as the car first shoomped into it, then ignored the fans entirely. Somehow Jake had managed not to overturn the trailer, although its cargo had been screaming with fear for several minutes.

"Hold up," Worzer ordered suddenly as he swung his weapon toward the left-hand bank. The wash was about thirty meters wide at that point, sides sheer and a meter high. Rob glanced forward to see that a small screen to Worzer's left on the bulkhead, previously dark, was now crossed by three vari-colored lines. The red one was bouncing frantically.

"They got an entrance, sure 'nough," Leon said. He aimed his powergun at the same point, then snapped his face shield down. "Watch it, kid," he said. The black's right hand fumbled in a metal can welded to the blower's side. Most of the paint had chipped from the stenciled legend: GRENADES. What appeared to be a lazy overarm toss snapped a knobby ball the size of a child's fist straight and hard against the bank.

Dirt and rock fragments shotgunned in all directions. The gully side burst in a globe of black streaked with garnet fire, followed by a shock wave that was a physical blow.

"Watch your side, kid!" somebody shouted through the din, but Rob's bulging eyes were focused on the collapsing bank, the empty triangle of black gaping suddenly through the dust—the two ravening whiplashes of directed lightning ripping into it to blast and scatter.

The barrel clusters of the two veterans' powerguns spun whining, kicking gray, eroded disks out of their mechanisms in nervous arcs. The bolts they shot were blue-green flashes barely visible until they struck a target and exploded it with transferred energy. The very rock burst in droplets of glassy slag splashing high in the air and even back into the war-car to pop against the metal.

Leon's gun paused as his fingers hooked another grenade. "Hold it!" he warned. The sergeant, too, came off the trigger, and the bomb arrowed into the now-vitrified gap in the tunnel mouth. Dirt and glass shards blew straight back at the bang. A stretch of ground sagged for twenty meters beyond the gully wall, closing the tunnel the first explosion had opened.

Then there was silence. Even the flirts, huddled in a terrified heap on the floor of their cage, were soundless.

Glowing orange specks vibrated on Rob's retinas; the cyan bolts had been more intense than he had realized. "Via," he said in awe, "how do they dare . . . ?"

"Bullet kills you just as dead," Worzer grunted. "Jake, think you can climb that wall?"

"Sure. She'll buck a mite in the loose stuff." The gully side was a gentle declivity, now, where the grenades had blown it in. "Wanna unhitch the trailer first?"

"Negative, nobody gets off the blower till we cleaned this up."

"Umm, don't want to let somebody else in on the fun, maybe?" the driver queried. If he was tense, his voice did not indicate it. Rob's palms were sweaty. His glands had understood before his mind had that his companions were considering smashing up, unaided, a guerrilla stronghold.

"Cop," Leon objected determinedly. "We found it, didn't we?"

"Let's go," Worzer ordered. "Kid, watch your side. They sure got another entrance, maybe a couple."

The car nosed gently toward the subsided bank, wallowed briefly as the driver fed more power to the forward fans to lift the bow. With a surge and a roar, the big vehicle climbed. Its fans caught a few pebbles and whanged them around inside the plenum chamber like a rattle of sudden gunfire. At half speed, the car glided toward another fenced grainplot, leaving behind it a rising pall of dust.

"Straight as a plumb line," Worzer commented, his eyes flicking over his sensor screen. "Bastards'll be waiting for us."

Rob glanced at him—a mistake. The slam-spang! of shot and ricochet were nearly simultaneous. The recruit whirled back, bawling in surprise. The rifle pit had opened within five meters of him, and only the haste of the dark-featured guerrilla had saved Rob from his first shot. Rob pivoted his powergun like a hammer, both thumbs mashing down the trigger. Nothing happened. The guerrilla ducked anyway, the black circle of his foxhole shaped into a thick crescent by the lid lying askew.

Safety, *safety!* Rob's mind screamed and he punched the button fat-fingered. The rifleman raised his head just in time to meet the hose of fire that darted from the recruit's gun. The guerrilla's head exploded. His brains, flash-cooked by the first shot, changed instantly from a colloid to a blast of steam that scattered itself over a three-meter circle. The smoldering fragments of the rifle followed the torso as it slid downward.

The combat car roared into the field of waist-high grain, ripping down twenty meters of woven fencing to make its passage. Rob, vaguely aware of other shots and cries forward, vomited onto the floor of the compartment. A colossal explosion nearby slewed the car sideways. As Rob raised his eyes, he noticed three more swarthy riflemen darting through the grain from the right rear of the vehicle.

"Here!" he cried. He swiveled the weapon blindly, his hips colliding with Worzer in the cramped space. A rifle bullet cracked past his helmet. He screamed something again but his own fire was too high, bluegreen droplets against the clear sky, and the guerrillas had grabbed the bars while the flirts jumped and blatted.

The rifles were slamming but the flirts were in the way of Rob's gun. "Down! Down!" he shouted uselessly, and the red-haired flirt pitched across the cage with one synthetic breast torn away by the bullet she had leaped in front of. Leon cursed and slumped across Rob's feet, and then it was Chero Worzer shouting, "Hard left, Jake," and leaning across the fallen gunner to rotate his weapon. The combat car tilted left as the bow came around, pinching the trailer against the left rear of the vehicle— in the path of Worzer's powergun. The cage's light alloy bloomed in superheated fireballs as the cyan bolts ripped through it. Both tires exploded together, and there was a red mist of blood in the air. The one guerrilla who had ducked under the burst dropped his rifle and ran.

Worzer cut him in half as he took his third step.

The sergeant gave the wreckage only a glance, then knelt beside Leon. "Cop, he's gone," he said. The bullet had struck the big man in the neck between helmet and body armor, and there was almost a gallon of blood on the floor of the compartment.

"Leon?" Jake asked.

"Yeah. Lord, there musta been twenty kilos of explosive in that satchel charge. If he hadn't hit it in the air . . ." Worzer looked back at the wreck of the trailer, then at Rob. "Kid, can you unhitch that yourself?"

"You just *killed* them," Rob blurted. He was half blinded by tears and the after-image of the gunfire.

"Via, they did their best on us, didn't they?" the sergeant snarled. His face was tiger striped by dust and sweat.

"No, not them!" the boy cried. "Not them—the girls. You just—"

Worzer's iron fingers gripped Rob by the chin and turned the recruit remorselessly toward the carnage behind. The flirts had been torn apart by their own fluids, some pieces flung through gaps in the mangled cage. "Look at 'em, Jenne!" Worzer demanded. "They ain't human but if they was, if it was *Leon* back there, I'd a done it."

His fingers uncurled from Rob's chin and slammed in a fist against the car's armor. "This ain't heroes, it ain't no coppy game you play when you want to! You do what you got to do, 'cause if you don't, some poor bastard gets killed later when he tries to."

"Now get down there and unhitch us."

"Yes, sir." Rob gripped the lip of the car for support. Worzer's voice, more gentle, came through the haze of tears: "And watch it, kid. Just because they're keeping their heads down don't mean they're all gone." Then, "Wait." Another pause while the sergeant unfastened the belt and holstered handgun from his waist and handed it to Rob. Leon wore a similar weapon, but Worzer did not touch the body. Rob wordlessly clipped the belt, loose for not being fitted over armor, and swung down from the combat car.

The hitch had a quick-release handle, but the torqueing it had received in the last seconds of battle had jammed it. Nervously aware that the sergeant's darting-eyed watchfulness was no pretense, that the shot-scythed grainfield could hide still another guerrilla, or a platoon of them, Rob smashed his boot heel against the catch. It held. Wishing for his driller's sledge, he kicked again.

"Sarge!" Jake shouted. Grain rustled on the outer side of the combat car, and against the sky beyond the scarred armor loomed a parcel. Rob threw himself flat.

The explosion picked him up from the ground and bounced him twice, despite the shielding bulk of the combat car. Stumbling upright, Rob steadied himself on the armored side.

The metal felt odd. It no longer trembled with the ready power of the fans. The car was dead, lying at rest on the torn-up soil. With three quick strides, the recruit rounded the bow of the vehicle. He had no time to inspect the dished-in metal, because another swarthy guerrilla was approaching from the other side.

Seeing Rob, the ex-farmer shouted something and drew a long knife. Rob took a step back, remembered the pistol. He tugged at its unfamiliar grip and the weapon popped free into his hand. It seemed the most natural thing in the world to finger the safety, placed just as the tribarrel's had been, then trigger two shots into the face of the lunging guerrilla. The snarl of hatred blanked as the body tumbled facedown at Rob's feet. The knife had flown somewhere into the grain.

"Ebros?" a man called. Another lid had raised from the ground ten meters away. Rob fired at the hole, missed badly. He climbed the caved-in bow, clumsily one-handed, keeping the pistol raised. There was nothing but twisted metal where the driver had been. Sergeant Worzer was still semi-erect, clutched against his powergun by a length of structural tubing. It had curled around both his thighs, fluid under the stunning impact of the satchel charge. The map display was a pearly blank, though the window above it still read incongruously 614579 and the red line on the detector screen blipped in nervous solitude. Worzer's helmet was gone, having flayed a bloody track across his scalp as it sailed away. His lips moved, though, and when Rob put his face near the sergeant's he could hear, "The red . . . pull the red tab . . ."

Over the left breast of each set of armor were a blue and a red tab. Rob had assumed they were decorations of some sort. He shifted the sergeant gently. The tab was locked down by a cotter pin which he yanked out. Something hissed in the armor as he pulled the tab, and Sergeant Worzer murmured, "Oh lord. Oh lord." Then, "Now the stimulant, the blue tab."

After the second injection sped into his system, the sergeant opened his eyes. Rob was already trying to straighten the entrapping tube. "Forget it," Worzer ordered weakly. "It's inside, too . . . damn armor musta flexed. Oh lord." He closed his eyes, opened them in time to see another head peak cautiously from the tunnel mouth. "Bastard!" he rasped, and faster than he spoke he triggered his powergun. Its motor whined spitefully though the burst went wide. The head disappeared.

"I want you to run back to the gully," the sergeant said, resting his eyes again. "You get there, you say 'Fire Central.' That cuts in the arty frequency automatic. Then

you say, 'Bunker complex . . . ' " Worzer looked down.
" 'Six-one-four, five-seven-nine,' Stay low and wait for
a patrol."

"It won't bend!" Rob snarled in frustration as his
fingers slid again from the blood-slick tubing.

"Jenne, get your ass out of here, *now*."

"Sergeant— "

"Lord curse your soul, get out or I'll call it in myself!
Do I look like I wanna live?"

"Oh, Via . . ." Rob tried to reholster the pistol he had
set on the bloody floor. It slipped back with a clang. He
left it, gripping the sidewall again.

"Maybe tell Dad it was good to see him," Worzer
whispered. "You lose touch in this business, Lord knows
you do."

"Sir?"

"The priest . . . you met him. Sergeant-Major Worzer,
he was. Oh Lord, *move it—*"

At the muffled scream, the recruit leaped from the
smashed war-car and ran blindly back the way they had
come. He did not know he had reached the gully until
the ground flew out from under him and he pitched
spread-eagled onto the sand. "Fire Central," he sobbed
through strangled breaths, "Fire Central."

"Clear," a strange voice snapped crisply. "Data?"

"Wh-what?"

"Lord and martyrs," the voice blasted, "if you're screwing around on firing channels, you'll wish you never saw
daylight!"

"S-six . . . oh Lord, yes, six-one-four, five-seven-nine,"
Rob sing-songed. He was staring at the smooth sand.
"Bunkers, the sergeant says it's bunkers."

"Roger," the voice said, businesslike again. "Ranging
in fifteen."

Could they really swing those mighty guns so swiftly,
those snub-barreled rocket howitzers whose firing looked
so impressive on the entertainment cube?

"On the way," warned the voice.

The big tribarrel whined again from the combat car, the silent lash of its bolts answered this time by a crash of rifle shots. A flattened bullet burred through the air over where Rob lay. It was lost in the eerie, thunderous shriek from the northwest.

"Splash," the helmet said.

The ground bucked. From the grainplot spouted rock, smoke and metal fragments into a black column fifty meters high.

"Are we on?" the voice demanded.

"Oh, Lord," Rob prayed, beating his fists against the sand, "Oh Lord."

"Via, what is this?" the helmet wondered aloud. Then, "All guns, battery five."

And the earth began to ripple and gout under the hammer of the guns.

Rolling Hot

Chapter One

The camera threw the shadows of the Slammers' officer harshly across the berm which the sun had colored bronze a few moments ago as it set. Her hair was black and cut as short as that of a man.

"For instance, Captain Ranson," Dick Sullin said, "here at Camp Progress there are three thousand national troops and less than a hundred of your mercenaries, but—"

shoop

Ranson's eyes widened, glinting like pale gray marble. Fritzi Dole kept the camera focused tightly on her face. He'd gotten an instinct for a nervous subject in the three years he'd recorded Suilin's probing interviews.

"—the cost to our government—"

shoop-shoop

"—is greater for your handful of—"

"Incoming!" screamed Captain June Ranson as she

dived for the dirt. It wasn't supposed to be happening here—

But for the first instant, you *never* really believed it could be happening, not even in the sectors where it happened every bleeding night. And when things were bad enough for one side or the other to hire Hammer's Slammers you could be pretty sure that there were no safe sectors.

Camp Progress was on the ass end of Prosperity's inhabited continent—three hundred kilometers north of the coast and the provincial capital, Kohang, but still a thousand kays south of where the real fighting went on in the areas bordering the World Government enclaves. Sure, there'd been reports that the Conservatives were nosing around the neighborhood, but nothing the Yokel troops themselves couldn't handle if they got their thumbs out.

For a chance.

Camp progress was a Yokel—was a National Army—training and administrative center, while for the Slammers it served as a maintenance and replacement facility. In addition to those formal uses, the southern sector gave Hammer a place to post troops who were showing signs of having been at the sharp end a little too long.

People like Junebug Ranson, for instance, who'd frozen with her eyes wide open during a firefight that netted thirty-five Consies killed-in-action.

So Captain Ranson had been temporarily transferred to command the Slammers' guard detachment at Camp Progress, a "company" of six combat cars. There'd been seventeen cars in her line company when it was up to strength; but she couldn't remember a standard day in a war zone that they *had* been up to strength . . .

And anyway, Ranson knew as well as anybody else that she needed a rest before she got some of her people killed.

shoop

But she wasn't going to rest here.

The bell was ringing in the Slammers' Tactical Operations Center, a command car in for maintenance. The vehicle's fans had all been pulled, leaving the remainder as immobile as a 30-tonne iridium boulder; but it still had working electronics.

The Yokel garrison had a klaxon which they sounded during practice alerts. It was silent *now* despite the fact that camp security was supposedly a local responsibility.

Slammers were flattening or sprinting for their vehicles, depending on their personal assessment of the situation. The local reporter gaped at Ranson while his cameraman spun to find out what was going on. The camera light sliced a brilliant swath through the nighted camp.

Ranson's left cheek scraped the gritty soil as she called, "All Red Team personnel, man your blowers and engage targets beyond the berm. Blue Teams—" the logistics and maintenance people "—prepare for attack from within the camp."

She wasn't wearing her commo helmet—that was in her combat car—but commands from her mastoid implant would be rebroadcast over her command channel by the base unit in the TOC. With her free hand, the hand that wasn't holding the submachinegun she always carried, even here, Ranson grabbed the nearer of the two newsmen by the ankle and jerked him flat.

The Yokel's squawk of protest was smothered by the blast of the first mortar shell hitting the ground.

"I said *hold* it!" bellowed Warrant Leader Ortnahme, his anger multiplied by echoes with the tank's plenum chamber. "Not slide the bloody nacelle all across the bloody baseplate!"

"Yessir," said Tech 2 Simkins. "Yes, Mr. Ortnahme!"

Simkins gripped his lower lip between his prominent front teeth and pushed. The flange on the fan nacelle slid a little farther from the bolt holes in the mounting baseplate. "Ah . . . Mr. Ortnahme?"

It was hot and dry. The breeze curling through the access port and the fan intakes did nothing but drift grit into the eyes of the two men lying on their back in the plenum chamber. It had been a hard day.

It wasn't getting any easier as it drew to a close.

The lightwand on the ground beneath the baseplate illuminated everything in the scarred, rusty steel cavern—including the flange, until Simkins tried to position the nacelle and his arms shadowed the holes. The young technician looked scared to death. The good Lord knew he had reason to be, because if Simkins screwed up one more time, Ortnahme was going to reverse his multitool and use the welder end of it to—

Ortnahme sighed and let his body relax. He set down the multitool, which held a bolt ready to drive, and picked up the drift punch to realign the cursed holes.

Henk Ortnahme was tired and sweaty, besides being a lot older and fatter than he liked to remember . . . but he was also the Slammers' maintenance chief at Camp Progress, which meant it was his business to get the job done instead of throwing tantrums.

"No problem, Simkins," he said mildly. "But let's get it right this time, huh? So that we can knock off."

The tank, *Herman's Whore*, had been squarely over the blast of a hundred-kilogram mine. The explosion lifted the tank's 170-tonne mass, stunning both crewmen and damaging the blades of five of the six fans working at the time.

By themselves, bent blades were a field repair job— but because the crew'd been knocked silly, nobody shut down the system before the fans skewed the shafts . . . which froze the bearings . . . which cooked the drive motors in showers of sparks that must've been real bloody impressive.

Not only did the entire fan nacelles have to be

replaced now—a rear echelon job by anybody's standards—but three of the cursed things had managed to weld their upper brackets to the hull, so the brackets had to be replaced also.

It was late. Ortnahme'd kept his assistant at it for fourteen hours, so he couldn't rightly blame Simkins for being punchy . . . and the warrant leader knew his own skills and judgment weren't maybe all they bloody oughta be, just at the moment. They should've quit an hour before; but when this last nacelle was set, they were done with the cursed job.

"I got it, kid," he said calmly.

Simkins hesitated, then released the nacelle and watched nervously as his superior balanced the weight on his left palm. The upper bracket was bolted solidly, but there was enough play in the suspension to do real harm if the old bastard dropped—

A bell rang outside in the company area—rang and kept on ringing. Simkins straightened in terrified surmise and banged his head on the tank's belly armor. He stared at Ortnahme through tear-blinded eyes.

The warrant leader didn't move at all for a moment. Then his left biceps, covered with grit sticking to the sweat, bunched. The nacelle slid a centimeter and the drift punch shot through the realigned holes.

"Kid," Ortnahme said in a voice made tight by the tension of holding the fan nacelle, "I want you to get into the driver's seat and light her up, but don't—"

White light like the flash of a fuse blowing flickered through the intakes. The *blam!* of the mortar shell detonating was almost lost in the echoing clang of shrapnel against the skirts of the tank. Two more rounds went off almost simultaneously, but neither was quite as close.

Ortnahme swallowed. "But don't spin the fans till I tell you, right? I'll finish up with this myself."

"S—" Simkins began. Ortnahme had left the drift punch slide down and was groping for the multitool again. His arm muscles, rigid under their covering of fat, held the unit in place.

Simkins set the multitool in his superior's palm, bolt dispenser forward, and scuttled for the open access plate. "Yessir," he called back over his shoulder.

The multitool whirred, spinning the bolt home without a shade of difficulty.

Simkin's boots banged on the skirts as the technician thrust through the access port in the steel wall. It was a tight enough fit even for a young kid like him, and as for Ortnahme—Ortnahme had half considered cutting a double-sized opening and welding the cover back in place when he was done with this cursed job.

Just as well he hadn't done that. With a hole that big venting the plenum chamber, the tank woulda been anchored until it was fixed.

Tribarrels fired, the thump of expanding air preceded by the hiss of the energy discharge that headed a track to the target. Another salvo of mortar shells landed, and an earthshock warned of something more substantial hitting in the near distance.

Not a time to be standing around outside, wielding a patch on a tank's skirts.

With the first bolt in place, the second was a snap. Or maybe *Herman's Whore* had just decided to quit fighting him now that the shooting had started. The bitch was Slammers equipment, after all.

The tank shuddered. It was just Simkins hitting the main switch, firing up the containment/compression lasers in the fusion bottle that powered the vehicle, but for a moment Ortnahme thought the fan he held was live.

And about to slice the top half of his body into pastrami as it jiggled around in its mounting.

Shrapnel glanced from the thick iridium of the hull. It made a sharp sound that didn't echo the way pieces did when they rang on the cavernous steel plenum chamber. Ortnahme found the last hole with the nose of a bolt and triggered the multitool. The fastener spun and stopped too soon. Not home, not aligned.

Another earthshock, much closer than the first. *Herman's Whore* shuddered again, and the bolt whirred the last centimeter to seat itself properly.

Warrant Leader Henk Ortnahme, wheezing with more than exertion, squirmed on his belly toward the access port. He ignored the way the soil scraped his chest raw.

He started to lift himself through the access port—carefully; the mine had stripped half the bolts holding down the cover plate, so there was sharp metal as well as a bloody tight fit.

Tribarrels ripped outward, across the berm. To the south flares and tracers—mostly aimed high, way too high—from the Yokel lines brightened the sky.

Ortnahme was halfway through the access port when, despite the crash and roar of gunfire, he heard the whisper of more incoming mortar shells.

The 20cm main gun of another tank fired, blotting every other sight and sound from the night with its thunderous cyan flash.

When Ranson hit the deck, Dick Suilin's first reaction was that the woman officer was having convulsions. He turned to call for help, blinking because Fritzi's light had flared across him as the cameraman spun to record a new subject: half-clad soldiers sprinting or sprawling all across the detachment area. Somebody was ringing a raucous bell that—

Ranson, flat on the ground, grabbed Suilin's right ankle and jerked forward.

"Hey!" the reporter shouted, trying to pull away.

Standing straight, the woman didn't even come up to his collarbone, but she had a grip like a wire snare. Suilin overbalanced, flailing his arms until his butt hit the coarse soil and slammed all the air out of his lungs.

There was a white flash, a bang, and—about an inch

above Suilin's head—something that sounded like a bandsaw hitting a pineknot. Fritzi grunted and flung his camera in the opposite direction. It's floodlights went out.

"Fritzi, what are you—" Suilin shouted, stopping when his words were punctuated by two more blasts.

They were being *shelled* for God's sake! Not two hours' ride from Kohang!

The Slammers' captain had disappeared somewhere, but when Suilin started to get up to run for cover, Fritzi Dole fell across him and knocked him flat again.

Suilin started to curse, but before he got the first word out a nearby combat car lighted the darkness with a stream of bolts from a tribarrel.

The chunk of shrapnel which grated past Suilin a moment before had chopped off the back of his cameraman's skull. Fritzi's blood and brains splashed Suilin's chest.

Dick Suilin had seen death before; he'd covered his share of road accidents and nursing home fires as a junior reporter. Even so, he'd been on the political beat for years now. *This* was a political story; the waste of money on foreign mercenaries when the same sums spent on the National Army would give ten times the result.

And anyway, covering the result of a tavern brawl wasn't the same as feeling Fritzi's warm remains leak over the neat uniform in which Suilin had outfitted himself for this assignment.

He tried to push the body away from him, but it was heavy and as flexible as warm bread dough. He thought he heard the cameraman mumbling, but he didn't want to think that anyone so horribly wounded wouldn't have died instantly. Half of Fritzi's brains were gone, but he moaned as the reporter thrust him aside in a fit of revulsion.

Suilin rolled so that his back was toward the body.

The ground which he'd chosen for his interview was bare of cover, but a tank was parked against the berm twenty meters from him. He poised to scuttle toward the almost astronomical solidity of the vehicle and cower under the tarpaulin strung like a lean-to from its flank.

Before the reporter's legs obeyed his brain's decision, a man in the Slammers dull khaki ran past. The mercenary was doubled over by the weight of equipment in his arms and fear of shrapnel.

He was the only figure visible in what had been a languorously busy encampment. Suilin ran after him, toward the combat car almost as close as the tank, though to the opposite side.

The reporter needed companionship now more than he needed the greater bulk of steel and iridium close to his yielding flesh.

The combat car's driver spun its fans to life. Dust lifted, scattering the light of the tribarrel firing from the vehicle.

Three more mortar shells struck. Through the corner of his eye, Suilin saw the tarp plastered against the side of the tank.

The cloth was shredded by the blast that had flung it there.

"Hey, snake," said DJ Bell, smiling like he always had, though he'd been dead three months. "How they hangin'?"

Sergeant Birdie Sparrow moaned softly in his sleep. "Go away, DJ," his dream-self murmured. "I don't need this."

"Via, Birdie," said the dead trooper. "You need all the friends you can get. We—"

The short, smiling man started to change, the way he did in this dream.

"—all do."

Birdie didn't sleep well in the daytime, but with a tarp shading him, it was OK, even with the heat.

He couldn't sleep at all after dark, not since DJ bought it but kept coming back to see him.

DJ Bell was a little guy with freckles and red hair. He kept his helmet visor at ninety degrees as an eyeshade when he rode with his head and shoulders out of the commander's hatch of his tank, but his nose was usually peeling with sunburn anyways.

He'd had a bit of an attitude, DJ did; little-guy stuff. Wanted to prove he was as tough as anybody alive, which he was; and that he could drink anybody under the table—which he couldn't, he just didn't have the body weight, but he kept trying.

That stuff only mattered during stand-downs, and not even then once you got to know DJ. Birdie'd known DJ for five years. Been his friend, trusted him so completely that he never had to think about it when things dropped in the pot. DJ'd covered Birdie's ass a hundred times. They were the kind of friends you only had when you were at the sharp end, when your life was on the line every minute, every day.

It'd been a routine sweep, G Company's combat cars had pushed down a ridgeline while the tanks of M Company's 3rd Platoon held a blocking position to see what the cars flushed. One tank was deadlined with problems in its main-gun loading mechanism, and Lieutenant Hemmings had come down with the rolling crud, so Birdie Sparrow was in charge of the platoon's three remaining tanks.

Being short a tank didn't matter, G Company blew a couple of deserted bunkers, but they couldn't find any sign of Consies fresher than a month old. The combat cars laagered for the night on the ridge, while the tanks headed back for Firebase Red.

They were in line abreast. Birdie'd placed his own *Deathdealer* on the right flank, while DJ's *Widowmaker* howled along forty meters away in the center of the short line. They were riding over fields that'd been abandoned years before when the National Government cleared the area of civilians in an admission that they could no longer defend it from Conservative guerrillas slipping across the enclave borders.

All three tank commanders were head-and-shoulders out of their cupolas, enjoying the late afternoon sun. DJ turned and waved at Birdie, calling something that wasn't meant to be heard over the sound of the fans.

The motion sensor pinged a warning in Birdie's helmet, but it was too late by then.

Later—there was plenty of time later to figure out what had happened—they decided that the stand-off mine had been set almost three years before. It'd been intended to hit the lightly-armored vehicles the Yokels had been using in the region back then, so its high-sensitivity fuze detonated the charge 200 meters from the oncoming tanks.

Birdie's tanks didn't have—*none* of the Hammer's tanks had—its detection apparatus set to sweep that far ahead, because at that range the mine's self-forging projectile couldn't penetrate the armor even of a combat car. What the motion sensor had caught was the warhead shifting slightly to center on its target.

The mine was at the apex of an almost perfect isosceles triangle, with the two tanks forming the other corners. It rotated toward *Widowmaker* instead of *Deathdealer*.

Both tank commander's minds were reacting to the dirty, yellow-white blast they saw in the corner of their eyes, but there hadn't been time for muscles to shift enough to wipe away DJ's grin when the projectile clanged against Widowmaker's sloping turret and glanced upward. It was a bolt of almost-molten copper, forged from a plate into a spearpoint by the explosive that drove it toward its target.

DJ wore ceramic body armor. It shattered as the projectile coursed through the trooper's chest and head.

As Birdie Sparrow hosed the countryside with both his tribarrel and main gun, trying to blast an enemy who'd been gone for years, all he could think was, *Thank the Lord it was him and not me.*

"Look, y' know it's gonna happen, Birdie," said DJ's ghost earnestly. "It don't mean nothin'."

His voice was normal, but his chest was a gaping cavity and his face had started to splash—the way Birdie'd seen it happen three months before; only slowly, very slowly.

DJ had a metal filling on one of his molars. It glittered as it spun out through his cheek.

"DJ, you gotta stop doin' this," Birdie whimpered. His body was shivering and he wanted to wake up.

"Yeah, well, you better get movin', snake," DJ said with a shrug of his shoulders almost separated from what was left of his chest. The figure was fading from Birdie's consciousness. "It's starting again, y'know."

shoop

Birdie was out of his shelter and climbing the recessed steps to *Deathdealer*'s turret before he knew for sure he was awake. He was wearing his boots—he hadn't taken them off for more than a few minutes at a time in three months—and his trousers.

Most troopers kept their body armor near their bunks. Birdie didn't bother with that stuff anymore.

Despite the ringing alarm bell, there were people still standing around in the middle of the company area; but that was their problem, not Birdie Sparrow's.

He was diving feet-first through the hatch when the first mortar shell went off, hurling a figure away from its blast.

The body looked like DJ Bell waving good-bye.

When the third mortar shell went off, June Ranson rolled into a crouch and sprinted toward her combat car. The Consies used 100mm automatic mortars that fired from a three-round clip. It was a bloody good weapon—a lot like the mortar in Hammer's infantry platoons, and much more effective than the locally-made tube the National Army used.

The automatic mortar fired three shots fast, but the weight of a fresh clip stretched the gap between rounds three and four out longer than it would have been from a manually-loaded weapon.

Of course, if the Consies had a *pair* of mortars targeted on Ranson's detachment area, she was right outta luck.

Guns were firing throughout the encampment now, and the Yokels had finally switched on their warning klaxon. A machine-gun sent a stream of bright-orange Consie tracers snapping through the air several meters above Ranson's head. One tracer hit a pebble in the earthen berm and ricocheted upward at a crazy angle.

A strip charge wheezed in the night, a nasty, intermittent sound like a cat throwing up. A drive rocket was uncoiling the charge through the wire and minefield on which the Yokels depended for protection.

The charge went off, hammering the ground and blasting a corridor through the defense. It ignited the western sky with a momentary red flash like the sunset's afterthought.

Ranson caught the rear hand-fold of her combat car, *Warmonger*—Tootsie One-three—and swung herself into the fighting compartment. The fans were live, and both wing guns were firing.

Beside the vehicle were the scattered belongings of an evening meal: a catalytic cooker, open ration packets, and three bottles of local beer spilled to stain the dust. *Warmonger's* crew had been together for better than two year. They did everything as a team, so Ranson could be nearly certain her command vehicle could be up to speed in an emergency.

She was odd-man out: apart from necessary business, the crewmen hadn't addressed a dozen words to her in the month and a half since she took over the detachment.

Ranson didn't care. She'd seen too many people die herself to want to get to know any others closely.

Hot plastic empties ejecting from Stolley's left-wing gun spattered over here. One of the half-molten disks clung to the hair on the back of her wrist for long enough to burn.

Ranson grabbed her helmet, slapped the visor down over her face, and thumbed it from optical to thermal so that she could see details again. That dickheaded Yokel reporter had picked a great time to blind her with his camera light . . .

A mortar shell burst; then everything paused at the overwhelming crash of a tank's main gun. At least one of the panzers sent to Camp Progress for maintenance was up and running.

Figures, fuzzy and a bilious yellow-green, leaped from concealment less than a hundred meters from the berm. Two of them intersected the vivid thermal track of Stolley's tribarrel. The third flopped down and disappeared as suddenly as he'd risen.

A cubical multi-function display, only thirty centimeters on a side and still an awkward addition to the clutter filling the blower's fighting compartment, was mounted on the front bulkhead next to Ranson's tribarrel. She switched it on and picked up her back-and-breast armor.

"Janacek!" She ordered her right gunner over the pulsing thump-*hiss* of the tribarrels to either side of her. "Help me on!"

The stocky, spike-haired crewman turned from the spade grips of his gun and took the weight of Ranson's ceramic armor. She shrugged into the clamshell and latched it down her right side.

All six blowers in the guard detachment were beads of light in the multi-function display. Their fusion bottles were pressurized, though that didn't mean they had full crews.

"Now your own!" she said, handing the compartment's other suit to Janacek.

"Screw it!" the gunner snarled as he turned to his tribarrel.

"*Now*, trooper!" Ranson shouted in his ear.

Janacek swore and took the armor.

Two bullets clanged against the underside of the splinter shield, a steel plate a meter above the coaming of the fighting compartment. One of the Consie rounds howled off across the encampment while the other disintegrated in red sparks that prickled all three of the Slammers.

Stolley triggered a long burst, then a single round. "*My* trick, sucker!" he shouted.

The air was queasy with the bolts' ionized tracks and the sullen, petrochemical stink of the empty cases.

The blowers of the guard detachment were spaced more or less evenly around the 500-meter arc of the Slammers' area, because they were the only vehicles Ranson could depend on being combat ready. Two tanks were in Camp Progress for maintenance, and a third one—brand new—had been delivered here for shakedown before being sent on to a line company.

All three of the panzers *might* be able to provide at least fire support. If they could, it'd make a lot of difference.

Maybe the difference between life and death.

Ranson poked the control to give her all units with live fusion powerplants in a half-kilometer area. She prayed she'd see three more lights in her display—

Somebody who at least *said* he was Colonel Banyussuf, the camp commander, was bleating for help on the general channel. ". . . *are overrunning headquarters! They're downstairs now!*"

Likely enough, from the crossfire inside the berm at the other end of the camp. And Banyussuf's own bloody problem until Ranson had her lot sorted out.

There were ten blips: she'd forgotten the self-propelled howitzer in because of a traversing problem. Somebody'd brought it up, too.

Ranson switched on her own tribarrel. A blurred figure rose from where the two Consies Stolley'd killed were cooling in her visor's image. She ripped the new target with a stream of bolts that flung his arm and head in the air as his torso crumpled to the ground.

They were Hammer's Slammers. They'd been brought to Prosperity to kick ass, and that's just what they were going to do.

Chapter Two

Hans Wager, his unlatched clamshell flapping against his torso, lifted himself onto the back deck of his tank and reached for the turret handhold.

He hated mortars, but the shriek of incoming didn't scare him as much as it should've. He was too worried about the bleeding cursed, *huge* whale of a tank he was suddenly in charge of in a firefight.

And Wager was pissed: at Personnel for transferring him from combat cars to tanks when they promoted him to sergeant; at himself, for accepting the promotion if the transfer came with it; and at his driver, a stupid newbie named Holman who'd only driven trucks during her previous six months in the regiment.

The tank was brand new. It didn't have a name. Wager'd been warned not bother naming the vehicle, because as soon as they got the tank to D Company it'd be turned over to a senior crew while he and Holman were given some knackered junk.

Wager grabbed the hatch—just in time, because the tank bucked as that dickhead Holman lifted her on the fans instead of just building pressure in the plenum chamber. "Set—" Wager shouted. The lower edge of his body armor caught on the hatch coaming and jolted the rest of the order out as a wheeze.

Curse this bloody machine that didn't have any bloody *room* for all its size!

The berm around the Yokel portion of Camp Progress was four meters high—good protection against incoming, but you couldn't shoot over it. They'd put up guard towers every hundred meters inside the berm to cover their barbed wire and minefields.

As Wager slid at last into his turret, he saw the nearest tower disintegrate in an orange flash that silhouetted the bodies of at least three Yokel soldiers.

Holman had switched on the turret displays as soon as she boarded the tank, so Wager had access to all the data he could possibly want. Panoramic views in the optical, enhanced optical, passive thermal, active infrared, laser, millimetric radar, or sonic spectra. Magnified views in all the above spectra.

Three separate holographic screens, two of which could be split or quadded. Patching circuits that would display similar data fed from any other Slammer vehicle within about ten kays.

Full readouts through any of the displays on the status of the tank's ammunition, its fans, its powerplant, and all aspects of its circuitry.

Hans Wager didn't understand *any* of that cop. He'd only been assigned to this mother for eighteen hours.

His commo helmet pinged. "This is Tootsie six," said the crisp voice of Captain Ranson from the guard detachment. "Report status. Over."

Ranson didn't have a callsign for Wager's tank, so she was highlighting his blip on her multi-function display before sending.

Wager didn't have a callsign either.

"Roger, Tootsie six," he said. "Charlie Three-Zero—" the C Company combat car he'd crewed for the past year as driver and wing gunner "—up and running. Over."

Holman'd got her altitude more or less under control, but the tank now hunched and sidled like a dog unused to a leash. Maybe Wager ought to trade places with Holman. He figured from his combat car experience that he could *drive* this beast, so at least one of the seats'd be filled by somebody who knew his job.

Wager reached for the seat lever and raised himself out of the cold electronic belly of the turret. He might not have learned to be a tank commander yet, but . . .

The night was bright and welcoming. Muzzle flashes erupted from the slim trees fringing the stream 400 meters to Swager's front. Short bursts without tracers. He set his visor for persistent display—prob'ly a way to do that with the main screens, too, but who the cop cared?—to hold the aiming point in his vision while he aligned the sights of the cupola tribarrel with them.

The first flash of another burst merged with the crackling impact of Wager's powergun. There wasn't a second shot from *that* Consie.

Wager walked his fire down the course of the stream, shattering slender tree trunks and igniting what had been lush grass an instant before the ravening cyan bolts released their energy. The tank still wasn't steady, but Wager'd shot on the move before. He knew *his* job.

A missile exploded, fuel and warhead together, gouging a chunk out of the creekbank where the tribarrel had found it before its crew could align it to fire.

Hans Wager's job was to kill people.

The helmeted Slammers' trooper—with twenty kilos of body armor plus a laden equipment belt gripped in his left arm—caught the handle near the top of the car's shield, put his right foot in the step cut into the flare of the plenum chamber skirt, and swung himself into the vehicle.

Suilin's skin was still prickling from the hideous, sky-devouring flash/*crash!* that had stunned him a moment before. He'd thought a bomb had gone off, but it was a tank shooting because it happened again. He'd pissed his pants, and that bothered him more than the way Fritzi was splashed across the front of his uniform.

Suilin grabbed the handle the way the soldier had. The metal's buzzing vibration startled him; but it was the fans, of course, not a short circuit to electrocute him. He put his foot on the step and jumped as he'd seen the soldier do. He *had* to get over the side of the armor which would protect him once he was there.

His chest banged the hard iridium, knocking the breath out of him. His left hand scrabbled for purchase, but he didn't have enough strength to—

The trooper Suilin had followed to the combat car leaned over and grabbed the reporter's shoulder. He jerked Suilin aboard with an ease that proved it was as much a knack as pure strength—

But the fellow *was* strong, and Dick Suilin was out of shape for this work. He didn't belong here, and now he was going to die in this fire-struck night . . .

"Take the left gun!" shouted the trooper as he slapped the armor closed over his chest. He lowered his helmet visor and added in a muffled voice, "I got the right!"

A trio of sharp, white blasts raked the National Army area. Something overflew the camp from south to north with an accelerating roar that dwarfed even the blasts of the tank gun. It was visible only as the dull glow of a heated surface.

Suilin picked himself up from the ice chest and stacked boxes which halved the space available within the fighting compartment. One man was already bent over the bow gun, ripping the night in short bursts. Suilin's guide seized the grips of the right-hand weapon and doubled the car's weight of fire.

Two of the guard towers were burning. Exploding flares and ammunitions sent sparkles of color through the smoky orange flames. The fighting platforms were armored, but the towers were constructed of wood. Suilin had known that—but he hadn't considered until now what the construction technique would mean in a battle.

There wasn't supposed to *be* a battle, here in the South.

Suilin bent close to the third tribarrel, hoping he could make some sense of it. He'd had militia training like every other male in the country over the age of sixteen, but Prosperity's National Army wasn't equipped with powerguns.

He took the double grips in his hands, that much was obvious. The weapon rotated easily, though the surprising mass of the barrels gave Suilin's tentative swings more inertia than he'd intended.

When his thumbs pressed the trigger button between the grips, nothing happened. The tribarrel had a switch or safety somewhere, and in the dark Suilin wasn't going to be able to overcome his ignorance.

The gun in a tank's cupola snapped a stream of cranyan fire south at a flat angle. There was a huge flash and a separate flaring red streak in the sky above the National Army positions. Two other missiles detonated on the ground as three of the earlier salvo had done.

The mercenaries claimed they could shoot shells and missiles out of the air. Suilin hadn't believed that was more than advertising puffery, but he'd just seen it happen. The Slammers' vehicles couldn't protect the National Army positions, but missiles aimed high enough to threaten the mercenaries' own end of Camp Progress were being gutted by computer-aimed powerguns.

The back of Suilin's mind shivered to realize that just now he really didn't care what happened to his fellow citizens, so long as those Consie missiles couldn't land on *him*.

The tribarrel was useless—the reporter knew he was useless with it—but a short-barreled grenade launcher and bandolier lay across the ice chest beside him. He snatched it up and found the simple mechanical safety with his left thumb.

Suilin had never been any good with a rifle, but his shotgun had brought down its share of birds at the estates of family friends. In militia training he'd taken to grenade launchers like a child to milk.

A bullet passed close enough to crack in Suilin's left ear. He didn't have any idea where the round came from, but both the other men in the fighting compartment swung their tribarrels and began hosing a swale only a hundred meters from the berm. So . . .

Suilin lifted his grenade launcher and fired. He didn't bother with the sights, just judged the angle of the barrel. The *chook!* of the shot was a little sharper than he'd expected; the Slammers used lighter projectiles with a higher velocity than the weapons he'd been trained on.

They used a more potent bursting charge, too. The grenade's yellow flash, fifty meters beyond Suilin's point of aim, looked like an artillery piece firing.

He lowered the muzzle slightly and squeezed off. This time the projectile burst just where he wanted it, in the swale whose lips were lighted by the tribarrel's crackling bolts.

Suilin didn't see the figure leap from concealment until the powerguns clawed the Consie dazzlingly apart.

"That's right!" his guide screamed from the right-hand gun. "Flush the bastards for us!"

The grenade launcher's recoil woke a similar warmth from the reporter's shoulder. He swung his weapon slightly and walked three shots down the hidden length of the swale. The last was away before the first was cratering the darkened turf.

An empty clip ejected from the weapon after the fifth round. Both tribarrels fired. There was a disemboweled scream as Dick Suilin reached for the bandolier, groping for more ammunition . . .

✧   ✧   ✧

The turret hatch clanged above Birdie Sparrow; he wasn't shivering any more. Albers, his driver, hadn't boarded yet, so Birdie brought *Deathdealer* up himself by touching the main switch. The displays lighted softly on auxiliary power while the fusion bottle built pressure.

Deathdealer's hull deadened most sounds, but mortar fragments rang on her skirts like sleet on a window. "Booster, Screen Three," Birdie said, ordering the tank's artificial intelligence to bring up Screen Three, which he habitually used for non-optical sensor inputs.

The tracks of mortar shells were glowing holographic arcs, red for the first salvo and orange for the second. Birdie computed a vector and overlaid it on his main screen at the same time he fed the data to fire control. The turret began to rotate on its frictionless magnetic bearings; the breech of the main gun raised a few centimeters as the muzzle dipped onto its aiming point.

Deathdealer grunted as her fans took a first bite of air. Albers had boarded, so they were fully combat ready.

Light enhancement on the main screen showed the shell tracks arcing from a copse 1800 meters from the berm at a deflection of forty-three degrees east of true north. The orange pipper on Screen Two, the gunnery display, was centered on that point.

The Consies might be in a gully hidden by the trees, and there was a limit to the amount of dirt and rock even a 20cm powergun could excavate, but—

Birdie rocked his foot switch, sending two rounds from his main gun crashing downrange.

Deathdealer shook. The amount of copper plasma being expelled was only a few grams, but when even that slight mass was accelerated to light speed, its recoil force shifted the tank's 170 tonnes. Spent casings ejected onto the turret floor, overwhelming the air conditioning with the stench of hot matrix.

The copse exploded in a ball of fire and live steam.

A tree leaped thirty meters skyward, driven by the gout of energy that had shattered the bole at root level.

Birdie chuckled and coughed in the atmosphere of reeking plastic. The mortar crew might not've bought it this time, but they bloody sure weren't going to call attention to themselves for a while. DJ'd have appreciated that.

The main screen highlighted movement in blue: two figures hunched with the weight of the burden they carried between them toward the berm.

Birdie's left thumb rocked the gun control from main to coax while his right hand expertly teased the joystick to bring the pipper onto his targets. They went to ground just as his foot was tensing on the gunswitch, disappearing into a minute dip that meant the difference between life and death.

Birdie started to switch back to the main gun and do the job by brute force, but—

Y' know it's gonna happen, DJ had said in his dream. Birdie waited, ten seconds, twenty. . . .

The Consies popped up from cover, their figures slightly blurred by phosphor delays in the enhanced hologram. Birdie's foot pressed down the rest of the way. A drive motor whirred as the cupola tribarrel thumped out its five-round burst. Cyan impacts flung the targets to left and right as parts of their bodies vaporized explosively.

Death had waited; thirty seconds for that pair, years for other men. But Death didn't forget.

Birdie was safe. He was inside the heaviest piece of land-based armor in the human universe.

Three artillery rockets hit in the near distance. A fourth rumbled overhead, shaking *Deathdealer* and Birdie's vision of safety. Those were definitely big enough to hurt anything in their impact zone.

Even a tank.

The reflexes of five years' combat, including a year

as platoon sergeant, took over. Birdie kept one eye on the panoramic main screen while his hands punched data out of his third display.

The other tanks in the encampment were powered up. The tribarrel couldn't override it without codes he didn't have. The third tank, an H Company repair job named *Herman's Whore*, didn't respond when he pinged it, and a remote hook-up indicated nobody was in the turret.

From his own command console, Birdie rotated the *Whore's* tribarrel to the south and slaved it to air defense. Until somebody overrode his command, the gun would engage any airborne targets her sensors offered her.

That left Birdie to get back to immediate business. An alarm pinged to warn him that a laser rangefinder painted *Deathdealer's* armor. The gunnery computer was already rotating the turret, while a pulsing red highlight arrowed the source: an anti-tank missile launcher twelve hundred meters away, protected only by night and distance.

Which meant unprotected.

Deathdealer's close-in defense system would detonate the missile at a distance with a sleet of barrel-shaped steel pellets, but the Consies needed to learn that you didn't target Colonel Hammer's tanks.

Birdie Sparrow thumbed the gunswitch, preparing to teach the Consies a main-gun lesson.

Henk Ortnahme, panting as he mounted the turret of *Herman's Whore*, didn't notice the cupola tribarrel was slewed until the bloody thing ripped out a bloody burst that almost blew his bloody head off.

The plasma discharge prickled his scalp and made the narrow fringe that was all the hair he had stand out like a ruff.

Ortnahme ducked blindly, banging his chin on the

turret. He couldn't see a bloody thing except winking afterimages of the bolts, and he was too stunned to be angry.

The southern sky flashed and bled as one warhead detonated vainly and another missile's fuel painted the night instead of driving its payload down into the Slammers' positions. Sure, somebody'd slaved the cupola gun to air defense, and that was fine with Ortnahme.

Seeing as he'd managed to survive learning about it.

He mounted the cupola quickly and lowered himself into the turret, hoping the cursed gun wouldn't cut loose again just now. The hatch was a tight fit, but it didn't have sharp edges like the access port.

The port had torn Ortnahme's coveralls so he looked like he'd been wrestling a tiger. Then the bloody coverplate—warped by the mine that deadlined the tank to begin with—hadn't wanted to bolt back in place.

But Ortnahme was in the turret now, and *Herman's Whore* was ready to slide.

The radio was squawking on the command channel. Ortnahme'd left the hatch open, and between the racket of gunfire and incoming—most of *that* well to the south by now—the warrant leader couldn't hear what was being said. If he'd known he was in for a deal like this, he'd've brought the commo helmet stashed in his quarters against the chance that someday he'd get back out in the field . . .

For now he rolled the volume control up to full and blasted himself with, "DO YOU HAVE A CREW? O—"

Ortnahme dumped some of the volume.

"—ver."

"Roger, Tootsie Six," the warrant leader reported. "*Herman's Whore* is combat ready. Over."

He sat down, the first chance he'd had to do that since sun-up, and leaped to his feet again as the multitool he'd stowed in his cargo pocket clanged against the frame of the seat. Blood and martyrs!"

Ortnahme was itching for a chance to shoot something, but he'd spent too long with the fan and the coverplate. There weren't any targets left on *his* displays, and he suspected that most of the bolts still hissing across the berm were fired by kids who didn't have the sense God gave a goose.

The Consies had hit in a rush, figuring to sweep over the encampment by sheer speed and numbers. You couldn't *do* that against the firepower the Slammers put out.

The rest of Camp Progress, though. . . .

"Tootsie Six to all Red and Blue personnel," Junebug Ranson continued. "The Yokels report that bandits have penetrated their positions. Red units will form line abreast and sweep south through the encampments. Mobile Blue units—"

The three tanks. Ortnahme's tank, by the Lord's blood!

"—will cross the berm, form on the TOC, and sweep counterclockwise from that point to interdict bandit reinforcements. *Deathdealer* has command."

Sergeant Sparrow. Tall, dark, and as jumpy as a pithed frog. Usually Ortnahme got crewmen to help him when he pulled major maintenance on their vehicles, but he'd given Sparrow a wide berth. *That* boy was four-plus crazy.

"Remaining Blue elements," Ranson concluded, "hold what you got, boys. We got to take care of this now, but we'll be back. Tootsie Six over."

Remaining Blue elements. The maintenance and logistics people, the medic and the light-duty personnel. The people who were crouched now in bunkers with their sidearms and their prayers, hoping that when the armored vehicles shifted front, the Consies wouldn't be able to mount another attack on the Slammer positions.

"*Deathdealer*, roger."

"Charlie Three-zero, roger."

"*Herman's Whore*, roger," Ortnahme reported. He didn't much like being under the command of Birdie Sparrow, a flake who was technically his junior, but Sparrow was a flake because of years of line service, and it wasn't a point that the warrant leader would even think of mentioning after it all settled down again.

Assuming.

He switched to intercom. "You heard the lady, Simkins," he said. "Lift us over the bloody berm!"

And as the fan note built from idle into a full-throated roar, Ortnahme went back to looking for targets.

The combat car drove a plume of dust from the berm as it started to back and swing. The man who'd been firing the forward tribarrel turned so that Dick Suilin could see the crucifix gilded onto the plastron of his body armor. He flipped up his visor and said, "Who the cop're you?"

"I'm, ah—" the reporter said.

His ears rang. Afterimages like magnified algae rods filled his eyes as his retinas tried to redress the chemical imbalances burned into them by the glaring powerguns.

He waggled the smoking muzzle of the grenade launcher.

That must have been the right response. The man with the crucifix looked at the trooper who'd guided Suilin to the vehicle and said, "Where the cop's Speed, Otski?"

The wing gunner grimaced and said, "Well, Cooter, ah—his buddy in Logistics got in, you know, this morning."

"Bloody buggered *fool!*" Cooter shouted. He'd looked a big man even when he hunched over his tribarrel; straightening in rage made him a giant. "*Tonight* he's stoned?"

"Cut him some slack, Cooter," Otski said, looking aside rather than meeting the bigger soldier's eyes. "This ain't the Strip, you know."

Suilin rubbed his forehead. The Strip. The no-man's-
land surrounding the Terran Government enclaves in the
north.

"Tonight it's the bleeding Strip!" Cooter snapped.

Cooter's helmet spoke something that was only a tiny
rattle to Suilin. "Tootsie Three, roger," the big man said.
Otski nodded.

A multiple explosion hammered the center of the
camp. Munitions hurled themselves in sparkling tracks
from a bubble of orange flame.

"Blood 'n martyrs," Cooter muttered as angry light
bathed his weary face.

He lifted a suit of hard armor from the floor of the
fighting compartment. "Here," he said to Suilin, "put this
on. Wish I could give you a helmet, but that dickhead
Speed's got it with him."

Their combat car was sliding across the packed earth
keeping its bow southward—toward the flames and the
continued shooting. The car passed close to where Fritzi
Doyle lay. The photographer's clothing swelled in the
draft blasting from beneath the plenum chamber.

Dust whipped and eddied. The other combat cars
were maneuvering also, forming a line. Here at the
narrow end of the encampment, the separations between
vehicles were only about ten meters apiece.

"That gun work?" Cooter demanded, patting the
breech of the tribarrel as Suilin put on the unfamiliar
armor. The clamshell seemed to weigh more than its
actual twenty kilos; it was chafing over his left collarbone
even before he got it latched.

"Huh?" the reporter grunted. "I think—I mean, I
don't—"

Making a bad guess *now* meant someone might die
rather than just a libel suit.

Meant Dick Suilin might die.

"Oh, right," Cooter said easily. He poked with a big
finger at where the gun's receiver was gimbaled onto its

pedestal. A green light glowed just above the trigger button. "No sweat, turtle. I'll just slave it to mine. You just keep bombin' 'em like you been doing."

The helmet buzzed again. "Tootsie Three, roger," Cooter repeated. He tapped the side of his helmet and order, "Move out, Shorty, but keep it to a walk, right?"

Cooter and Otski bent over their weapons. When the big trooper waggled his handgrips, the left tribarrel rocked in parallel with his own.

"What are we doing?" Suilin asked, swaying as the combat car moved forward. The big vehicle had the smooth, unpleasant motion of butter melting as a grill heats.

The reporter pulled another loaded clip from the bandolier to have it ready. He squinted toward the barracks ahead of them, silhouetted in orange light.

"Huh?" said Cooter. His face was a blank behind his lowered visor as he looked over his shoulder in surprise.

"We're gonna clear your Consie buddies outta Camp Progress," Otski said with a feral grin in his voice.

"Yeah, right, you don't have a commo," Cooter said/apologized. "Look, anybody you see in a black uniform, zap him. Anybody shoots at us, *zap* him. Fast."

"Anything bleedin' *moves*," said Otski, "you zap it. Any mistake you gotta make, make it in favor of *our* ass, right?"

Suilin nodded tightly. There was a howl and *whump!* behind them. For a moment he thought the noise was a shell, but it was only one of the huge tanks lifting its mass over the berm.

A combat car on the right flank fired down one of the neat boulevards which served the National Army's portion of the camp.

"Hey, turtle?" the right wing gunner said. "You got a name?"

"Dick," Suilin said. He'd lifted the grenade launcher to his shoulder twice already, then lowered it because he felt like a fool to be aiming at no target. The noise around him was hideous.

"Don't worry, Dick," Otski said. "We'll tell yer girl you were brave."

He chuckled, then lighted the wide street ahead of them with a burst from his tribarrel.

"You must send the 4th Armored Brigade to relieve us!" Colonel Banyussuf was ordering his superiors in Kohang. Since June Ranson's radio was picking up the call down in the short-range two-meter push, there was about zip possibility that anybody 300 kilometers away could hear the Yokel commander's panicked voice.

Two men in full uniform poked their rifles gingerly southward, around the corner of a barracks. Light reflected from their polished leather and brightly-nickeled Military Police brassards. The MP's stared in open-mouthed amazement as the combat car slid past them.

"About zip" was still a better chance than that District Command in Kohang would do anything about Banyussuf's problems.

Trouble here meant there was *big* trouble everywhere on Prosperity. District Command wasn't going to send the armored brigade based on the coast near Kohang haring off into the sticks to relieve Banyussuf.

"Watch it," Willens, their driver, warned.

Warmonger slid into an intersection. A crowd of thirty or so women and children screamed and ran a step or two away from them, then screamed again and flattened as another car crossed at the next intersection east. Dependents of senior non-coms, looking for a place to hide. . . .

Ranson wouldn't have minded having a Yokel armored brigade for support, but it'd take too long to reach here. Her team could do the job by themselves.

"Two o'clock!" she warned. Movement on the second

floor of a barracks, across the wide boulevard that acted as a parade square every morning for the Yokels.

The left corner of her visor flashed the tiny red numeral 2. Her helmet's microprocessor had gathered all its sensor inputs and determined that the target was of Threat Level 2.

Cold meat under most circumstances, but in Camp Progress there were thousands of National Army personnel who looked the same as the Consies to scanners. With her visor on thermal, Ranson couldn't tell whether the figure wore black or a green-on-green mottled Yokel uni—

The figure raised its gun. 2 blinked to 1 in Ranson's visor, then vanished—

Because a dead man doesn't have any threat level at all. Ranson's burst converged with Janacek's; the upper front of the barracks flew apart as the powerguns ignited it.

Willens slewed the car left. Somebody leaned out of a window of the same barracks and fired—missed even the combat car except for one bullet ricocheting from the dirt street to whang on the skirts.

Ranson killed the shooter; letting *Warmonger*'s forward motion walk the flashing cyan cores of her burst down the line of barracks windows. Janacek was raking the lower story, and as they came abreast of the building, the One-five blower to *Warmonger*'s right laid on a crossfire from two of its tribarrels.

A single bolt from the other car sizzled through gaps already blown in the structure and hit the barracks on the other side of the street. The cyan track missed Ranson by little enough that the earphones in her helmet screamed piercingly with harmonics from the energy release.

She noticed it was the way she'd noticed a reflection in a shop window. Everything around her seemed to be reflected or hidden behind sheets of thick glass. Nothing touched her. Her skin felt warm, the way it did when she was on the verge of going to sleep.

A tank's main gun flashed beyond the berm. Ranson would've liked the weight of the panzers with her to push the Consies out, but their 20cm cannon were too destructive to use within a position crammed with friendly troops and their dependents. If things got hot enough that the combat cars needed a bail-out—

She'd give the orders she had to give and worry about the consequences later. But for now. . . .

A group of armed men ran from a cross street into the next intersection. Some of them were still looking back over their shoulders when *Warmonger*'s three tribarrels lashed them with converging streams of fire.

Figures whirled and disintegrated individually for a moment before a bloom of white light—a satchel charge, a buzzbomb's warhead; perhaps just a bandolier strung with grenades—enveloped the group. The shockwave slammed bodies and body fragments in every direction.

Ranson was sure they'd been wearing black uniforms. Pretty sure.

"—*must help me!*" whimpered the radio. "*They have captured the lower floor of my headquarters!*"

She hand-keyed the microphone and said, "Progress Command, this is Slammers' Command. Help's on the way, but be bloody sure your own people don't shoot at *us*. Out."

Or *else*, her mind added, but she didn't want that threat on record. Anyway, even the Yokels were smart enough to know what happened when somebody shot at the Slammers. . . .

"Tootsie Six to Red elements," Ranson heard herself ordering. "Keep moving even if you're taking fire. Don't let 'em get their balance or they'll chop us."

Her voice was echoing to her down corridors of glass.

Chapter Three

Callsign Charlie Three-zero hit halfway up the berm's two-meter height. Holman had the beast still accelerating at the point of impact.

Even though Wager'd seen it coming and had tried to brace himself, the collision hurled his chest against the hatch coaming. His clamshell armor saved his ribs, but the shock drove all the breath from his body.

Air spilled from the tilted plenum chamber. The tank sagged backward like a horse spitted on a wall of pikes.

Hans Wager hoped that the smash hadn't knocked his driver's teeth out. He wanted to do that much himself, as soon as things got quiet again.

"Holman," he wheezed as he keyed his intercom circuit. He'd never wanted to command a tank. . . . "Use lift, not your bloody speed. You can't—"

Dust exploded around Charlie Three-zero as if a bomb had gone off. Holman kept the blades' angle of attack flat to build up fan speed before trying to raise the vehicle again. She wasn't unskilled, exactly; she just wasn't used to moving something with this much inertia.

"—just ram through the bloody berm!" Wager concluded; but as they backed, he got a good look at the chunk they'd gouged from the protective dirt wall and had to wonder. They bloody near *had* plowed their way through, at no cost worse than bending the front skirts.

Rugged mother, this tank was. Might be something to be said for panzers after all, once you got to know 'em.

And got a bleedin' driver who knew 'em.

Something in the middle of the Yokel positions went off with walloping violence. Other people's problems weren't real high on Hans Wager's list right now, though.

The acting platoon leader, Sergeant Sparrow, had assigned Wager to the outside arc of the sweep and taken the berm side himself. Wager didn't like Sparrow worth spit. When Wager arrived at Camp Progress, he'd tried to get some pointers from the experienced tank sergeant, but Sparrow was an uncommunicative man whose eyes focused well beyond the horizon.

The dispositions made sense, though. The action was likely to be hottest right outside the camp. Sparrow's reflexes made him the best choice to handle it. Wager wasn't familiar with his new hardware, but he was a combat trooper who could be trusted to keep their exposed flank clear.

The middle slot of the sweep was a tank cobbled into action by the maintenance detachment. The lord *only* knew what they'd be good for.

The Red team's six combat cars had formed across the detachment area and were starting toward the bubbling inferno of the Yokel positions. As they did so, Sparrow's *Deathdealer* eeled over the berm with only two puffs where the skirts dug in and kicked dirt high enough for it to go through the fan intakes.

Even the blower from maintenance had made the jump without a serious problem. While Wager and his *truck*driver—

Holman had the fans howling on full power. A lurching *clack* vibrated through Charlie Three-zero's fabric as the driver rammed all eight pitch controls to maximum lift.

"Via!" Wager screamed over the intercom. "Give her a *little* for—"

Their hundred and seventy tonnes rose—bouncing on thrust instead of using the cushion effect of air under pressure in the plenum chamber. The tank teetered like a plate spinning on a broomhandle.

"—ward!"

The stern curtsied as Holman finally tilted two of her fan nacelles to direct their thrust to the rear. Charlie Three-zero slid forward, then hopped up as the skirts gouged the top of the berm like a cookie cutter in soft dough.

The tank sailed off the front of the berm and dropped like the iridium anvil she was as soon as her skirts lost their temporary ground effect. They hit squarely, ramming the steel skirts ten centimeters into the ground and racking Wager front and back against the coaming.

Somehow Holman managed to keep a semblance of control. The tank's bow slewed right—and Charlie Three-zero roared off counterclockwise, in pursuit of the other two members of their platoon.

They continued to bounce every ten meters or so. Their skirts grounded, rose till there was more than a hand's breadth clearance beneath the skirts—and spilled pressure in another hop.

But they were back in the war.

The reason Warrant Leader Ortnahme fired into the rockpile 300 meters to their front was that the overgrown mount—a dump for plowed-up stone before the government took over the area from Camp Progress—was a likely hiding place for Consie troops.

The reason Ortnahme fired the main gun instead of the tribarrel was that he'd never had an excuse to do *that* before in his twenty-three years as a soldier.

His screens damped automatically to keep from being overloaded, but the blue flash was reflected onto Ortnahme through the open hatch as *Herman's Whore* bucked with the recoil.

The rockpile blew apart in gobbets of molten quartz and blazing vegetation. There was no sign of Consies.

Via! but it felt good!

Simkins was keeping them a hundred meters outside Sparrow's *Deathdealer*, the way the acting platoon leader had ordered. Simkins had moved his share of tanks in the course of maintenance work, but before now, he'd never had to drive one as fast as twenty kph. He was doing a good job, but—

"Simkins!" he ordered. *"Don't* jink around them bloody bushes like they was the landscaping at headquarters. Just drive over 'em!"

But the kid was doing fine. The Lord *only* knew where the third tank with its newbie crew had gotten to.

The air of the Yokels' high berm crackled with hints of cyan, the way invisible lightning backlighted clouds during a summer storm. The Red team was finding somebody to mix with.

The tanks might as well be practicing night driving techniques. The Consies that'd hit this end of the encampment must all be dead or runnin' as fast as they could to save their miserable—

WHANG!

Herman's Whore slewed to the right and grounded, then began staggering crabwise with the left side of her skirts scraping. They'd been hit, *hard*, but there wasn't any trace of the shot in the screens whose sensors should've reported the event even if they hadn't warned of it.

"Sir, I've lost plenum chamber pressure," Simkins said, a triumph of the obvious that even a bloody civilian with a bloody *rutabaga* for a brain wouldn't've bothered to—

"Did the access door blow open again?" Simkins continued.

Blood and Martyrs. Of course.

"Lord, kid, I'm sorry," the warrant leader blurted, apologizing for what he hadn't said—and for the fact he hadn't been thinking. "Put 'er down and I'll take care of it."

The tank settled. Ortnahme raised his seat to the top of its run, then prepared to step out through the hatch. Down in the hull, the sensor console pinged a warning.

Ortnahme couldn't see the screens from this angle, and he didn't have a commo helmet to relay the data to him in the cupola.

He didn't need the electronic sensors. His eyes and the sky-glow from the ongoing destruction of Camp Progress showed him a Consie running toward *Herman's Whore* with an armload of something that wasn't roses.

"Simkins!" the warrant leader screamed, hoping his voice would carry either to the driver or the intercom pick-up in the hull. "Go! Go! Go!"

The muscles beneath Ortnahme's fat bunched as he swung the tribarrel. The gun tracked as smoothly as wet ice, but it was glacially slow as well.

Ortnahme's thumbs clamped on the trigger, lashing out a stream of bolts. The Consie flopped down. None of the bolts had cracked through the air closer than a meter above his head. The bastard was too close for the cupola gun to hit him.

Which the Consie figured out just as quick as Ortnahme did. The guerrilla picked himself up and shambled toward the tank again, holding out what was certainly a magnetic mine. It would detonate a few seconds after he clamped it onto the *Whore's* steel skirts.

Ortnahme fired again. His bolts lit the camouflaged lid of the hole in which the Consie was hidden—twenty meters from where the target was now.

There was a simple answer to this sort of problem; the close-in defense system built into each of Hammer's combat vehicles, ready to blast steel shot into oncoming missiles or men who'd gotten too close to be handled by the tribarrel.

Trouble was, Ortnahme was a very competent and experienced mechanic. He'd dismantled the defense system before he started the rebuild. If he hadn't he'd've risked killing himself and fifty other people if his pliers slipped and sent a current surge down the wrong circuit. He'd been going to reconnect the system in the morning, when the work was done. . . .

The intake roar of the fans resumed three Consie steps before the tank began moving, but finally *Herman's Whore* staggered forward again. They were a great pair for a race—the tank crippled, and the man bent over by the weight of the mine he carried. A novelty act for clowns. . . .

Down in the hull the commo was babbling something—orders, warnings; Simkins wondering what the *cop* his superior thought he was up to. Ortnahme didn't dare leave the cupola to answer—or call for help. As soon as they drew enough ahead of the Consie, he'd blast the bastard and then fix the access plate so they could move properly again.

The trouble with *that* plan was that *Herman's Whore* had started circling. The tank moved about as fast as the man on foot, but the Consie was cutting the chord of the arc and in a few seconds—

The warrant leader lifted himself from the hatch and let himself slide down the smooth curve of the turret. He fumbled in his cargo pocket. Going in this direction, his age and fat didn't matter. . . .

The Consie staggered forward, bent over his charge, in a triumph of will over exhaustion. He must have been blowing like a whale, but the sound wasn't audible over the suction of the tank's eight fans.

Ortnahme launched himself from the tank and crushed the guerrilla to the ground. Bones snapped, caught between the warrant leader's mass and the mine casing.

Ortnahme didn't take any chances. He hammered until the grip of the multitool thumped slimy dirt instead of the Consie's head.

Herman's Whore was circling back. Ortnahme tried to stand, then sat heavily. He waved his left arm.

By the time Simkins pulled up beside him, the warrant leader would be ready to get up and *weld* that cursed access cover in place.

Until then, he'd figured he'd just sit and catch his breath.

Terrain is one thing on a contour map, where a dip of three meters in a hundred is dead flat, and another thing on the ground, where it's enough difference to hide an object the size of a tank.

Which is just what it seemed to have done to callsign Tootsie Four, the maintenance section's vehicle, so far as Hans Wager could tell from his own cupola.

It wasn't Holman's fault.

What with the late start, they'd had to drive like a bat outta Hell to get into position. It would've taken the Lord and all his martyrs to save 'em if they'd stumbled into the Consies while Wager was barely able to hang on, much less shoot.

But since they caught up, she'd been keeping Charlie Three-zero about 300 meters outboard of Sparrow's blower, just like orders. Only thing was, there was supposed to be another tank between them.

Sparrow was covering a double arc, with his tribarrel swung left and his main gun offset to the right. It was the main gun that fired, kicking a scoopload of fused earth skyward in fiery sparkles.

Wager didn't see what the platoon leader'd shot at, but three figures jumped to their feet near the point of impact. Wager tumbled them to the ground again as blazing corpses with a burst from his tribarrel.

They were doing okay. Wager was doing okay. His facial muscles were locked in a tight rictus, and he took his fingers momentarily from the tribarrel's grips to massage the numbness out of them.

His driver was doing all right too, now that it was just a matter of moving ahead at moderate speed, *Deathdealer* was traveling at about twenty kph, and Holman had been holding Charlie Three-zero to the same speed since they caught up with the rest of the platoon.

Because Sparrow's tank was on the inside of the pivot, it was slowly drawing ahead of them. Wager felt the hull vibration change as Holman fiddled with her power and tilt controls, but the tank's inertia took much longer to adjust.

The fan note built into a shriek.

Wager scanned the night, wishing he had the eyes of two wing gunners to help the way he would on a combat car. Having the main gun was all well and good, but he figured the firepower of another pair of tribarrels—

Via! What did Holman think they were doing? Running a race?

—would more than make up for a twenty centimeter punch in *this* kind of war.

"Holman!" he snarled into his intercom. "Slow us bloody—"

Charlie Three-zero's mass had absorbed all the power inputs and he was now rocketing through the night at twice her previous speed. *Way* too fast in the dark for anything but paved roads. Rocks clanged on the skirts as the tank crested a knoll—

And plunged down the other side, almost as steep as the berm they'd crashed off minutes before.

"*—down!*"

The ravine was full of Consies, jumping aside or flattening as Charlie Three-zero hurtled toward them under no more control than a 170-tonne roundshot.

Wager's bruised body knew *exactly* how the impact would feel, but reflex kept that from affecting anything he did. Charlie Three-zero hit, bounced. Wager's left hand flipped the protective cage away from the control on the tribarrel's mount—the same place it was on a combat car. He rammed the miniature joystick straight in, firing the entire close-in defense system in a single white flash from the top of the skirts.

Guerrillas flew apart in shreds.

The door of a bunker gaped open in the opposite side of the gully. Holman had been trying to raise Charlie Three-zero's bow to slow their forward motion. As the tank hopped forward, the bow *did* lift enough for the skirts to scrape the rise instead of slamming into it the way they had when trying to get out of Camp Progress.

"Bring us—" Wager ordered as he rotated his tribarrel to bear on the Consies behind them, some squirming in their death throes but others rising again to point weapons.

—*around*, he meant to say, but Holman reversed her fans and sucked the tank squarely down where she'd just hit. The unexpected impact rammed Wager's spine against his seat. His tribarrel was aimed upward.

"You dickheaded fool!" he screamed over the intercom as he lowered his weapon and the tank started to lift in place.

A Consie threw a grenade. It bounced off the hull and exploded in the air. Wager felt the hot *flick* of shrapnel beneath the cheekpiece of his helmet, but the grenadier himself flopped backward with most of his chest gone.

The tribarrel splattered the air, then walked its long burst across several of the guerrillas still moving.

Holman slammed the tank down again. They hit with a crunch, followed by a second shudder as the ground collapsed over the Consie bunker.

Holman rocked her fans. Dust and quartz pebbles flew back, covering the corpses in the gully like dirt spurned by a cat over its dung.

"Sergeant?" called the voice in Wager's intercom. "Sergeant? Want to make another pass?"

Wager was trying to catch his breath. "Negative, Holman," he managed to say. "Just bring us level with *Deathdealer* again."

"Holman," he added a moment later. "You did just fine."

Their position in line was second from the left, but Dick Suilin glimpsed at the remaining combat car on his side only at intersections—and that rarely.

Its powerguns lit the parallel street in a constant reminder of its lethal presence. A burst quivering like a single blue flash showed Suilin a hump on what would have been the straight slope of a barracks roofline across the next intersection.

The reporter fired; the empty clip ejected with the *choonk* of his weapon.

Before Suilin's grenade had completed its low-velocity arc toward its target, the figure fired back with a stream of tracers that looked the size of bright orange baseballs. They sailed lazily out of the flickering muzzle flashes, then snapped past the reporter with dazzling speed.

The splinter shield above Suilin rang, and impacts sparkled on the iridium side armor. *How could the Consie have missed*— the reporter thought.

A tremendous blow knocked him backward.

His grenade detonated on the end wall of the building, a meter below the machinegunner. Cooter, screaming curses or orders to their driver, squeezed his trigger button. Cyan fire ripped from both the weapon he gripped and the left wing gun, slaved to follow the point gun's controls.

Suilin didn't hurt, but he couldn't feel anything between his neck and his waistband. He tried to say, "I'm all right," to reassure himself, but he found there was no air in his lungs and he couldn't breathe. There were glowing dimpled in the splinter shield where the machinegun had hammered it.

I'm dead, he thought. It should have bothered him more than it did.

His grenade had missed the Consie. Tracers sprayed

harmlessly skyward as the fellow jumped back while keeping a deathgrip on his trigger.

Cooter's powerguns lit and shattered rooftiles as they sawed toward, then through, their target. The machinegun's ammunition drum blew up with a yellow flash.

Suilin's hands hurt like *Hell*. "Via!" he screamed. A flash of flaming agony wrapped his chest and released it as suddenly, leaving behind an ache many times worse than what he remembered from the time he broke his arm.

Both the mercenaries, faceless in their visored helmets, were bending over him. "Where you hit?" Cooter demanded as Otski lifted the reporter's right forearm and said, "Via! But it's just fragments, it's okay."

Cooter's big index finger prodded Suilin in the chest. "Yeah," he said. "No penetration." He tugged at something.

Suilin felt a cold, prickling sensation over his left nipple. "What're you—" he said, but the Slammers had turned back to their guns.

The car must have paused while they checked him. Now it surged forward faster than before.

They swept by the barracks. Cooter's long double burst had turned it into a torch.

Suilin lay on his back. He looked down at himself. There was a charred circle as big as a soup dish in the fabric cover of his clamshell. In the center of *that* was a thumb-sized crater in the armor itself.

The pockmark in the ceramic plate had a metallic sheen, and there were highlights of glittering metal in the blood covering the backs of both Suilin's hands. When the bullet hit the clamshell armor and broke up, fragments splashed forward and clawed the reporter's bare hands.

He rose, pushing himself up with his arms. For a moment, his hands burned and there were icepicks in his neck and lower back.

Coolness spreading outward from his chest washed over the pain. There were colored tabs on the breast of the armor. Suilin had thought they were decorations, but the one Cooter had pulled was obviously releasing medication into Suilin's system.

Thank the Lord for that.

He picked up the grenade launcher and reloaded it. Shock, drugs, and the tiny bits of metal that winked when he moved his fingers made him clumsy, but he did it.

Like working against a deadline. Your editor didn't care why you *hadn't* filed on time; so you worked when you were hung over, when you had flu. . . .

When your father died before you had had time to clear things up with him. When your wife left you because you didn't care about *her*, only your cursed *stories*.

Dick Suilin raised his eyes and his ready weapon just as both the combat car and the immediate universe opened up with a breathtaking inferno of fire.

They'd reached the Headquarters of Camp Progress.

It was a three-story building at the southern end of the encampment. Nothing separated the pagoda-roofed structure from the berm except the camp's peripheral road. The berm here, like the hundred-meter square in front of the building, had been sodded and was manicured daily.

There were bodies sprawled on the grass. Suilin didn't have time to look at them, because lights flared in several ground-floor windows as Consies launched buzzbombs and ducked back.

The grenade launcher's dull report was lost in the blurred crackling of the three tribarrels, but the reporter knew he'd gotten his round away as fast as the veterans had theirs.

Unlike the rest of Camp Progress, the Headquarters building was a masonry structure. At least a dozen powerguns were raking the two lower floors. Though the stones spattered out pebbles and molten glass at every impact, the walls themselves held and continued to protect the Consies within them.

The grenade was a black dot against the window lighted by bolts from the powerguns. It sailed through the opening, detonated with a dirty flash, and flung a guerrilla's corpse momentarily into view.

The oncoming buzzbomb filled Suilin's forward vision. He saw it with impossible clarity, its bulbous head swelling on a thread of smoke that trailed back to the grenade-smashed room.

The close-in defense system went off, spewing miniature steel barrels into the path of the free-flight missile. They slashed through the warhead, destroying its integrity. When the buzzbomb hit the side of the combat car between the left and center gun positions, the fuze fired but the damaged booster charge did not.

The buzzbomb bounced from the armor with a bell sound, then skittered in tight circles around the grass until its rocket motor burned out.

Cooter's driver eased the vehicle forward, onto the lawn, at barely walking speed. The square was normally lighted after sunset, but all the poles had been shot away.

Dick Suilin had spent three days at or close to the Headquarters building while he gathered the bulk of his story. Clean-cut, *professional* members of the National Army, doing their jobs with quiet dedication—to contrast with ragged, brutal-looking mercenaries (many of whom were female!), who absorbed such a disproportionate share of the defense budget.

"Hey turtle!" Otski called. "Watch that—"

To either side of the grassed area were pairs of trailers, living quarters for Colonel Banyussuf and his favored staff. The one on the left end was assigned to Sergeant-Major Lee, the senior non-com at Camp Progress. Suilin was billeted with him. The door was swinging in the light breeze, and a dozen or so bulletholes dimpled the sidewall at waist height, but Suilin could at least hope he'd be able to recover his gear unharmed when this was over.

The car to their left fired a short burst at the trailer. The bolts blew the end apart, shattering the plywood panels and igniting the light metal sheathing. The reporters swore at the unnecessary destruction.

The air criss-crossed with machinegun bullets and the smoke trails of at least a dozen buzzbombs. All four of the silent trailers were nests of Consie gunners.

Suilin ducked below the car's armored side.

Bullets hit the iridium and rang louder than things that small could sound. The defense system, a different portion of the continuous strip, went off. The light reflected from the underside of the splinter shield was white and orange and cyan, and there was no room in the universe for more noise.

The reporter managed to raise himself, behind the muzzle of his grenade launcher, just in time to see Sergeant-Major Lee's trailer erupt in a violent explosion that showered the square with shrapnel and blew the trailer behind it off its slab foundation.

There was a glowing white spot on the armor of the combat car to Suilin's left. As he watched, the driver's hatch popped open and a man scrambled out. Another crewman rolled over the opposite sidewall of the fighting compartment.

The car blew up.

Because the first instants were silent, it seemed a drawn-out affair, though the process couldn't have taken more than seconds from beginning to end. A streak of blue-green light shot upward, splashed on the splinter shield and *through* the steel covering almost instantaneously.,

The whole fighting compartment became a fireball that bulged the side armor and lifted the remnants of the shield like a bat-wing.

A doughnut of incandescent gas hung for a moment over the wreckage, then imploded and vanished.

Suilin screamed and emptied the clip of his grenade launcher into the other trailer on his side. It was already burning; Cooter didn't bother to fire into its crumpled remains as their car accelerated toward the Headquarters building.

Two flags—one white, the other the red-and-gold of the National Government—fluttered from the top floor of the building on short staffs. No one moved at those windows.

Now the lower floors were silent also. Otski raked the second story while Cooter used the car's slow drift to saw his twin guns across the lowest range of windows. Cooter's rotating iridium barrels were glowing white, but a ten-meter length of the walls collapsed under the point-black jackhammer of his bolts.

Suilin reloaded mechanically. He didn't have a target. At this short range, his grenades were more likely to injure himself and the rest of the crew than they were to find some unlikely Consie survivor within the Headquarters building.

He caught motion in the corner of his eye as he turned.

The movement came from a barracks they'd passed moments before, on the north side of the square. Tribarrels, Otski's and that of the next combat car in line, had gnawed the frame building thoroughly and set it alight.

A stubby black missile was silhouetted against those flames.

Gear on the floor of the fighting compartment trapped the reporter's feet as he tried to swing his grenade launcher. The close-in defense system slammed just above the skirts. The buzzbomb exploded in a red flash, ten meters away from the combat car.

A jet of near-plasma directed from the shaped-charge warhead skewered the night.

The spurt of light was almost lost to Suilin's retinas, dazzled already by the powerguns, but the blast of heat was a shock as palpable as that of the bullet that had hit him in the chest.

Otski fell down. Something flew past the reporter as he reeled against the armor.

The barrel of the grenade launcher was gone. Just gone, vaporized ten centimeters from the breech. If the jet had struck a finger's breadth to the left, the grenade would have detonated and killed all three of them.

The shockwave had snatched off Otski's helmet. The gunner's left arm was missing from the elbow down. That explained the stench of burned meat.

Suilin vomited onto his legs and feet.

"I'm all right," Otski said. He must have been screaming for Suilin to be able to hear him. "It don't mean nothin'."

A line was charred across the veteran's clamshell armor. A finger's breadth to the left, and . . .

There were two tabs on the front of Otski's back-and-breast armor. Suilin pulled them both.

"Is it bleeding?" Cooter demanded. "Is it bleeding?"

The bone stuck out a centimeter beyond where the charred muscle had shrunk back toward the gunner's shoulder. "He's—" Suilin said. "It's—"

"Right," shouted Cooter. He turned back to his tribarrel.

"I'm all right," said Otski. He tried to push himself erect. His stump clattered on the top of an ammunition box. His face went white and pinched in.

Don't mean nothin', Otski's lips formed. Then his pupils rolled up and he collapsed.

The combat car spun in its own length and circled the blasted Headquarters building. There were figures climbing the berm behind the structure. Cooter fired.

Dick Suilin leaned over Otski and took the grips of his tribarrel. Another car was following them; a third had rounded the building from the other side.

When Suilin pressed the thumb button, droplets of fire as constant as a strobe-lit fountain streamed from his rotating muzzles.

Sod sprouted in a line as the reporter walked toward the black-clad figure trying desperately to climb the steep berm ahead of them. At the last moment the guerrilla turned with his hands raised, but Suilin couldn't have lifted his thumbs in time if he'd wanted to.

Ozone and gases from the empty cases smothered the stink of Otski's arm.

For a moment, Consies balanced on top of the berm. A scything crossfire tumbled them as the tanks and combat cars raked their targets from both sides.

When nothing more moved, the vehicles shot at bodies in case some of the guerrillas were shamming. Twice Suilin managed to explode the grenades or ammunition that his targets carried.

Cooter had to pry the reporter's fingers from the tribarrel when Tootsie Six called a ceasefire.

Chapter Four

"I've got authorization," said Dick Suilin, fumbling in the breast pocket of his fatigues. The *"Extend all courtesies"* card signed by his brother-in-law, Governor Samuel Kung, was there, along with his Press ID and his Military Status Papers.

Suilin's military status was Exempt-III. That meant he would see action only in the event of a call-up of all male citizens between the ages of sixteen and sixty.

He was having trouble getting the papers out because his fingers were still numb from the way they'd been squeezing the tribarrel's grips.

For that matter, the National Government might've proclaimed a general call-up overnight—if there *was* still a National Government.

"Buddy," snarled the senior non-com at the door of the communications center, "I can't help you. I don't care if you got authorization from God 'n his saints. I don't care if you *are* God 'n his saints!"

"I'm not that," the reporter said in a soft, raspy voice. Ozone and smoke had flayed his throat. "But I need to get through to Kohang—and it's your ass if I don't."

He flicked at his shirtfront. Some of what was stuck there came off.

Suilin's wrist and the back of his right hand were black where vaporized copper from the buzzbomb had recondensed. All the fine hairs were burned off, but the skin beneath hadn't blistered. His torso was badly bruised where the bullet-struck armor had punched into him.

The butt of the pistol he now carried in his belt prodded the bruise every time he moved.

"Well, I'm not God neither, buddy," the non-com said, his tone frustrated but suddenly less angry.

He waved toward his set-up and the two junior technicians struggling with earphones and throat mikes. "The land lines're down, the satellites're down, and there's jamming right across all the bands. If you think *you* can get something through, you just go ahead and try. But if you want my ass, you gotta stand in line."

The National side of Camp Progress had three commo centers. The main one was—had been—in the shielded basement of Headquarters. A few Consies were still holed up there after the rest of the fighting had died down. A Slammers' tank had managed to depress its main gun enough to finish the job.

The training detachment had a separate system, geared toward the needs of homesick draftees. It had survived, but Colonel Banyussuf—who'd also survived—had taken over the barracks in which it was housed as his temporary headquarters. Suilin hadn't bothered trying to get through the panicked crowd now surrounding the building.

The commo room of the permanent maintenance section at Camp Progress was installed in a three-meter metal transport container. It was unofficial—the result of scrounging over the years. Suilin hadn't ever tried to use it before; but in the current chaos, it was his only hope.

"What do you mean, the satellites are down?" he demanded.

He was too logy with reaction to be sure that what he'd heard the non-com say was as absurd as he thought it was. The microwave links were out? Not all of them, surely. . . .

"Out," the soldier repeated. "Gone. Blitzed. Out."

"Blood and martyrs," Suilin said.

The Consie guerrillas couldn't have taken down all the comsats. The Terran enclaves had to have become directly involved. That was a stunning escalation of the political situation—

And an escalation which was only conceivable as part of a planned deathblow to the National Government of Prosperity.

"I've *got* to call Kohang," said Dick Suilin, aloud but without reference to the other men nearby. All he could think of was his sister, in the hands of Consies determined to make an example of the governor's wife. "Suzi . . ."

"You can forget bloody Kohang," said one of the techs as he stripped off his headphones. He ran his fingers through his hair. The steel room was hot, despite the cool morning and the air conditioner throbbing on the roof. "It's been bloody overrun."

Suilin gripped the pistol in his belt. "What do you mean?" he snarled as he pushed past the soldier in the doorway.

"They said it was," the technician insisted. He looked as though he intended to get out of his chair, but the reporter was already looming over him.

"*Somebody* said it was," argued the other tech. "Look, we're still getting signals from Kohang, it's just the jamming chews the bugger outta it."

"There's fighting all the hell over the place," said the senior non-com, putting a gently restraining hand on Suilin's soldier. " 'Cept maybe here. Look, buddy, nobody knows what the hell's going on anywhere just now."

"Maybe the mercs still got commo," the first tech said. "Yeah, I bet they do."

"Right," said the reporter. "Good thought."

He walked out of the transport container. He was thinking of what might be happening in Kohang.

He griped his pistol very hard.

The chip recorder sitting on the cupola played a background of guitar music while a woman wailed in Tagalog, a language which Henk Ortnahme had never bothered to learn. The girls on Esperanza all spoke Spanish. And Dutch. And English. Enough of it.

The girls all spoke money, the same as everywhere in the universe he'd been since.

The warrant leader ran his multitool down the channel of the close-in defense system. The wire brush he'd fitted to the head whined in complaint, but it never quite stalled out.

It never quite got the channel clean, either. Pits in the steel were no particular problem—*Herman's Whore* wasn't being readied for a parade, after all. But crud in the holes for the bolts which both anchored the strips and passed the detonation signals . . . that was something else again.

Something blew up nearby with a hollow sound, like a grenade going off in a trash can. Ortnahme looked around quickly, but there didn't seem to be an immediate problem. Since dawn there'd been occasional shooting from the Yokel end of the camp, but there was no sign of living Consies around here.

Dead ones, sure. A dozen of 'em were lined up outside the TOC, being checked for identification and anything else of intelligence value. When that was done—done in a pretty cursory fashion, the warrant leader expected, since Hammer didn't have a proper intelligence officer here at Camp Progress—the bodies would be hauled beyond the berm, covered with diesel, and barbecued like the bloody pigs they were.

Last night had been a bloody near thing.

Ortnahme wasn't going to send out a tank whose close-in defenses were doubtful. Not after he'd had personal experience of what that meant in action.

He bore down harder. The motor protested; bits of the brush tickled the faceshield of his helmet. He'd decided to wear his commo helmet this morning instead of his usual shop visor, because—

Via, why not admit it? Because he'd really wished he'd had the helmet the night before. He couldn't change the past, couldn't have all his gear handy back *then* when he needed it; but he could sure as hell have it on him now for a security blanket.

There was a 1cm pistol in Ortnahme's hip pocket as well. He'd never seen the face of the Consie who'd chased him with the bomb, but today the bastard leered at Ortnahme from every shadow in the camp.

The singer moaned something exceptionally dismal. Ortnahme backed off his multitool, now that he had a sufficient section of channel cleared. He reached for a meter-long strip charge.

Simkins, who should've been buffing the channels while the warrant leader bolted in charges, had disappeared minutes after they'd parked *Herman's Whore* back in her old slot against the berm. The kid'd done a bloody good job during the firefight—but that didn't mean he'd stopped being a bloody maintenance tech. Ortnahme was going to burn him a new asshole as soon as—

"Mr. Ortnahme?" Simkins said. "Look what I got!"

The warrant leader turned, already shouting. "Simkins, where in the name of all that's holy have—"

He paused. "Via, Simkins," he said. "Where did you get that?"

Simkins was carrying a tribarrel, still in its packing crate.

"Tommy Dill at Logistics, sir," the technician answered brightly. "Ah, Mr. Ortnahme? It's off the books, you know. We set a little charge on the warehouse roof, so Tommy can claim a mortar shell combat-lossed the gun."

Just like that was the only question Ortnahme wanted to ask.

Though it was sure-hell *one* of 'em, that was God's truth.

"Kid," the warrant leader said calmly, more or less. "What in the bloody hell do you think you're gonna do with that gun?"

From the way Simkins straightened, "more or less" wasn't as close to "calmly" as Ortnahme had thought.

"Sir!" the technician said. "I'm gonna mount it on the bow. So I got something to shoot, ah . . . you know, the next time."

The kid glanced up at the blaring recorder. He was holding the tribarrel with no sign of how much the thing weighted. He wouldn't been able to do that before Warrant Leader Ortnahme started running his balls off to teach him his job.

Ortnahme opened his mouth. He didn't know which part of the stupid idea to savage first.

Before he figured out what to say, Simkins volunteered, "Mister Ortnahme? I figured we'd use a section of engineer stake for a mount and weld it to the skirt. Ah, so we don't have to chance a weld on the iridium, you know?"

Like a bloody puppy, standin' there waggling his tail—

and *how* in bloody hell had he got Sergeant Dill to agree to take a tribarrel off manifest?

"Kid," he said at last, "put that down and start buffing this channel for me, all right"

"Yes, Mister Ortnahme."

The klaxon blurted, then cut off.

Ortnahme and every other Slammer in the compound froze. Nothing further happened. The Yokels must've been testing the system now that they'd moved it.

The bloody cursed fools.

"Sir," the technician said with his face bent over the buzz of his own multitool. "Can I put on some different music?"

"I like what I got on," Ortnahme grunted, spinning home first one, then the other of the bolts that locked the strip of explosive and steel pellets into its channel.

"Why, sir?" Simkins prodded unexpectedly. "The music, I mean?"

Ortnahme stared at his subordinate. Simkins continued to buff his way forward, as though cleaning the channel were the only thing on his mind.

"Because," Ortnahme said. He grimaced and flipped up the faceshield of his helmet. "Because that was the kinda stuff they played in the bars on Esperanza my first landfall with the regiment. Because it reminds me of when I was young and stupid, kid. Like you."

He slid another of the strip charges from its insulated packing, then paused. "Look," he said, "this ain't our tank, Simkins."

"It's our tank till they send a crew to pick it up," the technician said over the whine of his brush. "It's our tank tonight, Mister Ortnahme."

The warrant leader sighed and fitted the strip into place. It bound slightly, but that was from the way the skirt had been torqued, not the job Simkins was doing on the channel.

"All right," Ortnahme said, "but we'll mount it solid

so you swing the bow to aim it, all right? I don't want you screwing around with the grips when you oughta be holding the controls."

Simkins stopped what he was doing and turned. "*Thank* you, Mister Ortnahme!" he said, as though he'd just been offered the cherry of the most beautiful women on the bloody planet.

"Yeah, sure," the warrant leader said with his face averted. "Believe me, you're gonna do the work while I sit on my butt 'n watch."

Ortnahme set a bolt, then a second. "Hey kid?" he said. "How the hell did you get Tommy to go along with this cop?"

"I told him it was you blasted the Consie with the satchel charge when Tommy opened his warehouse door."

Ortnahme blinked, "Huh?" he said. "Somebody did that? It sure wasn't me."

"Tommy's got a case of real French brandy for you, sir," the technician said. He turned and grinned. "And the tribarrel. Because I'm your driver, see? And he didn't want our asses swingin' in the breeze again like last night."

"Bloody hell," the warrant leader muttered. He placed another bolt and started to grin himself.

"We won't use engineer stakes," he said. "I know where there's a section of 10cm fuel-truck hose sheathing. We'll cut and bend that. . . ."

"Thank you, Mister Ortnahme."

"And I guess we could put a pin through the pivot," Ortnahme went on. "So you could unlock the curst thing if, you know, we got bogged down again."

"*Thank* you, Mister Ortnahme!"

Cursed little puppy. But a smart one.

Two blocks from the commo room, Dick Suilin passed the body of a man in loose black garments. The face of the corpse was twisted in a look of ugly surprise. And old scar trailed up his cheek and across an eyebrow, but there was no sign of the injury that had killed him here.

The Slammers' TOC was almost two kilometers away. Suilin was already so exhausted that his ears buzzed except when he tried to concentrate on something. He decided to head for the infantry-detachment motor pool and try to promote a ride to the north end of the camp.

It occurred to the reporter that he hadn't seen any vehicles moving in the camp since the combat cars reformed and howled back to their regular berths. As he formed the thought, a light truck drove past and stopped beside the body.

A lieutenant and two soldiers wearing gloves, all of them looking morose, got out. Before they could act, a group of screaming dependents, six women and at least as many children, swept around the end of one of the damage buildings. They pushed the soldiers away, then surrounded the corpse and began kicking it.

Suilin paused to watch. The enlisted men glanced at one another, then toward the lieutenant, who seemed frozen. One of the men said, "Hey, we're s'posed to take—"

A woman turned and spat in the soldier's face.

"Murdering Consie bastard! Murdering little Consie bastard!"

Two of the older children were stripping the trousers off the body. A six-year-old boy ran up repeatedly, lashed out with his bare foot, and ran back. He never quite made contact with the corpse.

"Murdering Consie Bastard!"

The officer drew his pistol and fired in the air. The screaming stopped. One woman flung herself to the ground, covering a child with her body. The group backed away, staring at the man with the gun.

The officer aimed at the guerrilla's body and fired. Dust puffed from the shoulder of the black jacket.

The officer fired twice more, then blasted out the remainder of his ten-round magazine. The hard ground sprayed grit in all directions; one bullet ricocheted and spanged into a door jamb, missing a child by centimeters at most.

The group of dependents edged away. Bullets had disfigured still further the face of the corpse.

"Well, get on with it!" the lieutenant screamed to his men. His voice sounded tinny from the muzzle blasts of his weapon.

The soldiers grimaced and grasped the body awkwardly with their gloved hands. A glove slipped as they swung the guerrilla onto the tailgate of the truck. The body hung, about to fall back.

The lieutenant grabbed a handful of the Consie's hair and held it until the enlisted men could get better grips and finish their task.

Suilin resumed walking toward the motor pool. He was living in a nightmare, and his ears buzzed like wasps. . . .

"Now, to split the screen," said squat Joe Albers, *Deathdealer*'s driver, "you gotta hold one control and switch the other one whatever way."

Hans Wager set his thumb on the left HOLD button and clicked the right-hand magnification control of the main screen to x4. The turret of the unnamed tank felt crowded with two men in it, although Wager himself was slim and Albers was stocky rather than big.

"Does it matter which control you hold?" asked Holman, peering down through the hatch.

"Naw, whichever you want," Albers said while Wager watched the magical transformations of his screen.

The left half of the main screen maintained its portion of a 360 degree panorama viewed by the light available in the human visual spectrum. Broad daylight, at the moment. The right portion of the screen had shrunk into a 90 degree arc whose field of view was only half its original height.

Wager twisted the control dial, rotating the magnified sector slowly around the tank's surroundings. Smoke still smoldered upward from a few places beyond the berm; here and there, sunlight glittered where the soil seared by powerguns had enough silicon to glaze.

The berth on the right side of the tank was empty. The combat car assigned there had bought it in the clearing operation. Buzzbombs. The close-in defense system hadn't worked or hadn't worked well enough, same difference. Albers said a couple of the crew were okay. . . .

Wager's field of view rolled across the Yokel area. The barracks nearest the Slammers were in good shape still; but by focusing down one of the streets and rolling the magnification through *x16* and *x64*, he could see that at least a dozen buildings in a row had burned.

A few bolts from a powergun and those frame structures went up like torches. . . .

The best protection you had in a combat car wasn't armor or even your speed; it was the volume of fire you put on the other bastard and anywhere the other bastard might be hiding.

Tough luck for the Yokels who'd been burned out. Tougher luck, much tougher, for the Consies who'd tried to engage Hammer's Slammers.

"For the driver," Albers said with a nod up toward Holman's intent face, "it's pretty much the same as a combat car."

"The weight's not the bloody same," Holman said.

"Sure, you gotta watch yer inertia," the veteran driver agreed, "but you do the same things. You get used to it."

He looked back over at Wager. The right-half screen was now projecting a magnified slice of what appeared at one-to-one on the left.

On the opposite side of the encampment, a couple

of the permanent maintenance staff worked beside another tank. The junior tech looked on while his boss, a swag-bellied warrant three, settled a length of pipe in the jig of a laser saw.

"Turret side, though," Albers went on, "you gotta be careful. About half what you know from cars, that's the wrong thing in the turret of a panzer."

"I don't like not having two more pair of eyes watchin' my back," Wager muttered as his visuals swam around the circumference of the motionless tank.

The screens'll watch for you," Albers said gently.

He touched a key without pressing it. "You lock one of 'em onto alert at all times. The AI in here, it's like a thousand helmet systems all at once. It's faster, it catches more, it's better at throwing out the garbage that just looks like it's a bandit."

The hatches of the Tactical Operations Center, a command car without drive fans, were open, but from the angle Wager couldn't see inside. The backs of two Slammers, peering within from the rear ramp, proved there was a full house—a troop meeting going on. What you'd expect after a contact like last night's.

"Not like having tribarrels pointing three ways, though," Holman said. Dead right, even though she'd never crewed a combat vehicle before.

Albers looked up at her. "If you want," he said, "you can slave either of the guns to the threat monitor. It'll swing 'em as soon as it pops the alert."

Deathdealer, Alber's own tank, was parked next to the TOC. A tarpaulin slanted from the top of the skirts tot he ground, sheltering the man beneath. "Via," Wager muttered. "He's racked out now?"

Birdie Sparrow's right hand was visible beneath the edge of the tarp. It was twitching. Albers looked at the magnified screen, then laid his fingers over Wager's on the dial and rolled the image away.

"Birdie's all right," the veteran driver said. "He takes

a little getting used to, is all. And the past couple months, you know, he's been a little, you know . . . loose."

"That's why they sent you back here with the blower instead of using some newbies for transit?" Holman asked.

Bent over this way, Holman had to keep brushing back the sandy brown curls that fell across her eyes. Her hair was longer than Wager had thought, and the strands appeared remarkably fine.

"Yeah, something like that, I guess," Albers admitted. "Look, Birdie's great when it drops in the pot like last night. Only . . . since his buddy DJ got zapped, he don't sleep good, is all."

"Newbies like us," Wager said bitterly. *Not new to war, not him at least; but new to this kind of war.*

"I can see this gear can do everything but tuck me goodnight. But I'm bloody sure that *I* won't remember what to do the first time I need to. And that's liable to be my ass." He glanced upward. "Our ass."

Holman flashed him a tight smile.

"Yeah, well," Albers agreed. "Simulators help, but on the job training's the only game there's ever gonna be for some things."

Albers rubbed his scalp, grimacing in no particular direction. "You know," he went on, "you can take care a' most stuff if you know what button to push. But some things, curst if I know where the button is."

It seemed to Hans Wager that Albers' eyes were searching for the spot on the main screen where his tank commander lay shivering beneath a sunlit tarp.

When Dick Suilin was twenty meters from the motor pool, a jeep exploded within the wire-fenced enclosure. The back of the vehicle lurched upward. The contents of its fuel tank sprayed in all directions, then *whoomped* into a fireball that rose on the heat of its own combustion.

No one was in the jeep when it blew up, but soldiers throughout the area scattered, bawling warnings.

A few men simply cowered and screamed. One of them continued screaming minutes after the explosion.

Suilin resumed walking toward the entrance.

The combined motor pool held well over three hundred trucks, from jeeps to articulated flat-beds for hauling heavy equipment. The only gate in and out of Camp Progress was visible a block away. A pair of bunkers, massive structures with three-meter walls of layered sandbags and steel planking, guarded the highway where it passed through the wire, minefields, and berm.

The sliding barrier was still in place across the road. When the Consies came over the berm, they took the bunkers from behind. Satchel charges through the open doors set off the munitions within, and the blasts lifted the roofs.

The bunkers had collapsed. The craters were still smoldering.

One of the long sheds within the motor pool had been hit by an artillery rocket. The blast fold back its metal roof in both directions. Grenades and automatic weapons had raked and ignited some of the trucks parked in neat rows, but there were still many undamaged vehicles.

A three-tonne truck blew up. The driver jumped out of the cab and collapsed. Diesel from the ruptured fuel tank gushed around him in an iridescent pool. Nobody moved to help, though other soldiers stared in dazed expectation.

Two officers were arguing at the entrance while a number of enlisted men looked on. A lieutenant wearing the green collar tabs of Maintenance & Supply said in a voice that wavered between reasonableness and frustration, "But Major Schaydin, it isn't *safe* to take any of the vehicles yet. The Consies have booby—"

"God curse you for a fool!" screamed the major. His Summer Dress uniform was in striking contrast to the lieutenant's fatigues, but a nearby explosion had ripped away most of the right trouser leg and blackened the rest. "*You* can't deny me! I'm the head of the Intelligence Staff! My orders supersede any you may have received. Any orders at all!"

Schaydin carried a pair of white gloves, thrust jauntily through his left epaulet. His hat hadn't survived the events of the evening.

"Sir," the lieutenant pleaded, "this isn't orders, it isn't *safe*. The Consies boobytrapped a bunch of the vehicles during the attack, time delays and pressure switches, and they—"

"You bastards!" Schaydin screamed. "D' you want to find yourselves playing pick-up-sticks with your butt cheeks?"

He stalked past the lieutenant, brushing elbows as though he really didn't see the other man.

A sergeant moved as though to block Schaydin. The lieutenant shook his head in angry frustration. He, his men, and Suilin watched the major jump into a jeep, start it, and drive past them in a spray of dust.

"I need a jeep and driver," Suilin said, enunciating carefully. "To carry me to the Slammers' TOC." He deliberately didn't identify himself.

The lieutenant didn't answer. He was staring after Major Schaydin.

Instead of following the road, the intelligence officer pulled hard left and drove toward the berm. The jeep's engine lugged for a moment before its torque converter caught up with the demand. The vehicle began to climb, spurning gravel behind it.

"He'd do better," said the lieutenant, "if he at least tried it at a slant."

"Does he figure just to drive through the minefields?" asked one of the enlisted men.

"The Consies blew paths all the cop through the mines," said a sergeant. "If he's lucky, he'll be okay."

The jeep lurched over the top of the berm to disappear in a rush and a snarl. There was no immediate explosion.

"Takes more 'n luck to get through the Consies themselfs," said the first soldier. "Wherever he thinks he's going. Bloody officers."

"I don't need an argument," said Dick Suilin quietly.

"Then take the bloody jeep!" snapped the lieutenant. He pointed to a row of vehicles. "Them we've checked, more or less, for pressure mines in the suspension housings and limpets on the gas tanks. They must've had half a dozen sappers working the place over while their buddies shot up the HQ."

"No guarantees what went *into* the tanks," offered the sergeant. "Nothin' for that but waiting—and I'd as soon not wait on it. You want to see the mercs so bad, why don't you walk?"

Suilin looked at him. "If it's time," the reporter said, "it's time."

The nearest vehicle was a light truck rather than a jeep. He sat in the driver's seat, feeling the springs sway beneath him. No explosion, no flame. Suilin felt as though he were manipulating a marionette the size and shape of the man he had been.

He pressed the starter tit on the dash panel. A flywheel whirred for a moment before the engine fired normally.

Suilin set the selector to Forward and pressed the throttle. No explosion, no flame.

As he drove out of the motor pool, Suilin heard the sergeant saying, ". . . no insignia and them eyes—he's from an Insertion Patrol Group. Just wish them and the Consies'd fight their war and leave us normal people alone. . . ."

"Here he is, Captain Ranson," said the hologram of

the commo tech at Firebase Purple. The image shifted.

Major Danny Pritchard looked exhausted even in hologram, and he was still wearing body armor over his khaki fatigues. He rubbed his eyes. "What do you estimate the strength of the attack on Camp Progress, Junebug?" he asked.

"Maybe a battalion," Ranson replied, wondering if her voice was drifting in and out of timbre the way her vision was. "They hit all sides, but it was mostly on the south end."

"Colonel Banyussuf claims it was a division," Pritchard said with a ghost of a smile. "He claims his men've killed over five thousand Consies already."

An inexperienced observer could have mistaken for transmission noise the ripping sounds that shook the hologram every ten or twenty seconds. Even over a satellite bounce, Ranson recognized the discharge of rocket howitzers. Hammer's headquarters was getting some action too.

Cooter laughed. "If the Yokels killed anybody, it was when one of 'em fell out a window and landed on 'im. We got maybe three hundred."

"Stepped on?" demanded the image of Hammer's executive officer—and some said, heir.

"Stepped on and gun camera, maybe two hundred," Ranson said. "But there's a lot of stuff won't show up till they start sifting the ashes. Cooter's right, maybe three. It was a line battalion, and it won't be bothering anybody else for a while."

The command car was crowded. Besides Ranson herself, it held a commo Tech named Bestwick at the console, ready if the artificial intelligence monitoring the other bands needed a human decision; Cooter, second in command of the detachment; and Master Sergeant Wylde, who'd been a section leader before, and would be again as soon as his burns healed.

Wylde was lucky to be alive after the first buzzbomb hit his car. He shouldn't have been present now; but he'd insisted, and Ranson didn't have the energy to argue with him. Anyway, between pain and medications, Wylde was too logy to be a problem except for the room his bandaged form took up.

"Hey?" said Cooter. He lifted his commo helmet slightly with one hand so that he could knuckle the line of his sweat-darkened auburn hair. "Major? What the hell's happening, anyway? Is this all over?"

Danny Pritchard smiled a great deal; usually it was a pleasant expression.

Not this smile.

"They hit the three firebases and all but one of the line companies," the major said. "We told everybody hold what they got; and then the hogs—" Pritchard nodded; a howitzer slashed the sky again from beyond the field of view "—scratched everybody's back with firecracker rounds. Each unit swept its circuit before the dust settled from the shellbursts."

The smile hardened still further. "Kinda nice of them to concentrate that way for us."

Ranson nodded, visualizing the white flare of precisely-directed cluster bomblets going off. The interlocking fields of fire from Firebases Red, Blue, and Purple covered the entire Strip. Guerrillas rising in panic, to be hosed down by the tribarrels in the armored vehicles. . . .

"Yeah," said Sergeant Wylde in a husky whisper. The wounded man's face didn't move and his eyes weren't focused on the hologram. "But how about the Yokels? Or is this a private fight fer us 'n the Consies?"

"Right," said Pritchard with something more than agreement in his tone of voice. "Hold one, Junebug."

The sound cut off abruptly as somebody hit the muting switch of the console at HQ. Major Pritchard turned his head. Ranson could see Pritchard's lips moving in profile as he talked to someone out of the projection field. She was in a dream, watching the bust of a man who spoke silently. . . .

What's your present strength in vehicles and trained crews?

Junebug?

Captain Ranson?

Ranson snapped alert. Cooter had put his big arm around her shoulders to give her a shake.

"Right," she said, feeling the red prickly flush cover her, as though she'd just fainted and come around. She couldn't remember where she was, but in her dream somebody had been asking—

"We've got—" Cooter said.

"We're down a blower," Ranson said, facing Pritchard's worried expression calmly. "A combat car."

"Mine," said Wylde to his bandaged hands. Ranson wasn't sure whether or not the sergeant was within the hologram pick-up.

"My crews, two dead," Ranson continued. "Three out for seven days or more. Sergeant Wylde, my section leader, he's out."

"Oh-yew-tee," Wylde muttered. "Out."

"Can you pick anybody up from the Blue side?" Pritchard asked.

"There's the three panzers," Ranson said. "Only one's got a trained crew, but they came through like gangbusters last night."

She frowned, trying to concentrate. "Personnel, though. . . . Look, you know, we're talking newbies and people who're rear echelon for a reason."

People even farther out of it than Captain June Ranson, who nodded off while debriefing to Central. . . .

"Look, sir," Cooter interjected. "We shot the cop outta the Consies. I don't know about no 'five thousand dead' cop, but if they'd had more available, they'd a used it last night. They bloody sure don't have enough left to try anytime soon."

"I believe you, Lieutenant," Pritchard said wearily. "But that's not the only problem." He rubbed the palms of his hands together firmly. "Hold one," he repeated as he got up from the console.

Colonel Alois Hammer sat down in Pritchard's place.

The hologram was as clear as if Hammer were in the TOC with Ranson. The Colonel was madder than hell; so mad that his hand kept stabbing upward to brush away the tic at the corner of his left eye.

"Captain . . ." Hammer said. He fumbled with the latches of his clamshell armor to give himself time to form words—or at least to delay the point at which he had to speak them.

He glared at June Ranson. "*We* kicked the Consies up one side and down the other. The National Army had problems."

"That's why they hired us, sir," Ranson said. She was very calm. Thick glass was beginning to form between her and the image of the regimental commander.

"Yeah, that's why they did, all right," Hammer said. He ground at his left eye.

He lowered his hand. "Captain, you saw what happened to the structure of Camp Progress during the attack?"

"What structure?" Cooter muttered bitterly.

Ranson shivered. The glass wall shivered also, falling away as shards of color that coalesced into Hammer's face.

"Sir, the Consies were only a battalion," Ranson said. "They could've done a lot of damage—they did. But it was just a spoiling attack, they couldn't 've captured the base in the strength they were."

"They can capture Kohang, Captain," Hammer said. "And if they captured a district capital, the National Government is gone. The people who pay us."

Ranson blinked, trying to assimilate the information.

It didn't make any sense. The Consies were beat—beaten *good*. Multiply what her teams had done at Camp Progress by the full weight of the Regiment—with artillery and perfect artillery targets for a change—and the Conservative Action Movement on Prosperity didn't have enough living members to bury its dead. . . .

"Nobody was expecting it, Captain Ranson," Hammer said. The whiskers on his chin and jowls were white, though the close-cropped hair on the colonel's head was still a sandy brown. "The National Government wasn't, *we* weren't. It'd been so quiet the past three months that we—"

His eye twitched. *"Via!"* he cursed. *"I* thought, and if anybody'd told me different I'd 've laughed at them. I thought the Consies were about to pack it in. And instead they were getting ready for the biggest attack of the war."

"But Colonel," Cooter said. His voice sounded desperate. "They *lost*. They got their butts kicked."

"Tell that to a bunch of civilians," Hammer said bitterly. "Tell that to your Colonel Banyussuf—the bloody fool!"

Somebody at Central must have spoken to Hammer from out of pick-up range, because the colonel half-turned and snarled, "Then *deal* with it! Shoot 'em all in the neck if you want!"

He faced around again. For an instant, Ranson stared into eyes as bleak and merciless as the scarp of a glacier. Then Hammer blinked, and the expression was gone; replaced with one of anger and concern. Human emotions, not forces of nature.

"Captain Ranson," he resumed with a formality that would have been frightening to the junior officer were she not drifting again into glassy isolation. "In a week, it'll all be over for the Consies. They'll have to make their peace on any terms they can get—even if that means surrendering for internment by the National Government.

But if a district capital falls, there won't *be* a National Government in a week. All they see—"

Hammer's left hand reached for his eye and clenched a fist instead. "All they see," he repeated in a voice that trembled between a whisper and a snarl, "is what's been lost, what's been destroyed, what's been disrupted. You and I—"

His hand brushed out into a slighting gesture. "We've expended some ammo, we've lost some equipment. We've lost some people. Objectives cost. Winning costs."

Sergeant Wylde nodded. Blood was seeping from cracks in the Sprayseal which replaced the skin burned from his left shoulder.

"But the politicians and—and what passes for an army, here, they're in a panic. One more push and they'll fold. The people who pay us will fold."

One more push. . . . Ranson thought/said; she wasn't sure whether the words floated from her tongue or across her mind.

"Captain Ranson," Hammer continued, "I don't like the orders I'm about to give you, but I'm going to give them anyway. Kohang has to be relieved soonest, and you're the only troops in position to do that job."

June Ranson was sealed in crystal, a tiny bead that glittered through the universe. "Sir," said the voice from her mouth, "there's the 4th Armored at Camp Victory. A brigade. There's the Yokel 12th and 23rd Infantry closer than we are."

Her voice was enunciating very clearly. "Sir, I've got eight blowers."

"Elements of the 4th Armored are attempting to enter Kohang from the south," Hammer said. "They're making no progress."

"How hard are they trying?" shouted Cooter. "How hard are they bloody trying?"

"It doesn't matter," Ranson thought/said.

"Lieutenant, that doesn't matter," said Hammer,

momentarily the man who'd snarled at an off-screen aide. "They're not doing the job. We're going to. That's what we're paid to do."

"Cooter," said Ranson, "shut up."

She shouldn't say that with other people around. Screw it. She focused on the hologram. "Sir," she said, "what's the enemy strength?"

"We've picked up the callsigns of twenty-seven Consie units in and around Kohang, company-size or battalion," Hammer said, in a tone of fractured calm. "The data's been downloaded to you already."

Bestwick glanced up from the console behind the projected image and nodded; Ranson continued to watch her commanding officer.

"Maybe three thousand bandits," Ranson said.

"Maybe twice that," Hammer said, nodding as Ranson was nodding. "Concentrated on the south side and around Camp Victory."

"There's two hundred thousand people in Kohang," Ranson said. "There's three thousand *police* in the city."

"The Governmental Compound is under siege," Hammer said coldly. "Some elements of the security forces appeared to be acting in support of the Consies." He paused and rubbed his eye.

"A battalion of the 4th Armored left Camp Victory without orders yesterday afternoon," he continued. "About an hour before the first rocket attack. Those troops aren't responding to messages from their brigade commander."

"Blood and martyrs," somebody in the TOC said. Maybe they all said it.

"Sir," said Ranson, "we can't, we can't by ourself—"

"Shoot your way into the compound," Hammer said before she could finish. "Reinforce what's there, put some backbone into 'em. They *got* enough bloody troops to do the job themselves, Captain . . . they just don't believe it."

He grimaced. "Even a couple blowers. That'll do the trick until G and H companies arrive. Just a couple blowers."

"Cop," muttered Wylde through his bandages.

"Bloody hell," muttered Cooter with the back of his hand tightly against his mouth.

"May the Lord have mercy on our souls," said/thought June Ranson.

"Speed's essential," Hammer resumed. "You have authorization to combat-loss vehicles rather than slow down. The victory bonus'll cover the cost of replacement."

"I'll be combat-lossing crews, Colonel," Ranson's voice said, "but they're replaceable too. . . ."

Cooter gasped. Wylde grunted something that might have been either laughter or pain.

Hammer opened his mouth, then closed it with an audible clop. He opened it again and spoke with a lack of emotion as complete as the white, colorless fury of a sun's heart. "You are not to take any unnecessary risks, Captain Ranson. It *is* necessary that you achieve your objective. You will accept such losses as are required to achieve your objective. Is that understood?"

"Yes sir," said Ranson without inflection. "Oh, yes sir."

Hammer turned his head. The viewers at Camp Progress thought their commander was about to call orders or directions to someone on his staff. Instead, nothing happened while the hologram pick-ups stared at the back of Alois Hammer's head.

"All right," Hammer said at last, beginning to speak before he'd completely faced around again. His eyes were bright, his face hard. "The Consies' night vision equipment isn't as good as ours for the most part, so you're to leave as soon as it's dark. That gives you enough time to prepare and get some rest."

"*Rest*," Wylde murmured.

"The World Gov satellites'll tell the Consies where we

are to the millimeter," Ranson said. "We'll have ambush teams crawling over us like flies on a turd, all the way to Kohang."

Or however far.

"Junebug," said Hammer, "I'm not hanging you out to dry. Thirty seconds before you start your move, all the WG satellites are going to go down, recce and commo both. They'll stay down for however long it suits me that they do."

Ranson blinked, "Sir," she said hesitantly, "if you do that . . . I mean, that means—"

"It means that our commo and reconnaissance is probably going to go out shortly thereafter, Captain," Hammer said. "So you'll be on your own. But you don't have to worry about tank killers being vectored into your axis of advance."

"Sir, if you hit their satellites—" Ranson began.

"They'll take it and smile, Captain," Hammer said. "Because if they don't, there won't *be* any Terran World Government enclaves here on Prosperity to worry about. I guarantee it. They may think they can cause me trouble on Earth, but they *know* what I'll do to them here!"

"Yessir," June Ranson said. "I'll check the status of my assets and plot a route, then get back to you."

"Captain," Hammer said softly, "if I didn't think it could be done, I wouldn't order it. No matter how much it counted. Good luck to you and your team."

The hologram dissolved into a swirl of phosphorescent mites, impingement points of the carrier wave itself after the signal ceased. Bestwick shut down the projector.

"Cooter," Ranson said, "get the guard detachment ready. I'll take care of the tanks myself."

Cooter nodded over his shoulder. The big man was already on the way to his blower. It was going to be tricky, juggling crews and newbies to fill the slots that last night's firefight had opened. . . .

If Hammer took on the World Government, he was going to lose. Not here, but in the main area of politics and economics on Earth.

That bothered June Ranson a lot.

But not nearly as much as the fact that the orders she'd just received put her neck on the block, sure as Death itself.

Chapter Five

Speedin' Steve Riddle sat by Platt's cot in the medical tent, listening to machines pump air in and out of his buddy's lungs.

And thinking.

They sat on the lowered tailgate of Platt's truck, staring at the sky and giggling occasionally at the display. At first there'd been only the lesser moon edging one horizon while the other horizon was saffron with the sunset.

Lights, flames . . . streaks of tracers that painted letters in the sky for the drug-heightened awareness of the two men. Neither Platt nor Riddle could read the words, but they knew whatever was being spelled was excruciatingly funny. . . .

"Speed," called Lieutenant Cooter, "get your ass back to the blower and start running the prelim checklist. We're moving out tonight."

"Wha . . . ?" Riddle blurted, jerking his head up like an ostrich surprised at a waterhole. He was rapidly going bald. To make up for it, he'd grown a luxuriant moustache that fluffed when he spoke or exhaled.

"Don't give me any lip, you stupid bastard!" Cooter snapped, though Speed's response had been logy rather than argumentative. "If I didn't need you bad, you'd be findin' your own ticket back to whatever cesspit you call home."

"Hey, El-Tee!" Otski called, sitting up on his cot despite the gentle efforts of Shorty Rogers to keep him flat. "How they hangin', Cooter-baby?"

He waggled his stump.

"Come on, Otski," Rogers said. Shorty was *Flamethrower*'s driver and probably the best medic in the guard detachment as well as being a crewmate of the wounded man. "Just take it easy or I'll have to raise your dosage, and then it won't feel so good. All right?"

The medicomp metered Platt's breathing, in and out.

"Hey, lookit," Otski burbled, fluttering his stump again though he permitted Shorty to lower him back to the cot.

An air injector spat briefly, but the gunner's voice continued for a moment. "Lookit it when I wave, Cooter. I'm gonna get a flag. Whole bunch flags, stick 'em in there 'n wave 'n wave. . . ."

"Shorty, you're gonna have to get back to the car too," Cooter said. "We'll turn 'em over to the Logistics staff until they can be lifted out to a permanent facility."

"Cop! None a' the Logistics people here'd know—"

Riddle thought:

The parts shed bulged around a puff of orange flame. The shockwave threw Riddle and Platt flat on the sloping tailgate; they struggled to sit up again. It was hilarious.

The Consie sapper rose from his crouch, silhouetted by the flaming shed he'd just bombed. He carried a machinepistol in a harness of looped rope, so that the weapon swung at waist height. His right hand snatched at the grip.

"Lookie, Speed!" Platt cackled. "He's just as bald as you are! Lookie!"

"Lookie!" Riddle called. He threw up his arms and fell backward with the effort.

The machinepistol crackled like the main truss of a

house giving way. Its tracers were bright orange, lovely orange, as they drew spirals from the muzzle. One of them ricocheted around the interior of the truck box, dazzling Riddle with its howling beauty. He sat up again.

"Beauty!" he cried. Platt was thrashing on his back. Air bubbled through the holes in his chest.

The machinepistol pointed at Riddle. Nothing happened. The sapper cursed and slapped a magazine into the butt-well to replace the one that had ejected automatically when the previous burst emptied it.

The Consie's body flung itself sideways, wrapped in cyan light as a powergun from one of the combat cars raked him. The fresh magazine exploded. A few tracers zipped crazily out of the flashing yellow ball of detonating propellant.

"Beauty," Steve Riddle repeated as he fell backward. Platt's chest wheezed.

"—a medicomp when it bit 'em on the ass!"

Air from the medicomp wheezed in and out of Platt's nostrils.

"Screw you!" called a supply tech with shrapnel wounds in his upper body.

"Then get 'em over to the Yokel side!" Cooter said. "They got facilities. Look, I'm not lookin' for an argument: we're movin' out at sunset, and none of my able-bodied crew are stayin' to bloody screw around here. All right?"

"Yeah, all right. One a the newbies had some training back home, he says." Rogers stood up and gave a pat to the sleeping Otski. "Hey, how long we gonna be out?"

"Don't bloody ask," Cooter grunted bitterly. "Denzil, where's your driver?"

The left wing gunner from Sergeant Wylde's blower turned his head—all the motion of which he was capable the way he was wrapped. "Strathclyde?" he said. His voice sounded all right. The medicomp kept his coverings flushed and cool with a bath of nutrient fluid. "Check over to One-one. He's got a buddy there."

"Yeah, well, One-five needs a driver," Cooter explained. "I'm going to put him on it."

Shorty Rogers looked up. "What happened to Darples on One-five?" he asked.

"Head shot. One a the gunners took over last night, but I figure it makes sense to transfer Strathclyde for a regular thing."

"Cop," muttered Rogers. "I'll miss that snake." Then, "Don't mean nuthin'."

"Riddle!" Cooter snarled. "What the bloody hell are you doing still here? Get your ass moving, or you won't bloody have one!"

Riddle walked out of the medical tent. The direct sunlight made him sneeze, but he didn't really notice it.

Bright orange tracers, spiraling toward his chest.

He reached his combat car, *Deathdealer*. The iridium armor showed fresh scars. There was a burnished half-disk on the starboard wall of the fighting compartment— copper spurted out by a buzzbomb. The jet had cooled from a near-plasma here on the armor. Must've been the round that took out Otski. . . .

Riddle sat on the shaded side of the big vehicle. No one else was around. Cooter and Rogers had their own business. They wouldn't get here for hours.

Otski wouldn't be back at all. Never at all.

Bright orange tracers. . . .

Riddle took a small cone-shaped phial out of his side pocket. It was dull gray and had none of the identifying stripes that marked ordinary stim-cones, the ones that gave you a mild buzz without the aftereffects of alcohol.

He put the flat side of the cone against his neck, feeling for the carotid pulse. When he squeezed the cone, there was a tiny hiss and a skin-surface prickling.

Riddle began to giggle again.

✧ ✧ ✧

Troops were moving about the Slammers' portion of the encampment in a much swifter and more directed fashion than they had been the afternoon before, when Dick Suilin first visited this northern end of Camp Progress.

The reporter glanced toward the bell—a section of rocket casing—hung on top of the Tactical Operations Center. Perhaps it had rung, unheard by him while he drove past the skeletons of National Army barracks . . . ?

The warning signal merely swayed in the breeze that carried soot and soot smells even here, where few sappers had penetrated.

Suilin had figured the commo gear would be at the TOC, where Captain Ranson was there or not. In the event, the black-haired female officer sat on the back-ramp of the vehicle, facing three male soldiers who squatted before her.

She stood, thumping out of her closing orders, as Suilin pulled up; the men rose a moment later. None of the group paid the local reporter any attention.

Suilin didn't recognize the men. One of them was fat, at least fifty standard years old, and wore a grease-stained khaki jumpsuit.

"No problem, Junebug," he called as he turned away from the meeting. "We'll be ready to lift—if we're left alone to *get* ready, all right? Keep the rest a your people and their maintenance problems off my back—" he was striding off toward a parked tank, shouting his words over his shoulder "—and we'll be at capacity when you need us."

Suilin got out of his truck. *They called their commanding officer Junebug?*

"Yeah, well," said another soldier, about twenty-five and an average sort of man in every way. He lifted his helmet to rub his scalp, then settled the ceramic/plastic pot again. "What do you want for a callsign? Charlie Three-zero all right?"

Ranson shook her head. "Negative. You're Blue Three," she said flatly.

Blue Three rubbed his scalp again. "Right," he said in a cheerless voice. "Only you hear 'Charlie Three-zero,' don't have kittens, okay? I got a lot to learn."

He turned morosely, adding, "And you know, this kinda on-the-job training ain't real survivable."

Suilin stood by, waiting for the third male mercenary to go before he tried to borrow the Slammers' communications system to call Kohang.

Instead of leaving, the soldier turned and looked at the reporter with a disconcertingly slack-jawed vacant-eyed stare. The green-brown eyes didn't seem to focus at all.

Captain Ranson's eyes followed her subordinate's. She said angrily, "Who the bloody hell are you?"

It wasn't the same face that Suilin had been interviewing the night before.

There were dark circles around Ranson's eyes, and her left cheek was badly scratched. Her face, her hands, and her neck down to the scallop where she'd been wearing armor, where dingy with fouling spewed from the breeches of her tribarrel when jets of nitrogen expelled the empty cases.

Ranson had been angry at being forced into an interview. She'd known the power was in the reporter's hands: the power to probe for answers she didn't want to give; the power to twist questions so that they were hooks in the fabric of her self-esteem; the power to make a fool out of her, by the words he tricked her into saying—or the form into which he edited those words before he aired them.

Now . . .

Now Suilin wondered what had happened to Fritzi Dole's body. He was *almost* certain that this small, fierce mercenary wouldn't shoot a reporter out of hand to add to the casualty count, no matter how angry and frustrated she was now. . . .

"I'm, ah," he said, "Dick Suilin. I'm, ah, we met yesterday when the—"

"The reporter," Ranson said. "Right, the bloody fool who didn't know t' hit the dirt for incoming. The interview's off."

She started to turn. "Beat it," she added.

"It's not—" Suilin said. "Captain Ranson, I need to talk to somebody in Kohang, and your commo may be the—"

"Buddy," said Ranson with a venom and disgust that shocked the reporter more than the content of the words did, "you must be out of your mind. Get *out* of here."

The other soldier continued to watch without expression.

"Captain, you don't understand," Suilin called to Ranson's back. "I need to make sure my sister's all right."

The woman bend to re-enter the immobile command blower.

"Curse it! She's the wife of the District Governor. *Now* will you—"

Ranson turned. The reporter thought he'd seen her angry before.

"The District Governor," she repeated softly. "The District Bleeding Governor."

She walked toward Suilin. He poised, uncertain as to what the female officer intended.

She tapped him on the chest as she said, "Your brother-in-law doesn't have any balls, buddy." The tip of her index finger was like a mallet.

"Captain—"

"He's got a brigade of armor," Ranson continued, "and maybe ten battalions of infantry and gendarmes, according to the order of battle in my data banks."

She tapped even harder. Suilin backed a step. "But no balls a'tall."

The reporter set his leg to lock him into place. "Captain, you can't—"

Ranson slapped him, forehand and then back across the other cheek. Her fingers were as hard as the popper of a bullwhip. "And he's got an ass, so we're going to get *our* ass shot off to save his!"

She spun on her heel. "Sparrow, get him out of my sight," she called over her shoulder as she entered her TOC.

Suilin viewed the world through a blur of tears. Sparrow put a hand on his shoulder and turned him with a detached gentleness that felt like compassion to the reporter at the moment.

"S'okay, turtle," the mercenary said as he walked Suilin toward the truck he'd borrowed. "We just got orders to relieve the District Governor ourself, and we got bugger-all t' do it with."

"What?" the reporter said. "In Kohang?"

His right cheek burned, and his left felt as if someone had flayed the skin from it. He wondered if Ranson had been wearing a ring. "Who's relieving Kohang?"

Sparrow waved an arm as deliberately as a stump speaker gesturing. "You're lookin' at it, turtle," he said. "Three tanks, five cars . . . and maybe crews for most of 'em."

The veneer of careless apathy dropped away. Sparrow shivered. He was tall and thin with an olive complexion several shades darker than Suilin's own.

"Via," the mercenary muttered. "Via!"

Sparrow turned and walked, then trotted in a loose-limbed way toward the tank across the enclosure from the TOC. He climbed the shallow steps up its skirts and battered hull, then popped into the turret with the haste of a man boarding under fire.

The hatch clanged loudly behind him.

Dick Suilin sat in his truck, blinking to clear his eyes and mind. He started the vehicle and turned it in a tight circle, heading back toward National Army Headquarters.

His own gear had been destroyed in the firefight, but he thought the barracks in which Fritzi Doyle was billeted had survived. The cameraman had worn fatigues. One of his spare sets would fit Suilin well enough.

Fritzi wouldn't mind.

The corpse of a National Army sergeant was sprawled at the doorway of a bombed-out building. He'd thrown on a uniform shirt, but he had no shoes or trousers. His left arm was outstretched while his right was folded under his face as though cushioning it from the ground.

He'd been carrying a grenade launcher and a satchel of reloads for it. They lay beside his body.

Suilin stopped the truck, picked up the weapon and ammunition, and set the gear on the passenger seat. As an afterthought, he tried to lift the dead man. The body was stiff and had already begun to blacken in the bright sun.

Someone whose job it was would deal with the sergeant. Not Dick Suilin.

Suilin's hands felt slimy. He accelerated away, kicking gravel over the corpse in his haste to be shut of it.

"Blue one," said Captain June Ranson, checking the artificial intelligence in her multi-function display. A digit on the holographic map blinked twice in yellow, then twice more in blue light when the transponder in *Deathdealer* answered the call automatically.

"Go ahead, Tootsie Six," said Sergeant Sparrow's voice.

"Linkage check," Ranson said, "Blue two."

Deathdealer led the line-to-be, quivering on its fans just ahead of Ranson's *Warmonger.*

There wasn't enough room in the Slammers' end of the encampment to form up completely until the blowers started to move south, toward the gate. Sound, re-echoing from the berm and the sloped iridium sides of the vehicles, vibrated the flesh of everyone around.

Exclusion circuits in Ranson's commo helmet notched

out as much of the fan's racket as possible, but the sound of multiple drive nacelles being run up to speed created an ambiance beyond the power of electronics to control. Air forced beneath the lips of eight plenum chambers picked up grit which ricocheted into standing waves where the currents from two or three blowers intersected.

Deathdealer's turret was already buttoned up. Nothing wrong with that—it'd be quieter inside, thought the fan-driven chaos would penetrate even the massive iridium castings that stopped all but direct pointblank hits by the largest powerguns.

Ranson had never seen Birdie Sparrow man his tank from the open cupola. A tank's electronics were better than human senses, even when those senses were augmented by the AI and sensors in a commo helmet. The screens within a panzer's turret gave not only crisper definition on all the electro-opical bands but also gave multiple simultaneous options.

That information glut was one of the reasons most tank commanders chose to fight their vehicles from the cupola instead of the closed turret whenever possible.

It was difficult to get experienced crewmen to transfer from combat cars to panzers, even though it usually meant promotion. Most tank commanders were promoted from driver, while the driver slots were filled by newbies with no previous combat experience in the Slammers.

Ranson had checked Birdie Sparrow's personnel file— this afternoon; she'd had no reason to call up the records from Central's database before. . . .

Before Colonel Hammer handed her command of a suicide mission.

Sparrow had five standard years, seven months, service with the Regiment. All but the training in the first three months had been in line companies, so there was no need to wonder how he handled combat: *just fine or he wouldn't 've lasted out his fourth month*. Hammer's

Slammers weren't hired by people who needed them to polish their gear in barracks.

A few problems on stand-down; a more serious one with a platoon leader in the field that had cost Sparrow a pay-grade—but it was the lieutenant who'd been transferred back to Central and, after the discrete interval required for discipline, out of the Slammers. Sparrow had an excellent record and must have been in line for his own platoon—

Instead of which, he'd been sent down here to the quiet South for a little time off.

Junebug Ranson had an even better service record than Sparrow did. She knew curst well what *she* was doing down here at Camp Progress.

Task Force Ranson was real lucky to have a company commander as experienced as Junebug Ranson to lead the mission, and a tanker as good as Birdie Sparrow to head up the unit's tank element.

The trouble was, they were both bughouse bleeding crazy, and Ranson knew it.

It was her job to know it, and to compensate the best way she could.

"Roger, Tootsie Six," said her helmet in the voice of Warrant Leader Ortnahme as the digit 2 flickered on the map display.

"Linkage check," responded Captain Ranson. "Blue Three."

Needs must, when the Devil drives.

"Cooter," said Chief Lavel over the commo helmet's Channel 3. It was a lock-out push normally reserved for vehicle intercoms, so that even Tootsie Six couldn't overhear without making a point of it. "I found 'im. The sonuvabitch."

Flamethrower shuddered violently and began to skid as the tank to starboard ran up its fans to full pitch and thrust for a test.

The panzer's drivers had his nacelles vertical, so the hundred and seventy tonnes of tank simply rose a hand's breadth off the ground. The air bleeding beneath the skirts was at firehose pressure, though; the smack of it pushed the lighter combat car away until Shorty Rogers grounded *Flamethrower* to oppose the friction of steel on soil to the blast of the wind.

Cooter keyed Channel 3 and said, "Can you get him here, Chief? We're gonna get the word any time now."

"Cooter," said his friend, "I think you better take a look at this one yourself."

Chief Lavel had been a gun captain. He knew about time and about movement orders; and he knew what he was saying.

"Cop!" Cooter swore. "He in his doss, then?"

The tank, the nameless one crewed by a couple newbies, settled back onto its skirts. The sergeant in the cupola looked down at Cooter. In formation, they'd be running well ahead of *Flamethrower*'s tailass Charlie slot.

"Negative," said Chief. "He's in his buddy's bunk—you know, Platt's? In the Logistics doss."

Night fell like an axe at Camp Progress. Except for the red blur on the western horizon, the sun had disappeared completely in the past three minutes.

Cooter switched his visor to enhancement and checked to make sure the nameless tank was between him and Tootsie Six, then cut back to standard optical.

Depth perception was never quite as good on enhanced mode. There were enough lights on in the encampment for Cooter to find his way to the Logistics bunker/barracks.

Cooter tapped the shoulder of Gale, the right-wing gunner from Tootsie One-four, transferred to *Flamethrower* now that Otski and the other blower had both become casualties. Speaking on 12, the other lock-out push, to be heard over the fan noise, Cooter said,

"Hold the fort, Windy. I'll be back in a couple minutes max."

"We'll be bloody *gone* in a couple minutes, Cooter," Gale replied.

He was an older man, nearly thirty; not a genius, but bright and competent enough that he'd 've had a blower of his own years before had he not adamantly refused the promotion.

"Yeah, well," Cooter said, climbing awkwardly past Speed Riddle's clamshell and helmet stacked in front of the left tribarrel. "We're last in line. Worst case, Shorty'll have to make up a little time."

Worst case, Captain Ranson would notice her second-in-command hadn't pulled out on time and would check *Flamethrower's* own sensors. If she found Cooter gone from his post now, she'd have him dragged behind a blower all the way back to Camp Progress as soon as the mission was over.

Which was pretty much what Cooter had in mind for Speed Riddle.

He lumbered across the ground, burdened by his armor and half-blinded by dust despite is lowered visor. Cooter was a big man, but no man was significant in an area packed with the huge, slowly-maneuvering masses of armored vehicles.

Logistics section—the warehouses, truck park, and bunkered sleeping quarters for the associated personnel—formed the boundary between the Slammers' positions and the remainder of Camp Progress. Sappers who'd gotten through the Yokel defenses had bombed a parts shed and shot up a few trucks, but the Red section's counterattack put raid to the Consies here before they'd really gotten rolling.

The doss—half dug into the berm, half sandbagged—was undamaged except for six plate-sized cups where one round had splashed a Consie sapper instead of hitting the sandbags.

Chief Lavel stood in the doorway. He gestured to Cooter but hunched his way into the doss before the lieutenant arrived.

Chief tried to give himself a little advantage when there was anything tricky to do, like negotiating the double step that put the floor of the doss below ground level for safety. He got around amazingly well for a man missing his left arm and leg, though.

Outside the bunker, armored vehicles filled the evening with hot lubricant and the sharpness of ozone arcing away from dirty relays. The bunker's interior stank of human waste.

"What the . . . ?" Cooter muttered as he followed Chief down the narrow hallway along the front wall of the structure. A glowstrip was tacked to the ceiling; Cooter's helmet scraped it. He swore, ducked, and then straightened to bump again.

Board partitions made from packing cases divided the doss into rooms—decent-sized ones for Lavel and his permanent staff and, at the far end, tiny cubicles to house transients like the drivers making supply runs. The rooms were empty; the personnel were either involved with the departure or watching it.

Except for the last cubicle, where Speed Riddle lay sprawled on a cot with a broad smile. The balding gunner had fouled himself thoroughly enough that waste was dripping from his pants' leg onto the floor.

Riddle's fingers held a drug phial. Two more empties lay beside his hand.

Cooter stared at the gunner for several seconds. Then he turned around and strode back down the aisle.

His helmet brushed the glowstrip. He punched upward with his knotted right fist, banging the flat fixture against the ceiling of steel plank and causing grit to drift down through the perforations from the sandbagged topcover.

"Coot!" Lavel called, stumping along behind him. "Hey Coot. Slow down."

"Chief," Cooter said without slowing or turning, "I want that bastard tied up until he can be delivered to Central. With wire. Barbed wire'd be fine. Somthin' happens to me, you take care of the Court Martial, right?"

The end of Lavel's long crutch shot across the doorway, blocking Cooter's exit. "*Wait* a bloody minute!" Chief said.

Lavel was leaning against the right wall. The crutch was strapped to his stump, since he didn't have a left hand with which to grip it. He lowered it, a slim wand of boron monocrystal, when Cooter turned at last to face him.

"Going to use one of the newbies in Riddle's place?" he asked.

Cooter shook his head violently, as much to clear it as for a gesture. "Put the last one I could trust on One-five for a driver," he said. "I'll be better off watching that side myself than trusting some hick who's still got both thumbs up his ass."

"Take me, Cooter," said Chief Lavel.

Cooter looked at his friend with a cold lack of passion. Chief was so tall that he also had to duck to clear the ceiling. His shoulders were massive. Lavel had been thin when he was a whole man, but the inertia of his years of injury gave him a grotesque pot bell.

"Please, Coot," he said. "You won't regret it."

"I need you here, Chief," Cooter said as he turned. "You take care of Riddle, you hear?"

"*Coot?*"

"Gotta go now," Cooter muttered as he took both steps to the exterior with one stretch of his long, powerful legs.

The armored vehicles were snorting, running up the speed of their fans again; and, as Cooter strode toward *Flamethrower*, a tank fired its main gun skyward.

There were too bloody many vehicles in too little space, and the bloody drivers had too much on their minds.

A combat car was drifting toward *Herman's Whore*. The lighter vehicle was already so close that Ortnahme had to crank down his display to read the number stenciled on its skirts. "Tootsie One-two!" he snarled. "You're fouling—"

The tank lurched. For an instant, Ortnahme thought Simkins was trying to back away from the oncoming car. That wouldn't work, because Herman's Whore had rotated in place and her skirts were firmly against the berm.

"—us, you dickheaded—"

The man in the fighting compartment of Tootsie One-two turned, his face a ball of blank wonder as he stared at the tank looming above him. He was probably gabbling to his driver over the intercom, but there was no longer time to avoid the collision. The skirts of both vehicles were thick steel, but the combined mass would start seams for sure.

"—fool! Watch your—"

The bow of *Herman's Whore* lifted slightly. Simkins had run up his fans and vectored them forward. The tank couldn't slide backward because of the berm, so its bow skirts blasted a shrieking hurricane of air into the combat car.

Tootsie One-two, *Flamethrower*, pitched as though it had just dropped into a gully. The trooper in the fighting compartment bounced off the coaming before he could brace himself on the grips of two of the tribarrels.

Why in blazes was there only *one* man in the back of *Flamethrower* when the task force was set to move out?

The combat car slid two meters under the thrust of the tank's fans before Shorty Rogers dumped his own ground effect and sparked to a halt on bits of gravel in the soil.

The figure in the fighting compartment stood up again and gave *Herman's Whore* an ironic salute. "Blue two," said Ortnahme's helmet. "Sorry 'bout that."

"Tootsie One-two," the warrant leader responded. He

felt expansive and relieved, now that he was sure they wouldn't be deadlined at the last instant by a stupid mistake. "No harm done. It's prob'ly my bloody fault for not seeing your nacelles were aligned right when we had time to screw with 'em."

Herman's Whore settled, a little abruptly. Their skirts gave the ground a tap that rattled Ortnahme's teeth and probably cut a centimeter-deep oval in the hard soil.

"Simkins—" the warrant leader began, the word tripping the helmet's artificial intelligence to intercom mode.

"Sir, I'm sorry," his driver was already blurting. "I let the sucker—"

"Blood 'n martyrs, Simkins," Ortnahme interrupted, "don't worry about that! Where dja learn that little maneuver, anyhow?"

"Huh?" said the helmet. "Sir, it was just, you know, the leverage off the berm . . . ?"

He sounded like he thought Ortnahme was gonna chew his head off. Which had happened maybe a little too often in the past . . . but bloody hell, you had t' break 'em in the start. . . .

"Sir?" Simkins added in a little voice.

"Yeah?"

"Sir, I really like tanks. D'ye suppose that—"

"Like bloody hell!" the warrant leader snapped. "Look, kid, you're more good to me and Colonel Hammer right where you bloody are!"

"Yessir."

Which, come t' think about it, was driving a panzer. Well, there'd be time t' worry about that later.

Or there wouldn't.

The turret interior had darkened as the sky did, because the main screen was set on direct optical. Ortnahme frowned, then set the unit for progressive enhancement, projecting images at 60% of average daylight ambiance.

The visual display brightened suddenly, though the

edges of the snarling armored vehicles lacked a little of the definition they would have had in unaided sunlight. No matter what the sky did—sun, moons, or the Second Coming—the main screen would continue to display at this apparent light level until Ortnahme changed its orders.

Henk Ortnahme *knew* tanks. He knew their systems backward and forward, better than almost any of the panzers' regular crews.

Line troops found a few things that worked for them. Each man used his handful of sensor and gunnery techniques, ignoring the remainder of his vehicle's incredibly versatile menu. You don't fool around when your life depends on doing instinctively something that works *for you*.

The maintenance chief had to be sure that everything worked, every time. He'd spent twenty years of playing with systems that most everybody else forgot. He could run the screens and sensors by reflex and instantly critique the performance of each black box.

What the warrant leader *hadn't* had for those twenty years was combat experience. . . .

"Sir," said the helmet. "Ah, when are we supposed to pull out?"

A bloody stupid question.

Sunset, and Simkins could see as well as Ortnahme that it was sunset plus seven. Captain Ranson had said departure time would be coordinated by Central, so probably the only people who knew why Task Force Ranson was on hold were a thousand kilometers north of—

Screen Two, which in default mode—as now—was boresighted to the main gun, flashed the orange warning DIRECTOR CONTROL. As the letters appeared, the turret of *Herman's Whore* began to rotate without any input from Warrant Leader Ortnahme.

The turret was being run by Fire Central, at

Headquarters. Henk Ortnahme had no more to say about the situation than he did regarding any *other* orders emanating directly from Colonel Hammer.

"Sir?" Simkins blurted over the intercom.

"Blue Two—" demanded at least two other vehicles simultaneously, alerted by the squealing turret and rightly concerned about what the hell was going on. Screwing around with a tank's main gun in these close quarters wasn't just a *bad* idea.

"Simkins," Ortnahme said. His fingers stabbed buttons. "It's all right. The computer up in Purple's just took over."

As he spoke, Ortnahme set his gunnery screen to echo on Screen Three of the other tanks and the multi-function displays with which the combat cars made do. That'd answer their question better 'n anything he could say—

And besides, he was busy figuring out what Central thought it was doing with his tank.

The warrant leader couldn't countermand the orders coming from Firebase Purple, but he *could* ask his own artificial intelligence to tell him what firing solution was being fed to it. Screen Three obligingly threw up the figures for azimuth, elevation, and range.

"Blood 'n martyrs," Henk Ortnahme whispered.

Now he knew why the departure of Task Force Ranson had been delayed.

They had to wait for the Terran World Government's recce satellite to come over the horizon—

Herman's Whore fired its main gun; cyan lightning and a thunderclap through the open hatch, a blast of foul gases within the turret.

—so they could shoot it down.

The unexpected bolt didn't blind Cooter because his visor reacted in microseconds to block the intense glare. The shock stunned him for a moment anyway; then the big man began to run through the mass of restive vehicles.

A tank—*Deathdealer*, Blue One—slid forward. When

the big blower was clear, entering the Yokel area between the demolished shed and a whole one, Captain Ranson's *Warmonger* fell in behind it. It was as though the echoing blast from *Herman's Whore* had triggered an iridium avalanche.

The third vehicle, another combat car, sidled up to the line of departure. That'd be One-five, its driver a newbie on whom Cooter had decided to take a chance. The fellow was matching his blower's speed to that of the leading vehicles, but he had his bow pointing thirty degrees off the axis of motion.

Some dickhead Yokel had parked a light truck just inside the Slammer's area. One-five's tail skirts managed to tap the little vehicle and send it spinning halfway up the berm, a graphic illustration of the difference between a tonne at rest and thirty tonnes in motion.

Cooter reached his car panting with exertion, anger, and a relieved awareness of how bloody *near* that asshole Riddle had made him cut it. One-one was already pulling into line for the run through Camp Progress, though the second and third combat cars would spread left and right as outriders as soon as they left the gate.

A Yokel wearing fatigues cut for somebody shorter put a hand on Cooter's shoulder as he set his foot on *Flamethrower*'s skirt. The fellow carried a slung grenade launcher, a kitbag, and a satchel of ammunition.

Cooter had never seen him before.

"Who the hell are you?" he snarled over the fans' intake howl. The skirts were quivering with repressed violence, and the nameless Blue Three was already headed into the Yokel compound.

"I'm Dick," the fellow shouted. "From last night. Lieutenant, can you use a grenadier for this run?"

Cooter started at him a second, five seconds . . . ten. One-six was pulling out. . . .

"You bet your ass I can, turtle," Cooter said. "Welcome aboard!"

Chapter Six

The upper half of June Ranson's visor showed a light-enhanced view of her surroundings. It flicked from side to side as her head bobbed in the nervous-pigeon motions of somebody with more things to worry about than any human being could handle.

Deathdealer led the column. Even from 200 meters ahead, the wake of the tank's vast passage rocked *Warmonger*'s own considerable mass. Willens was driving slightly left of the center of *Deathdealer*'s track, avoiding some of the turbulence and giving himself a better direct view forward. It raised the danger from mines, though; the tank would set off anything before the combat car reached it, if their tracks were identical. . . .

She let it go for now. The roadway between Camp Progress and the civilian settlement over the ridge had been cleared in the fighting the night before.

Stolley had his tribarrel cocked forward, parallel to the car's axis of motion instead of sweeping the quadrant to the left side like he ought to. Stolley figured— and they all figured, Junebug Ranson as sure as her wing gunner—that first crack at any Consies hereabouts would come from the front.

But a ninety percent certainty meant one time in ten you were dead. *Deathdealer* and the bow gunner, June Ranson, could handle the front. Stolley's job—

Ranson put her fingers on the top barrel of Stolley's weapon, well ahead of the mounting post, and pushed.

The wing gunner's hands tightened on the grips for a moment before he relaxed with a curse that he didn't even try to muffle. The gun muzzles swung outward in the direction they ought to be pointed.

Stolley stared at his commanding officer. His face was a reflecting ball behind his lowered visor.

"If you don't like your job," Ranson said, speaking over the wind noise instead of using intercom, "I can arrange for you to drive. Another blower."

Stolley crouched behind his gun, staring into the night.

Ranson nodded in approval of the words she'd been listening to, the words coming from her mouth. Good command technique—under the circumstances, under field conditions where it was more important to be obeyed than to be liked. This crew wasn't going to like its blower captain anyway . . . but they'd obey.

Ranson shook her head violently. She wasn't an observer, watching a holographic record from command school on Friesland. She was . . .

The images on the lower half of her visor wobbled at a rate different from that of the combat car and didn't change when Ranson darted her head to the left or right. She'd slaved its display to that of the sensors on *Deathdealer* in the lead. The tank's intakes sucked the tops of low bushes toward her from the roadside. Then, as *Deathdealer* came alongside, the air leaking beneath her skirts battered them away.

Moments later, *Warmonger* swept by the bushes. The top of Ranson's visor repeated the images of the lower section as if on a five-second delay.

Ranson shook her head again. It didn't help.

By an emergency regulation—which had been in place for fourteen years—there were to be no private structures within two kilometers of a military base. Colonel Banyussuf had enforced that reg pretty stringently. There'd been drink kiosks all along the road to within a hundred meters of the gate, but they were daylight use only.

Since the panzers swept through the night before,

nothing remained of the flimsy stands but splinters and ash that swirled to the passage of Task Force Ranson.

Permanent civilian dwellings, more serious entertainment—whores, hard drugs, gambling—as well as the goods and services you'd normally find in a town the size of Camp Progress, were in Happy Days. That settlement was just over the ridge the road climbed as it ran southeast from the camp. Technically, Happy Days was within the two-kilometer interdict; but out of sight, out of mind.

Being over the ridge meant line-of-sight bolts from the Slammers' powerguns wouldn't 've hurt the civilians. The National Army might've dropped some indirect fire on Happy Days during the fighting, but Ranson doubted the Yokels had been that organized.

Janacek had taped a red-patterned bandanna to the lower rear edge of his commo helmet. At rest, it kept sun from the back of his neck, but when the car was moving, it popped and fluttered like a miniature flag.

When Task Force Ranson got beyond the settlement, they could open their formation and race cross-country through the night, but the only practical place to cross the wooded ridge was where the road did.

There were probably Consies hidden among the civilians of Happy Days. One of them might try a shot as the armored vehicles howled past. . . .

The lead tank crested the rise in a cloud of ash and charred wood. There'd been groves of mighty trees to either side of the road. Panels of bright silk strung from trunk to trunk sectioned the copses into open-air brothels in fine weather.

Before. During the previous night, return fire and the backblasts of bombardment rockets had torched the trees into ash and memories. That permitted *Deathdealer*'s driver to swing abruptly to the right, off the roadway and any weapons targeted on it, just before coming into sight of Happy Days.

Debris momentarily blanked the lower half of Ranson's

visor. It cleared with a view of the settlement. The ground across the ridge dropped away more steeply than on the side facing Camp Progress, so the nearest of the one- and two-story houses were several hundred meters away where the terrain flattened.

Happy Days was a ghost town.

Deathdealer was proceeding at forty kph, fractionally slower than her speed a few moments before. *Warmonger* started to close the 200-meter separation, but Willens throttled back and swung to the left of the road as the combat car topped the rise. Ranson's left hand switched her visor off remote; her right was firm on the tribarrel's grip.

Happy Days hadn't been damaged in the previous night's fighting. The buildings crowded the stakes marking the twenty-meter right of way, but their walls didn't encroach—another regulation Banyussuf had enforced, with bulldozers when necessary.

Half the width was road surface which had been stabilized with a plasticizer, then pressure-treated. The lead tank slipped down the incline on the right shoulder behind a huge cloud of dust.

Nothing moved in the settlement.

A few of the structures were concrete prefabs, but most were built of laths covered with enameled metal. Uncut sheets already imprinted with the logo of soups or beers gleamed in an array more colorful than that of a race course. Behind the buildings themselves, fabric barriers enclosed yards in which further business could be conducted in the open air.

The lead tank was almost between the rows of buildings. Ranson's visor caught and highlighted movement of the barred window of a popular knocking-shop across the street and near the far end of the strip. She switched her display to thermal.

Stolley swung his tribarrel toward the motion.

"No!" June Ranson shouted.

The wing gunner's short burst snapped through the air like a single streak of cyan, past *Deathdealer* and into a white coruscance as the window's iron grillwork burned at the impacts.

A buzzbomb arced from the left and exploded in the middle of its trajectory as the tank's close-in defense system fired with a vicious crackling.

At least twenty automatic weapons volleyed orange tracers from Happy Days. The bullets ricocheted from *Deathdealer* and clanged like hammerblows on *Warmonger*'s hull and gunshields.

"All Tootsie elements!" Ranson shouted. Willens had chopped his throttles; *Warmonger*'s skirts tapped the soil. "Bandits! Blue One—"

But it was too late to order Blue One to lay a mine-clearing charge down the road. The great tank accelerated toward Happy Days in a spray of dust and pebbles, tribarrel and main gun blasting ahead of it.

"Hey, snake?" said DJ Bell from the main screen as bolts from a powergun cracked past *Deathdealer*. "Watch out for the Pussycat, OK?"

"Go 'way, DJ!" Birdie Sparrow shouted. "Albers! Goose it! Fast! Fast!"

The sound of bullets striking their thick armor was lost in the roar of the fans whose intakes suddenly tried to gulp more air than fluid flow would permit. The impacts quivered through Sparrow's boots on the floorplate like the ticks of a mechanical clock gone haywire.

Sparrow gripped a gunnery joystick in either hand. Most tankers used only one control, thumb-switching from main gun to tribarrel and back at need. He'd taught himself years ago to operate with both sticks live. You didn't get sniper's precision that way, but—

"Bandits!" cried the captain. "Blue One—"

Whatever she wanted would wait.

—when it was suppressing fire you needed, like now—

Whatever anybody else wanted could wait.

Using the trigger of the right joystick, Sparrow rapped a five-round burst from the tribarrel across a shop midway down the Strip on the left side. Sheet metal blew away from the wood beneath it, fluttering across the street as if trying to escape from the sudden blaze behind it.

The main screen was set on a horizontally-compressed 360 degree panorama. Sparrow was used to the distortion. He caught the puff of a buzzbomb launch before his electronics highlighted the threat.

A defensive charge blasted from above *Deathdealer*'s skirts. It made the hull ring as none of the hostile fire had managed.

Sparrow's tribarrel raked shop-fronts further down the Strip in a long burst. The bolts flashed at an increasing separation because the tank was accelerating.

Deathdealer's turret rotated counter-clockwise, independently of the automatic weapon in the cupola. The left pipper, the point-of-aim indicator for the main gun, slid backward across the facade of one of the settlement's sturdier buildings.

The neon sign was unlighted, but Sparrow knew it well—a cat with a Cheshire grin, gesturing with a forepaw toward her lifted haunches.

That was where the buzzbomb had come from. Three more sparks spat in the darkness—light, lethal missiles, igniting in the whorehouse parlor—just as Sparrow's foot stroked the pedal trip for his 20cm cannon.

Deathdealer's screens blacked out the cyan flash. The displays were live again an instant later when dozens of ready missiles went off in a secondary explosion that blew the Pussycat's walls and roof into concrete confetti.

"Blue Three," the command channel was blatting, "move forward and—"

Albers brought *Deathdealer* into the settlement with

gravity aiding his desperately-accelerating fans. He was hugging the right side of the Strip, too close for a buzzbomb launched from that direction to harm. Anti-personnel mines banged harmlessly beneath them.

"—lay a clearing charge before anybody else proceeds!"

Across the roadway, shopfronts popped and sizzled under the fire of Sparrow's tribarrel and the more raking bolts of combat cars pausing just over the ridgeline as Tootsie Six had ordered.

Deathdealer brushed the front of the first shop. The building collapsed like a bomb going off.

The tank accelerated to eighty kph. Albers used his mass and the edge of his skirts like a router blade, ripping down the line of flimsy shops. The fragments scattered in the draft of his fans.

A Consie took two steps from a darkened tavern, knelt, and aimed his buzzbomb down the throat of the oncoming tank.

Sparrow's foot twitched on the firing pedal. The main gun crashed out a bolt that turned a tailor's shop across the road into a fireball with a plasma core. The blast was twenty meters from the rocketeer, but the Consie flung away his weapon in surprise and tried to run.

A combat car nailed him, half a pace short of the doorway that would have provided concealment if not protection.

Sparrow had begun firing with his tribarrel at a ten o'clock angle. As *Deathdealer* raced toward the far end of the settlement, he panned the weapon counter-clockwise and stuttered bursts low into shop fronts. Instants after the tribarrel raked a facade, his main gun converted the entire building into a self-devouring inferno.

Two controls, two pippers sliding across a compressed screen at varying rates. The few bullets that still spattered the hull were lost in the continuous rending impact of Albers' 170-tonne wrecking ball.

Choking gases from the cannon breech, garbled orders and warnings from the radio.

No sweat, none of it. Birdie Sparrow was in control, and they couldn't none of 'em touch him.

Another whorehouse flew apart at the touch of *Deathdealer*'s skirt. A meter by three-meter strip of metal enameled with a hundred and fifty bright Lion Beer logos curled outward and slapped itself over the intake of #1 Starboard fan.

The sudden loss of flow dipped the skirt to the soil and slewed *Deathdealer*'s bow before plenum-chamber pressure couldn't balance the mass it carried. The stern swung outward, into the *clang-clang* impact of bolts from a combat car's tribarrel. Fist-sized chunks vaporized from iridium armor that had ignored Consie bullets.

Sparrow rocked in his turret's stinking haze, clinging grimly to the joysticks and bracing his legs as well. The standard way to clear a blocked duct was to reverse the fan. That'd ground *Deathdealer* for a moment, and with the inertia of their present speed behind *that* touchdown—

Albers may have chopped his #1S throttle but he didn't reverse it—or try to straighten *Deathdealer*'s course out of the hook into which contact had canted it. They hit the next building in line, bow-on at seventy kph—shattering panels of pre-stressed concrete and sweeping the fan duct clear in the avalanche of heavy debris.

Deathdealer bucked and pitched like a bull trying to pin a tiger to the jungle floor. The collision was almost as bad as the one for which Sparrow had prepared himself, but the tank never quite lost forward way. They staggered onward, cascading chunks of wall, curtains, and gambling tables.

The tank's AI threw up a red-lit warning on Screen Three. *Deathdealer*'s ground-penetrating radar showed a thirty-centimeter tunnel drilled beneath the road's hard surface from the building they'd just demolished. The cavity was large enough to contain hundreds of kilos of explosive—

And it almost certainly did.

Without the blocked fan, *Deathdealer* would've been over the mine before the Consie at the detonator could react—that was the advantage of speed and the shattering effect of heavy gunfire, the elements Sparrow'd been counting on to get them through.

And their armor. Even a mine that big. . . .

"All Mike—T-tootsie elements," Sparrow warned. "The road's mined! Mine!"

He'd frozen the gunnery controls as he waited for the collision. Now, while Albers muscled the tank clear of the wreckage and started to build speed again, Sparrow put both pippers on the building across the road from them. He vaporized it with a long burst and three twenty-centimeter rounds, just in case the command detonator was there rather than in the shattered gambling den.

It might have a pressure or magnetic detonator. Speed wouldn't 've helped *Deathdealer* then. If luck hadn't slewed them off the road at the right moment.

"Can't touch us!" Birdie Sparrow muttered as he fired back over the tank's left rear skirts. "Can't touch us!"

"Not this time, snake," said DJ Bell as bitter gases writhed through the turret.

If he'd bothered to look behind him, Hans Wager could've seen that the tail end of the column had yet to pass the gates of Camp Progress.

Just over the ridge, all hell was breaking loose.

Wager's instinctive reaction was the same as always when things really dropped in the pot: to hunker down behind his tribarrel and hope there were panzers close enough to lend a hand.

It gave him a queasy feeling to realize that this time, *he* was the tank element and it was for him, Blue Three, that the CO was calling.

"—move forward and lay a clearing charge!"

Something big enough to light the whole sky orange blew up behind the ridge. Pray the Lord it was Consies eating some of their own ordnance rather than a mine going off beneath a blower.

The lead tank and Tootsie Six had both dropped over the ridgeline. One-five and One-one pulled forward. The first car slid to the right in a gush of gray-white ash colored blue by gunfire while the other accelerated directly up the road.

Blue Three shuddered as her driver poured the coal to her. Through inexperience, Holman swung her fan nacelles rearward too swiftly. Their skirts scraped a shower of sparks for several meters along the pavement.

Wager found his seat control, not instinctively but fast enough. He dropped from cupola level while the tank plowed stabilized with a sound like mountains screaming.

Tracers stitched the main screen and across the sky overhead, momentary flickers through the open hatch.

One-five vanished behind the crest. One-one swung to the right and stopped abruptly with a flare of her skirts, still silhouetted on the ridgeline. Blue Three was wallowing toward the same patch of landscape under full power.

Wager shouted a curse, but Holman had their mount under control. The nameless tank pivoted left like a wheeled vehicle whose back end had broken away, avoiding the combat car. They could see now that One-one had pulled up to keep from overrunning Tootsie Six.

Blue Three began to slide at a slight sideways angle down the ridge they'd just topped. The three cars ahead of them were firing wildly into the smoke and flying debris of the settlement.

Sparrow's Blue One had just smashed a building. It pulled clear with the motion of an elephant shrugging during a dust bath.

"All Mike—T-tootsie elements," came a voice that a mask on the main screen would identify (if Wager wondered) as Blue One, used to his old callsign. "Mines! Mines!"

"Blue Three!" snarled Captain Ranson. "Lay the bloody charge! Now!"

If the bitch wanted to trade jobs, she could take this cursed panzer and all its cursed hardware! She could take it and shove it up her ass!

It wasn't that Hans Wager had never used a mine-clearing charge before. On a combat car, though, they were special equipment bolted to the bow skirts and fired manually. All the tanks were fitted with integral units, controlled by the AI. So. . . .

"Booster," Wager ordered crisply. "Clearance charge."

The gunsight pipper on Screen Two dimmed to half its previous orange brilliance. ARMED appeared in the upper left corner of the screen, above RANGE TO TARGET and LENGTH OF FOOTPRINT.

Magenta tracks, narrowed toward the top by foreshortening, overlay the image of the settlement toward which Blue Three was slipping with the slow grace of a beerstein on a polished bar.

Instead of aligning with the pavement, the aiming tracks skewed across the right half of the Strip.

"Holman!" Wager screamed. "Straighten up! Straighten the fuck out! With the road!"

Sparrow's *Deathdealer* had reached the end of the built-up Strip. The turret was rotated back at a 220 degree angle to the tank's course. Its main gun fired, a blacked-out streak on Blue Three's screens and a dazzle of cyan radiance through her open hatch.

Wager heard the fan note rise as his driver adjusted nacelles #1S and #2S and boosted their speed. The nameless tank seemed to hesitate, but its attitude didn't change.

"Range," Wager called to his artificial intelligence. They were about a hundred meters from the nearest buildings. Since they were still moving forward maybe he ought to—

Whang!

Wager looked up in amazement. The bullet that had flattened itself against the cupola's open hatch dropped onto his cheek. It was hotter than hell.

"Sonuvabitch!" Wager shouted.

"Blue Two," ordered the radio, "move into position and lay down a clearance charge!"

"Sergeant," begged Holman over the intercom channel, "do you want me to stop us or—"

She'd straightened 'em out all right, for about a millisecond before the counter-clockwise rotation began to swing the tank's bow out of alignment again in the opposite direction. The aiming tracks marched across the screen with stately precision.

The volume of fire from the combat cars slackened because Wager's tank blocked their aim. Another bullet rang against the hatch; this one ricocheted glowing into the darkness. Bloody good thing Wager wasn't manning the cupola tribarrel himself just now. . . .

"Fire!" Wager ordered his AI.

He didn't know what the default setting was. He just knew he wasn't going to wait in his slowly-revolving tank and get it right some time next week.

Blue Three chugged, a sound much like that of a mortar firing nearby. The charge, a net of explosive filaments deploying behind a sparkling trio of rocket drivers, arched from a bow compartment.

As soon as the unit fired, the computed aiming tracks transformed themselves into a holographic overlay of the charge being laid—the gossamer threads would otherwise have been invisible.

The net wobbled outward for several seconds, shuddering in the flame-spawned air currents. It settled, covering five-hundred meters of pavement, the road's left shoulder, and the fronts of most of the buildings on the left side.

Muzzle flashes continued to wink from the stricken ruins of Happy Days.

The charge detonated with a white flash as sudden as that of lightning. Dust and ash spread in a dense pall that was opaque in the thermal spectrum as well as to normal optics.

Hundreds of small mines popped and spattered gravel. The explosive-filled cavity whose image, remoted from *Deathdealer* and frozen for reference on Wager's screen Three, didn't go off.

Fuckin' A.

Hans Wager shifted Screen Two to millimetric radar and gripped his gunnery control. "Holman, drive on," he ordered, aware as he spoke that Blue Three was already accelerating.

Holman hadn't waited to be told. She knew as sure as Wager did that if the big mine went off, it was better that a tank take the shock than the lesser mass of a combat car.

Better for everybody except maybe the tank's crew.

Wager triggered the main gun and coaxially-locked tribarrel simultaneously, throwing echoing swirls onto his display as the dense atmosphere warped even the radar patterns.

"Tootsie Six," he said as he felt the tank beneath him build to a lumbering gallop. "This is Blue Three. We're going through."

Flamethrower cleared the rise. The settlement was a scene from Bruegel's Hell, and Dick Suilin was being plunged into the heart of it.

Cooter looked back over his shoulder at the reporter. His voice in Suilin's earphones said, "Watch the stern, turtle. Don't worry about the bow—we'll go through on Ortnahme's coattails."

Gale, the veteran trooper, had already shifted his position behind the right win gun so that he was facing backward at 120 degrees to the combat car's direction of travel. Suilin obediently tried to do the same, but he found that stacked ammo boxes and the large cooler made it difficult for him to stand. By folding one knee on the cooler, he managed to aim at the proper angle, but he wasn't sure he'd be able to hit anything if a target appeared.

Flamethrower was gathering speed. They'd crawled up the slope, matching their speed to that of the tank ahead of them. That vehicle in turn was trying not to overrun the combat cars pausing at the hillcrest.

The first series of the loud shocks occurred before Suilin's car was properly beyond the berm of Camp Progress. After that, the hidden fighting settled down to the vicious sizzle of powerguns. Each bolt sounded like sodium dropping into water in blazing kilogram packets.

When *Flamethrower* topped the ridgeline, offset to the left of the last tank in Task Force Ranson, Suilin saw the remains of Happy Days.

Four days before, he'd thought of the place as just another of the sleazy Strips that served army bases all over Prosperity—all over the human universe. Now it was a roiling pit, as smoky as the crater of a volcano and equally devoid of life.

"Blue Two," said a voice in Suilin's earphones, "this is Tootsie One-two. We're comin' through right up yer ass, so don't change yer mind, all right?"

It was probably Cooter speaking, but the reporter couldn't be sure. The helmets transmitted on one side-band, depriving the voices of normal timbre, and static interrupted the words every time a gun fired.

"Roger that, Tootsie One-two," said a different speaker. "Simkins, you heard the man. Keep yer bloody foot in it, right?"

Suilin's visual universe was a pattern of white blurs against a light blue background. The solidity and intensity of the white depended on the relative temperature of the object viewed.

I put it on thermal for you, Gale had said as he

slapped a commo helmet onto the reporter's head with the visor down.

The helmet was loose, slipping forward when Suilin dipped his head and tugging back against its chin strap in the airstream when the combat car accelerated uphill. There was probably an adjustment system, but Suilin didn't know where it was . . . and this wasn't the time to ask.

Their own car, *Flamethrower*, slid over the crest and slowed as a billow of dust and ash expanded from the bow skirts like half a smoke ring. The driver had angled his fans forward; they lifted the bow slightly and kicked light debris in the direction opposite to their thrust against the vehicle's mass.

The tank had offset to the right on the hilltop as *Flamethrower* pulled left. Now it blew forward a similar but much larger half-doughnut. The arc of dust sucked in on itself, then recoiled outward when the cannon fired. The gun's crash was deafening to Suilin, even over the howl of the fans.

There was nothing to see on the flank Suilin was supposed to be guarding except the slight differential rate at which rocks, gravel, and vegetation lost the heat they'd absorbed during daylight. He risked a look over his shoulder, just as the tank fired again and Cooter ripped a burst from his tribarrel down the opposite side of what had been the settlement.

A combat car was making the run through Happy Days. The preceding vehicle of the task force waited in line abreast of the rising ground to the east of the settlement. Their hulls, particularly the skirts and fan intakes, were white; the muzzles of their powerguns were as sharp as floodlights.

The settlement was a pearly ambiance that wrapped and shrouded the car speeding through its heart. A gout of rubble lifted. It had fused to glass under the impact of the tank's twenty-centimeter bolt.

Suilin couldn't see any sign of a target—for the big

gun or even for Cooter's raking tribarrel. The car racing through the wreckage was firing also, but the vehicles waiting on the far side of the gauntlet were silent, apparently for fear of hitting their fellow.

The road was outlined in flames over which smoke and ash swept like a dancer's veils. Molten spatters lifted by the tank cannon cooled visibly as they fell. There was no return fire or sign of Consies.

There were no structures left in what had been a community of several thousand.

The tank beside *Flamethrower* shrugged like a dog getting ready for a fight. Dust and ash puffed from beneath it again, this time sternward.

"Hang on, turtle!" a voice crackled in Suilin's ears as *Flamethrower* began to build speed with the deceptive smoothness characteristic of an air cushion vehicle.

Suilin gripped his tribarrel and tried to see something—*anything*—over the ghost-ring sight of the weapon. The normal holographic target display wasn't picked up by his visor's thermal imaging. The air stank of ozone and incomplete combustion.

The car rocked as its skirts clipped high spots and the debris flung from the buildings. The draft of *Flamethrower*'s fans and passage shouldered the smoke aside, but there was still nothing to see except hot rubble.

Cooter and Gale fired, their bursts producing sharp static through Suilin's headset. The helmet slipped back and forth on the reporter's forehead.

In desperation, Suilin flipped up his visor. Glowing smoke became black swirls, white flames became sullen orange. The bolts from his companion's weapons flicked the scene with an utter purity of color more suitable for a church than this boiling inferno.

Suilin thumbed his trigger, splashing dirt and a charred timber with cyan radiance. He fired again, raising his sights, and saw a sheet of metal blaze with the light of its own destruction.

They were through the settlement and slowing again. There were armored vehicles on either side of *Flamethrower*. Gale fired a last spiteful burst and put his weapons on safe.

Suilin's hands were shaking. He had to grip the pivot before he could thumb the safety button.

It'd been worse than the previous night. This time he hadn't known what was happening or what he was supposed to do.

"Tootsie Six to all Tootsie elements," said the helmet. "March order, conforming to Blue One. Execute."

The vehicles around them were moving again, though *Flamethrower* held a nervous, greasy balance on its fans. They'd move out last again, just as they had when Task Force Ranson left the encampment.

Minutes ago.

"How you doing, turtle?" Lieutenant Cooter asked. He'd raised his visor also. "See any Consies?"

Suilin shook his head. "I just . . ." he said. "I just shot, in case . . . Because you guys were shooting, you know?"

Cooter nodded as he lifted his helmet to rub his scalp. "Good decision. Never hurts t' keep their heads down. You never can tell. . . ."

He gazed back at the burning waste through which they'd passed.

Suilin swallowed. "What's this 'turtle' business?" he asked.

Gale chuckled through his visor.

Cooter smiled and knuckled his forehead again. "Nothin' personal," the big lieutenant said. "You know, you're fat, you know? After a while you'll be a snake like the rest of us."

He turned.

"Hey," the reporter said in amazement. "I'm not fat! I exercise—"

Gale tapped the armor over Suilin's ribs. "Not fat

there, turtle," the reflective curve of the veteran's visor said. "Newbie fat, you know? Civilian fat."

The tank they'd followed from Camp Progress began to move. "Watch your arcs, both of you," Cooter muttered over the intercom. "They may have another surprise waiting for us."

Suilin's body swayed as the combat car slipped forward. He still didn't know what the mercenaries meant by the epithet.

And he was wondering what had happened to all the regular inhabitants of Happy Days.

"Go ahead, Tootsie," said the voice of Slammer Six, hard despite all the spreads and attentuations that brought it from Firebase Purple to June Ranson's earphones. "Over."

"Lemme check yer shoulder," said Stolley to Janacek beside her. "C'mon, crack the suit."

"Roger," Ranson said as she checked the positioning of her force in the multi-function display. "We're OK, no casualties, but there was an ambush at the strip settlement just out the gate."

Blue One was ghosting along 200 meters almost directly ahead of *Warmonger* at sixty kph. That was about the maximum for an off-road night run, even in this fairly open terrain.

One-one and One-five had taken their flanking positions, echeloned slightly back from the lead tank. The remaining four blowers were spaced tank-car, tank-car, behind *Warmonger* like the tail of a broadly diamond-shaped kite.

Just as it ought to be . . . but the ratfuck at Happy Days had cost the task force a good hour.

"We couldn't 've avoided it," Ranson said, "so we shot our way through."

If she'd known, *known*, there was a company of Consies in Happy Days, she'd 've bypassed the place by heading north cross-country and cutting east, then south, near Siu Mah. It'd 've been a hundred kilometers out of their way, but—

"Look, bugger off," said Janacek. "I'm fine. I'll take another pill, right?"

"Any of the bypass routes might've got you in just as deep," said Colonel Hammer, taking a chance that, because of the time lag, his satellited words were going to step on those of his junior officer. "It's really dropped in the pot, Captain, all the hell over this country. But you don't see any reason that you can't carry out your mission?"

The question was so emotionless that concern stuck out in all directions like barbs from a burr. "Over."

"Quit screw'n around, Checker," Stolley demanded. "You got bits a jacket metal there. I get 'em out and there's no sweat."

Ranson touched the scale control of her display. The eight discrete dots shrank to a single one, at the top edge of a large-scale moving map that ended at Kohang.

Latches clicked. Janacek had opened his clamshell armor for his buddy's inspection. A bullet had disintegrated on the shield of Janacek's tribarrel during the run through Happy Days; bits of the projectile had sprayed the wing gunner.

Ranson felt herself slipping into the universe of the map, into a world of electronic simulation and holographic intersections that didn't bleed when they dropped from the display.

That was the way to win battles: move your units around as if they *were* only units, counters on a game board. Do whatever was necessary to check your enemy, to smash him, to achieve your objective.

Commanders who thought about blood, officers who saw with their mind's eye the troops they commanded screaming and crawling through muck with their intestines dangling behind them . . . those officers might be squeamish, they might be hesitant to give the orders needful for victory.

The commander of the guerrillas in this district understood that perfectly. Happy Days was a deathtrap for anybody trying to defend it against the Slammers. There was no line of retreat, and the vehicles' powerguns were sure to blast the settlement into ash and vapor, along with every Consie in it.

The company or so of patriots who'd tried to hold Happy Days on behalf of the Conservative Action Movement almost certainly didn't realize that; but the man or woman who gave them their orders from an office somewhere in the Terran Government enclaves on the North Coast did. The ambush had meant an hour's delay for the relief operation, and that was well worth the price—on the North Coast.

Men and munitions were the cost of doing business. You needed both of them to win.

You needed to spit them both in the face of the enemy. They could be replaced after the victory.

Stolley's hand-held medikit began to purr as it swallowed bits of metal that it had separated from the gunner's skin and shoulder muscles. Janacek cursed mildly.

Colonel Hammer knew the rules also.

"Slammer Six," June Ranson's voice said, "we're continuing. I don't know of any . . . I mean, we're not worse off than when we received the mission. Not really."

She paused, her mouth miming words while her mind tried to determine what those words should be. Hammer didn't interrupt. "We've got to cross the Padma River. Not a lotta choices about where. And we'll have the Santine after that, that'll be tricky. But we'll know more after the Padma."

Warmonger's fans ruled the night, creating a cocoon of controlled sound in which the electronic dot calling itself Junebug Ranson was safe with all her other dots.

Her chestplate rapped the grips of the tribarrel. She'd started to doze off again.

"Tootsie Six, over!" she said sharply. Her skin tingled, and all her body hairs were standing up straight.

There was a burst of static from her headset, but no response.

"Tootsie Six, over," she repeated.

Nothing but carrier hum.

Ranson craned her neck to look upward, past the splinter shield. There was a bright new star in the eastern sky, but it was fading even as she watched.

For fear of retribution, the World Government had spared the Slammers' recon and comsats when they swept the Yokels' own satellites out of orbit. When Alois Hammer raised the stakes, however, the Terrans stayed in the game.

"Now a little Sprayseal," Stolley muttered, "and we're done. Easier 'n bitchin', ain't it?"

Task Force Ranson was on its way now.

But they'd been on their own from the start. Troops at the sharp end were always on their own.

"Awright, then latch me up, will ya?" Janacek said. Then, "Hey, Stolley. When ya figure we get another chance t' kick butt?"

Warmonger howled through the darkness.

Chapter Seven

"I think it's a little tight now," Suilin said, trying gingerly to lift the commo helmet away from his compressed temples.

"Right," said Cooter. "Now pull the tab over the left ear. Just a cunt hair."

"Time t' stoke the ole furnaces," said Gale, handing something small to Cooter while the reporter experimented with the fit of his helmet.

When Suilin drew down on the tab as directed, the helmet lining deflated with an immediate release of pressure. It felt good—but he didn't want the cursed thing sliding around on his head, either; so maybe if he pulled the right tab again, just a—

"And one for you, buddy," Gale said, offering Suilin a white-cased stim cone about the size of a thumbnail. "Hey, what's your name?"

"Dick," the reporter said. "Ah—what's this?"

Cooter set the base of his cone against the inner side of his wrist and squeezed to inject himself. "Wide-awakes," he said. "A little something to keep you alert. Not much of a rush, but it beats nodding off about the time it all drops in the pot."

"Like Tootsie Six," Gale said, thumbing forward with a grin.

The front of the column was completely hidden from *Flamethrower*. Task Force Ranson had closed to fifty-meter separations between vehicles as soon as they entered the forest, but even Blue Two, immediately ahead of them, had been only a snorting ambiance for most of the past hour.

"Junebug's problem ain't she's tired," Cooter said with a grimace. "She's . . ." he spun his finger in a brief circle around his right ear. "It happens. She'll be okay."

"But won't this . . . ?" Suilin said, rolling the stim cone between his fingers. "I mean, what are the side effects?"

As a reporter, he'd seen his share and more of burnouts, through his business and in it.

Cooter shrugged. "After a couple days," the big man said, raising his arm absently to block a branch swishing past his gunshield, "it don't help any more. And your ears ring like a sonuvabitch about that long after. Better 'n getting your ass blown away."

"Hey," said Gale cheerfully. "Promise me I'll be *around* in a couple days and I'll drink sewage."

Suilin set the cone and squeezed it. There was a jet of cold against his skin, but he couldn't feel any other immediate result.

Flamethrower broke into open terrain, a notch washed clean when the stream below was in spate. The car slid down the near bank, under control but still fast enough that their stern skirts sparked and rattled against the rocky soil. Water exploded in a fine mist at the bottom as Rogers goosed his fans to lift the car up the far side. They cleared the upper lip neatly, partly because the bank had already been crumpled into a ramp by the passage of earlier vehicles.

Blue Two had been visible for a moment as the tank made its own blasting run up the bank. Now *Flamethrower* was alone again, except for sounds and the slender-boled trees through which the task force pushed its way.

"Lord, why can't this war stop?" Dick Suilin muttered.

"Because," said Cooter, though the reporter's words weren't really meant as a question, "for it to stop, either your folks or the World Government has gotta throw in the towel. Last we heard, that hadn't happened."

"May a bloody happened by now," Gale grunted, looking sourly at the sky where stars no longer shared their turf with commo and recce satellites. "Boy, wouldn't that beat hell? Us get our asses greased because we didn't know the war was over?"

"It's *not* the *World* Government," the reporter snapped. "It's the Terran Government, and that hasn't been the government on *this* world for the thirty years since we freed ourselves."

Neither of the mercenaries responded. Cooter lowered his head over his multi-function display and fiddled with its dials.

"Look, I'm sorry," Suilin said after a moment. He lifted

his helmet and rubbed his eyes. Maybe the Wide-awake was having an effect after all. "Look, it's just that Prosperity could be a garden spot, a paradise, if it weren't for outsiders hired by the Terrans."

"Sorry, troop," said Gale as he leaned past Suilin to open the cooler on the floor of the fighting compartment. "But that's a big negative."

"Ninety percent of the Consies 're born on Prosperity," Cooter agreed without looking up. "And I don't mean in the Enclaves, neither."

"Ninety-bloody-eight percent of the body count," Gale chuckled. He lifted the cap off a beer by catching it on the edge of his gunshield and thrusting down. "Which figures, don't it?"

He sucked the foam from the neck of the bottle and handed it to Cooter. When he opened and swigged from the second one, Gale murmured, "I'll say this fer you guys. You brew curst good beer."

He gave the bottle to Suilin.

It was a bottle of 33, cold and wonderfully smooth when the reporter overcame his momentary squeamishness at putting his lips on the bottle that the mercenary had licked. Suilin didn't realize how dry his throat was until he began to drink.

"Look," he said, "there's always going to be malcontents. They wouldn't be a threat to stability if they weren't being armed and trained in the Enclaves."

"Hey, what do I know about politics?" Gale said. He patted the breech of his tribarrel with his free hand.

A branch slapped Suilin's helmet; he cursed with doubled bitterness. "If Coraccio'd taken the Enclaves thirty years ago, there wouldn't be any trouble now."

"Dream on, turtle," Gale said over the mouth of his own beer.

"Coraccio *couldn't* take the WG's actual bases," Cooter remarked, quickly enough to forestall any angry retort. "The security forces couldn't hold much, but they sure-hell weren't givin' up the starports that were their only chance of going home to Earth."

Gale finished his beer, belched, and tossed the bottle high over the side. The moonlit glitter seemed to curve backward as *Flamethrower* ground on, at high speed despite the vegetation.

"You shoulda hired us," he said. "Well, you know—somebody like us. But we'll take yer money now, no sweat."

Suilin sluiced beer around in his mouth before he swallowed it. "Only a fraction of the population supported the Consies," he said. "The Conservative Action Movement's just a Terran front."

"Only a fraction of the people here 're really behind the Nationals, either," Cooter said. He raised his hand, palm toward Suilin in bar. "All right, sure a bigger fraction. But what most people want's for the shooting to stop. Trust me, turtle. That's how it *always* is."

"We've got a right to decide the government of our own planet!" the reporter shouted.

"You bet," agreed the big lieutenant. "And that's what you're paying Hammer's Slammers for. So their fraction gets tired of havin' its butt kicked quicker 'n your fraction does."

"They're payin' us," said Gale, caressing his tribarrel again, "because there's nodamnbody in the Yokel army who's got any balls."

Suilin flushed. His hand tightened on his beer bottle.

"All Tootsie elements," said a voice from Suilin's commo helmet. "We're approaching Phase Line Mambo, so look sharp."

The reporter didn't fully understand the words, but he knew by now what it meant when both mercenaries gripped their tribarrels and waggled the muzzles to be sure they turned smoothly on their gimbals.

Dick Suilin dropped the bottle with the remainder of his beer over the side. His hands were clammy on the grips of his weapon.

That was the trouble with his learning to understand things. Now he knew what was coming.

When Henk Ortnahme rocked forward violently, he reacted by bracing his palms against the main screen and opening his mouth to bellow curses at Tech 2 Simkins.

Herman's Whore didn't ground 'er bloody skirts, though, as Simkins powered her out of the unmanned gully between Adako Creek and the Padma River . . . and Warrant Leader Ortnahme wouldn't a been bouncing around the inside of his tank like a pea in a whistle if he'd had brains enough to strap himself into his bloody seat.

He didn't shout the curses. When he rehearsed them in his mind, they were directed as much at himself as the kid, who was doing pretty good. Night, cross-country, through forested mountains—pretty *bloody* good.

"*All Tootsie elements,*" boomed the command channel. "*We're approaching Phase Line Mambo, so look sharp.*"

Phase Line Mambo: Adako Beach, and the only bridge for a hundred kays that'd carry tanks over the Padma River. Consie defenses for sure. Maybe alerted defenses.

Simkins wasn't the only guy in *Herman's Whore* who was getting a crash course tonight in his new duties.

"Company," said somebody on the unit push, musta been Sparrow, because the view remoted onto Ortnahme's Screen Three had the B1 designator in its upper left corner.

The lead tank overlooked the main east-west road through the forest; Sparrow must've eased forward until *Deathdealer* was almost out of the trees. Half a dozen light vehicles were approaching from the east, still a kilometer away. They were moving at about fifty kph— plenty fast enough for anything on wheels that had to negotiate the roads in this part of the continent.

A dull blue line began jumping through the remoted

image, three centimeters from the right edge of the screen. Nothing wrong with the equipment: *Deathdealer*'s transmission was just picking up interference from another circuit, the one that aligned the tank's main gun. . . .

"*Don't Shoot!*" June Ranson snarled on the command channel before she bothered with proper communications procedures.

Then, "Tootsie Six to all Tootsie elements. Form on Blue One, east along the roadcut. *Don't* expose yourselves, and don't shoot without *my* orders. These're probably civilians. We'll wait till they clear the bridge, then we'll blast through ourselves while the guards 're relaxing."

Herman's Whore rocked as Simkins shifted a bit to the left, following the track of the car ahead. They'd intended to enter the roadcut in line ahead, where the slope was gentlest; now they'd have to slide down abreast.

A sputter of static on the commo helmet indicated one of the subordinate leaders, Sparrow or Cooter, was talking to Tootsie Six on a lock-out channel.

Ranson didn't bother to switch off the command push to reply, "Negative, Blue One. Getting there twenty minutes later doesn't matter. The bridge guards'll 've seen the truck lights too; they'll be trigger-happy until they see there's no threat to them."

No big deal. Line abreast was a little trickier for the drivers, but it was about as fast . . . and it put Task Force Ranson in a perfect ambush position, just in case the trucks weren't civilian after all.

Herman's Whore nosed to the edge of the trees, swung to her port side to the roadcut, and halted. She quivered in dynamic stasis.

Ortnahme cranked up the magnification on his gunnery screen, feeding enhanced ambient light to his display. He had a better angle on the trucks than Blue One did, and when he focused on the figures filling the canvas-topped bed of the lead vehicle—

Blood 'n martyrs!

"Tootsie Six," hissed the general unit push before Ortnahme could call his warning, "this is One-Six. They ain't civilians."

The leading truck had National Army fender stencils and a Yokel crest on the passenger door, but the troops in back wore black uniforms. Ortnahme scanned their faces at a hundred magnifications. Bored, nervous—yeah, you could be both at the same time, he knew that bloody well himself. And very bloody young.

"Roger," said the command channel crisply. "All Tootsie elements, I'm highlighting your primary targets. On command, take 'em out before you worry about anybody else."

That truckload wasn't going to get much older.

Ortnahme's remote screen pinged as the view from *Deathdealer* vanished and was replaced by the corner tag R-for-Red 6 and a simple string of magenta beads, one for each truck. The second bead from the end was brighter and pulsing.

"Blue Two, roger," the warrant leader said, knowing the AI would transmit his words as a green dot on Ranson's display—even if all seven responses came in simultaneously.

"When the shooting starts, team," the command channel continued, "go like hell. Six out."

The first soft-skin had passed beneath *Herman's Whore* and was continuing toward the bridge. The armored vehicles would have burning trucks to contend with in their rush, but Ortnahme realized Ranson couldn't pop the ambush until all six targets were within the killing ground.

The second truck was a civilian unit with a mountain landscape painted on the passenger door and MASALLAH in big metalized letters across the radiator. Other than that, it was the same as the first: a stake-bed with twelve rubber tires and about sixty bloody Consies in back.

MASALLAH. God help us. They'd *need* God's help when the tribarrels started slicing into 'em.

The third truck came abreast with its gearbox moaning. Yokel maintenance was piss-poor, at least from what Ortnahme'd seen of it. Guess it didn't matter, not if they were handing over their hardware to the Consies.

Nobody in the trucks looked up, though they were within fifty meters of Task Force Ranson. Half the distance was vertical . . . which was a problem in itself for Ortnahme, since the guns in the turret and cupola of *Herman's Whore* couldn't depress as low as the pintle-mounted weapons of the combat cars.

"Tootsie, this is Blue One," said the radio. "Vehicles approaching the bridge from the west, too."

"Bloody marvelous," somebody muttered on the general push. It might have been the warrant leader himself.

"Roger, Blue One," replied Ranson coolly. "They're stopping, so it shouldn't affect us. Six out."

The gunnery pipper didn't bear on the trucks when they were directly below *Herman's Whore*. Life being what it bloody was, that's where Ortnahme's target would be when the balloon went up.

"Simkins," the warrant leader said, "when I give the word, get us over the edge. Got that? Not even a bloody eyeblink later."

"Yessir," agreed the intercom. "Ah, sir . . . ?"

Ortnahme grimaced. The fourth truck was below them. "Go ahead."

"Sir, won't the guards be even more alerted if we start shooting before we cross the bridge? Than if we'd gone sooner, I mean?"

"Yeah," Ortnahme said, stating the bloody obvious, but this wasn't the time to tear a strip off the kid. "But we don't want a Consie battalion waiting for us on the other side, do we? It's the hand we got, kid, so we play it."

"Yessir," Simkins agreed. "I just wondered."

From his voice, that's all it was.

Maybe Simkins hadn't figured out that one *real* likely response from his altered guard detachment would be to blow the bloody bridge—maybe with most of Task Force Ranson learning to fly a hundred meters above the Padma River.

The fifth truck, Yokel Army again, grunted and snarled its way onto Screen Two. Ortnahme's pipper quivered across the canvas top, bloody useless unless the Consies all died of fright when the main gun ripped over their heads, but he still had a view of the troops. There was something funny about this lot. They were wearing armbands, and their uniforms—

"*All Tootsie elements—*"

"Simkins, *go!*" the warrant leader shouted.

Herman's Whore lurched sideways and down. Startled faces glanced upward in the magnified display, warned at last but only a microsecond before the command push added, "*Fire!*"

The pure, heart-wrenching blue of powerguns firing saturated the roadcut. Ortnahme's foot took up the slack in the gun pedal as his tank slid—and the orange pipper slid down onto one of the mouths screaming in the back of the fifth truck.

The 20cm bolt merged with a white and orange explosion. The whole truck was a fireball. Heated by the plasma, the steel chassis blazed with even greater venom than the contents of the fuel tanks and the flesh of the soldiers at the point of impact.

Ortnahme switched to his tribarrel as the tank rushed down the slope, its fans driving into a sea of flame.

Not that it mattered, but the troops in the truck he'd just destroyed weren't wearing black uniforms.

Three blazing figures lurched out of the inferno. Ortnahme shot them down, more as an act of mercy than of war.

They were in camouflaged National Army fatigues with black armbands, and they were carrying National Army assault rifles.

Not that it mattered.

"Fire!" June Ranson heard her voice say. Her visor opaqued, shutting out the double microsecond dazzles of *Deathdealer's* main gun firing almost on top of her, but the momentary blindness didn't matter. The battle was taking place within a holographic screen while Ranson watched it from above.

Her tribarrel scissored bolts across those of Stolley's weapon, turning fist-sized chunks of the leading truck into meter-diameter flashes colored by material that vaporized and burned: rubber/metal/wood across the truck; cloth/flesh/munitions as the muzzles lifted into the bed.

Metals burned with a gorgeous intensity of color, white and red and green.

The target exploded into a lake of fire that screamed. Willens kept *Warmonger* as high on her fans as he could as the combat car entered the roadcut at a barely-controlled slide and cranked hard right to follow *Deathdealer* up the bridge approach.

The filters of Ranson's helmet snapped into place as flames *whuffed* out like crinolines encircling the combat car. For a moment, everything was orange and hot; then *Warmonger* was through.

Junebug Ranson was back in the physical world in which her troops were fighting.

The Adako beach community was a few hovels on this east side of the Padma River. There were twenty or thirty more dwellings, still unpretentious, beyond the gravel strand across the stream. The bridge itself was a solid concrete structure with a sandbagged blockhouse on the far end and a movement-control kiosk in the center of the span.

The blockhouse and kiosk had been added in re-action to the worsening security situation. When *Deathdealer*'s main gun punched the center of the blockhouse twice, the low building blew apart with an enthusiasm which the ammunition going off within did little more than color. Swatches of fiberglass fabric from the sandbags burned red as they drifted in the updraft.

A bus was waiting on the other side to cross the bridge. It lurched off the road and heeled slowly over onto its side, its headlights still burning. The truck behind it didn't move, but both cab doors flew open and fig-ures scuttled out.

A man without pants ran from one of the huts near the bridge approach and began firing an automatic rifle at *Deathdealer*. Sparrow ignored—or was unaware of—the fleabites, but Stolley triggered a burst in the Consie's direction.

The hovel disintegrated into burning debris under the touch of the cyan bolts. The Consie dropped flat and continued firing, sheltered by the rocky irregularity of the ground. Another set of muzzleflashes sparkled yellow from closer to the streambed. A bullet rang on *Warmonger*'s hull.

The long span between the concrete guardrails of the bridge had been narrowed by coils of concertina wire, reducing the traffic flow to a single lane past the cen-tral checkpoint. A round, pole-mounted signal board, white toward the east and presumably red on the other face, reached from the kiosk.

An attendant bolted out of the kiosk, waving his empty hands above his head. He was running toward the armored vehicles rather than away, but he didn't have a prayer of reaching safety in either direction.

The flash of *Deathdealer*'s main gun ended the pos-sibility of a threat lurking within the kiosk and crisped the attendant on his third stride.

"All Tootsie!" Ranson shouted. "Watch the left of the near side, there's bandits!"

The gunners on her combat cars were momentarily blind as they bucked out of the fireball to which they had reduced the trucks. That made them a dangerously good target for the riflemen firing from the downslope.

Those Consies were good. Caught completely by surprise, hideously outgunned—and still managing to make real pests of themselves. Hammer could use more recruits of their caliber—

To replace the troops this run was going to use up.

Sparks cascaded in all directions as *Deathdealer* entered the bridge approach and Albers, the only experienced tank drier in the task force, dropped his skirts so low they scraped. The truck-width passage across the bridge was too narrow for the blowers, and there wasn't time for the lengthy spooling and restringing of the barriers that would've been required during a normal down-time move.

June Ranson felt the satisfaction common to any combat soldier when circumstances permit him to use the quick and dirty way to achieve his objective. But that didn't mean there weren't risks. . . .

Deathdealer hit the first frame and smashed it to kindling while loops of wire humped like terrified caterpillars. Strands bunched and sparkled. The tank slid forward at forty kph, grinding the concertina wire between the guardrail and the vehicle's own hundred and seventy tonnes.

The wire couldn't *stop* a tank or even a combat car, but any loop that snaked its way into a fan intake would lock up the nacelle as sure as politicians lie. A bulldozer with treads for traction was the tool of choice for clearing this sort of entanglement; but, guided by a driver as expert as Albers, a tank would do the job just fine.

Warmonger followed *Deathdealer* at a cautious fifty meters, in case a strand of wire came whipping back unexpectedly. Willens drove with his hatch buttoned up above him, while Ranson and her two gunners crouched behind their weapons. The blades of a drive fan weren't the only thing you could strangle with a loop of barbed wire.

Steel rubbed concrete in an aural counterpart of the hell-lit road the task force had left behind them. Sparks ricocheted in wild panic, scorching when they touched. Ranson smelled a lock of her hair that had grown beyond the edge of her helmet.

Deathdealer's tribarrel fired. Ranson didn't bother remoting an image of Sparrow's target, and there was nothing to see from behind the tank's bulk now.

"Six," said her commo helmet, "Blue One. The bus 'n truck 're—"

Deathdealer swung onto the western approach, pushing as well as dragging tangled masses of concertina wire. The tank shook herself like a whore waggling a come-on. A touch of her skirts pulverized half a meter of bridge abutment.

"—civvie, no threat. Over."

As Albers accelerated forward, *Deathdealer's* stern rebounded from the concrete and slapped the three-axled truck that had been waiting to cross the bridge. The lighter vehicle danced away from the impact with the startled delicacy of a horse shying. Ten meters from the pavement, the crumpled wreckage burst into flame.

"All Tootsie elements," Ranson relayed. "Vehicles at the west approach are no threat, repeat, no threat. Six out."

Warmonger blasted through a cloud of powdered concrete as Willens pulled them clear of the bridge. Blue One fired his tribarrel into the houses to the right. There was no sign of hostile activity or even occupation. A ball of wire still dragged twenty meters behind the tank, raising a pall of dust.

One of the tires of the overturned bus revolved lazily. The vehicle lay on both its doors. Figures were climbing out of the windows. They flattened as *Warmonger* swept by behind the tank.

Stolley's tribarrel snapped over the civilians as he fired across the river, trying to nail the Consie riflemen from this better angle. Rock flashed and gouted, but the muzzleflashes bloomed again.

A trooper screamed on the unit push.

Junebug Ranson's eyes were glazed. Her mouth was open.

Ozone and matrix residues from her tribarrel flayed her throat as she fired into the village, shattering walls and roofslates.

It was very beautiful in the hologram of her mind.

Five-year-old Dickie Suilin screamed, "*Suzi!*" as his older sister squeezed his nostrils shut and clapped her other hand over his mouth. The flames arcing over the skirts of *Flamethrower* roared their laughter.

He could breathe after all. A mask of some sort had extended from the earpieces of the commo helmet as soon as the inferno waved an arm of blazing diesel fuel to greet the combat car plunging toward it. Suilin could breathe, and he could see again when overload reset his visor from thermal display to optical.

Though there wasn't much to see except flames curling around black steel skeletons, the chassis of trucks whose flammable portions were already part of the red/orange/yellow/white billows.

Even steel burned when Suilin raked it with his tribarrel. Faces bloomed into smears of vapor and calcined bones. . . .

Blue Two grunted head-on down the road, spewing a wake of blazing debris to either side. Cooter's driver followed, holding *Flamethrower* at a forty-five degree angle along the edge of the cut.

The slant threw the men in the fighting compartment toward the fire their vehicle was skirting. Gale clung to the starboard coaming. Cooter must have locked his tribarrel in place, because he was frozen like a statue of Effort on its grips.

And Dick Suilin, after a hellish moment of feeling his torso swing out and down toward the bellowing flames, braced his feet against the inner face of the armor and grabbed Cooter by the waist. If the big lieutenant minded, they could discuss it later.

Something as soft-featured and blast as a tar statue reached out of the flames and gripped the coaming to either side of Suilin's tribarrel. The only parts of the figure that weren't black were the teeth and the great red cracks writhing in what had been the skin of both arms. The thing fell away without trying to speak.

Only a shadow. Only a sport thrown by the flames.

"Help me, Suzi," the reporter whispered. "Help me, Suzi."

Blue Two sucked fire along with it for an instant as the tank cleared the ambush site. Then the return flow, cool sweet air, pistoned Hell back into its proper region and washed Suilin in its freedom as well.

This car was *Flamethrower*. For the first time, Suilin realized how black was the humor with which the Slammers named their vehicles.

The driver brought them level with a violence that banged the skirts on the roadway. Suilin grunted. He reached for the grips of his tribarrel, obeying an instinct to hang onto something after he lost his excuse to hold Cooter.

Powerguns punctuated the night with flashes so intense they remained for seconds as streaks across the reporter's retinas. His mind tried desperately to process the high-pitched chatter from the commo helmet mixture of orders, warnings and shouted exclamations.

It was all meaningless garbage; and it was all terrifying.

The downslope to the left of the roadway was striped

orange by the firelight and leaping with shadows thrown from outcrops anchored too firmly in the fabric of the planet to be uprooted with the Padma River flooded. Muzzleflashes pulsed there, shockingly close.

A bottle-shaped yellow glow swelled and shrank as the gunman triggered his burst. The gun wasn't firing tracers, but the corner of Suilin's eyes caught a flicker as glowing metal snapped from the muzzle.

Specks of light raked the car ahead of Blue Two. Red sparks flashed up the side armor.

On the commo helmet, someone screamed *lordlordlord*.

The tribarrel wouldn't swing fast enough. Dick Suilin was screaming also. He unslung his grenade launcher.

Blue Two's main gun lit the night. Rock and the damp soil beneath it geysered outward from the point of impact, a white track glowing down the slope for twenty meters.

Flamethrower's driver flinched away from the bolt, throwing the thirty-tonne car into a side-step as dainty as that of a nervous virgin.

Blue Two and the combat car both accelerated up the bridge approach. The tank's turret continued to rotate to bear on the cooling splotch which its first bolt had grazed. If it fired from *that* angle, the bolt would pass within ten meters of *Flame*—

The tribarrel in Blue Two's cupola fired instead of the main gun.

Suilin straightened and fired a burst from his own tribarrel in the same general direction. He'd dropped the grenade launcher when he ducked in panic behind the hull armor. He was too rattled now to be embarrassed by his reaction.

And anyway, both the veterans sharing the fighting compartment had ducked also.

You couldn't be sure of not being embarrassed unless you were dead. The past night and day had been a gut-wrenching exposition of just what it meant to be dead. Dick Suilin would do anything at all to avoid *that*.

Traces of barbed wire clung to the cast-in guardrail supports. Large sections of the rail had been shattered by gunfire or smashed at the touch of behemoths like *Flamethrower*. Blue Two swung its turret forward again, releasing a portion of the fear that knotted Suilin's stomach, but only a portion.

Gale fired his tribarrel over *Flamethrower's* stern. Bolts danced off the left guardrail and streaked through the ambush scene. Their cyan purity glared even in the heart of the kerosene pyre which consumed the trucks and their cargo. The bolts vanished only when they touched something solid.

Flamethrower was the last vehicle in the column. Suilin turned also and hosed the fire-shot darkness, praying that there would be no wobbling muzzleflashes to answer as a Consie rifleman raked *Flamethrower* as he had the car ahead of them.

They slid past the further abutments at fifty kph. There'd been a blockhouse there, but it lay in steaming ruins licked by rare red tongues of flame. A truck burned brightly, well down the steep embankment supporting the approach to the bridge.

On its side, between *Flamethrower* and the truck, lay a tipped-over bus. A Consie gunman silhouetted by the truck, aimed at Suilin from a bus window.

Liquid nitrogen sprayed into the chambers of Suilin's tribarrel as it cycled, kicking out the spent cases and cooling the glowing iridium of the chamber before the next round was loaded. The gas was a hot kiss blowing back across the reporter's hands as he horsed his weapon onto the unexpected threat. The tribarrel was heavy despite being perfectly balanced on its gimbals, and it swung with glacial torpor.

"*Not that*—" screamed Suilin's headset. Two cm bolts ripped across the undercarriage of the bus, bright flashes that blew fuel lines, air lines, hydraulic lines into blazing tangles and opened holes the size of tureens in the sheet metal.

The line of bolts missed by millimeters the man whose raised hand had been shadowed into a weapon by the flames behind him. The civilian fell back into the interior of the bus.

No-no-no—

Suilin's screams didn't help any more than formal prayers would have done if he'd had leisure to form them.

When it first ignited, the ruptured fuel tank engulfed the rear half of the bus. The flames had sped all the way to the front of the vehicle before any of the flailing figures managed to crawl free.

Somebody patted the reporter's forearms; gently at first, but then with enough force to detach his deathgrip from the tribarrel.

"S'okay, turtle," a voice said. "All okay. Don't mean nothin'."

Suilin opened his eyes. He'd flipped up his visor, or one of the mercenaries had raised it for him. Cooter was holding his forearms, while Gale watched the reporter with obvious concern. He wasn't sure which of the veterans had been speaking.

The river lay as a black streak behind them as the road climbed. Adako beach was a score of dull fires, big enough to throw orange highlights on the water but nothing comparable to the holocaust of the truck convoy.

And the similar diesel-fed rage which consumed the bus.

"No sweat," Cooter said gently. "Don't mean nothin'."

"It means something to *them!*" the reporter screamed. He couldn't see for tears, but when he closed his eyes every terrified line of the civilian at the bus window cleared from the surface of his mind. *"To them!"*

"Happens to everybody, turtle," Gale said. "There's always somebody don't get the word. This time it was you."

"It won't matter next century," Cooter said. "Don't sweat that you can't change."

Flamethrower slowed as Blue Two entered the woods ahead. When the trees closed around the combat car, Dick Suilin could no longer see the flames.

Memory of the fire began to dull. Only a minute. Only a few seconds. . . .

"Trust me, turtle," Gale added with a chuckle. "You stick with us and it won't be the last time, neither."

Chapter Eight

Birdie Sparrow curled and uncurled his hands, working out the stiffness from their grip on the gunnery joysticks.

Gases from the breech of the main gun swirled as if fleeing the efforts of the air-conditioning fans which tried to scavenge them. The twisted vapors picked up the patterns glowing in the holographic screens, mixed and softened the colors, and turned the turret interior into a sea of gentle pastels.

The radio crackled with reports of damage and casualties. That didn't touch Birdie. *Deathdealer's* finish had been scratched by a bullet or two, and there were some new dents in her skirts; but the Consies hadn't so much as fired a buzzbomb.

Tough about the crew of One-six, but a combat car . . . what'd they expect? That was worse 'n ridin' with your head out the cupola.

DJ Bell pointed from a whisp of mauve vapor toward the yellow warning that had just blinked alive in the corner of Screen Two.

Sparrow hit the square yellow button marked Automatic Air Defense—easy to find now, because it started to glow a millisecond after the *Aircraft Warning* header came up on the gunnery screen. The tribarrel in the cupola whined, rousing to align itself with the putative target.

Piss off, DJ, Sparrow thought/said to the phantom of his friend that grinned until the inevitable change smeared its features.

Aloud, certainly aloud, Sparrow reported, "Tootsie Six, this is Blue One. Aircraft warning. Sonic signature only."

He was reading off the data cascading in jerks down the left edge of his screen like the speeded-up image of a crystal glowing. The pipper remained in the center of the holofield, but the background displayed on the screen jumped madly. The tracking system was trying to find gaps that would permit it to shoot through the dense vegetation.

"AAD has a lock but not a window." Sparrow paused then pursed his lips. "Signature is consistent with a friendly recce drone. We expectin' help? Over."

The bone-deep hum of *Deathdealer* grinding her way southward was the only response for several seconds.

"Blue One," Captain Ranson's voice said at last, "it may be friendly—but let your AAD make the choice. I'd rather shoot down a friendly drone with a bad identification transponder than learn the Terrans were giving some smart-help to their Consie buddies. Out."

The pipper jumped and quivered among the tree images, like an attack dog straining on its leash.

"No, sweat, snake," whispered DJ Bell. "It's all copacetic. This time . . ."

"Blue Two lock," said Ranson's headset as the B2 designator glowed air-defense yellow in her multifunction display.

Warmonger went airborne for an unplanned instant.

Willens boosted his fans when he realized the ground had betrayed him, but the car landed again like a gymnast dropping three meters onto a mat.

The three mercenaries in the fighting compartment braced for it, splay-legged and on their toes. Shock gouged the edge of Ranson's breastplate into the top of her thighs.

"Blue Three, ah, locked," said Sergeant Wager, but the designator *didn't* come on, not for a further five seconds.

Wager, the recent transfer from combat cars, was having problems with his hardware. Understandable but a piss-poor time for it. His driver, that was Holman, she wasn't any better. The nameless Blue Three kept losing station, falling behind or speeding up to the point the tank threatened to overrun the car directly ahead of it.

"Janacek!" Ranson snapped. "Don't point your gun! Now! Lower it!"

"Via, Cap'n—" the wing gunner said fiercely. His tribarrel slanted upward at a thirty degree angle on the rough southwest vector he'd gleaned from seeing *Deathdealer's* cupola gun rouse.

"*Lower* it, curse you!" Ranson repeated. "And then take your cursed hands away from it. *Now!*"

There was almost nil chance of a hand-aimed tribarrel doing any good if three tank units failed on air-defense mode. There was a bloody good chance that a human thumb would twitch at the wrong time and knock down a friendly drone whose IFF handshake had passed the tank computers, though . . .

Deathdealer had to be the leading panzer. Blue Three in the rear-guard slot wouldn't tear gaps the way it did in the middle of the line, but Wager's inexperience could be an even worse disaster there if the task force were hit from behind. Maybe if she put *Deathdealer's* driver in the turret of Blue Three and moved an experienced drier from one of the cars to—

Command exercises. Arrange beads of light in a chosen order, then step back while the grading officer critiques your result.

"*Tight-ass bitch*," the intercom muttered. Handkeyed, Janacek or Stolley, either one, or even Willens.

Veterans don't like to be called down by their new CO. But veterans screw up too, just like newbies . . . just like COs who drift in and out of an electronic nonworld, where the graders snarl but don't shoot.

Ranson thought she heard the aircraft's engine over the howl of *Warmonger*'s fans and the constant slap of branches against their hull. That was impossible.

"Six, its friendly!" Sparrow called, echoing the relayed information that flashed on the display which in turn cross-checked the opinion of the combat car's own electronics. And they could all be wrong, but—

The aircraft *was* friendly. Its data dump started.

Maps and numerals scrolled across the display, elbowing one another aside as knowledge became chaos by its volume. Ranson was so focused on her attempt to sort the electronic garbage with a combat car's inadequate resources that she didn't notice the drone when it passed overhead a few seconds later.

The Slammers' reconnaissance drones were slow, loping along at less than a thousand kph instead of sailing around the globe at a satellite's ninety-minute rate. On the other hand, no satellite could survive in a situation where the enemy had powerguns and even the very basic fire-direction equipment needed to pick up a solid object against the vacant backdrop of interstellar space.

Stolley whispered inaudibly as the drone flicked past, barely visible along the slats of the trees. The aircraft had a long, narrow-chord wind mounted high so as not to interfere with the sensors in its belly.

The drone's high-bypass turbofan sighed rather than roaring, and the exhaust dumped from its twin outlets was within fifty degrees C of ambient. Except for the panels covering the sensor bays, the plastic of the wings and fuselage absorbed radio—radar—waves, and the material's surface adapted its mottled coloration to whatever the background might be.

Task Force Ranson could still have gulped the drone down with the ease of a frog and a fly. The Consies operating here weren't nearly as sophisticated—

And that was good, because even a cursory glance at the downloaded data convinced June Ranson that the task force was cold meat if it continued along the course she'd planned originally.

Information wriggled on her multi-function display. Task Force Ranson didn't have a command car, but the electronics suite of one of the panzers would do about as well. . . .

"Blue One," she ordered, "how close is the nearest clearing where we can laager for—half an hour? Six over."

That should be time enough. There were wounded in One-six to deal with besides. Cooter could shift crews while she—

"Six," said Sparrow in his usual expressionless voice, "there's a bald half a kay back the way we came. It'll give us a clear shot over two-seventy, maybe three-hundred degrees. Blue One over."

"Roger, Blue One," Ranson said. Weighing the alternatives, knowing that the grader would demonstrate that any decision she made was the wrong one, because there are no right decisions in war.

Knowing also that there is no decision as bad as no decision at all.

"All Tootsie elements," her voice continued, "halt and prepare to reverse course."

Warmonger bobbed, its fan chuffing as Willens tried to scrub off momentum smoothly while his eyes darted furiously over the display showing his separation from the huge tanks before and behind him.

"Tootsie, One-two, lead on the new course as displayed." Better to have a tank as a lead vehicle, but there wasn't much chance of trouble here in the boonies, and it was only half a kilometer. . . .

Warmonger touched the ground momentarily, then began to rotate on its axis. A twenty-centimeter treebole, thick for this area, this forest, this planet, obstructed the turn. Willens backed them grudgingly to the altered course.

Anyway, she wasn't sure she wanted Blue Two leading. Ortnahme didn't have much field experience either.

"We'll laager on the bald. Break. Blue Three, I'll be borrowing your displays. I want you to take over my position while we're halted. Over."

"Roger, Tootsie Six. Blue Three out."

"All Tootsie elements, execute new course. Tootsie Six out."

She'd get an eighty percent for that. Down on reversing, down on halting, down on not swapping Cooter's combat car for one of the panzers. But she'd be down on those points whichever way she'd chosen. . . .

Ranson rubbed her eyes vaguely surprised to find that they were open. Her body braced itself reflexively as Willens brought *Warmonger* up to speed.

She'd use Blue Three's displays. And she'd use the tank's commo gear also, because that was going to get tricky.

Of course, it was always tricky to talk with Colonel Hammer.

The bald was a barren, hundred-meter circle punched in the vegetation of a rocky knoll by fire, disease, or the chemistry of the underlying rock strata. *Flamethrower* scudded nervously across the clearing and settle, not to the ground on idle but in a dynamic stasis with its fans spinning at high speed.

Cooter spoke to his multi-function display, then poked a button on the side of it. Suilin's tribarrel shivered.

"Just let it be," the big lieutenant said, nodding toward the weapon. "I put all the guns on air defense." He gripped the rear coaming and swung his leg over the side of the vehicle.

"There's not much chance of 'em helping, using car sensors," he added. "But it's what we got till the panzers arrive."

As Cooter spoke, Blue Two came bellowing out of the trees. The tank's vast size was emphasized by the narrow compass of the bald. The warrant leader from Maintenance, his bulky form unmistakable, waved from the cupola as his driver pulled to a location 120 degrees around the circle from *Warmonger*. Further vehicles were following closely.

"What's going on?" the reporter asked Gale. "Why are we in the, the clear?"

In only a few hours, Suilin had gotten so used to the forest canopy that he felt naked under the open sky. Both moons were visible, though wisps of haze blotted many of the stars. He didn't suppose the leaves really provided much protection—but, like his childhood bedcovers, they'd served to keep away the boogeymen of his imagination.

The veteran gestured toward the horizon dominated by a long ridge twenty kilometers away. "Air attack," he said. "Or arty. While we're movin' it's okay, but clumpin' all together like this, we could get our clocks cleaned. If we see it comin', we're slick, we shoot it down. But with powerguns, if a leaf gets in the way, the bolt don't touch the incoming shell it's s'posed t' get, does it?"

"The Consies don't have air . . . ?" Suilin began, but he broke the statement off on a rising inflection.

Gale grinned viciously. "Right," he said. "Bet on that and kiss yer ass goodbye."

He glanced at the combat car which had just pulled up beside them and grounded. "Not," he added, "like we're playin' it safe as is."

Cooter clambered aboard the grounded car. Its sides were scratched, like those of all the vehicles, but the words *Daisy Belle* could be read on the upper curve of the armorplate.

A cartoon figure had been drawn beside the name, but it would have been hard to make out even under better lighting. A bullet had struck in the center of the drawing, splashing the paint away without cratering the armor. A second bullet had left a semicircle of lead on the coaming.

There was only one mercenary standing erect in the fighting compartment to greet Cooter.

"Wisht we had a better field that way," Gale mused aloud, nodding toward the crags that lurched up to the immediate north of the bald, cutting off vision in that direction. "Still, with the panzers—" a second tank had joined Blue Two and the third was an audible presence "—it oughta be okay. Whatever hardware does best, them big fuckers does best."

Suilin climbed out of the fighting compartment and jumped to the ground. He staggered when he found himself on footing that didn't vibrate. Despite the weight of his armor, the reporter mounted the rear slope of *Daisy Belle* without difficulty. He'd learned where the steps in the armor were—

And he was no longer entering an alien environment.

Cooter was examining the right forearm of the standing crewman. The trooper's sleeve had been torn away. The bandage across the muscles was brilliantly white in the moonlight except for the dots of blood on opposite sides.

He must have bandaged himself, because the other two crewmen lay on the floor of the fighting compartment—one dead, the other breathing but comatose.

"I'm okay," the wounded man said sullenly.

"Sure you are, Titelbaum," Cooter replied. "Tootsie One-five," he continued, keying his helmet. "This is

Tootsie Three. Tommy, send one a' your boys—send Chalkin—to One-six. Over."

"I kin *handle* it!" Titelbaum insisted as the lieutenant listened to the reply.

"One-five," Cooter said in response to a complaint Suilin couldn't hear. "*I'd* like to be in bed with a hooker. Get Chalkin over here, right? I need 'im to take over. Three out."

"I kin—"

"You got one hand," Cooter snapped. "Just shut it off, okay?"

"I'm left—"

"You're a bloody liar." Cooter looked at Suilin, balanced on the edge of the armor, for the first time. "Good. Gimme a hand with McGwire. We'll sling her to the skirts and get a little more space for Chalkin."

Suilin nodded. He didn't trust himself to speak.

"Here, take the top," Cooter said. He reached beneath McGwire's shoulders and lifted the corpse with surprising gentleness.

McGwire had been a small woman with sharp features and a fine shimmer of blond hair. Her head was bare. A bullet had entered beneath her right mastoid at an upward slant that lifted the commo helmet when it exited with a splash of brains.

McGwire's flesh was still warm. Suilin kept his face rigid as his hands took the weight from Cooter.

"Titelbaum," the lieutenant said, "where's your—oh."

The wounded crewman was already offering a flat dispenser of cargo tape. Cooter thrust it into a pocket and grasped the corpse by the boots.

"Okay, turtle," he said as he raised his leg over the side coaming—careful not to step on the comatose soldier on the floor of the compartment. "Easy now. We'll fasten her to the tarp tie-downs."

Cooter paused for a moment on the edge, using a tribarrel to support his elbow. Then he swung his other leg clear and slid from the bulge of the skirts to the ground without jerking or dropping his burden.

Suilin managed to get down with his end also. It was a difficult job, even though he had proper steps for his feet.

Gear—stakes, wire mesh, bedding and the Lord knew what all else—was fastened along the sides of all the combat cars. Cooter spun a few centimeters of tape into a loop and reached behind a footlocker to hook the loop to the hull. He took two turns around McGwire's ankles before snugging them tight to the same tie-down.

A trooper carrying a submachinegun and a bandolier of ammunition jogged up to *Daisy Belle*, glancing around warily at the vehicles which snorted and shifted across the bald. "This One-six?" he demanded. "Oh, hi, Coot."

"Yeah, try 'n keep Titelbaum trackin', will you?" the lieutenant said. "He's takin' it pretty hard, you know?"

"Aw, cop," the newcomer muttered, looking past Suilin. "Nandi bought it? Aw, cop."

"Foran's not in great shape neither, but he'll be okay," Cooter said.

The lieutenant's big, capable fingers wrapped tape quickly around McGwire's shoulders.

The corpse leaked on Suilin's hands and wrist. The reporter's face didn't move except for a slight flaring of his nostrils.

Chalkin climbed into the fighting compartment. The barrel of his submachinegun rang against the armor. "Dreamer," he said. "None of us'll be okay unless some fairy godmother shows up real quick."

"Okay, let's get back," Cooter said. He touched the reporter's shoulder, turned him. "Dunno how long Junebug's gonna stay here."

He glanced up at the moons. "No longer 'n she has to, I curst well hope."

Suilin found he had a voice. "It gets easier from here?" he asked.

"Naw, but it gets over," the big man said as he waved Suilin ahead of him at the steps of their vehicle.

Suilin paused, looking at the hull beneath the tribarrel he served. He hadn't had a good look at the cartoon painted on the sides of the combat car before. Above *Flamethrower* in crude Gothic letters, a wyvern writhed so that its tail faced forward. Jets of blue fire spouted from both nostrils, and the creature farted a third flame as well.

He wondered whether a bullet would blast away the grinning drawing an instant before another round lifted the top of Dick Suilin's head.

"It gets over," Cooter mused aloud. "One way or the other."

"Sir, are we s'posed to be watchin' this?" Simkins murmured through the intercom link. The map sliding across the main turret screen was reproduced in miniature on one of the driver's displays as well.

"Junebug didn't put a bloody lock on it, did she?" Ortnahme grunted. "Besides, we got all the data the drone dumped ourselfs."

But the men on *Herman's Whore* didn't know what the Task Force commander was going to do with the recce data; and therefore, what she was going to do with them.

Warrant Leader Ortnahme was pretty sure Captain Ranson didn't realize *Herman's Whore* was echoing the displays from Blue Three; but as he'd told Simkins, she hadn't thrown the mechanical toggle that would've prevented them from borrowing the signals.

And Hell, it was their asses too!

"Sir," said Simkins, "where 're we?"

"We're, off-screen, kid," Ortnahme replied, just as the image rotated eight degrees from Grid North to place as much as possible of the River Santine on the display at one time. The Estuary was on the right edge of the screen.

Symbols flashed at a dozen points—bridges, ferries; fords if there'd been any, which there weren't, not this far down the Santine's course.

The image jerked leftward under June Ranson's control in the nameless tank. More symbols, but not so very many more; and none of 'em a bloody bit of good until you'd gone 300 kays in the wrong bloody direction. . . .

"Which way are we going to go, sir?" the technician asked.

The display lurched violently back to the southward. The image jumped as Ranson shrank the map scale, focusing tightly on la Reole. The numeral I overlay the main bridge in the center of the town. The symbol was flashing yellow.

"Which bloody way do you think we're gonna go?" Ortnahme snarled. "You think we're pushin' babycarts? There's only one tank-capable bridge left on the Santine till you've gone all the way north t' bloody Bumfuck! And *that* bridge's about to fall into the river by itself, it looks!"

"W-warrant Leader Ortnahme? I'm sorry, sir."

Blood 'n martyrs.

It musta been lonely, closed up in the driver's compartment.

The Lord knew it was lonely back here in the turret. Wonder if the background whisper of a voice singing in Tagalog came through the intercom circuit?

"S'okay, kid," Ortnahme muttered. "Look, its just— ridin' on air don't mean we're light, you see? There's still a hundred seventy tonnes t' support, even if the air cushion spreads it out as good as you can. And there's not a bloody lotta bridges that won't go flat with that much weight on 'em."

Ortnahme stared grimly at the screens. Beside la Reole, there were two "I" designators—bridge of unlimited capacity—across the lower Santine, as well as four Category II bridges that might do in a pinch. Updated information from the drone had colored all six of those symbols red—destroyed.

"Specially with the Consies blowing every curst thing up these coupla days," he added.

"I see, sir," the technician said with the nervous warmth of a puppy who's been petted after being kicked. "So we're going through la Reole?"

Ortnahme stared glumly at the screen. The bridge designators weren't the only unpainted symbols the reconnaissance drone had painted on the map from the Slammers' database.

"Well, kid," the warrant leader said, "there's some problems with that, too. . . ."

"Tootsie Six to Slammer Six," June Ranson said, loading the cartridge that would be transmitted to Firebase Purple in a precisely-calculated burst. "Absolute priority."

Even if you got your dick half into her, Colonel, you need to hear this now.

"The only tank crossing point on the lower Santine is la Reole, which is in friendly hands but is encircled by dug-in hostiles. The forces at my disposal are not sufficient to overwhelm the opposition, nor is it survivable to penetrate the encirclement and proceed to the bridge with the bulk of the hostile forces still in play behind us."

She paused, though the transmission would compress the hesitation out of existence. "Unless you can give us some support, Colonel, I'm going to have to swing north till the river's fordable. It'll add time." *Three days at least.* "Maybe two days."

A deep breath, drawn against the unfamiliar, screen-lighted closeness of the tank turret. "Tootsie Six, over."

Would the AI automatically precede the transmission with a map reference so that the Colonel could respond?

"Slug the transmission with our coordinates and execute," she ordered the unit as she stared bleakly at the holographic map filling her main screen.

Nothing else was working out the way she wanted. Why should the tank's artificial intelligence have the right default?

"Tootsie Three, this is Six," she said aloud. "You got One-six sorted out, Cooter?"

It might be minutes before her own message went out, and the wait for Hammers' response would be at least that long again. The heavens had their own program. . . .

"Tootsie Six, roger," her second-in-command replied, panting slightly. "I gave Chalkin the blower. Me—"

The transmitting circuit *zeep*ed, pulsing Ranson's message skyward in a tight packet which would bounce from the ionized track that a meteor had just streaked in the upper atmosphere.

Meteorites, invisible to human eyes during daytime, burned across the sky every few seconds. It would give the signal the narrowest, least interceptible path to the desired recipient. . . .

"—Gwire bought it and Foran's not a lot better, but there's no damage to the car. Over."

"Tootsie Three, how are the mechanicals holding—"

The inward workings of the console beneath Screen Three gave a satisfied chuckle; its amber Stand-by light flashed green.

That quick.

"Cooter," Ranson said, "forget—no—" she threw a toggle "—listen in."

Staring at the screen—though she knew the transmission would be voice only—she said, "Play burst."

Despite the nature of the transmission, the voice was as harshly clear as if the man speaking were stuffed into the turret with his task force commander. For intelligibility, the AI expanded the bytes of transmitted information with sound patterns from its database. If the actual voice wasn't on record, the AI created a synthesis that attempted to match sex, age, and even accent.

In this case, the voice of Colonel Alois Hammer was readily available for comparison with the burst transmission.

"Slammer Six to Tootsie Six," the Colonel rasped. "Absolute priority. You must not, I say again, must not, delay. I believe we can provide limited artillery support for you when you break through at la Reole. If that isn't sufficient, I'm ordering you to detach your tank element and proceed with your combat cars by the quickest route feasible to the accomplishment of your mission. I repeat, I order you to carry on with combat cars alone if you can't cross your tanks at la Reole. Over."

Over indeed.

"Send target overlay," June Ranson said aloud. Her index finger traced across the main screen the symbols of Consie positions facing la Reole. "Execute."

Artillery support? Had Hammer sent down a flying column including a hog or two, or was he expecting them to risk their lives—and mission—on Yokel tubes crewed by nervous draftees?

The transmitter squealed again.

She didn't like being inside a tank. The view was potentially better in every respect than what her eyes and helmet visor could provide from *Warmonger*'s deck, but it was all a simulation. . . . "What do you think, Lieutenant Cooter?" Ranson said, as though she were testing him for promotion.

"Junebug," the lieutenant's worried voice replied, "let's run the gauntlet at la Reole, even with the bridge damaged. Trying t' bust what they got at Kohang without the panzers, that'll be our butts sure."

So, Lieutenant. . . . You'd commit your forces on a vague suggestion of artillery support—when you know that the enemy is in bunkers, with heavy weapons already targeted on the route your vehicles must take from the point you penetrate the encirclement?

Ranson slapped blindly to awaken herself, wincing with pleasure and a rush of warmth when her fingers rapped something hard. Her skin was flushed.

"Right," she said—aloud, alert. "Let's see what kind of artillery we're talking about."

She looked at the blank relay screen. "Tootsie Six to Hammer Six," *No need for priority now.* "I and my XO judge the Blue Element to be necessary for the successful completion of our mission. Transmit details of proposed artillery support. Over."

Ranson rubbed her eyes. "Execute," she ordered the AI.

"Blue Two to Tootsie Six," her headset said.

She should've involved Ortnahme—and Sparrow, he was Blue Element Leader—in the planning. She had to think like a task force commander, not a grading officer. . . .

"Junebug, if the friendlies can lay some sorta surface covering on the bloody water," the warrant leader was saying, "agricultural film on a wood frame, that'd do, just enough to spread the effect, we can—"

"Negative, Blue Two," Ranson interrupted. "This is a river, not a pond. The current'd disrupt any covering they could cobble together, even if the Consies weren't shelling. I don't want you learning to swim. Over."

"Tootsie Six," grunted Ortnahme: twice her age and in a parallel—though non-command—pay grade. "That bloody bridge has major structural damage. I don't want to learn to dive bloody tanks from twenty meters in the air, neither. Blue Two out."

If you want it safe, Blue Two, you're in the wrong line of work tonight.

Chuckle; green light.

"Play burst."

"Slammer Six to Tootsie Six. There's an operable hog at Camp Progress with nineteen rounds in storage. Using extended-range boosters, it can cover la Reole. One of the transit-company staff is ex-artillery; he's putting together a crew. By the time you need some bunkers hit, the tube'll be ready to do it."

Zip from the console, as the AI replaced the pause which the burst compression had edited out.

"Speed is absolutely essential. If you don't get to Kohang within the next six hours, we may as well all have stayed home. Over."

"Tootsie Six to Slammer Six," Ranson said with textbook precision. She could feel her soul merging with that of the nameless tank, viewing the world through its sensors and considering her data in an electronic balance. "Task Force Ranson will proceed in accordance with the situation as it develops. We will transmit further data if a fire mission is required. Tootsie Six, out. Execute."

She was the officer on-site. She would make the final decision. And if Colonel Hammer didn't like it, what was he going to do? Put her in command of a suicide mission?

"Tootsie Six," said her headset, "this is Blue Two. The hog's operable, all right. The trouble's in the turret-traversing mechanism, and that won't matter for a few rounds to a single point. But I dunno about the bloody crew. Over."

"Six, Three," Cooter's voice responded. "Chief Lavel's solid as they come. He'll handle the fire control, and the rest—that's just lift 'n carry, right? Getting the shells on the conveyor? Nothin' even a newbie with a room-temperature IQ going t' screw up. Over."

She would make the final decision.

"All Tootsie elements," June Ranson heard her voice ordering calmly. Her touch shrank the map's scale; then her index finger traced the course to la Reole on the screen.

"Transmit," she said. "We will proceed on the marked trace to Phase Line Piper—" fingertip stroking the crest across a shadowy valley from the Consie positions above the beleaguered town on the Santine Estuary "—and punch through enemy lines to the bridge after a short artillery preparation. Prepare to execute in five minutes. Tootsie Six out."

She used the seat as a step instead of raising herself to the hatch with its power lift. Clouds streaked the sky, but the earlier thin overcast was gone.

The Lord have mercy on our souls.

Chapter Nine

"Sarge," said Holman on the intercom, "why aren't we just crossing the river instead of fooling with a damaged bridge? When I was in trucks, we'd see the line companies go right around us while we was backed up for a bridge. Down, splash, up the far bank and gone."

Now that the task force has moved into open country, Holman was doing a pretty good job of keeping station. You couldn't take somebody straight out of a transport company and expect them to drive blind *and* over broken terrain—with no more than forty hours of air-cushion experience to begin with.

If your life depended on it, though, that was just what you did expect.

"Combat cars have that much lift," Wager explained bitterly. "*These* mothers don't. Via! but I wish I was back in cars."

He was down in the turret, trying to get some sort of empathy with his screens and controls before the next time he needed them. He was okay on mine-clearing, now; he had the right reflexes.

But the next time, Tootsie Six wouldn't be ordering

him to lay a mine-clearance charge, it'd be some other cursed thing. It'd be the butt of Hans Wager and the whole cursed task force when he didn't know what the hell to do.

"Look, Holman," he said, because lift was something he *did* understand, lift and tribarrels laying fire on the other mother before he corrected his aim at you. "We're in ground effect. The fans pressurize the air in the plenum chamber underneath. The ground's the bottom of the pressure chamber, right? And that keeps us floating."

"Right, but—"

Holman swore. The column was paralleling the uphill side of a wooded fenceline. She'd attempted to correct their tank's tendency to drift downslope, but the inertia of 170 steel and iridium tonnes had caught up with her again. One quadrant of Wager's main screen exploded in a confetti of splintered trees and fence posts.

"Bleedin' motherin' martyrs!" snarled the intercom as Holman's commo helmet dutifully transmitted to the most-recently accessed recipient.

Friction from the demolished fence and vegetation pulled the tank farther out of its intended line, despite the driver's increasingly violent efforts to swing them away. When the cumulative over-corrections swung the huge pendulum *their* way, the tank lurched upslope and grounded its right skirt with a shock that rattled Wager's head above the breech of the main gun.

Bloody amateur!

Like Hans Wager, tank commander.

Blood and martyrs.

"S'okay, Holman," Wager said aloud, more or less meaning it. "Any one you walk away from."

He'd finally cleared the mines at Happy Days, hadn't he?

"Look, the lift," he went on. "Without something pretty solid underneath, these panzers drop. Sink like stones.

But combat cars, the ones you been watchin', they've got enough power for their weight they can use thrust to keep 'em up, not just ground effect."

Wager wriggled the helmet. It'd gotten twisted a little on his brow when he bounced a moment ago. Their tank was now sedately tracking the car ahead, as though the mess behind them had been somebody else's problem.

"Only thing is," Wager continued, "a couple of the cars, they're runnin' short a fan or two themselves by now. Talkin' to the guys on One-one while we laagered. Stuff that never happens when you're futzing around a firebase, you get twenty kays out on a route march and *blooie*."

"We're all systems green," Holman said. "Ah, sarge? I think I'm gettin' the hang of it, you know? But the weight, it still throws me."

"Yeah, well," Wager said, touching the joystick cautiously so as not to startle the other vehicles. The turret mechanism whined restively; Screen Two's swatch of rolling farmland, centered around the orange pipper, shifted slightly across the panorama of the main screen.

"Look, when we get to the crossing point, if we do, get across that cursed bridge *fast*, right?" he added. "It's about ready to fall in the river, see, from shelling? So put'cher foot on the throttle 'n keep it there."

"No, sarge."

"*Huh?*"

"Sarge, I'm sorry." Holman said, "but if we do that, we bring it down for sure. And us. Sarge, look, I'm, you know, I'm not great on tanks. But I took a lotta trucks over piddly bridges, right? We'll take it slow and especially no braking or acceleration. That'll work if anything does. I promise. Okay?"

She sounded nervous, telling a veteran he was wrong.

She sounded like she curst well thought she was right, though.

Via, maybe she was. Holman didn't have any line

experience . . . but that didn't mean she didn't have *any* experience. They needed everything they could get right now, her and him and everybody else in Task Force Ranson. . . .

"They say she's a real space cadet," Wager said aloud. "Her crew does. Cap'n Ranson, I mean."

"Because she's a woman," Holman said flatly.

"Because she flakes out!" Wager snapped. "Because she goes right off into dreamland in the middle a' talking."

He looked at the disk of sky speeding past his open hatch. It didn't seem perceptibly brighter, but he could no longer make out the stars speckling its sweep.

"At least," said Holman with a touch more emotion than her previous comment, "Captain Ranson isn't so much of a flake that she'd go ahead with the mission without her tanks."

"Yeah," said Sergeant Hans Wager in resignation. "Without us."

Camp Progress stank of death: the effects of fire on scores of materials; rotting garbage that had been ignored among greater needs; and the varied effluvia each type of shell and cartridge left when it went off.

There was also the stench of the wastes which men voided as they died.

It was a familiar combination to Chief Lavel, but some of the newbies in his work crew still looked queasy.

A Consie had died of his wounds beneath the tarp covering the shells off-loaded from the self-propelled howitzer. It wasn't until the shells were needed that the body was found. The corpse's skin was as black as the cloth of the uniform which the gas-distended body stretched.

They'd get used to it. They'd better.

Lavel massaged the stump of his right arm with his remaining hand as he watched eight men cautiously lift a 200mm shell, then lower it with a clank onto the gurney. They paused, panting.

"Go on," he said, "One more and you've got the load."

"Via!" said Riddle angrily. There were bright chafe lines on both of the balding man's wrists. "We can rest a bloody—"

"Riddle!" Lavel snapped. "If you want to be wired up again, just say the word. Any word!"

Two of the work crew started to lower their clamp over the remaining shell in the upper of the two layers. The short, massive round was striped black and mauve. Ridges impressed in the casing showed where it would separate into three parts at a predetermined point in its trajectory.

"Not that one!" Lavel ordered sharply. "Nor the other with those markings. Just leave them and bring the— bring one of the blue-and-whites."

Firecracker rounds that would rain over four hundred anti-personnel bomblets apiece down on the target area. No good for smashing bunkers, but much of the Consies' hasty siegeworks around la Reole lacked overhead cover. The Consies'd die in their trenches like mice in a mincer when the firecracker rounds burst overhead. . . .

Lavel stumped away from the crew, knowing that they could carry on well enough without him. He was more worried about the team bolting boosters onto the shells already loaded onto the hog. A trained crew could handle the job in a minute or less per shell, but the scuts left at Camp Progress when the task force pulled out. . . .

Scuts like Chief Lavel, a derelict who couldn't even assemble artillery rounds nowadays. A job he could do drunk in the dark a few years ago, back when he'd been a man.

But he had to admit, he felt alive for almost the first time since Gresham's counter-battery salvo got through the net of cyan bolts that should've swept it from the sky. It wasn't any part of Lavel's fault, but he'd paid the price.

That's how it was in war. You trusted other people and they trusted you . . . so when you screwed up—

—and Chief knew he'd screwed up lots of times in the past, you couldn't live and not transpose a range figure *once*—

—it was some other bastard got it in the neck.

Or the arm and leg. What goes around, comes around.

Lavel began whistling *St. James' Infirmary* between his teeth as he approached the self-propelled howitzer. *His* self-propelled howitzer for the next few hours.

Craige and Komar, transit drivers who hadn't been promoted to line units after a couple years service each, seemed to have finished their task. Six assembled rounds waited on the hog's loading tray.

Between each 200mm shell (color-coded as to type) and its olive-drab base charge was a white-painted booster. The booster contained beryllium-based fuel to give the round range sufficient to his positions around la Reole.

Lavel checked each fastener while the two drivers waited uneasily.

"All right," he said at last, grudging them credit for the task he could no longer perform. "All right. They should be coming with the next load now."

He climbed the three steps into the gun compartment carefully. The enclosure smelled of oil and propellant residues. It smelled like home.

Lavel powered up, listening critically to the sound of each motor and relay as it came live. The bank of idiot lights above the targeting console had a streak of red and amber with a green expanse: the traversing mechanism failed regularly when the turret was rotated over fifteen degrees to either side.

Thank the Lord for that problem. Without it, the howitzer wouldn't 've been here in Camp Progress when it was needed.

Needed by Task Force Ranson. Needed by Chief Lavel.

He sat in the gun captain's chair, then twisted to look over his shoulder. "Are you clear?" he shouted to his helpers. "Keep clear!"

For choice, Lavel would have stuck his head out the door of the gun compartment to make sure Craige and Komar didn't have their hands on the heavy shells. That would mean picking up his crutch and levering himself from the chair again. . . .

Level touched the EXECUTE button to start the loading sequence.

The howitzer had arrived at Camp Progress with most of a basic load of ammunition still stowed in its hull. For serious use, the hog would have been fed from one or more ammunition haulers, connected to the loading ramp by conveyor belts.

No problem. The nineteen rounds available would be enough for *this* job.

Seventeen rounds. Two of the shells couldn't be used for this purpose. But seventeen was plenty.

The howitzer began to swallow its meal of ammunition, clanking and wobbling on its suspension. Warrant Leader Ortnahme had ordered the shells off-loaded and stored at a safe distance—from him—as soon as the hog arrived for maintenance. That quantity of high explosive worried most people.

Not Chief Lavel, who'd worked with it daily—until some other cannon-cocker got his range.

CLUNK. CLUNK. The first six rounds would go into the ready-use drum, from which the gun could cycle them in less than fifteen seconds.

CLUNK. CLUNK. Each round would be launched as an individually-targeted fire mission. The hog's computer chose from the ready-use drum the shell that most nearly matched the target parameters.

For bunkers, an armor-piercing shell or delay-fused high explosive if no armor piercing was in the drum. So on down the line until, if nothing else were available, a paint-filled practice round blasted out of the tube.

CLUNK. The loading system refilled the ready-use drum automatically, until the on-board stowage was exhausted and the outside tray no longer received fresh rounds. Lavel could hear the second gurney-load squealing closer.

CLUNK.

The drum was loaded—six green lights on the console. He could check the shell-types by asking the system, but there was no need. He'd chosen the first six rounds to match the needs of his initial salvo.

A touch threw the target map up on the screen above the gunnery console. The drone's on-board computer had processed the data before dumping it.

Damage to buildings within la Reole—shell-burst patterns as well as holes—provided accurate information as to the type and bearing of the Consie weapons. When that data was superimposed on the raw new siege works, it was easy for an artificial intelligence to determine the location of the enemy's heavy weapons, the guns that were dangerous to an armored task force.

One more thing to check. "TOC," Lavel said to his commo helmet.

No response for ten seconds, thirty. . . . The first shell of the new batch clanged down on the loading ramp.

"Tech 2 Helibrun," a harried voice responded at last. "Go ahead, Yellow Six."

Yellow Six. Officer in command of Transit, Lavel's lips curled.

"I'm waiting for the patch to Tootsie Six," he said, more sharply than the delay warranted. "Why haven't I been connected?"

"The bl—" the commo tech began angrily. He continued after a pause to swallow. "Chief, the patch is in place. We don't have contact with the task force yet, is all. From the data we've got from Central, it'll be about an hour before they're on ground high enough that we can reach them from here."

Another pause; instead of an added, *you cursed fool*, simply, "We'll connect you when we do. Over."

Lavel swallowed his own anger. He was getting impatient; which was silly, since he'd waited more than seven years already. . . .

"Roger," he said. "Yellow Six out."

Another shell dropped onto the ramp. There would be plenty of time to load and prepare all seventeen round before the start of the fire mission.

Over an hour to kill, and to kill. . . .

The lower half of June Ranson's visor was a fairy procession of lanterns. They hung from tractor-drawn carts and bicycles laden with cargo.

"Action front!" Ranson warned. She was probably the only person in the unit who was trying to follow a remote viewpoint as well as keeping watch on her immediate surroundings.

The reflected cyan crackle from *Deathdealer*'s stabilized tribarrel provided an even more effective warning.

The main road from the southwest into la Reole and its bridge across the Santine Estuary was studded with figures and crude vehicles. Hundreds of civilians, guided—guarded—by a few black-clad guerrillas, were lugging building materials uphill to the Consie siege lines.

The lead tank of Task Force Ranson had just snarled into view of them.

Sparrow's first burst must have come from the bellowing darkness so far as the trio of Consies, springing to their feet from a lantern lit guardpost, were concerned. The guerrillas spun and died at the roadside while civilians gaped in amazement. Without light-enhanced optics, the tank cresting a plowed knoll 500 meters away was only sound and a flicker of lethal cyan.

Civilians flung down their bicycles and sought cover in the ditches beside the road. Bagged cement; hundred-kilo loads of reinforcing rods; sling-loads of brick—building materials necessary for a work of destruction—lay as ungainly lumps on the pavement.

The loads had been pushed for kilometers under the encouragement of armed Consies. Bicycle wheels spun lazily in the air.

A rifleman stood up on a tractor-drawn cart and fired in the general direction of *Deathdealer*. Sparrow's tribarrel spat bolts at a building on the ridgeline, setting off a fuel pump in a fireball.

Ranson, Janacek, and at least two gunners from car One-five, the left outrider, answered the rifleman simultaneously.

The Consie's head and torso disappeared with a blue stutter. The canned goods which filled the bed of the carp erupted in a cloud of steam. The tractor continued its plodding uphill progress. Its driver had jumped off and was running down the road, screaming and waving his arms in the air.

There were no trucks or buses visible in the convoy. The Consies must have commandeered ordinary transport for more critical purposes, using makeshifts to support the sluggish pace of siegework.

In the near distance to the east of Task Force Ranson, the glare of a powergun waked cyan echoes from high clouds. One of the weapons which the Consies had brought up to bombard la Reole—a pedestal-mounted powergun. The weapon was heavy enough to hole a tank or open a combat car like a can of sardines. . . .

"Booster!" Ranson shouted to her AI. "Fire mission Able. Break. Tootsie Three, call in Fire Mission Able directly—in clear—as soon as you raise Camp Progress. Break. All Tootsie elements, follow the road. They can't 've mined it if they're using it like this. Go! Go! Go!"

Warmonger bucked and scraped the turf before clear-

ing a high spot. Willens had wicked up his throttles.
Though he'd lifted the car for as much ground clearance
as possible, *Warmonger*'s present speed guaranteed a
bumpy ride on anything short of a pool table.

Speed was life now. These terrified civilians and their
sleepy guards had nothing to do with the mission of Task
Force Ranson, but a single lucky slug could cause an
irreplaceable casualty. Colonel Hammer was playing this
game with table stakes. . . .

In the roar of wind and gunfire, Ranson hadn't been
able to hear the chirp of her AI transmitting.

If it *had* transmitted. If the electronics of a combat
car jolting along at speed were good enough to bounce
a transmission a thousand kays north from a meteor track.
If Fire Central would relay the message to Camp
Progress in time. If the hog at Camp Progress. . . .

Two men shot at *Warmonger* from the ditch across
the road.

Ranson fired back. Bolts ripped from the rotating
muzzles of her powergun and vanished from her sight.
It wasn't until the lower half of her visor blacked
momentarily and the upper half quivered with cyan reflections that she realized that she'd been aiming at the
remote image from *Deathdealer*.

Part of June Ranson's mind wondered what her bolts
had hit, might have hit. The part in physical control
continued to squeeze the butterfly trigger of her
powergun and watch the cyan light vanish in the divided
darkness of her mind. . . .

The night ahead of Dick Suilin was lit spitefully by
the fire of the other armored vehicles. He clung to the
coaming of *Flamethrower*'s fighting compartment with his
left hand; his right rested on the grip of his tribarrel,
but his thumb was curled under his fingers as if to
prevent it from touching the trigger.

There were no signs of Consies shooting back, but a

farm tractor had collapsed into a fuel fire that reminded
Suilin of the bus after his bolts raked it.

Oh dear Lord. Oh dear Lord.

Gale was lighting his quarter with short bursts. So
far as the reporter could tell, the veteran's bolts were
a matter of excitement rather than a response to real
targets. Lieutenant Cooter gripped the armor with both
hands and shouted so loudly into his helmet microphone that Suilin could hear the sounds though not
the words.

Both veterans had a vision of duty.

Dick Suilin had his memories.

When the armored vehicles prickled with cyan bolts,
they re-entered the reporter's universe. It had been very
easy for Suilin to believe that the three of them in the
back of *Flamethrower* were the only humans left in the
strait bounds of existence. The darkness created that
feeling; the darkness and the additional Wide-awake he'd
accepted from Gale.

Perhaps what most divorced Suilin from that which
had been reality less than two days before was the
buzzing roar of the fans. Their vibration seemed to jelly
both his minds and his marrow.

Since the driver slid his throttles to the top of their
range, *Flamethrower*'s skirt jolted repeatedly against the
ground. Suilin found the impacts more bearable than the
constant, enervating hum of the car at moderate speed.

Task Force Ranson swung raggedly at an angle to the
left. Each armored vehicle followed a separate track,
though the general line was on or parallel to the paved
highway.

Suilin had ridden the la Reole/Bunduran road a
hundred times in the past. It was easy to follow the road's
course now with his eyes, because of the fires lit by
powerguns all along its course. The truckers cafe and fuel
point at the top of the ridge, three kilometers from la
Reole, was a crown of flames.

Flamethrower lurched over a ditch and sparked her skirts on the gravel shoulder. The driver straightened his big vehicle with port, then starboard sidethrusts. The motion rocked Suilin brutally but seemed to be expected by the veterans with him in the fighting compartment.

Gale shot over the stern, and Cooter's weapon coughed bursts so short it appeared to be clearing its triple throats.

A dozen civilians huddled in the ditch on Suilin's side of the car. All but one of them were pressed face-down in the soft earth. Their hands were clasped over the back of their heads as if to force themselves still lower.

The exception lay on her back. A powergun had decapitated her.

Suilin tried to scream, but his throat was too rigid to pass the sound.

"Shot!" crackled his headphones, but there was shooting everywhere. As armored vehicles disappeared over the brow of the ridge, all their weapons ripped the horizon in volleys. Cooter had explained that the Consie siegeworks were just across a shallow valley from where Task Force Ranson would regain the road.

A Consie wearing crossed bandoliers rolled up-right in the ditch fifty meters ahead of *Flamethrower*. He aimed directly at Suilin.

Cooter saw the guerrilla, but the big lieutenant had been raking the right side of the road while Gale covered the rear. He shouted something and tried to turn his tribarrel.

Suilin's holographic sights were a perfect image of the Consie, whose face fixed in a snarl of hate and terror. The guerrilla's cheeks bunched and made his moustache twitch, as though he were trying to will his rifle to fire without pulling the trigger.

The muzzle flashes were red as heart's blood.

Flamethrower jolted over debris in the road. A bicycle flew skyward; the air was sharp with quicklime as bags of cement ruptured. Three bullets rang on the armor in front of Dick Suilin and ricocheted away in a blaze of sparks.

As the car settled again, Suilin's tribarrel lashed out: one bolt short, one bolt long . . . and between them, the guerrilla's hair and the tips of his moustache ablaze to frame what had been his face.

Flamethrower was past.

The sky overhead began to scream.

Hans Wager was strapped into his seat. He hated it, but at least the suspended cradle preserved him from the worst of the shocks.

The tank grounded on the near ditch; sparked its skirts across the pavement in red brilliance; and grounded sideways on the ramp of the drainage ditch across the road. Holman hadn't quite changed their direction of travel, though she'd pointed them the right way.

The stern skirts dragged a long gouge up the road as Holman accelerated with the bow high. The main screen showed a dazzling roostertail of sparks behind the nameless tank. Wager didn't care. He had too much on his own plate.

Deathdealer fired its main gun.

That was all right for Birdie Sparrow, an experienced tanker and riding the lead vehicle. Wager'd set the mechanical lock-out on his own 20cm weapon.

He didn't trust the electronic selector when there were this many friendly vehicles around. A bolt from the main gun would make as little of a combat car as it would of a church choir.

Hans Wager was determined that he'd make this *cursed, bloody* tank work for him. Nothing would ever convince him that a tank's sensors were really better than three sets of human eyeballs, sweeping the risks of a battlefield—

But there weren't three sets of eyeballs, just his own, so he *had* to make the hardware work.

The threat sensor flashed a Priority One carat onto

the main screen. Wager couldn't tell what the target was in the laterally-compressed panorama. The cupola gun, slaved to the threat sensor the way Albers explained it could be, was already rotating left. It swung the magnified gunnery display of Screen Two with it.

Two bodies and one body still living, a Consie huddling beside what had been a pair of civilian females. The guerrilla's rifle was slung across his back, forgotten in his panic. He was too close for the tribarrel to bear.

The tank's skirts swept a bicycle and sling-load of bricks from the road, flinging the debris ahead and aside of its hundred-and-seventy-tonne rush. Chips and brickdust pelted the Consie. He leaped up.

His chest exploded in cyan light and a cloud of steam which somersaulted the corpse a dozen meters from the ditch.

There'd been a major guardpost at the truckstop on the hill, but *Deathdealer* and the crossfire of the two leading combat cars had already ended any threat from that quarter. Fuel roared in an orange jet from the courtyard pump. The roof of the cafe had buried whoever was still inside when tribarrels cut the walls away.

"*Shot*," said his commo helmet. The voice of whoever was acting as fire control was warning that friendly artillery would impact in five seconds.

Three bodies sprawled: a step, another step, and a final step, from the front door of the cafe.

Deathdealer dropped over the hill. Its main gun lighted the far valley. The nameless tank topped the ridgeline with a roar. Their speed and Holman's inexperience lofted the vehicle thirty centimeters into the air at the crest.

Hans Wager, bracing himself in his seat, toggled the main gun off safe.

The low ridge a kilometer away paralleled the Santine River and embraced the western half of la Reole. The

Consies had used the road to bring up their heavy weapons and building materials for substantial bunkers.

Three shells, dull red with the friction of their passage through air, streaked down onto the enemy concentration. The earth quivered.

The initial results were unremarkable. A knoll shifted settled; a hundred meters south of that knoll, dust rose in a spout like that of a whale venting its lungs; a further hundred meters south, black smoke puffed—not from the hilltop but well beneath the crest where raw dirt marked the mouth of a recently-excavated tunnel.

The knoll erupted, then settled again into a cavity that could have held a tank.

Blue light fused and ignited dust as a store of powergun ammunition devoured itself and the weapon it was meant to feed.

The tunnel belched orange flame; sucked in its breath and blazed forth again. The second time, the edge of the shock wave propelled a human figure.

Three more shells streaked the sky. One of them hit well to the south. The others were aimed at targets across the estuary.

Deathdealer raked the far ridge with both main gun and tribarrel. The combat cars shot up sandbag covered supply dumps on both sides of the road. Most of the armed Consies would be in bunkers, but any figure seen *now* was fair game for as many guns as could bear on it.

Long before they topped the ridge, Wager had known what his own target would be.

A mortar firing at night illuminates a thirty-meter hemisphere with its skyward flash. There'd been such a flash, needlessly highlighted by the tank's electronics, before the Consies realized they were being taken in the rear.

Wager hated mortars. Their shells angled in too high to be dealt with by the close-in defense system, and a direct hit would probably penetrate the splinter shield of a combat car.

Now a mortar and its crew were in the center of Wager's gunnery screen.

Normally the greatest danger to a mortar was counterfire from another mortar. A shell's slow, arching trajectory was easy for radar to track, and the most rudimentary of ballistic computers could figure a reciprocal. The guerrillas here had been smart: they'd mounted their tube on the back of a cyclo, a three-wheeled mini-truck of the sort the civilians on Prosperity used for everything from taxis to hauling farm produce into town.

At the bottom of the slope, work crews had cleared a path connecting several firing positions. The cyclo had just trundled into a revetment. Shell cartons scattered outside the position 200 meters up the track showed where the crew had fired the previous half-dozen rounds.

The Consie mortarmen were turned to stare with amazement at the commotion behind them. The sparkling impact as Wager's tank landed, half on the pavement and half off, scattered the crew a few paces, but the tanker's shot was in time. . . .

The center of the cyclo vanished: Wager had used his main gun. The 20cm bolt was so intense that the explosion of cases of mortar ammo followed as an anticlimax.

Several of the mortar shells were filled with white phosphorous. None of the crewmen had run far enough to be clear of the smoky tendrils whose hearts would blaze all the way through the victims on which they landed.

The nameless tank swept past flaming heaps of food, bedding, and material. Ammunition burned in harmless corkscrews through the sky and an occasional *ping* on the armor.

More shells from Camp Progress howled overhead and detonated, six of them almost simultaneously this time.

A curtain of white fire cloaked the siegelines as hundreds
of antipersonnel bomblets combed crevices to lick Consie
blood.

The leading vehicles, *Deathdealer* and two combat
cars, had slowed deliberately to let the salvo land.
Holman matched her tank's attitude to the slope and
drew ahead with the inertia she'd built on the downgrade.
She spun the nameless tank with unexpected delicacy
around the shell crater gaping at the hillcrest.

The artillery had flung dozens of bodies and bodyparts
out of eviscerated bunkers. Holman slowed to a crawl
so that Wager could pick his targets on the reverse slope.

Men in black uniforms were climbing or crawling from
trenches which shells had turned into abattoirs. Wager
ignored them. His AI highlighted the firing slits of
bunkers which the shells had spared.

Every time his pipper settled, his foot trod out another
20cm bolt.

Jets of plasma from powerguns traveled in a straight line
and liberated all their energy on the first solid object they
touched. Wager's bolts couldn't penetrate the earth the way
armor-piercing projectiles did—but their cyan touch could
shake apart hillsides in sprays of volcanic gas.

The interior of a bunker when a megajoule of plasma
spurted through the opening was indescribable Hell.

Deathdealer pulled over the crest a hundred meters
to the left of Wager's tank. Its main gun spat bolts at
the pace of a woodpecker hammering. Sparrow's experience permitted him to fire in a smooth motion, again
and again, without any pause greater than that of his
turret rotating to bear on the next target.

La Reole sprawled half a kilometer away. The nearest buildings had been shattered by shellfire and the first
flush of hand-to-hand fighting before the Consies
retreated to lick their wounds and blast the Yokel garrison into submission.

Smoke lifted from a dozen points within the town. A

saffron hint of dawn gaped on hundreds of holes in the tile roofs.

An amphibious landing vehicle pulled down from the protection of a courtyard in the town and opened fire with its machinegun. Consies emerging from a shell-ravaged bunker stumbled and fell. Wager remembered the Yokels had a marine Training Unit here at la Reole . . .

The tank's turret was thick with fumes. Wager breathed through filters, though he didn't remember them clamping down across his mouth and nose.

He stamped on the firing pedal. The gun wheezed instead of firing: he'd shot off the entire thirty-round basic load, and the tank had to cycle more main gun ammunition from storage deep in the hull.

There weren't any worthwhile targets anyway. Every slit that might have concealed a cannon or powergun was a glowing crater. Streaks of turf smoldered where bolts had ripped them.

Deathdealer was advancing again. The muzzle of its main gun glowed white.

"Sarge, should I . . . ?" Wager's intercom demanded.

"Go, go!" he snapped back. "And Via! be careful with the bridge!"

He hoped the Yokels would have sense enough not to shoot at them. For the moment, that seemed like the worst danger.

Three more shells from Camp Progress screamed overhead.

The howitzer still rocked with the sky-tearing echoes of its twelfth round. Chief Lavel was laughing. Only when he turned and met Craige's horrified eyes did he realize that he wasn't alone in the crew compartment.

Craige massaged her ears with her palms. "Ah," she said. "The guys wanta know, you know . . . are we dismissed now?"

Drives moaned as the gun mechanism filled its ready-use drum with the remaining shells in storage. Lavel put his palm against an armored side-panel to feel every nuance of the movement. It was like being reborn. . . .

"Not yet," he said. "When the last salvo's away, we'll police up the area."

The crew compartment was spacious enough to hold a full eight-man crew under armor when the howitzer was changing position. The 200mm shells and their rocket charges were heavy, and no amount of hardware could obviate the need for humans during some stages of the preparation process.

The actual firing sequence required only one man to pick the targets. The howitzer's AI and electromechanical drives did the rest.

It didn't even require a whole man. A ruin like Chief Lavel was sufficient.

He glanced at the panoramic screen mounted on the slanted armor above the gun mantlet. A light breeze had dissipated much of the smoke from the sustainer charges. They burned out in the first seven seconds after ignition. High in the heavens, streaking south were dense white trails where the ramjet boosters cut in.

The beryllium fuel was energetic—but its residues were intensely hygroscopic and left clouds thick enough to be tracked on radar.

The residues were lethal at extreme dilution as well . . . but the boosters ignited at high altitude, and it wasn't Alois Hammer's planet.

Besides, Via! this was a war, wasn't it? There was always collateral damage in war.

"Ah . . ." said Craige. "Sir? When are you going to shoot off the rest?"

"When I get the bloody update from the task force, aren't I?" Lavel snarled. He patted the console. "It's thirty-three seconds to splash from here. We don't fire the last five rounds will we see what still needs to be hit and where the bloody friendlies are!"

The console in front of Lavel began to click and whine. He had a voice link to the task force, but the electronically-sensed information, passed from one AI to another, was faster by an order of magnitude.

It was also less subject to distortion, even when, as now, it had to be transmitted over VHF radio.

Besides, the crews of Task Force Ranson had plenty to occupy them without spotting for the guns.

The new data swept all the previous highlights from the targeting overlay. Green splotches marked changes in relief caused by shell-bursts and secondary explosions. Denser pinheads of the same hue showed where bolts from the 20cm powerguns of tanks had glazed the terrain, sealing firing positions whether or not the bunkers themselves were destroyed.

No worthy targets remained on the west side of the Santine.

Lavel's light pen touched a bunker on the near bank of the estuary anyway. It had been build to hold a heavy gun, though the AI was sure nothing was emplaced in it yet. That accomplished, Lavel checked the eastern arc of the siege lines.

The east side was lightly held, because most of the Consie forces across the Santine were concentrated on Kohang. The Marine unit in la Reole could probably have broken out—but in doing so, they would have had to surrender the town and the crucial crossing point. Somebody—somebody with more brains and courage than any of the Yokels at Camp Progress had decided to hold instead of running.

Lavel had two high-explosive shells, one target solid, and a firecracker round remaining. He chose three eastside bunkers for the HE and the solid. The solid was intended to test the air-defense system of friendly units, but its hundred and eighty kilos weren't going to do anybody it landed on any good. He set his firecracker round to detonate overhead ten seconds after the others splashed.

The console chittered, then glowed green.

Green for ready. Probably the last time Chief Lavel would ever see that message.

He sighed and slapped EXECUTE.

The door to the crew compartment was open. Craige wasn't wearing a commo helmet, but she got her hands to her ears at the *chunk!* of the ignition charge expelling the first round from the tube.

The seven-second ROAR-R-R-R-R-R-R-R-R! of the sustainer motor shook the world.

The remaining four rounds blasted out at one-a-second intervals like beads on a rosary of thunder. Their backblasts shoved the howitzer down on its suspension and raised huge doughnuts of dust from the surrounding soil.

All done. The fire mission, and the last shred of meaning in Chief Lavel's life.

There was still a green light on the ready-use indicator.

"Booster!" Lavel snapped. "Shell status!"

"One practice ready," said the console in a feminine voice. "Zero rounds in storage."

Lavel turned, rising from his seat with a face like a skull. "You!" he said to Craige. "How many rounds did you load this last time?"

"What?" said Craige. "How . . . ? Six, six like you told us. Isn't that—"

"*You stupid bastards!*" Lavel screamed as his hand groped with the patch to Task Force Ranson, changing it from digital to voice. "Those last two shells were anti-tank rounds with seeker heads! You Killed 'em all!"

All the displays of *Herman's Whore* pulsed red with an Emergency Authenticator Signal. A voice Ortnahme didn't recognize bellowed, "Task Force! Shoot down the friendly incoming! Tank Killer rounds! Ditch your tanks! Ditch!"

Ortnahme pushed the air defense selector. It was already uncaged. He'd been willing to take the chance of bumping it by accident so long as he knew it would be that many seconds quicker to activate when he might need it.

Like now.

"Simkins," he said, surprised at his own calm, "cut your fans and ditch. *Soonest!*"

His calm wasn't so surprising after all. There'd been emergencies before.

There'd been the time a jack began to sink—thin concrete over a bed of rubble had counterfeited a solid base. Thirty tonnes of combat car settling toward a technician. The technician was dead, absolutely, if he did anything except block the low side of the car with the fan nacelle he'd been preparing to fit.

Ortnahme had said, "Kid, slide the fan under the skirt *now!*"—calmly—while he reached under the high side of the car. The technician obeyed as though he'd practiced the movement.

And for the moment that the sturdy nacelle supported the car's weight, Warrant Leader Ortnahme had gripped Tech 2 Simkins by the ankle and jerked him out of the deathtrap.

The kid was all thumbs when it came to powertools, but he took orders for a treat. *Herman's Whore* stuttered for a moment as the inertia of the air in her intake ducts drove the fans. The big blower grounded hard and skidded a twenty-meter trench in the soil as she came to rest.

Ortnahme's seat was raising him, not as fast as a younger, slimmer man could've jumped for the hatch without power assist—but Henk Ortnahme *wasn't* bloody young and slim.

He squeezed his torso out of the cupola hatch. The tribarrel was rotating on its Scarf ring, the muzzles lifting skyward in response to the air defense program.

Blood and martyrs! It was going to—

The powergun fired. Ortnahme couldn't help but flinch away. Swearing, bracing himself on the coaming, he tried to lever himself out of the hatch as half-melted plastic burned the back of his hands and clung to his shirtsleeves.

He stuck. His pistol holster was caught on the smoke grenades he'd slung from a wire where he could reach them easily when he was riding with the hatch open.

Blood and martyrs.

The northern sky went livid with cyan bolts and the white winking explosions they woke in the predawn haze. *Herman's Whore* and the other tanks were firing preset three-round bursts—not one burst but dozens, on and on.

The incoming shells had been cargo rounds. They had burst, spilling their sheafs of submunitions.

There were hundreds of blips, saturating the armored vehicles' ability to respond. Given time, the tribarrels could eliminate every target.

There wouldn't be that much time.

Simkins rolled to the ground, pushed clear by the tank's own iridium flank as its skirts plowed the sod. He stared up at the warrant leader in amazement.

Ortnahme sucked in his chest, settled onto the seat cushion to get a centimeter's greater clearance, and rose in a convulsive motion like a whale broaching. His knees rapped the coaming, but he would've chewed his legs bloody off it that was what it took to get away *now*.

Hundreds of targets. A firecracker round, antipersonnel and surely targeted on the opposite side of the river. Harmless except for the way the half-kilo bomblets screened the three much heavier segments of an antitank—

Ortnahme bounced from the skirt of *Herman's Whore* and somersaulted to the ground. His body armor kept him from breaking anything when he hit on his back, but his breath wheezed out in an animal gasp.

Two brighter, bigger explosions winked in the detonating mist above him.

The third anti-tank submunition triggered itself. It was an orange flash and a streak of white, molten metal reaching for *Deathdealer* like a mounting pin for a doomed butterfly.

It took Birdie Sparrow just under three seconds to absorb the warning and slap the air defense button. The worst things you hear for heartbeats before you understand, because the mind refuses to understand.

The tribarrel slewed at a rate of 100 degrees/second, so even the near one-eighty it turned to bear on the threat from the sky behind was complete in less than two seconds more.

Four and a half seconds, call it. *Deathdealer* was firing skyward scarcely a half second after small charges burst the cases of both cargo shells and spilled their submunitions in overwhelming profusion.

It wasn't the first time that the distance between life and death had been measured in a fraction of a second.

Albers cut the fans and swung *Deathdealer* sideways on residual energy so that they grounded broadside on, carving the sod like a snowplow and halting them with a haste that lifted the tank's off-side skirts a meter in the air.

Sparrow's seat cradled him in the smoky, stinking turret of his tank. Screen Two showed a cloud of debris that jumped around the pipper like snow in a crystal paperweight.

A red light winked in a sidebar of the main screen, indicating that *Deathdealer*'s integrity had been breached: the driver's hatch was open. In the panoramic display Albers, horizontally compressed by the hologram, was abandoning the vehicle.

"Better ditch too, Birdie," said the horribly-ruined corpse of DJ Bell. "This is when it's happening."

"Booster!" Sparrow screamed to his AI. "Air defense! Sort by size, largest first!"

If it'd been two anti-tank rounds, no sweat. The handful of submunitions in each cargo shell would've been blasted in a few seconds, long before they reached their own lethal range and detonated.

"Hey, there's still time." DJ's face was changing; but this time his features knitted, healed, instead of splashing slowly outward in a mist of blood and bone and brains. "Not a lot, but there's time. You just gotta leave, Birdie."

A pair of firecracker rounds, that was fine too. Their tiny bomblets wouldn't more than etch *Deathdealer*'s dense iridium armor when they went off. Hard lines for the combat cars, but that was somebody else's problem . . . and anyway, none of the bomblets were going to land within a kilometer of the task force.

The heavy anti-tank submunitions weren't aimed at this side of the river either. If the shell had been of ordinary construction, it would've impacted on a bunker somewhere far distant from the friendly tanks.

But the submunitions had seeker heads. As they spun lazily from the casing that bore them to the target area, sophisticated imaging systems fed data to their on-board computers.

A bunker would've done if no target higher in the computers' priorities offered.

A combat car would've done very well.

But if the imagine system located a tank, then it was with electronic glee that the computer deployed vanes to brake and guide the submunition toward that prime target.

Too little time.

Birdie Sparrow slammed the side of his fist into the buckle to disengage himself from the seat restraints. A fireball lighted the gunnery screen as *Deathdealer*'s reprogrammed tribarrel detonated a larger target than the antipersonnel bomblets to which the law of averages had aimed it.

"Birdie, *quick*," DJ pleaded. His face was almost whole again.

Sparrow sang back onto his seat as the screen flared again. "No," he whispered. "No. Not out there."

DJ Bell smiled at his friend and extended a hand. "Welcome home, snake," he said.

There was a white flash.

Chapter Ten

"Watch it," warned Cooter, ducking beneath the level of his gunshield. Part of Dick Suilin's mind understood, but he continued to stand upright and stare.

The dawn sky was filthy with rags of black smoke, tiny moth-holes streaming back in the wind when bomblets exploded. That was nothing, and the crackle of two tank tribarrels still firing as the remaining anti-personnel cloud impacted on the far ridge was little more.

Deathdealer was devouring itself.

The submunitions location, as well as its attitude and range in respect to *Deathdealer*, were determined by a computer more sophisticated than anything indigenously built on Prosperity. The computer's last act was to trigger the explosion that shattered it in an orange fireball high above the tank.

The blast spewed out a projectile that rode the shockwave, molten with the energy that forged and compressed it. It struck *Deathdealer* at a ninety degree angle where the tank's armor was thinnest, over the rear turtleback covering the powerplant.

Hammer's anti-tank artillery rounds were designed to

defeat the armor of the most powerful tanks in the human universe. This one performed exactly as intended, punching its self-forging fragment through the iridium armor and rupturing the integrity of the fusion bottle that powered the huge vehicle's systems.

Plasma vented skyward in a stream as intensely white as the heart of a star. It etched and ate away the edges of the hole without rupturing the unpierced portion of the armor. The internal bulkheads gave way.

Plasma jetted from the driver's hatch an instant before the cupola blew open. Stored ammunition flashed from underdeck compartments. It stained the blaze cyan and vaporized the joint between hull and skirts.

The glowing husk of what had been *Deathdealer* settled to the ground. Where the hull overlay portions of the skirt, the thick steel plates melted from the iridium armor's greater residual heat.

The entire event was over in three seconds. It would be days before the hull had cooled to the temperature of the surrounding air.

The thunderclap, air rushing to fill the partial vacuum of the plasma's track, rocked the thirty-tonne combat cars. Suilin's breastplate rapped the grips of his tribarrel.

Across the river, Consie positions danced in the light of hundreds of bomblets. They looked by contrast as harmless as rain on a field of poppies.

"All units," said Suilin's helmet. "Remount and move on. We've got a job to do. Six out."

Another combat car slid between *Deathdealer* and the figure of the tank's driver. He'd been running away from his doomed vehicle until the initial blast knocked him down. He rose to his feet slowly and climbed aboard the car whose bulk shielded him both from glowing metal and remembrance of what had just happened/almost happened.

Flamethrower rotated on its axis so that all three tribarrels could cover stretches of the bunker line the task force had just penetrated.

"We're the rear guard," Cooter said. "Watch for movement."

The lieutenant triggered a short burst at a figure who stumbled along the ridgeline—certainly harmless since he'd crawled from a shatter bunker; probably unaware even when the two cyan bolts cut him down.

Suilin thought he saw a target. He squinted. It was a tendril of smoke, not a person.

He wasn't sure he would have fired anyway.

Other cars were advancing toward the town, but it took some moment for the crews of the surviving tanks to reboard. One of the tanks jolted forward taking *Deathdealer*'s former place at the head of the column.

The fat maintenance officer who captained *Herman's Whore* was still climbing into the cupola of the other giant vehicle. His belt holster flapped loosely against his thigh.

"Here," said Gale, handing Suilin an open beer.

Cooter was already drinking deeply from a bottle. He fired a short burst with his left hand, snapping whorls in the vapor above the ridge.

The Consie siege lines were gray with blasted earth and the smoke of a thousand fires. There must have been survivors from the artillery and the pounding, bunker-ripping fury of the powerguns, but they were no longer a danger to Task Force Ranson.

Suilin's beer was cold and so welcome to his parched throat that he'd drunk half of it down before he realized that it tasted—

Tasted like transmission fluid. Tasted worse than the plastic residues of the empty cases flung from his tribarrel. He stared at the bottle in amazement.

Flamethrower spun cautiously again and fell to behind *Herman's Whore*. Cooter dropped his bottle over the side of the vehicle. He began talking on the radio, but Suilin's numbed ears heard only the laconic rhythm of the words.

Gale broke a ration bar in half and gave part to the reporter. Suilin bit into it, feeling like a fool with the food in one hand and a horribly-spoiled beer in the other. He thought about throwing the bottle away, but he was afraid the veteran would think he was spurning his hospitality.

The ration bar tasted decayed.

Gale, munching stolidly, saw the reporter's eyes widen and said, "Aw, don't worry. It always tastes like that."

He wiped his mouth with the back of his hand, grimy with recondensed vapors given off when his tribarrel fired. "It's the Wide-awakes, you know." He fished more of the cones from the pouch beside the cooler, distributing two of them to Cooter and Suilin.

Suilin dropped the cone into a sidepocket. He forced himself to drink the rest of his beer. It was horrible, as horrible as everything else in this bleeding dawn.

He nodded back toward *Deathdealer*, still as bright as the filament of an incandescent lightbulb. "Is it always like . . . ? Is it always like that?"

"Naw, that time, they got the fusion bottle, y'know?" Gale said, gazing at the hulk with only casual interest.

Internal pressures lifted *Deathdealer*'s turret off its ring. It slid a meter down the rear slope before welding itself onto the armor at a skew angle. "S' always differ'nt, I'd say."

"Except for the guys who buy it," Cooter offered, looking backward also. "Maybe it's the same for them."

Suilin bit another piece from the chalk-textured, vile-flavored ration bar.

"I'll let you know," he heard his voice say.

"Blue Two," said Captain June Ranson, watching white light from *Deathdealer* quiver on the inner face of her gunshield, "this is Tootsie Six. You're acting head of Blue Section. Six out."

"Roger, Tootsie."

Sergeant Wager's nameless tank, now the first unit in Task Force Ranson, was picking its way through rubble and shell craters at the entrance to la Reole. It had been a new vehicle at the start of this ratfuck. Now it dragged lengths of barbed wire—and a fencepost—and its skirts were battered worse than those of *Herman's Whore*.

The tank's newbie driver swung wide to pull around a pile of bricks and roof tiles. Too wide. The wall opposite collapsed in a gout of brick dust driven by the tank's fans. Uniformed Yokels, looking very young indeed, scurried out of the ruin, clutching a machinegun and boxes of ammunition.

Warmonger slid into the choking cloud. Filters clapped themselves over Ranson's nose. Janacek swore. Ranson hoped Willens had switched to sonic imagine before the dust blinded him.

Dust enfolded her in a soft blur. Static charges kept her visor clear, but the air a millimeter beyond the plastic was as opaque as the silicon heart of a computer.

Sparrow was dead, vaporized; out of play. But his driver had survived, and she could transfer him to Blue Three. Take over from the inexperienced driver—or perhaps for Sergeant Wager, also inexperienced with panzers but an asset to the understrength crew of One-six.

Mix and match. *What is your decision on this point, Candidate Ranson . . . ?*

Something jogged her arm. She could see again.

The tracked landing vehicle had blacked into a cross-street again, making way for the lead tank. The dust was far behind *Warmonger*. The third car in line was stirring it back to life.

A helmeted major in fatigues the color of mustard greens—a Yokel Marine—waved toward them with a swagger stick while he shouted into a hand communicator.

"Booster, match frequencies," Ranson ordered.

She saw through the corners of her eyes that Stolley and Janacek were exchanging glances. How long had her eyes been staring blankly before Stolley's touch brought her back to the physical universe?

". . . onsider yourselves under my command as the ranking National officer in the sector!" the headphones ordered Ranson as her AI found the frequency on which the major was broadcasting. "Halt your vehicles now until I can provide ground guides and reform my defensive perimeter."

"Local officer," Ranson said, trusting her transmitter to overwhelm the hand-held unit even if the Yokel were still keying it, "this is Captain Ranson, Hammer's Regiment. That's a negative. We're just passing through."

The Yokel major was out of sight behind *Warmonger*. A ridiculous little man with creased trousers even now, and a coating of dust on his waxed boots and moustache.

A little man who'd held la Reole with a battalion of recruits against an attack much heavier than that which crumpled three thousand Yokels at Camp Progress. Maybe not so ridiculous after all. . . .

"Local officer," Ranson continued, "I think you'll find resistance this side has pretty well collapsed. We'll finish off anything we find across the river. Slammers out."

La Reole had been an attractive community of two- and three-story buildings of stuccoed brick. Lower floors were given over to shops and restaurants for bridge traffic. Shattered glass from display windows now jeweled the pavement, even where shellfire had spared the remainder of the structures.

The highway kinked into a roundabout decorated with a statue, now headless; and kinked again as it proceeded to the bridge approaches. The buildings on either side of the dogleg had been reduced to rubble. The Consie gunners hadn't been able to get a clear shot at the bridge with their direct-fire weapons or to stop the shells their mortars and howitzers lobbed toward the span.

"No! No! No!" shouted the major, his voice buzzy and attenuated by interference from drive fans. "You're needed here! I order you to stop—and anyway, you can't cross the bridge, it's too weak. Do you hear me! halt!"

Another landing vehicle sheltered in a walled forecourt with its diesel idling. The gunner lifted his helmet to scratch his bald scalp, then saluted Ranson. He was at least twice the age of any of the six kids in the vehicle's open bay, but they were all armed to the teeth and glaring out with wild-eyed fury.

The Consies had attempted a direct assault on la Reole before they moved their heavy weapons into position. That must've gotten interesting.

A few civilians raised their heads above window sills, but they ducked back as soon as any of the mercenaries glanced toward them.

"Local Officer," Ranson said as echoes of drive fans hammered her from the building fronts, "I'm sorry but we've got our orders. You'll have to take care of your remaining problems yourself. Slammers out."

She split her visor to take the remote from the new lead tank. The controls had reverted to direct view when transmission from *Deathdealer* ceased.

The bridge at la Reole was a suspension design with a central tower in mid-stream and slightly lower towers on either bank to support the cables. Consie gunners had battered the portions of the towers which stuck up above the roof peaks. They had shattered the concrete and parted the cable on the upstream side.

The span sagged between towers, but the lowest point of its double arc was still several meters above the water. The downstream cable continued to hold, although it now stretched over piles of rubble instead of being clamped firmly onto the towers. A guardpost of Marines with rocket launchers, detailed to watch for raft-borne Consies, gaped at the huge tank that approached them.

"Willens," Ranson ordered her driver, "hold up."

The lower half of her visor swayed as the tank moved onto the raise approach.

"All Tootsie units, hold up. One vehicle on the bridge at a time. Take it easy. Six out."

The lead tank was taking it easy. Less than a walking pace, tracking straight although the span slanted down at fifteen degrees to the left side. Flecks of gravel and dust flew off in the fan draft, then drifted toward the sluggish water.

There were cracks in the asphalt surface of the bridge. Sometimes the cracks exposed the girders beneath.

The Yokel major was shouting demands at June Ranson, but she heard nothing. Her eyes watched the bridge span swaying, the images in the top and bottom of her visor moving alternately.

"Just drive *through* it, kid," snarled Warrant Leader Ortnahme as he felt *Herman's Whore* pause. Close to the bridge, la Reole had taken a tremendous pasting from Consie guns. Here, collapsed buildings cascaded bricks and beams from either side of the street.

The tank seemed to gather itself on a quivering column of air. "Like everybloodybody else did!" Ortnahme added in a raised voice.

Simkins grabbed handfuls of his throttles instead of edging them forward in the tiny increments with which he normally adjusted the tank's speed and direction. The pause had cost them momentum, but *Herman's Whore* still had plenty of speed and power to batter through the obstacle.

Larger chunks of building material parted to either side of the blunt prow like bayou scum before a barge. Dust billowed out from beneath the skirts in white clouds. It curled back to feed through the fan intakes.

Behind the great tank, wreckage settled again. The pile had spread a little from the sweep of the skirts, but it was built up again by blocks and bits which the thunder of passage shook from damaged buildings.

"Sorry, sir," muttered Simkins over the intercom.

The kid's trouble wasn't that he couldn't drive the bloody tank: it was that he was too bloody careful. Maybe he didn't have the smoothness of, say, Albers from. . . .

Via. Maybe not think about that.

Simkins didn't have the smoothness of a veteran driver, but he had plenty of experience shifting tanks and combat cars in and out of maintenance bays where centimeters counted.

Centimeters didn't count in the field. All that counted was getting from here to there without delay, and doing whatever bloody job required to be done along the way.

Ortnahme sighed. The way he'd reamed the kid any time Simkins brushed a post or halted *in* the berm instead of *at* it, he didn't guess he could complain now if his technician was squeamish about dingin' his skirts.

Simkins eased them to a halt just short of the bridge approach. Cooter's blower was making the run—the walk, rather—and bleedin' Lord 'n martyrs, how the *Hell* did they expect that ruin to hold a tank?

The near span rippled to the rhythm of *Flamethrower*'s fans, and the span beyond the crumbling central support towers still danced with the weight of the car that'd crossed minutes before. This was bloody *crazy*!

The Yokels guarding the bridge must've though so too, from the way they stared in awe at *Herman's Whore*.

Ortnahme, hidden in the tank's belly, glared at their holographic images. They'd leaned their buzzbomb launchers against the sandbagged walls of their bunker.

Hard to believe that ten-kilo missiles could really damage something with the size and weight of armor of *Herman's Whore*, but Henk Ortnahme believed it. He'd rebuilt his share of tanks after they took buzzbombs the wrong way—and, regretfully, had combat-lossed others when the cost of repair would exceed the cost of buying a new unit in its place.

There were costs for crew training and, less tangibly, for the loss of experience with veteran crewmen; but those problems weren't in Ortnahme's bailiwick.

"Sir?" the intercom asked. "The . . . you know, the guns they been hitting this place with. Wasn't that a, you know, an awful lot?"

"Don't worry about it, kid," the warrant leader said smugly. "Our only problem now's this bloody bridge."

Ortnahme adjusted his main screen so that the panorama's stern view was central rather than being split between the two edges. The shattered bunkers were hidden by the same buildings that'd protected the bridge from Consie gunfire. Smoke, turgid and foul, covered the western horizon.

"Ah, sir?" Simkins said. "What I mean is, you, know, we been fighting guerrillas, right? But all this heavy stuff, this was like a war."

A Yokel jeep jolted its way over the rubble pile in the wake of Task Force Ranson. The driver was young and looked desperately earnest. The Marine major who'd gestured in fury as *Herman's Whore* swept into la Reole at the end of the Slammers' column sat/stood beside the driver.

The officer was covering his mouth and nose with a handkerchief in his left hand while his right gripped the windshield brace to keep his ass some distance in the air. The jeep could follow where air cushions had taken the Slammers, but the wheeled vehicle's suspension and seat padding were in no way sufficient to make the trip a comfortable one.

"This war's been goin' on for bloody years, kid," Ortnahme explained.

His thumb rotated the panorama back to its normal orientation. Bad enough watching the bridge sway, without having the screen's image split *Flamethrower* right down the middle that way.

"They got, the Consies, they been hauling stuff outta the Enclaves all that time, sockin' it away. Bit by bit till they needed it for that last big push. All that stuff—" Ortnahme nodded toward the roiling destruction behind them, though of course the technician couldn't see the gesture "—that means the Consies just shot their bolt."

Ortnahme scratched himself beneath the edge of his armor and chuckled. "Course, it don't mean they didn't *hit* when they shot their bloody bolt."

Cooter's blower had just reached the far end of the bridge—safely, Via! but this tank weight five, six, times as much—when the image on the main screen changed sharply enough to recall the warrant leader from his grim attempt to imagine the next few minutes.

Though *Herman's Whore* pretty well blocked the bridge approach, the driver of the Yokel jeep managed to slide around them with two wheels off on the slope of the embankment. As the jeep gunned its way back onto the concrete, its image filled a broad swath of Ortnahme's screen.

What the bloody *Hell?*

The major threw down his makeshift dust filter, rose to his full height, and began to shout and gesture toward the tank. The young Marines at the bunker beside *Herman's Whore* snapped to attention—eyes front, looking neither toward the tank nor their screaming officer.

Ortnahme could've piped the Yokel's words in through a commo circuit, scrubbed of all the ambient noise. Thing was, whatever the fellow was saying, it sure as hell wasn't anything Warrant Leader Henk Ortnahme wanted to hear.

"Simkins!" he said. "Can you get by these meatballs?"

"Ah . . . Without hitting the jeep?"

"Can you get bloody *by*, you dickhead?"

Herman's Whore shifted sideways like a beerstein on

a slick, wet bar. The fan note built for a moment; then, using all his maintenance-bay skills, Simkins slid them past the jeep closer than a coat of paint.

The wheeled vehicle shrank back on its suspension as the sidedraft from the plenum chamber buffeted it, but metal didn't touch bloody metal!

That Yokel major was probably still pissed off. Then the jeep bobbed in the windthrust, he fell sideways out of his seat. Let him file a bloody complaint with Colonel Hammer—in good time.

The left side of the tank tilted down, but that didn't bother the warrant leader near as much as the motion. It'd been bad watching the bridge sway when another vehicle was on it. The view on Ortnahme's screens hadn't made his stomach turn, thought, as the reality bloody well did. Bloody and martyrs, they were—

They were opening wide cracks in the asphalt surface as they passed over it. The tank's weight was stretching the underlying girders beyond their design limits.

The cracks spread forward, outrunning *Herman's Whore* in its sluggish progress toward the supporting pier in the center of the estuary.

And that *bloody* fool of a major had climbed back into his jeep. His driver had two wheels and most of the jeep's width on the narrow downstream sidewalk, using the span's tilt to advantage because it prevented the tank's sidedraft from flipping the lighter vehicle right through the damaged guardrail.

Those sum'bitch Yokels were trying to pull around the tank and block it on this shuddering nightmare of bridge.

"Kid," Ortnahme began, "don't let em—"

He didn't have to finish the warning, because Simkins was already pouring the coal to his fans.

The water of the Santine Estuary was sluggish and black with tannin from vegetable matter that fed it on the forested hills of its drainage basin. Glutinous white bubbles streaked the surface, giving the current's direction and velocity. The treetrunks, crates, and other solid debris were more or less hidden by the fluid's dark opacity.

Ortnahme had a very good view of the water because of the way *Herman's Whore* tilted toward it.

They were approaching the central pier now while the span behind them flexed like the E-string of a bass guitar. The jeep, caught in the pulses and without the tank's weight to damp them, bounced all four wheels off the gaping roadway while the two Yokels clung for dear life.

Consie shells and the bolts from their own bunkered powergun had reduced the central towers to half their original height. The Yokels at the guardpost there were already climbing piles of rubble to be clear of the oncoming tank. *Herman's Whore* wasn't rocketing forward, but a tank head-on at twenty kph looks like Juggernaut on a joyride.

Their speed was four times what Ortnahme had planned, given the flimsy structure of the bridge. He just hadn't realized *how* bloody flimsy.

They *had* to go fast!

Ortnahme's helmet crackled with angry demands from the east bank. He switched the sound off at the console.

Tootsie Six could burn him a new one if she wanted, just as soon as *Herman's Whore* reached solid ground again. Until then, he didn't give a hoot in Hell what anybody but his driver had to say.

They reached the central pier in a puff of dust and clanging gravel, debris from the towers. Task Force Ranson's previous vehicles had rammed a track clear, but the kid was moving too fast to be nice about what his skirts scraped.

The Yokel jeep halted on the solid pier. The major shook his fist, but he didn't seem to be ordering his guards to try buzzbombs where verbal orders had failed.

Via, maybe they were going to make it after all. That newbie crew in Blue Three had crossed, hadn't—

A cable parted, whanging loud enough to be clearly audible. A second *whang!*, a third—

The bow of *Herman's Whore* was tilting upward. The intake howl of her fans proved that Simkins had both throttle banks slid wideflatopen.

It wasn't going to be enough.

The cables parting were the short loops every meter or so, attaching the main support cable to the bridge span. Each time one broke, the next ahead took the doubled strain of the tank's weight—and broke in turn. The asphalt roadway crumbled instantly, but the unsupported stringers beneath continued to hold for a second or two longer—until they stretched beyond steel's modulus of tension.

Thirty meters behind *Herman's Whore*, the span fell away from the central pier and splashed into the estuary. Froth from its impact drifted sullenly downstream.

The tank was accelerating toward safety at fifty kph and rising, but their bow was pointing up at thirty-five, forty, forty-five—

For an instant, *Herman's Whore* was climbing at an angle of forty-seven degrees with the east tower within a hundred meters and the round, visored faces of everybody in the task force staring at them in horror. Then the spray of the tank bellying down into the estuary hid everything for the few seconds before her roaring fans stalled out in the thicker medium.

Warrant Leader Ortnahme lifted his foot to the top of his seat and thrust his panting body upward. His eyes had just reached the level of the cupola hatch when water rushing in the opposite direction met him.

Easy, easy. He was fine if he didn't bloody panic. . . . The catches of his body armor, top and bottom; shrugging sideways, feeling them release, feeling the ceramic weight drop away instead of sinking even *his* fat to a grave in the bottom muck.

The water was icy and tasted of salt. Bubbles of air

gurgled past Ortnahme as *Herman's Whore* gave its death rattle. Violet sparks flickered in the blackness as millions of dollars worth of superb, state-of-the-art electronics shorted themselves into melted junk.

Ortnahme's skin tingled. His diaphragm contracted, preventing him from taking the breath he intended as a last great gurgling shivered past his body to empty the turret of air. He shoved himself upward to follow the bubble to the surface.

He was halfway through the hatch when his equipment belt hooked on the string of grenades again.

The warrant leader reached down for the belt buckle. The drag of water on his shirtsleeves slowed the movement, but it was all going to be—

The belt had twisted. He couldn't find the buckle though his fingers scrabbled wildly and his legs strained upward in an attempt to break web gear from which Ortnahme's unconscious mind knew you could support a bloody *howitzer* in mid-air.

Air. Blood and martyrs. He tried to scream.

Herman's Whore grounded with a slurping impact that added mud to the taste of salt and blood in Ortnahme's mouth. They couldn't be more than three meters down; but a millimeter was plenty deep enough if it was over your mouth and nose.

Plenty deep enough to drown.

The darkness pressing the warrant leader's eyes began to pulse deep red with his heartbeats, a little fainter each time. He thought he felt something brush his chest, but he couldn't be sure and he didn't think his fingers were moving anymore.

The wire parted. A grip on Ortnahme's belt added its pull to the warrant leader's natural buoyancy.

Sunlight came as a dazzling explosion. Ortnahme bobbed, sneezed in reaction. Water sprayed from his nostrils.

Tech 2 Simkins was dog-paddling with a worried look.

he was trying to retract the cutting blade of his multitool, but his face kept dipping beneath the surface.

One of the combat cars had just waddled down the bank. It was poised to lift across the water as soon as the man in the stern—Cooter, it was, from his size and the crucifix on his breastplate—unlimbered a tow line for the swimmers to grab as the car skittered by.

"Sir," Simkins said. His face was wet from dunking, but Ortnahme would swear there were tears in his eyes as well. "Sir, I'm sorry. I tried to hold it but I—"

He was blubbering, all right, but the black water slapped him again when he forgot to paddle. Sometimes being hog fat and able to float had advantages. . . .

"Sir—" the kid repeated as his streaming visage lifted again.

"Via, kid!" Ortnahme said, almost choking on his swollen tongue. He'd bitten the bloody hell out of it as he struggled. "Will you shut yer bleedin' trap?"

Flamethrower roared as it moved onto the water.

"If I ever have a son," Ortnahme shouted over the fan noise, "I'll name the little bastard Simkins!"

Chapter Eleven

"I thought," said Dick Suilin, looking down at the silent trench line as *Flamethrower* accelerated past, "that we'd have to fight our way out of la Reole, too."

It must have rained recently, because ankle-deep mud slimed the bottom of the trench. Two bodies lay face down in it. Their black uniforms smoldered around the holes chewed by shell fragments.

The bruises beneath Suilin's armor itched unbearably.

"I wonder what my sister's doing," he added inconsequently.

"The Consies were just tacking the west bank down," Cooter said, his eyes on his multi-function display. "Nothin' serious."

"Nothin' that wasn't gonna run like rabbits when the shells hit—thems as could," Gale interjected with a chuckle.

"All their heavy stuff this side of the river," the lieutenant continued, "that's at Kohang."

He shrugged. "Where we'll find it quick enough, I guess."

"Where's your sister?" Gale asked. The veteran gunner poked a knifepoint into the crust around the ejection port of his tribarrel. Jets of liquid nitrogen were supposed to cool and expel powergun rounds from the chambers after firing. A certain amount of the plastic matrix remained gaseous until it condensed on the outside of the receiver, narrowing the port.

Suilin unlatched his body armor and began rubbing the raw skin over his ribs. His fatigue shirt was sweaty, but the drenching in salt spray from the estuary seemed to have made the itch much worse.

"She's in Kohang," the reporter said. It was hard to remember what he'd said to whom about his background, about Suzette. "She's married to Governor Kung."

The past two days were a blur of gray and cyan. Maybe fatigue, maybe the drugs he was taking against the fatigue.

Maybe the way his life had been turned inside out, like the body of the Consie guerrilla his tribarrel had centerpunched. . . .

"Whoo-ie!" Gale chorted. "Well, if that's who she is, I sure hope she don't mind meetin' a few good men. Er a few hundred!"

The reporter went cold.

Cooter reached over and took Gale's jaw between a

big thumb and forefinger. "Shut up, Windy," he said. "Just shut the fuck up, all right?"

"Sorry," muttered the wing gunner to Suilin. He brushed his mouth with the back of his hand. "Look, the place's still holdin', far as we know. We'll get there, no sweat."

He nodded to Cooter. "Anything on your box, El-tee?"

"Nothing yet. Junebug'll report in pretty quick, I guess."

The task force was moving fast in the open country between la Reole and Kohang further up the coast. A clump of farm buildings stood beneath an orchard-planted hillside two kilometers away.

Suilin found it odd to be able to see considerable distances with his normal eyesight. He felt as though he'd crewed *Flamethrower* all his life, but this was the first time he'd been aboard the combat car during daylight.

Almost daylight. The sun was still beneath the horizon. His fingertips massaged his ribs.

"You okay?" Gale asked unexpectedly.

"Huh?" Suilin said. He looked down at his bruises. Oh, yeah. I—the armor, last night a bullet hit it."

He saw Gale's eyes widen in surprise a moment before he realized the cause. "Oh," he corrected. "I mean the night before. At Camp Progress. I lost track. . . ."

Cooter handed out ration bars. The reporter stared at his with loathing, remembering the taste of the previous one.

"Go ahead," Cooter encouraged. "You need the calories. The Wide-awakes, they'll keep you moving, but you need the fuel to burn anyhow."

Suilin bit down, trying to ignore the flavor. This bar seemed to have been compressed from muck at the bottom of the estuary.

The two tankers they'd rescued wanted to stay together, so Cooter had transferred them both to One-six. The vehicles of Task Force Ranson were fully crewed at the moment—over-crewed, in fact.

Dick Suilin had seen at Adako Beach how quickly a short burst could wipe out the crew of a combat car. Without the firepower of the two tanks lost at la Reole. . . .

Funny to have another combat car directly ahead of *Flamethrower*. The only view of the task force the reporter'd had during most of the night was the stern of the tank which now lay at the bottom of the Santine.

"Will they raise her?" he asked. "The, that is, the tank that fell off the bridge?"

"Through the bloody bridge," Gale corrected.

"The hull's worth something," Cooter said.

His lips pursed in a moue. "Maybe the gun could be rebuilt to standard. But the really pricy stuff's the electronics, and that's all screwed for good 'n all. I figure the Colonel, he'll combat loss it and the other one both and try to squeeze a victory bonus outta your people to pay for 'em."

His eyes swept the horizon, looking for an enemy or a sign. "Lord knows we'll 've earned a bonus. If we win."

The display box beside Cooter's tribarrel clucked and spat.

"C'mon, El-tee," Gale demanded greedily. "What's she sayin'?"

"Give it a minute, will you?" the lieutenant said as he stared at his display. "It's a coded burst, right? And that takes a while."

Gale nodded to Suilin. "Tootsie's talkin' to the Old Man," the veteran explained. "Ain't meant for us to hear, but this close, we kin read anything she kin code."

He giggled. "The black box giveth and the black box taketh away."

"Bloody hell," Cooter muttered.

"Well, *c'mon!*"

"She told him we were across the Santine," Cooter

said, still watching the display where holograms spelled words decoded by the vehicle's AI. "She told him about the casualties. Told him we were going ahead with the mission."

"Well, what did ya bloody expect?" Gale snorted. "Come this far and settle down to rest 'n refit?"

Cooter turned to face the other two men. He looked very worn. "Also she told Central," he went on, "that we were getting messages from First of the Fourth Armored Brigade. They're ahead of us and they're requesting our positions so they can join up with us."

"Via," said Gale.

Dick Suilin blinked, "So we'll have a National armored battalion to support us in entering Kohang?" he said, puzzled at the mercenaries' attitude. "I didn't realize there were any friendly units this near the city."

"Via," Gale repeated. He scowled at the tribarrel, picking at the ejection port with a cracked fingernail. "How many bloody tanks in a Yokel battalion?"

In the frozen moment before anybody else spoke, Dick Suilin remembered the truck he'd ripped apart near the Padma, a National Army vehicle filled with troops in National Army uniforms.

"I said it was First of the Fourth," Cooter said. "I didn't say they were friendly."

Warmonger had settled into a reed-choked draw. The other vehicles were invisible, but June Ranson's display indicated that all of them were in place and awaiting her orders.

Steam rising from la Reole behind them was golden in the light of sunrise.

Janacek watched her expectantly; Stolley scanned the sky past the reed bracts with a scowl of displeasure. He knew there wasn't a prayer that he'd be able to hit any incoming with his tribarrel, but he was determined to try.

Blue Three was the only task force vehicle in the

open, poised 300 meters to the east on what passed for high ground in this coastal terrain. Its cupola gun quivered in air defense mode.

When their sole remaining tank could provide *sufficient* defense depended on what came through the air at the task force while its leader held the vehicles grounded for a council of war.

Maybe nothing would come. Probably nothing would come.

"Booster," said Junebug Ranson. "Council display, all Tootsie units."

Her multi-function display hummed and clicked. Faces glowed in the thirty-centimeter cube, replacing the holographic map and location beads. She'd have done better to use the tank's big screens, but she couldn't risk leaving her command vehicle here.

They were within twenty kays of Kohang. Everything that had occurred since they left Camp Progress, the danger and the losses, was only a prelude to what would happen in the next few hours.

Faces—the entire fighting-compartment crews of the other four combat cars, and the tense, tightlipped visage of Wager in the turret of Blue Three—crowded the multi-function display.

For a moment, no one spoke; the crews were waiting for Ranson, and June Ranson's mind was extending into a universe of phosphor dots.

The image of Cooter's face brightened and swelled slightly to highlight it as the lieutenant said, "Junebug, we gotta figure these guys've gone over to the Consies. They left Camp Victory without orders, just before the general attack. Only question is, do we go around 'em or do we fight 'em?"

"We're tasked to get there, not to fight, ain't we?" said Tillman, blower captain of One-five. At the best of times, Tillman was a thin, sallow man. The past two days had sweated off weight he couldn't afford to lose.

"Look, just in case they are friendly . . ." said Chalkin. He looked sour, partly because he was crowded in the fighting compartment of One-six with Ortnahme and Simkins as well as the shot-up survivors of the car's original crew. "I wouldn't mind havin' fifty tanks alongside us when we hit Kohang, even if it's Yokels."

"Max of forty-four tanks," interjected Warrant Leader Ortnahme, looking at something off-screen low, probable his clenched knuckles. There were problems on One-six, *Daisy Belle*; not just the crowding, but a fat noncombatant with a lot of rank, dropped on a blower commanded by a mere Senior Trooper on transfer.

"There were forty-four at their bloody laager when the drone overflew 'em," Ortnahme continued, looking straight at the pick-up in the car's multi-function display. "Some'll be dead-lined, twenty percent given what passes fer Yokel maintenance."

His fingers rose into the tiny field-of-view, ticking off the third point: "Some more drop out on the route march to block us when they've finl'ly get the lead out. So, say thirty-five max, maybe thirty."

"And," said Cooter's voice in the enfolding electronic tendrils of June Ranson's mind, "there's no bloody way—"

"—that those bastards're friendly," Cooter snapped at the hologram display beside his tribarrel while Dick Suilin shivered on the ribbed plastic crates of ammunition lining the interior of the fighting compartment.

At the signal to halt in dispersed order for council, *Flamethrower* had forced its way into a thicket of knotbushes. Their gnarled branches sprang back to full four-meter height behind the vehicle, concealing the combat car on all sides and even covering it fairly well from above.

"Look, just 'cause they sat out the last couple days—" argued a voice that had spoken earlier, not one that the reporter recognized.

The net wasn't wide open, as Suilin first thought. The computer—the AI— controlling the discussion cut off whoever was talking the instant someone higher in the hierarchy began to speak.

"There was *no* sign from the recce flight that they'd been hit," Cooter boomed onward. "With all the Consies did the other night, there was *no* chance they'd 've ignored a tank battalion—except it'd gone over or it was about t' go over."

Suilin's face was turned slightly away from the display. There was probably a way to magnify the images through his helmet visor, but he didn't much care.

He felt awful, as though he were in the midst of a bad bout of flu. Despite his chills, his throat felt parched. He gestured toward the cooler on which Gale sat.

The veteran shook his head, then nodded in explanation toward the display.

"Later," he said in a husky whisper that presumably wouldn't carry to the pick-up. He tossed Suilin another Wide-awake. "You're on the down side. No sweat. You'll get used t'it."

"Via, still wouldn't mind havin' the help," muttered a voice from the display. "*Some* cursed help."

The cone sent needles of delicious ice up the throat vein to which Suilin applied it. Gray fog cleared from his eyes. The holographic display sprang into focus, though the figures in it were featurelessly small.

He realized that Captain Ranson hadn't spoken during the discussion.

As thought the jolt of stimulant in the reporter's bloodstream had unblocked the commander's tongue, the mercenary captain's cool—cold—voice said, "We are nearly in contact with a force of uncertain loyalty, estimated to be a battalion of thirty to thirty-five armored vehicles."

Tiny, toothed birds jumped and chittered through the branches of the knotbushes, ignoring the iridium mon-

ster in their midst. Their wings were covered with pale
fur, familiar to Suilin but probably exotic to his mercenary companions.

"If the battalion is allied with the Conservative Action
Movement, it will threaten the rear of Task Force Ranson
as the task force performs its mission of breaking through
hostile forces encircling the Governmental Compound
in Kohang."

The sense of glacial well-being reached Suilin's fingertips. His hands stopped shaking.

Probably *not* exotic. The Lord only knew how many
worlds, how many life-forms, these scarred veterans had
seen uncaring on their career of slaughter for money. . . .

"The loyalty of the battalion must first be ascertained.
If hostile, the force must be engaged and neutralized
before Task Force Ranson proceeds with its primary
mission."

"Thirty bloody tanks," Cooter whispered.

"We will proceed as follows. First, I will inform the
armored battalion that we have received heavy casualties and have taken refuge in the settlement of Kawana."

"Even bloody Yokel tanks. . . ."

"Blue three—"

Hans Wager's head jerked up. You can only stay scared
for so long. Ranson's clop-clop mechanical delivery had
bored him, so his attention had been on the holographic
plan of a Yokel tank he'd called up on Screen Three.

"—will take a position north of Kawana, behind Chin
Peng Rise."

"Roger, Tootsie Six," Wager said, suddenly afraid that
he'd actually fallen asleep and missed some crucial part
of the Operations Order.

"Set your sensors for maximum sensitivity," Ranson's
voice continued without noticeable emotion. "You will
supply the precise location and strength of the other
force. In event the force proves hostile, you will be the

blocking element to prevent them breaking out to the north."

"Roger, Tootsie Six," Wager repeated in a whisper.

They didn't operate with Yokel armor—the difference in speed was too great, and the mercenaries had a well-justified concern about the fire discipline of the local forces in general.

Still, Wager'd looked over Yokel tanks out of curiosity. Memories echoed in his mind when his eyes rested on the holographic image.

"We can expect the other force to continue their approach from due south," Ranson's bored, boring voice continued. "Tootsie Three, you'll command the eastern element. Proceed with your blower and One-six clockwise from Chin Peng Rise, around Kawana by Hull Creek and Raider Camp Creek. Stay out of sight. Wait at the head of Radier Camp Creek, a kilometer east of Sugar Knob to the south of Kawana."

Via, thirty of them. If it wasn't thirty-five.

Or forty-four, despite Blue Two's scorn of the Yokel's ability to keep their hardware operational.

Each tank weighed sixteen point eight tonnes. They were track-laying vehicles with five road-wheels per side and the drive sprocket forward. Steel/ceramic sandwich armor. Diesel engine on the right side, opposite the driver. A two-man turret with either a high-velocity 60mm automatic cannon or a 130mm howitzer.

Lighweight vehicles, designed for the particular needs of the National Army in a guerrilla war that might at any moment burst into pitched battles with a foe equipped by the Terran World Government.

Nothing Wager's panzer couldn't handle, one on one. Nothing a combat car couldn't handle, one on one.

Thirty. Or Thirty-five. Or more.

"I will command the western element," Ranson said coolly. "Cars One-one, One-three, and One-five," We'll circle Kawana by Upper Creek and wait a kilometer west of Sugar Knob until the intentions of the other force become clear.

A shaped-charge round from the 130mm howitzer moved too fast for the close-in defense system to knock it down. A direct hit could penetrate the armor of a Slammer's tank.

The 60mm guns fired either high-explosive shells or armor-piercing shot. A single tungsten-carbide shot wouldn't penetrate Blue Three's hull or turret armor. Three hitting the same point might. Twelve on the same point *would* penetrate.

The clip-loaded 60mm cannon could cycle twelve rounds in twelve seconds.

"Blue Three," Ranson said, "if the other battalion is hostile, we will need *precise* data on enemy disposition before we launch our counterattack. This may require that you move into the open so that your sensors are unmasked. Do you understand?"

"Roger, Tootsie Six."

Hans Wager's hands were wiping themselves slowly against his pants legs. The rhythmic, unconscious gesture dried his palms for less than the time it took for his arms to move back and start the process again.

"Blue Three—" still no emotion in the voice "—if you like, for this operation I can replace you and your driver with more experienced—"

"Negative!" Wager snarled. He hand-keyed his helmet to break out of the council net. "Tootsie Six, that's a negative. We'll do our job. We understand. Out."

"Roger, Blue Three," said the voice. "All Tootsie units, courses and phase lines are being down-loaded into your AIs—now."

Wager's palms rubbed his thighs.

"Sarge?" whispered his intercom. "Thanks."

"Don't thank me, Holman," Wager said. "I think I just bought us both the farm."

Thirty or more guns aimed at them, and Blue

Three wouldn't be able to reply until the combat cars had the data needed to target every one of the enemy tanks.

Yeah, he understood all right.

Chapter Twelve

"D'ye got medics along?" the driver from Blue Three whined over the radio, a female voice in June Ranson's ears.

She sounded stunned and terrified, just as she was supposed to. The tank was the only vehicle of Task Force Ranson that would give a close-enough-to-correct reading of Yokel direction finders. . . .

"Via, we need medics. Via we need help. This is ah, Tootsie Six, over."

A game, a test program for the officer commanding 1st of the 4th armored. An electronic construct which was perfectly believable, like any good test program. The officer being tested would be judged on his reactions. . . .

"Booster," Ranson muttered. "Hostile Order of Battle."

She shouldn't have to speak. Electrons should flow from her nerve endings and race down the gold-foil channels of the artificial intelligence, then spring over high-frequency carrier waves to the sensor array of Blue Three. June Ranson should feel everything.

She should be the vehicles she commanded. . . .

"Tootsie Six, this is Delta three Mike four one," replied the voice that had been unfamiliar until it began whispering over the UHF Allied Common channel an hour before, requesting Task Force Ranson's position. "We have doctors and medical supplies. We're ten kilometers from Kawana. We'll bring your medical help in half an hour, but you must stay where you are. Do you understand? Mike four one over."

The water of Upper-Creek flared beneath *Warmonger* in a veil. The spray was iridescent where daggers of sunlight stabbed it through the low canopy. The two cars closely following *Warmonger* were hidden by the spray and the creek's wide loops.

Upper Creek drained the area south of Sugar Knob. The trees here had been cropped about ten years before so that their cellulose could be converted by bacteria to crude protein for animal feed. The second-growth trees that replaced the original forest were densely packed and had thin boles. They provided good cover, but they weren't obstacles for vehicles of the power and weight of combat cars.

Yokel tanks would find the conditions passable also, even if they left the trails worn by animals and the local populace.

"We can't go anywhere," Blue Three's driver whined. "We—"

Warmonger's artificial intelligence threw a print sidebar on the holographic condenser lens.

"—only got two cars left and they're shot t'bloody hell. We're right at the little store, where the road crosses the crik."

Willens, following the course Ranson and the AI set for him, nosed *Warmonger* against the north bank of the creek. The black, root-laced soil rose only a meter above the black, peat-rich water. The car snorted then mounted to firm ground through a bending wall of saplings.

The distance between barren Chin Peng Rise and the thin trees of Sugar Knob was about a kilometer and a half. Ranson's western element followed a winding three-kay course to stay low and unnoticed while encircling the Yokels' expected deployment area. Cooter and the two-car eastern element had an even longer track to follow to their hide . . . but the Yokel tanks seemed to be giving them the time they needed.

Willens advanced twenty meters further, to give room to One-five and One-one behind him, then settled with his fans on idle.

Task Force Ranson didn't want to stumble into contact before they knew where all their targets were.

Blue Three's sensors had greater range and precision by an order of magnitude than those crammed into the combat cars, but the cars could process the data passed to them by the larger vehicle. The sidebar on Ranson's multi-function display listed callsigns, isolated in the cross-talk overheard by the superb electronics of the tank pretending to be in Kawana while it waited behind Chin Peng Rise north of the tiny hamlet.

There were twenty-five individual callsigns. The AI broke them down as three companies each consisting of three platoons—but no more than four tanks in any platoon (five would have been full strength). Some platoons were postulated from a single callsign.

Not all the Yokel tanks would be indulging in the loose chatter that laid them out for Task Force Ranson like a roast for the carving; but most of them would, most of them were surely identified. The red cross-hatching that overlay the relief map in the main field of the display was the AI's best estimate thus far of the armored battalion's dispositions.

Blue Three was the frame of the trap and the bait within it; but the five combat cars of west and east elements were the spring-loaded jaws that would snap the rat's neck.

And this rat, Yokel or Consie, was lying. It was clear that the leading elements of 1st of the 4th were already deploying onto the southern slope of Sugar Knob, half a kilometer from the store and shanties of Kawana rather than the ten kays their commander claimed.

In the next few seconds, the commander of the armored battalion would decide whether he wanted to meet allied mercenaries—or light the fuse that would certainly detonate in a battle more destructive than any a citizen of Prosperity could imagine. He was being tested. . . .

The two sharp green beads of Lieutenant Cooter's element settled into position.

She heard a whisper in the southern sky. *Incoming*.

"All right, Holman, move us hull-down," Hans Wager ordered as his driver whined, "They're shooting at us! They're shooting at us!" over the Allied Common Channel and the scream of the incoming salvo wrote its own exclamation point in four crashing impacts on the valley below.

The nameless tank lifted, scraped, and hopped forward—up and out of its stand-by hide to a position so near the crest of Chin Peng Rise that the turret and sensor arrays had a clear sight across Kawana to the slumping mass of Sugar Knob beyond.

The hamlet had never been prepossessing. It was less so now that the ill-aimed Consie salvo had shaken down several shacks. Raider Camp Creek rolled with the muddy aftermath of the shell that had landed on it, and the footbridge paralleling the ford had collapsed into the turbid current.

Men and women in the sugarbush fields dropped their tools to run for their homes. The sandy rows in which the bushes were planted would've given better protection than the board walls of the shanties.

That much came to Wager's eyes from the direct view of his main screen. Screen Three displayed the data his chuckling AI processed, a schematic vision of the terrain behind Sugar Knob and the unseen Yokel tanks showing themselves to Wager's sensors.

A sidebar on the Main screen noted an incoming

second salvo, ten rounds but very ragged—even for Yokel artillery.

The Yokel vehicles were diesel-powered, so Wager's tank couldn't locate them precisely from sparkcoil emissions; but their diesels had interjector motors whose RF output could be pin-pointed by the Slammers' sensors.

Without the added shielding of Chin Peng Ridge to block Blue Three, the cross-hatched blur south of Sugar Knob on Screen Three began to coalesce into bright red beads: Yokel tanks, located to within a few meters.

Their disposition explained why the second salvo was so scattered. The Consies were using the 130mm howitzers on ten of their tanks to supplement regular artillery firing from the vicinity of Kohang.

For indirect fire, these tanks were concentrated in a tight arc along Upper Creek. They'd run their bows up on the north bank in order to get more elevation for their howitzers than their turret mechanisms would permit.

The tank shells scattered around Kawana, detonating with white flashes and the hollow *whoomps* characteristic of shape-charge antitank warheads. Sand spewed in great harmless fountains.

The store where the unpaved road forded the creek flung its walls sideways at a direct hit. Half a body arced into the water and sank.

"Six, this is Blue Three!" Wager shouted. "Am I clear to shoot?"

Then, though Ranson could see it herself as easily as Wager could if the crazy bitch saw *anything*, "Six, there's ten tanks a kilometer south of the Knob, just off the road, but the rest of the bastards are moving onto the crest!"

The Yokels were moving into direct-fire positions covering Kawana . . . and which covered the tank on Chin Peng Rise with no more cover than the fuzz on a baby's ass.

The saplings on Sugar Knob shifted with the weight

of black masses behind them, the dark-camouflaged bows of Consie tanks.

Two, three; seven tanks highlighted by Wager's AI. Their high-velocity 60mm cannons quested toward Kawana like the feelers of loathsome crustaceans. There were men in black uniforms riding on each turret.

If Wager fired, the plasma jolt from his powergun would blind and deafen the sensors on which the combat cars depended.

One of the long-barreled cannon suddenly lifted and turned. The tank commander had seen the gray gleam of the real enemy lurking behind Chin Peng Rise.

Red location beads were still appearing on Screen Three, the same view that was being remoted to the combat car AIs, but surely Ranson had enough data to—

"Tootsie Six!" Hans Wager cried, "Can you clear us?"

"Sarge, I'm backing—" Holman said.

"All Tootsie units," said the voice of Captain Ranson. "Take 'em."

The muzzle flash was a bright yellow blaze against the dark camouflage. The tungsten-carbide shot rang like a struck cymbal on the turret of Wager's nameless tank.

"Willens," said June Ranson, converting the holographic map on her display into a reality more concrete than the stems of young trees around her, "steer one-twenty degrees. West element, conform to my movements."

"Why we doin' this?" Stolley shouted, grabbing the captain's left arm and tugging to turn her.

Off to the left, only slightly muffled by intervening vegetation, the flat cracks of high velocity guns sounded from the crest of Sugar Knob.

Ranson slipped her arm from the wing gunner's grip. "Thirty seconds to contact," her voice said.

Warmonger's artificial intelligence had given her a

vector marker. Her eyes were on it, waiting for the vertical red line to merge with a target in her gunsights.

Stolley cursed and put his hands back on the grips of his tribarrel.

The gunfire from Sugar Knob doubled in intensity. *Warmonger* and the two cars accompanying it were headed away from the knob on a slating course. As *Warmonger* switched direction, the AI fed another target vector to each gunner's helmet.

A wrist-thick sampling flicked Ranson's tribarrel to the side. Her hands realigned the weapon with the vector. They acted by reflex, unaided by the higher centers of her brain which slid beads of light in a glowing three-dimensional gameboard.

Her solution to the Yokel attack had been as simple and risky as Task Force Ranson's lack of resources required. She was using Slammers' electronics and speed to accomplish what their present gunpower and armor could not.

So, Candidate Ranson. You've decided to divide your force before attacking a superior concentration. Rather like Colonel Custer's plan at the Little Big Horn, wouldn't you say?

But there was no choice. The Yokels would deploy along the ridge. Only by hitting them simultaneously from behind on both flanks could her combat cars roll up six or seven times their number of hostile tanks.

So, Candidate; you're confident that the opposing commander won't keep a reserve? If he does, it's your force—forces, I should say—that will be outflanked.

The Yokels hadn't held back a reserve . . . but the ten tanks lobbing shells over the knob from a kilometer to the rear would *act* as a reserve—if they weren't eliminated first.

Guns fired from Sugar Knob a kilometer away, guns on the Yokel left flank that Ranson had decided to bypass only thirty seconds before—

Warmonger burst into a clearing gray with powdersmoke and dust kicked up by the ten stubby howitzers firing at high angles.

The Yokel tanks had their engines forward and their turrets mounted well back, over the fourth pair of roadwheels. With their hulls raised fifteen degrees by the stream bank, the vehicles bucked dangerously every time they fired their heavy weapons. The water of Upper Creek slapped between the recoiling tanks and its gravel bed.

The tanks were parked in the creek to either side of the road. Less than a three-meter hill width separated each vehicle from its neighbors. While the turret crews fed their gun, the tank drivers stood on both ends of the line of vehicles, mixing with a dozen guerrillas in black uniforms.

The dismounted men covered their ears with their palms and opened their mouths to equalize pressure from the muzzle blasts. When the three combat cars slid from the forest, their hands dropped but their mouths continued to gape like the jaws of gaffed fish.

Men spun and fell, shedding body parts, as Ranson's tribarrel lashed them. The group on the east side of the lined-up tanks had time to shout and run a few steps before *Warmonger* raced down Upper Creek as though the gravel bed were a highway, giving Ranson and Stolley shots at them also.

The Yokel tanks couldn't react fast enough to be an immediate danger, but a single Consie rifleman could clear *Warmonger*'s fighting compartment.

Could *have*. When the last black-clad guerrilla flopped at the edge of the treeline, Willens spun *Warmonger* in a cataclysm of spray and the three tribarrels blazed into the backs on the renegade tanks.

One-one and One-five had followed *Warmonger* into the stream, but they hadn't had to worry about the dismounted enemy. Two of the left-side tanks were already wrapped in sooty orange palls of burning diesel fuel. The turret blew off a third as main gun ammunition detonated in the hull.

Ranson centered her projection sight on a tank's back deck, just behind the turret ring. The target's slope gave her a perfect shot. Cyan bolts streamed through the holographic image of her sight, splashing huge craters in thin armor designed only to stop shell splinters.

In gunnery simulators, the screaming tank crew didn't try to abandon their vehicle a second or two after it was to late. Ranson's bolts punched into the interior of the tank. A blast of foul white smoke erupted from the turret hatches and the cavity ripped by the tribarrel.

The tank commander and the naked torso of his gunner flew several meters in the air. The tank began to burn sluggishly.

June Ranson's hands swung from another target, but there were no targets remaining here.

The tanks' thickest armor was frontal. Striking from above and behind, the tribarrels ripped them as easily as so many cans of sardines.

Cans of barbecued pork. The gunnery simulators didn't provide the odor of close action, either.

All the ammunition on a Yokel tank detonated simultaneously, pushing aside the nearest vehicles and flinging the turret roof fifty meters in the air in a column of smoke.

"Willens, steer three hundred degrees," Ranson heard/ said. "West element, form on me."

Her eyes sought the multi-function display, while part of her mind wondered why she couldn't blend with Cooter's vehicles when she wanted to know their progress. . . .

Dick Suilin's ribs slammed hard against the edge of the fighting compartment as *Flamethrower* grounded heavily on its mad rush through the scrub forest. The reporter swore and wondered whether he'd be pissing blood in the morning, despite the clamshell armor that protected his kidney from the worst of the shock.

In the morning. He made a high-pitched sound somewhere between laughter and madness.

He'd fallen sideways because the only thing that he had to hang onto were the grips of his tribarrel. *That* was pointed over the left side, at ninety degrees to the combat car's direction of motion. The reporter swung back and forth as his weapon pivoted.

The blazing red-orange hairline on his visor demanded Suilin cover the left side. He horsed his gun in the proper direction again, wincing at the pain in his side, and tried to find a target in the whipping foliage.

There was no doubt where *Flamethrower*'s artificial intelligence wanted him to aim, though the rational part of the reporter's mind wondered why. They had—they were supposed to have—enveloped the enemy's right wing, so the first targets would be on the right side of *Flamethrower*. . . .

He supposed *Daisy Belle* was somewhere behind them. He supposed the other vehicles of the task force were somewhere also. He hadn't seen much of them. . . .

Dick Suilin supposed a lot of things; but all he knew was that his side hurt, his hands hurt from their grip on the automatic weapon, and that he really should've pissed in the minute while they waited for the go signal.

Flamethrower slid through a curtain of reeds. Two meters from the muzzle of Suilin's tribarrel, *that close*, was a tank with its hatches open, bogged in a swale. The soil was so damp that water gleamed in the ruts the treads had squeezed before being choked to a halt.

Right where the AI's vector had said it would be.

Suilin clamped his trigger so convulsively that he forgot for a moment that he was pointing a weapon. Two bolts splashed on the turret face, cyan and white, blazing steel, before several following swathes in the reeds with blasts of steam and flying cellulose.

Flamethrower grunted past the tank's bow at the speed of a running horse. The reporter pivoted to follow the target with his gun, ignoring the way he thrust himself against the sidearmor just as the impact had done moments before.

His sights steadied where a ball mantlet joined the tank's slim cannon to the target face. Panning like a photographer with a moving subject, Suilin kept the muzzles aligned as they spat cyan hell to within millimeters, bolt by bolt.

Suilin would have kept shooting, but the cannon barrel sagged and a sharp explosion lifted the turret a hand's breadth so that bright flame could flash momentarily all around the ring.

He didn't notice until they were past that there'd been a second tank on the other side of the swale, and that several men in National Army uniforms had been stringing tow cables between the vehicles. The second tank was burning fiercely. The crewmen were sprawled in the arc they'd managed to run before Gale's tribarrel searched them down.

Suilin thought the men were wearing black armbands, but he no longer really cared.

Dick Suilin heard the CRACK-CRACK-CRACK of automatic cannons upslope, the same timbre as machineguns firing but louder, much louder, despite the vegetation.

Shorty Rogers was running the valley south of Sugar Knob at a hellbent pace for the conditions. *Warmonger* cut to the right, bypassing some of the unseen tanks whose gunfire betrayed their presence.

Maybe the course was deliberate. Maybe *Daisy Belle* would take care of the other tanks. . . .

Suilin saw tank tracks slanting toward the crest an instant before he saw the tank itself, backing the way it had come. There was a guerrilla on the turret, hammering at the closed hatch. The Consie shouted something inaudible.

Suilin fired, aiming at the Consie rather than the tank. He missed both; his bolts sailed high to shatter trees on the crest.

That didn't matter. Cooter's helmet had given him the same target. The lieutenant's tribarrel focused on the hull where flowing script read *Queen of the South*. Paint blazed an instant before the armor collapsed and a fuel tank ruptured in a belch of flame.

Beyond *Queen of the South*, backing also, was a command vehicle with a high enclosed cap instead of a turret. Suilin caught only a glimpse of the vehicle before Gale's tribarrel punched through the thin vertical armor of the cab.

The rear door opened. Nothing came out except an arm flopping in its black sleeve.

They had almost reached the top of the knob. If *Daisy Belle* fired at them, the bolts would hit on Gale's side; but if *Flamethrower* was closing with the three cars in Captain Ranson's elements—

Dick Suilin aimed downhill because the glowing line directed him that way, but the artificial intelligence was using data now minutes old. The Consie tank was above them, backing around in the slender trees. It swung the long gun in its turret to cover the threat that bellowed toward it in a drumbeat of secondary explosions.

Suilin tried to point at the unexpected target. Cooter was firing as he swung his own weapon, but that tribarrel didn't bear either and the lash of cyan bolts across treeboles did nothing to disconcert the hostile gunner.

The cannon steadied on *Flamethrower*'s hull.

A twenty-centimeter bolt from Blue Three across the valley struck, and the whole stern of the light tank blew skyward.

The Yokel tank's shot was a white streak in the sky as it ricocheted from the face of Blue Three's turret.

Ragged blotches appeared on Wager's main screen as if the hologram were a mirror losing its silver backing. Booster spread the load of the damaged receptor heads among the remainder; the image cleared.

Hans Wager didn't see what was happening to his screen because he was bracing his head against it. He hadn't strapped himself into his seat, and Holman's attempt to back her hundred and seventy tonnes finally succeeded in a rush.

Wager wasn't complaining. His hatch was open and he could hear the *crack-crack* of two more hypersonic shots snapping overhead.

The Yokels' armor-piercing projectiles were only forty-three millimeters in diameter when they dropped their sabots at the gun's muzzle, but even here, a kilometer and a half away, they were traveling at 1800 meters per second. The shot that hit had smashed a dish-sized concavity from the face of Blue Three's armor.

"Holman!" Wager cried. "Open season! Get us Hulldown again."

They grounded heavily. Wager thought of the strain the tank's huge weight must be putting on the skirts and wondered if they were going to take it. Still, Holman wasn't the first tank driver to get on-the-job training in a crisis.

Anyway, the skirts'd better take it.

Chin Peng Rise had been timbered within the past two years. None of the scrub that had regrown on its loose, rock-strewn soil was high enough to conceal Blue Three's skirts, but the rounded crest itself would protect the hull from guns firing from the wooded knob across the valley.

The thing was, Holman had to halt them in the right place: high enough to clear their main gun but still far enough down the backslope that the hull was in cover.

Shells boomed among the shacks of Kawana. The residents wouldn't 've had any idea that two armies were maneuvering around them until the artillery started to land.

Innocent victims weren't Hans Wager's first concern right now. Via, it was their planet, their war, wasn't it?

His war too.

A plume of friable soil spewed from beneath the skirts as Holman fed power to her fans. Wager felt Blue Three twist as she lifted. *The silly bitch was losing control, letting 'em slide downhill instead of—*

"Holman!" he shouted. "Bring us up to firing level! They need us over—"

As Wager spoke the tank lifted—there'd been no downward motion, just the bow shifting. They climbed the twenty degree slope at a walking pace that brought a crisp view of Sugar Knob onto both the main and gunnery displays.

Shot and shells from Yokel cannon ripped the crest beside Blue Three, where the Slammers vehicle had lain hull-down before—and there they'd 've been now if Holman hadn't had sense enough to shift before she lifted them into sight again.

Wager could apologize later.

He'd locked his main and cupola guns on the same axis. His left hand rotated the turret clockwise with the gunnery screen's orange pipper hovering just above the projected crest of Sugar Knob. When the dark bulk of a Yokel tank slid into the sight picture, needlessly carated by the artificial intelligence, Wager thumbed his joystick control and laced the trees with cyan bolts from the tribarrel.

A bolt flashed white on the screen as it vaporized metal from the Yokel tank. Wager stamped on the pedal to fire his main gun.

Two more Yokel shots hit and glanced from Blue Three. Their impact was lost in the *crash* of the 20cm main gun firing.

Across the valley, the rear end of the Yokel tank jumped backward as the front became a ball of flowing gas.

Wager's main screen was highlighting at least a dozen targets, now. The Yokels had moved into positions overlooking Kawana so their direct fire could finish the tattered survivors of Task Force Ranson as soon as the artillery began to impact.

Some of the tank gunners were still focused on the innocent hamlet. Through the corner of his eye, Wager could see sporting tracks in the valley below as automatic cannons raked shacks and the figures running in terror among the sugarbushes they'd been tending.

Dirt blasted up in front of Blue Three an instant before the turret rang to a double hammerblow. Not all the Yokels were deceived as to their real enemy.

There wasn't time to sort 'em out, to separate the immediate dangers from the targets that might catch on in the next few seconds or minute. Hans Wager had to kill them all—

If he had time before they killed him.

Wager let the turret rotate at its own speed, coursing the further crest. He aimed with the cupola gun rather than the electronic pipper. During his years in combat cars, he'd gotten into the habit of hosing a tribarrel onto its target.

When things really drop in the pot, habit's the best straw to snatch.

Ignoring the shots that hit Blue Three and the shots that blasted grab-loads of dirt from the barren crest around them, Wager stroked his foot-trip again—

A tank exploded.

Again.

Too soon. The twenty-centimeter bolt ignited a swathe of forest beside the Yokel vehicle, but the tank's terrified crew was already bailing out. Wager's tribarrel spun their lifeless bodies into the blazing vegetation as his turret continued to traverse.

A huge pall of smoke leaped skyward from somewhere south of Sugar Knob. It mushroomed when the pillar of heated air could no longer support the mass of dirt, scrap metal, and pureed flesh it contained.

The ground-shock of the explosion rolled across Kawana in a ripple of dust.

Something hit Blue Three. Three-quarters of Wager's gunnery screen went black for a moment. He rocked forward on his foot-trip. The main gun fired, shocking the sunlight and filling the turret with another blast of foul gases from the spent case.

The screen brightened again, though the display was noticeably fuzzier. Another of the tanks on Sugar Knob had become a fireball.

The Yokels were running, backing out of the firing positions on the hillcrest that made them targets for Wager's main gun. He didn't know how the combat cars were doing, but there were columns of smoke from behind the knob where his own fire couldn't reach.

The cars'd have their work cut out for them, playing hide n' seek with the surviving Yokels in thick cover. At point-blank range, the first shot was likely to be the last of the engagement and the tank's thick frontal armor would be a factor.

A target backed in a gout of black diesel exhaust as Wager's sight picture slid over it. He tripped his main gun anyway, knowing that he'd hit nothing but foliage. His turret continued to traverse, left to right.

The Yokel tank snarled forward again, through the trees the twenty-centimeter bolt had vainly withered. *That sonuvabitch hadn't run, he'd just ducked back to shoot safe—*

In the fraction of a second it took Hans Wager to realize that *this* target had to be hit, that he *had* to reverse the smooth motion of his turret, yellow light flashed three times from the muzzle of the Yokel's cannon.

Hot metal splashed Wager and the intereior of the turret. The cupola blew off above him. The tribarrel's ammunition ripped a pencil of cyan upward as it burned in the loading tube.

The gunnery screen was dead, and the central half of the main screen pulsated with random phosphorescence. Motors whined as the turret began tracking counterclockwise across the landscape Wager could no longer see.

"*Blue Three, this is Tootsie Six—*"

Thousand one, thousand two—

"*—we had to bypass the east-flank hostiles. Cross the valley and help us soonest.*"

Wager trod his foot-trip. The gunnery screen cleared—somewhat—just in time to display the Yokel tank disintegrating with an explosion so violent that it snuffed the burning vegetation around the vehicle.

"Roger, Tootsie Six," Hans Wager responded. "Holman, move us—"

But Holman was already feeding power to her fans. You didn't have to tell her what her job was, not that one. . . .

Four more artillery shells burst in black plumes across the sandy furrows which Blue Three had to cross. The remains of Blue Three's cupola glowed white, and there was no hatch to button down over the man in the turret.

Hans Wager's throat burned from the gases which filled his compartment.

He didn't much care about that, either.

"Willens, bring us—" June Ranson began, breaking off as she saw the Yokel tank.

It was crashing through the woods twenty meters to *Warmonger*'s right, on an oppostie and almost parallel course. The 60mm cannon was pointed straight ahead, but the black-clad guerrilla riding on the turret screamed something down the gunner's open hatch as he unlimbered his automatic rifle.

Janacek's tribarrel was on target first. Half the burst exploded bits of intervening vegetation uselessly, but the remaining bolts sawed the Consie's legs off at the knee before hammering the sloped side of the turret.

The outer facing of the armor burned; its ceramic core spalled inward, through the metallic backing. It filled the turret like the contents of a shotgun loaded with broken glass. Smoke puffed from the hatches.

The tank continued to grind its way forward for another thiry seconds while Janacek fired into the hull without effect. The target disintegrated with a shattering roar.

Ranson's multi-function display indicated that both the remaining blowers in her element were within fifty meters of *Warmonger*, but she couldn't see any sign of them.

She couldn't *feel* them. They were real only as beads of light; and the red beads of hostile tanks were no longer where Blue Three had plotted them before the Yokels began to retreat. . . .

A tank ground through the screening foliage like a snorting rhinoceros, bow on with its cannon lowered. June Ranson willed a burst through the muzzle of her tribarrel. . . .

Cyan bolts slashed and ripped at glowing steel.

Stolley swung forward. His bolts intersected and merged with the captain's. The cannon's slim barrel lifted without firing and hurled itself away from the crater bubbling in the gun mantle.

"No!" Ranson screamed at her left wing gunner. "Watch your own—"

Another Yokel tank appeared to the left, its gun questing.

"—side!"

Leaves lifted away from the cannon's flashing muzzle. The blasts merged with the high-explosive charges of the shells which burst on *Warmonger's* side.

The combat car slewed to a halt. The holographic

display went dead; Ranson's tribarrel swung dully without its usual power assist.

For the first time in—months?—June Ranson truly saw the world around her.

The Yokel tank was within ten meters. It fired another three-round burst—shot this time. The rounds punched through the fighting compartment in sparkling richness and ignited the ammunition in Janacek's tribarrel.

The gunner bellowed in pain as he staggered back. Ranson grabbed the bigger man and carrried him with her over the side of the doomed vehicle. Leaf mould provided a thin cushion over the stony forest soil, but *Warmonger*'s bulk was between them and the next hammering blasts.

"Stolley," Janacek whispered. "Where's Stolley and Willens?"

June Ranson looked over her shoulder. Dunnage slung to *Warmonger*'s sides was ablaze. The thin, dangerous haze of electrical fires spurted out of the fan intakes and the holes shots had ripped in the full. Where Janacek's tribarrel had been, there was a glowing cavity in the iridium armor.

Willens had jumped from his hatch and collapsed. There was no sign of Stolley.

Ranson rose in a crouch. Her legs felt wobbly. She must have hit them against the coaming as she leaped out of the fighting compartment. She staggered back toward *Warmonger*.

Shots rang against the armor. A chip of white-hot tungsten ripped through both sides to scorch her thighs.

She tried to call Stolley, but her voice was a croak inaudible even to her over the roar of the flames in *Warmonger*'s belly.

The handgrips on the armor were hot enough to sear layers from her hands as she climbed back into the fighting compartment.

Stolley lay crumpled against the bulkhead. He was still breathing, because she could see bubbles forming in the blood on his lips. She gripped his shoulders and lifted, twisting her body.

The synthetic fabric of her trousers was being burned into her flesh as she balanced. Janacek crawled toward them, though what help he could be. . . .

Because her back was turned, June Ranson didn't see the tank's cannon rocked back and forth as it fired, aiming low into *Warmonger's* hull. She felt the impacts of armor-piercing shot ringing on iridium—

But only for an instant, because this burst fractured the car's fusion bottle.

Dick Suilin was looking over his should toward the bow of *Flamethrower* when the center of his visor blacked. Through the corners of his eyes, the reporter saw foliage withering all around him in the heat of the plasma fire. His hands and the part of his neck not shielded by visor or breastplate prickled painfully.

The gout of stripped atoms lasted only a fraction of a second. *Warmonger's* hull, empty as the shell of a fossil tortoise, continued to blaze white.

The Yokel tank, its cannon nodding for further prey, squealed past the wreckage.

Suilin's tribarrel was still pointed to cover the car's rear quadrant. Cooter's burst splashed upwards from the tank's glacis plate, blasting collops from the sheath and ceramic core.

Before the tribarrel could penetrate the armor at its point of greatest thickness, the tank's 60mm gun cracked out a three-round clip. Dick Suilin's world went red with a crash that struck him like a falling anvil.

The impact knocked him forward. He couldn't hear anything. The fighting compartment was brighter, because cannon shells had blown away the splinter shield overhead. The sun streamed down past the bare poles of plasma-withered trees.

The ready light over his tribarrel's trigger no longer glowed green. Suilin rotated the switch the way Gale had demonstrated a lifetime earlier. The metal felt cool on his fingertips.

The cannon's muzzle began to recoil behind a sound-less yellow flash. *Warmonger* shuddered as Suilin's thumbs pressed his butterfly trigger. Cyan bolts roiled the bottle-shaped flare of unburned powder, then carved the mantlet before the 60mm gun could cycle to battery and fire again.

Steel blazed, sucked inward, and blew apart like a bomb as the tank's ready ammunition detonated.

Suilin's tribarrel stopped firing. His thumbs were still locked on the trigger. A stream of congealed plastic drooled out of the ejection port. The molten cases had built up until they jammed the system.

The hull of the vehicle Dick Suilin had destoyed was burning brightly. Another tank crawled around it. The Consie on the second tank's turret was mouthing orders down the open hatch.

The long cannon swung toward *Flamethrower*.

Lieutenant Cooter rose to his hands and knees on the floor of the fighting compartment. His helmet was gone. There was a streak of blood across the sweat-darkened blond of his hair. He shook himself like a bear sur-rounded by dogs.

Gale sprawled, halfway out of the fighting compart-ment. A high-explosive round had struck him between the shoulderblades. It was a tribute to the trooper's ceramic body armor that one arm was still attached to what remained of his torso.

Suilin unslung his grenade launcher, aimed at the tank thirty meters away, and squeezed off. He couldn't hear his weapon fire, but the butt thumped satisfyingly on his shoulder. His eye followed the missile on its flat arc to the face of the tank's swivelling turret.

The grenades were dual purpose. Their cases were made of wire notched to fragment, but they were wrapped around a miniature shaped charge that could piece light armor.

Armor lighter than the frontal protection of a tank. The guerrilla flung his arms up and toppled, his chest clawed to ruins by shrapnel, but the turret face was only pitted.

The tank moved forward as it had to do so that as the turret rotated, the long gun would clear the burning wreckage of the sister vehicle.

Cooter dragged his body upright. He was still on his knees. The big man gripped the hull to either side of his tribarrel, blocking Suilin from any chance of using that weapon.

No time anyway. The reporter's grenades burst on the turret, white sparks that gouged the armor but didn't penetrate, couldn't penetrate.

Two hits, three—not a hand's breadth apart, remarkable rapid-fire shooting as the turret swung.

Suilin thought he could hear again, but the bitter crack of his grenades was lost in the howl of an oncoming storm. The ground shook and made the blasted trees shiver.

The last round in Suilin's clip flashed against the armor as vainly as the four ahead of it. The cannon's sixty-millimeter bore gaped toward *Flamethrower* like the gates of Hell.

Before the gun could fire, the great, gray bow of Blue Three rode downhill onto the revel tank, scattering treeboles like matchwood.

The clang of impact seemed almost as loud to Dick Suilin as that of the shells ripping *Flamethrower* moments before. The Slammers' tank, ten times the weight of the Yokel vehicle, scarcely slowed as it slid its victim sideways across the scarred forest.

A tread broke and writhed upward like a snake in its death throes. The hull warped, starting seams and rupturing the cooling system and fuel tanks in a gout of steam, then fire.

Metal screamed louder than men could. Blue Three's

skirts rode halfway up the shattered corpse of the rebel tank, fanning the flames into an encircling manacle. The Slammer's driver twisted the hundred and seventy tonnes she controlled like a booted foot crushing an enemy's face into the gutter.

Cooter stood up. Shorty Rogers raised his head from the bow hatch, glanced around, and disappeared again. A moment later, *Flamethrower* shuddered as her fans spun up to speed.

Blue Three backed away from the crackling inferno to which it had reduced its victim. Nothing else moved in the forest.

Dick Suilin's fingers were reflexively loading a fresh clip into his grenade launcher.

Chapter Thirteen

Task Force Ranson, consisting of one tank and four combat cars under Junior Lieutenant Brian Cooter, was within seven kilometers of the outskirts of Kohang when it received word that Consie resistance had collapsed.

The Governmental Compound within the city was relieved a few minutes later by elements of the 12th and 23rd Infantry Brigades of the National Army.

Chapter Fourteen

Dick Suilin looked at Kohang with eyes different from those with which he'd viewed the fine old buildings around the Park and Governmental Compound only days before.

The stone facades were bullet pocked now, but Suilin had changed much more than the city had during the intervening hours.

"Good thing we didn't have to fight through these streets," he said.

His voice was a croak from breathing powergun residues. He didn't know whether he'd ever regain the honey-smooth delivery that had been his greatest asset in the life of his past.

Tents had sprouted around the wheeled command vehicles in the central park fronting the Compound. There was a line of tarpaulin-covered bodies beside the border of shattered trees, but for the most part, the National Army soldiers looked more quizzical than afraid.

"Yeah," said Albers, now manning the right wing gun. He spoke in a similar rasping whisper. "Narrow streets and every curst one a those places built like a bunker. Woulda been a bitch."

"We'd've managed," said Cooter.

I doubt it, Suilin thought. *But we would have tried.*

The Compound's ornamental iron gates had been blown away early in the fighting. The makeshift barricade of burned-out cars which replaced them had already been pushed aside in the clean-up. Soldiers in clean fatigues bearing the collar flashes of the 23d Infantry stood aside as Task Force Ranson entered the courtyard.

Flamethrower settled wearily to the rubble-strewn cobblestones. The car gave a deep sigh as Rogers shut down its fans. The other vehicles were already parked within.

Blue Three listed to starboard since Kawana. The tank had brushed a stone gatepost to widen the Compound entrance, then dragged a sparking line across a courtyard-sized mosaic map of Southern District with all the major cities and terrain features described.

Flamethrower stank of burned plastic and blood. Gale's body was wrapped in his air-tight bedroll and slung to the skirts, but the part of him that had splashed over the interior of the fighting compartment didn't take long to rot in bright sunlight.

They took off their body armor. Suilin's fingers didn't want to bend. All three men were fumbling with their latches. Cooter gripped the edge of the hull armor and shivered.

"Blood and martyrs," he muttered tiredly. Then he said, "Tootsie One-five, this is Three. Take over here till I get back, Tillman. Colonel wants me to report t' Governor Kung."

Suilin heard the electronic click of an answer on a channel the AI didn't open to him. Surely assent. Nobody had the energy left to argue.

Cooter looked at the reporter. "You coming?" the mercenary asked.

Suilin shrugged. "Yeah," he said. "Yeah, sure. That's what I came for."

He didn't sound certain, even to himself.

"Albers," Cooter said as he climbed over the back of the combat car. "See if you can help Tillman line up billets and rations, okay?"

Albers nodded minusculy. He was sitting on the beer cooler. He didn't look at the big lieutenant. Except for the slight lift of his chin, he didn't move.

Suilin slid down the last step and almost fell. His legs didn't want to support him. They seemed all right after a few steps.

"The Consies 're asking for a cease fire," Cooter announced as he and the reporter walked toward the entrance to the Governor's Palace, the middle building of those closing the Compound on three sides. "Not just here. Their Central Command announced it."

"From the Enclaves," Suilin said, thinking aloud.

The soldiers at the entrance thirty meters away wore fatigues with the crossed-saber collar tabs of the Presidential Guard Force. They eyed the newcomers cautiously.

A buzzbomb had cratered the second floor of the Palace, directly above the entrance. Other than that, damage was limited to broken glass and bullet-pocks on the stone. The fighting hadn't been serious around here after all.

Dick Suilin now knew what buildings looked like when somebody really meant business.

"Will they get it?" he said aloud. "The cease fire, I mean."

Cooter shrugged. "I'm not a politician," he said.

Now that the reporter had taken off his clamshell armor, the sling holding his grenade launcher was too long. He adjusted the length.

The pink-faced captain commanding the guards blinked.

Cooter looked at his companion. "I'm not sure you'll need that in here," he said mildly.

"I'm not sure of anything," Dick Suilin replied without emotion. "Not any more."

"The hole in the skirt," said Warrant Leader Ortnahme in a judicious tone as he walked slowly toward Blue Three, "we can patch easy enough. . . ."

"Yessir," said Tech 2 Simkins through tight lips.

When a Yokel tank blew up three meters from Simkins' side of *Daisy Belle*, he'd been spattered with blazing diesel fuel. Bandages now covered the Sprayseal which replaced the skin of the technician's left arm.

He wasn't hurting, exactly; nobody carrying Simkins' present load of analgesics in his veins could be said to be in pain. Still, the technician had to concentrate to keep his feet moving in the right order.

"The bloody rest of it, though . . ." Ortnahme murmured.

Hans Wager had managed to find a can of black paint and a brush somewhere. He was painting something on the tank's bow skirts. His driver, a woman Ortnahme couldn't put a bloody name to, watched with a drawn expression.

The pair of 'em looked like they'd sweated off five kilos in the last two days. Maybe they had.

The tungsten-carbide shot that holed the skirt must have been so close to the muzzle that its fins hadn't had time to stabilize it. The shot was still yawing when it struck, so it'd punched a long oval in the steel instead of a neat round hole.

Ortnahme estimated the shot's probable further course with his eyes and called, "Did ye lose a bloody fan when that hit you?"

Wager continued painting, attempting a precision which was far beyond his present ability.

The driver turned slowly toward the pair of maintenance personnel. She said, "Yeah, that's right. Number 3 Port went out. That was okay, but the air spilling through the hole here—" nodding toward the gaping oval "—that was bad."

She paused for memory before she added, "Can you fix it?"

"Sure," the warrant leader said. "As soon as they ship in a spare." He shook his head. "A whole bloody lotta spares."

Simpkins nodded without speaking.

"What, ah . . . are you doing?" Ortnahme asked.

Wager turned at last. "We're putting the name on our tank," he croaked.

Wager's vacant expression turned to utter malevolence. "She's ours and we can call her anything we bloody please!" he shouted hoarsely. "They're not takin' her and givin' us some clapped out old cow instead, d'ye hear?

Not even the Old Man's gonna take her away from us!"

The warrant leader looked at the tank that had only been a callsign until now.

The turret had taken at least a dozen direct hits, most of them from armor-piercing shot. Ortnahme wondered if any part of the sensor array had survived.

One round had blasted a cavity in the stubby barrel of the main gun. It hadn't penetrated, but until the tube was replaced, firing the 20cm weapon would be as dangerous as juggling contact grenades.

Even a layman could see that the tribarrel's ammunition had chain-fired in its loading tube, vaporizing the weapon, the hatch, and the cupola itself. The warrant leader knew what a layman wouldn't: that when the bloody ammo went, it would've reamed its tubeway as wide as a cow's cunt, seriously weakening the turret forging itself. The whole bloody turret would have to be replaced before Ortnahme would certify *this* mother as fit for action.

Plus, of course, the fan nacelle. Pray Lord it was the only one gone when he and Simkins got underneath to look.

"No argument from me, snake," Henk Ortnahme said mildly. "I figure you guys earned the right to ride whatever you bloody well please."

Simkins had to keep moving for another half hour or so. Ortnahme nodded to the tankers, then walked on slowly with the technician's hand in his for guidance.

Behind them, Wager painted the last letter of *Nameless* on the skirt in straggling capitals.

Suzette, Lady Kung, wore neat fatigues and a look of irritation as she glanced over her shoulder toward the commotion by the door.

"Suzi!" Dick Suilin called, past the sergeant-major who blocked him and Cooter from the dignitaries milling in the conference room.

His sister's expression shifted blank amazement to a

mixture of love and horror. "Dick!" she cried. "Dick! Oh good Lord!"

She darted toward Suilin with her arms spread, striding fast enough to make her lustrous hair stream back from her shoulderblades.

The sergeant-major didn't know what was going on, but he knew enough to get out of the way of the governor's wife. He sprang to attention and repeated in a parade-ground voice what Cooter had told him: "Sir! The representatives of Task Force Ranson."

There were twenty-odd people in the room already, too many for the chairs around the map-stewn table. Most were officers of the National Army. A few civilian advisors looked up from the circle around Governor Kung.

Everyone was in fatigues, but several of the officers wore polished insignia and even medal ribbons.

Suzi hugged her brother fiercely, then gasped before she could suppress the reflex. Suilin had forgotten how he must smell. . . .

"Oh, Dick," his sister said. "It's been hard for all of us."

The reporter patted her hand and let her step away.

He pretended that he hadn't seen the look of disgust flash across her face. Couldn't blame her. He'd lived two days in his clothes, stinking of fear every moment of the time . . . and that was before the shell hit Gale beside him.

Cooter walked toward the conference table, parting the clot of advisors with the shockwave of his presence.

Governor Kung shoved his chair back and stood. He looked like a startled hiker who'd met a bear on a narrow trail.

"Sir," Cooter said, halting a meter from the Governor in a vain effort not to be physically threatening. "Colonel Hammer—"

"You're Ranson, then?" Kung said sharply, his tenor voice keyed higher than Suilin remembered having heard it before. "We were told you were going to relieve us. But I see you preferred to wait until General Halas had done the job!"

Dick Suilin moved up beside the mercenary. The edges of his vision were becoming gray, like the walls of a tunnel leading to the face of Governor Samuel Kung. Suilin's brother-in-law wasn't a handsome man, but his round, sturdy features projected unshakeable determination.

Cooter shook his head as if to clear it. "Sir," he said, "we got here as fast as we could. There was a lot of resis—"

"*My* troops met a lot of resistance, Captain," growled a military man—General Halas; Suilin had interviewed him a few weeks ago, during another life. "The difference is that we broke through and acomplished our mission!"

The tunnel of Dick Suilin's vision was growing red and beginning to pulse as his heart beat. Halas' voice came from somewhere outside the present universe.

"Sir," said Lieutenant Cooter, "with all respect—the Consies put the best they had in our way. When we broke that, broke *them*, the troops they had left in Kohang ran rather than face us."

"Nonsense!" snapped Kung. "General Halas and his troops from Camp Fortune kept up the pressure till the enemy ran. I don't know why we ever decided to hire mercenaries in the first place!"

"Don't you know why we hire mercenaries, Governor?" said Dick Suilin in a voice trembling like a fuel fire. "Don't you know?"

He stepped closer; felt the massive conference table against the front of his thighs, felt it slide away from his advance.

"Dick!" called Suzi, the word attenuated by the pounding walls of the tunnel.

"Because they fight, Governor!" Suilin shouted.

"Because they win, while your rear-echelon pussies wait to be save with their thumbs up their ass!"

Kung's face vanished. Suilin could see nothing but a core of flame.

"They save you, you worthless bastards!" he screamed in to the blinding darkness. "They saved us all!"

The reporter floated without volition or sight. "Reaction to the Wide-awakes," he heard someone, Cooter, murmur. "Had a pretty rough time. . . ."

A door closed, cutting off the babble of sounds. The air was cool, and someone was gently holding him upright.

"Suzi?" he said.

"You can't let 'em get t' you," said Cooter. His right arm was around Suilin's shoulders. His fingers carefully detached the grenade launcher from the reporter's grip. "It's okay."

They were back in the hallway outside the conference room. The walls were veneered with zebra-patterned marble, clean and cool.

"It's not okay!" screamed Dick Suilin. "You save all their asses and they don't care!"

"They don't have t' like us, snake," said Lieutenant Cooter, meeting Suilin's eyes. "They just have t' make the payment schedule."

Suilin turned and bunched his fist. Cooter caught his arm before he could smash his knuckles on the stone wall.

"Take it easy, snake," said the mercenary. "It don't mean nothin'."

Night March

Panchin heard Sergeant-Commander Jonas swear softly as he tried to coax anything more than a splutter from the ionization-track communicator. The wind blew a hiss of sand against *Hula Girl*'s iridium armor.

On a map of any practical scale this swatch of desert would look as flat as a mirror, but brush and rocky knobs limited Reg Panchin's view to a hundred meters in any direction from the combat car's right wing gun. Night stripped the terrain of all color but grays and purple grays. Panchin could have added false color to the light-amplified view through the faceshield of his commo helmet, but that would have made the landscape even more alien—and Panchin more lonely.

"I'm curst if I know what they're fighting over," muttered the driver, Trooper Rita Cortezar, over *Hula Girl*'s intercom channel. "I sure don't see anything here worth getting killed over."

Frosty Ericssen chuckled from the left gun. "Did you ever see a stretch of country that looked much better than this does, Tits?" he asked. "At least after we got through blowing it inside out, I mean."

Panchin was a Clerk/Specialist with G Company's headquarters section. He rode *Hula Girl* during the change of base because the combat car was short a crewman and HQ's command car was overloaded. You had to know Cortezar better than he did to call her "Tits" to her face.

Hula Girl carried three tribarreled powerguns—left wing, right wing, and the commander's weapon mounted on the forward bulkhead to fire over the driver's head. Space in the rear fighting compartment was always tight, but the change of base made the situation even worse than it would have been on a normal combat patrol.

A beryllium fishnet hung on steel stakes a meter above the bulkheads. It was meant to catch mortar bombs and similar low-velocity projectiles before they landed in the fighting compartment, but inevitably it swayed with the weight of the crew's personal baggage. More gear was slung to the outside of the armor, and the deck of the compartment was covered with a layer of ammo cans.

"They're fighting about power, not territory," Panchin said. Spiky branches quivered as wind swept a hillock, then danced toward *Hula Girl* in a dust devil that quickly dispersed. "Everybody on Sulewesi's a Malay, but they came in two waves—original colonists and the batch brought in three generations afterwards. The first lot claims to own everything, including the folks who came later. Eventually the other guys decided to do something about it."

Reg Panchin wasn't so much frightened as empty: he'd never expected to be out in the middle of a hostile nowhere like this. He supposed the line troopers were used to it. Talking about something he knew didn't help Panchin a lot, but it helped.

"We're working for the old guys, right?" Frosty said.

"Right," Panchin said. "Hammer's Slammers support the Sulewesi government. The rebels have a Council. I don't guess there's a lot to choose except who's paying who."

Sgt. Jonas straightened and patted the communicator. "Well, this thing's fucked," he said in a conversational tone. "I can't get more than three words at a time from Scepter Base. If they've got a better fix on the missing column than we do, they can't send it so I hear it."

Hula Girl's crew knew exactly where they were. Sulewesi had been mapped by satellite before the war broke out, and the combat car's inertial navigation system was accurate to within a meter in a day's travel. That didn't tell the Slammers where the missing platoon of local troops was, though.

"So let's go home," Frosty said. He relaxed a catch of his clamshell body armor to scratch his armpit. "I'm not thrilled being out alone in Injun Country like this."

"It might be the transmitter at Scepter Base," Panchin said. He squeezed the edge of the bulkhead between thumb and forefinger to remind himself of how thick the armor was between him and hostile guns. "Goldman was working on it before the move. She said the traverse was getting wonky."

"Fucking wonderful," Cortezar said. "Just wonderful."

Long-distance communications for Hammer's Slammers on Sulewesi were by microwaves bounced off the momentary ionization tracks meteors drew in the upper atmosphere. The commo bursts were tight-beam and couldn't be either jammed or intercepted by hostile forces.

That same directionality was the problem now. Unless the bursts were precisely aligned, they didn't reach their destination. *Hula Girl*'s crew had been out of communication with the remainder of the force ever since Captain Stenhuber sent them off to find a column that had gotten separated from the main body during the change of base.

"Rita, ease us forward a half klick on this heading," Jonas said. "We'll check again there. If that doesn't work we'll head for the barn."

He gave Ericssen a gloomy nod, then lifted his commo helmet with one hand to rub his scalp with the other. The sergeant was completely bald, though his eyebrows were unusually thick for a man of African ancestry.

"That won't be too soon for me," Frosty muttered.

Cortezar switched on the fans and let them spin for a moment before she flared the blades to lift the car. Even on idle the drive fans roared as they sucked air through the armored intake vents. There was no chance of hearing the missing column while the fans were running; though the acoustics of a landscape baffled with gullies, knolls, and clumps of brush up to four meters high made sound a doubtful guide here.

Hula Girl lifted with a greasy shudder. Sand sprayed through the narrow gap between the ground and the lower edge of the steel skirts enclosing the air cushion on which the combat car rode. A fusion bottle powered the eight drive fans. They in turn raised the pressure in the plenum chamber high enough to support the vehicle's thirty tonnes on ground effect. A combat car couldn't fly, but it could dance across quicksand or bodies of still water because the bubble of air spread the car's weight evenly over any surface.

"What did the locals do before they had us for guide dogs?" Cortezar asked as she took *Hula Girl* down one of the channels winding though the desert. The car wasn't moving much faster than a man could walk.

Wind and the occasional flash flood scoured away the soil here except where it was bound by rocks or the roots of plants. The desert vegetation stood on pedestals of its own making.

"They used positioning satellites," Panchin said. "The whole constellation got blasted as soon as the shooting started."

He'd read up on the planet when the Slammers took the Sulewesi Government contract. Mostly the line troopers didn't bother with the briefing materials. The information usually didn't affect mercenaries enough to matter more than a poker game did, but Panchin was interested.

"That puts both sides in the same leaky boat, don't it?" Frosty asked. "You'd think they could've figured that out and left the satellites up so that we could get some sleep."

"In a few minutes we'll head for Scepter Base," Jonas said in a reasonable tone. "I'll see if I can't keep us off perimeter watch for tonight. What's left of it."

The sergeant obviously didn't like the situation either, but his rank kept him from grumbling about orders. Ericssen would have probably acted the same as Jonas if their positions had been reversed. Mercenary soldiering had never been the easiest way to earn a living. People who didn't know that when they signed on with the Slammers learned it quick enough thereafter.

Hula Girl's intakes made the brush to either side wobble toward the vehicle. Gossamer fuzz as long as a man's fingers hung from the branches. The tendrils sucked moisture from the air at night when the relative humidity rose, though the vegetation only flowered after a rain.

It might not rain here for years.

"If they'd left the satellites up to begin with," Panchin said, "then one side or the other would've knocked them down when they thought that gave them an advantage. Maybe before an attack, when they had their people in position already. We'd still be out here."

War is a costly business. Importing mercenaries and their specialist equipment from off-planet is devastatingly expensive, but at least in the short run it costs less than losing. Both sides on Sulewesi had hired a few of the best and most expensive troops in the human universe. Hammer's Slammers were paid by the government, while the rebels had three comparable armored battalions from Brazil on Earth.

Four or five thousand soldiers, no matter how well

equipped, weren't enough to fight a war across the whole surface of a planet; locally-raised forces could only be trained as mechanized infantry because time was so short. To bridge the gap between the general mass and the highly-paid cutting edge, the government and rebels both used less sophisticated mercenaries. The mid-range troops provided weapons and communications of a higher order than those produced on Sulewesi, but at a tenth the cost of outfits like the Slammers and the Brazilians.

A tenth as effective too, the Slammers thought; but a pipe gun throwing a chunk of lead was still enough to splash your brains across the deck of a tank if you happened to be in the wrong place. War didn't stop being a dangerous business just because you were good at it.

Cortezar goosed the fans to take *Hula Girl* onto a ridge whose rocks had resisted the wind better than the light soil to either side. The skirts rubbed stones, clanking and throwing sparks. Ball-shaped vegetation flattened and shivered away from the gale that squirted under the plenum chamber.

Panchin held firmly onto the twin spade grips of his tribarrel as the deck slanted beneath his boots. "I don't see why they had to split the Regiment up this way," he said. "You can't blame Captain Stenhuber sending us out alone when all he's got to work with is seven combat cars and the G Company command vehicle."

"Yeah," Frosty agreed. "If we were all together we'd go through everything else on this planet like a spike through an eyeball."

"You bet we would," Jonas said in grim disapproval. "And while we were doing that, the rebels'd smash the rest of the government army, putting a platoon or two of Brazilian armor on point each time. The people who hired us want to win the war, not just one battle."

"The odometer says this is half a kilometer, sarge," Cortezar said with an edge in her voice. Reg Panchin felt alone, but really he was elbow to elbow with two fellow troopers. Cortezar sat by herself in the driver's compartment, and she was a meter closer to the most likely direction for a first shot besides.

"Yeah, all right," Jonas agreed. "I make Scepter Base forty-two degrees from here, but we'll want to dodge—"

A hand flare popped against the heavens and drained back to the desert floor as a shower of silver droplets. Panchin wasn't an expert at judging distances at night, but he didn't imagine the signal could have been launched from more than half a kilometer away.

"Bloody hell," said Ericssen. "We found them after all."

Jonas tilted the muzzles of his tribarrel skyward and tapped out three spaced rounds on the butterfly trigger between the grips. Each bolt of copper plasma lit the night cyan. Heated air cracked shut behind each hissing discharge.

"Head for the flare, Rita," the sergeant ordered. "But take it easy—I want to raise them with the laser communicator before we go barreling in."

Frosty nodded. "There's no such thing as friendly fire," he agreed. "And if they're not trigger happy, they ought to be with as many rebels as there are operating in this sandbox."

Three flares and at least a dozen bursts of automatic gunfire lofted skyward from the previous location northeast of *Hula Girl*. Distance thinned the muzzleblasts to a nervous rustling, like brushes stroking a drumhead. The tracers were the white used by local forces and a strobing pink that Panchin hadn't seen before.

He switched through the UHF and VHF bands on his commo helmet but only picked up static. He couldn't tell whether the problem was the helmet—even intercom was scratchy; this desert, where mineral deposits and temperature inversions played hell with everything in the electro-optical spectrum; or most likely, that nobody in the missing column was transmitting on any push that *Hula Girl*'s crew had been given for the operation.

The combat car ambled toward the flares as Sergeant Jonas bent over the multifunction display fixed to the bulkhead beside his tribarrel. Panchin echoed the display for a moment on his faceshield but cut back quickly to light amplification of his normal viewpoint. If he'd been in the Tactical Operations Center at Scepter Base where he belonged, it might have been interesting to watch blurs resolve into icons against a terrain map as the car processed sensor data on the column *Hula Girl* was approaching. Out here it might mean that Reg Panchin, right wing gunner, didn't see the hostile who was aiming a buzzbomb at *Hula Girl*.

Ericssen must have been thinking the same thing. He touched a button on the tribarrel's pintle. The barrel group rotated a third of a turn; a flat 2-cm disk clucked from the ejection slot. The disk was a polyurethane matrix holding an alignment of copper atoms which, when stripped in a powergun's chamber, streamed downrange as a ravening cyan plasma. Frosty was checking—again—to make sure that his weapon was loaded and ready.

There was nothing on Panchin's side of the car. Nothing but wind and desert.

"Hold here, Rita," Jonas ordered. He started to raise the communications mast even before *Hula Girl* settled on idling fans.

Panchin helped set the bracing wires of the telescoping five-meter mast; this was something he'd done before. Jonas used a joystick to align the transceiver head and began to speak into the separate microphone. The lens on top of the mast directed his words over the intervening brush and sand to the local column in the form of a modulated laser beam.

After a moment the sergeant straightened. "All right, they're expecting us," he said. "Take us in, Rita."

To save time he collapsed the mast without undoing the wires; they wound like spiderweb across the fighting compartment. Panchin coiled them quickly on their spools, smoothing kinks with his left hand.

Hula Girl wallowed over another crest. The column they'd been searching for was halted in the broad gully below. That was probably part of the reason they'd been out of communications for so long. Panchin had been a soldier too long to be surprised that nobody'd had sense enough to drive one of the working vehicles onto a ridge for a better signal.

There were four Sulewesi-built 6-wheeled armored personnel carriers and a command vehicle that was similar but slightly larger than the APCs; it had four axles instead of three. The recovery/repair vehicle with a crane and parts lockers used the longer chassis as well.

Besides the locals, the column contained three medium tanks with caterpillar tracks, ceramic armor, and a long coil gun in the hull. The tanks' turbine engines whined, but power for the coil guns must come from another source—probably magneto-hydrodynamic generators. A small cupola offset on the hull contained an automatic weapon.

One tank towed another. The third tank was towing an APC. The recovery vehicle towed a second APC; and, judging by the removed cover plates, the command vehicle had broken down also. Troops in a variety of uniforms stood around the vehicles. Some of them waved.

"Typical ratfuck," Jonas muttered. "Ninety klicks is too far for a change of base even when everybody knows what he's doing."

Hula Girl started down the slope. Cortezar deliberately broke away the gully rim to ease the angle. Sand and pebbles, some of them big enough to whang like bullets against the skirts, blasted ahead of the car in a spreading cloud.

"We going to be able to talk to these people?" Frosty asked. He had to use helmet intercom for Jonas to hear the question over the fan noise.

"The CO, Major Lebusan, spoke good Standard," Jonas said. "The rest of them, I dunno. Probably not."

Most rich people on Sulewesi were well educated and spoke Standard, the interstellar commercial language. Most rich people also managed to stay out of the military, at least the part of the military that might have to do some fighting. A few of the Slammers learned languages for fun, but nobody aboard *Hula Girl* knew more Malay than was necessary to ask for sex or a drink.

Cortezar slowed to a halt beside the command vehicle and cut the fans. A small man covered his face with a spotted bandanna until the dust had settled, then stepped forward. He wore a saucer hat with gold braid and his uniform was tailored; he'd probably been dapper some twenty hours earlier at the start of the march.

"I am Major Lebusan," the local said. "Can you fix my vehicle? That would be best."

"We're not mechanics, major," Sergeant Jonas said. He swung a leg over the bulkhead.

"I've worked on diesels," Cortezar said as she climbed out of the driver's compartment.

"We'll take a look then," Jonas said. He jumped to the ground. "Frosty, you keep an eye on the sensors, will you?"

Panchin took that as clearance for him to leave *Hula Girl* also. The ground would feel good for a change, and it'd be nice to have more elbow room than there was in the fighting compartment.

A burly man with a full black beard walked over to Panchin. He wore a ripple-camouflaged uniform of a style Panchin hadn't seen before. The holster across the center of his chest held a heavy sidearm with a folding stock.

"I Dolgov," the man said, extending a big hand to Panchin. Panchin took it, expecting—correctly—that Dolgov would squeeze hard as they shook. "Zaporoskiye Brigade. Tanks!"

Dolgov pointed to the tank being towed. "Electrics all go out, poof! Kaput. These Sulewesi monkeys, they not real mechanics. Good for nothing monkeys!"

Panchin wondered how well the Zaporoskiye maintenance section would do with *Hula Girl* if she broke down. The range in sophistication was no greater. Of course, the locals didn't seem able to repair their own command vehicle. Aloud he said, "We'll guide you to the firebase. Somebody there can fix you up, right?"

"Yah, monkeys," Dolgov said, shaking his head morosely. He spat into the night.

Before Panchin could figure out whether that was a "yes" or a "no," Jonas called, "Hey Panchin! Get over here, will you?"

He nodded to Dolgov and joined the group around the command vehicle. Cortezar had stepped away and the locals were closing the engine compartment again. A gas lantern hanging from a cable hook on a fender threw white light across the ground and nearby personnel from their waists down.

"You double-checked the base coordinates, didn't you?" Jonas asked bluntly. "The major here says it's grid A27, 4-4-9, 1-3-0."

"Negative!" Panchin said, feeling cold inside. He *had* checked the coordinates in the TOC before *Hula Girl* left Trident Base, though. "A-2-7, that's a roger, but the block was 6-2-1, 5-2-5."

Major Lebusan took off his fancy hat and slapped it angrily against his thigh. His uniform was green with a touch of mustard yellow. Though the major wore short-sleeved field kit except for the hat, an array of medal ribbons that spilled from his left breast to his right.

"That is not right!" he said. "Look, I show you!"

He snapped his fingers. An aide handed him a clipboard holding a map covered in clear plastic. Panchin and the sergeant both bent to read it. The crayon markings on the plastic were in cursive Malay script, but the circle drawn over Knoll 45/13 on the printed map was clear enough.

"Sarge," Frosty said over the intercom, "I'll bet they're in one of the outlying companies. I never saw those tanks at any of the firebases we've operated out of."

"I'll bet he's right," Panchin said. He wasn't sure if Zaporoskiye was a place or just the name of a freelance unit raised on some Slavic planet.

Sergeant Jonas lifted his helmet and rubbed his bare scalp again. "All right," he said tiredly. "Scepter Base is ten klicks away. I wasn't willing to tow this pig—"

He nodded at the command vehicle.

"—that far. But I guess we can manage three. Panchin, give me a hand. We'll use our own towlines."

Under his breath to Panchin as they walked to *Hula Girl*, the sergeant added, "Because their bloody cables won't be worth any more than any of the other bloody equipment on this bloody planet!"

"And you will carry me in your tank, please," Major Lebusan called after them.

Major Lebusan's presence made *Hula Girl*'s fighting compartment a little more cramped, but he was a small man and didn't wear body armor like the three Slammers. Panchin couldn't blame the major for riding with them. The broken-down command vehicle had no power for its communication devices, and *Hula Girl*'s fans kicked a quite astounding amount of sand and dust over it besides.

The grip of the Sulewesan vehicle's wheels meant that sometimes it jerked *Hula Girl* unexpectedly, even though the combat car was heavier and had plenty of excess power for the tow. Friction with the soil was a more efficient means of braking than the vectored thrust of an air-cushion vehicle like *Hula Girl*.

For three kilometers it was bearable. There were rebels all over this stretch of desert. Abandoning a broken-down vehicle could mean making the other side a gift of it.

"Are there going to be any friendlies at this outpost?" Cortezar asked over the intercom. "Slammers, I mean."

"Negative," Panchin said. "I'd have handled their supply requests if there were."

That was his job: supply clerk for the 1st and 2nd Platoons of G Company, Hammer's Slammers; assigned to the government's Desert Dragons combat group, a motley assortment of locals and off-planet mercenaries in roughly regimental strength. The Slammers' combat cars had been perimeter security for the main body during the change of base. It was *Hula Girl*'s bad luck that she was the nearest car to where the missing column was supposed to be; and Reg Panchin's bad luck that he happened to be riding her instead of another vehicle.

The column was echeloned back to the left of *Hula Girl* and her tow to avoid the worst of the dust. The personnel of broken-down vehicles were all packed onto others. A rebel ambush would mean a massacre; but again, Panchin understood why the weary locals wanted to escape choking discomfort even at the risk of their lives.

"Sarge, we ought to have a sight of them from the next rise," Cortezar said. Her compartment had a multifunction display like the commander's, so she didn't have to echo the terrain map on her faceshield as Panchin could have done.

"Right, I'm getting their signatures already," Jonas said. He sounded a little concerned. "Keep us hull down and I'll let the major talk us in on the laser. We don't have any of the codes for this laager."

Cortezar slowed *Hula Girl* carefully, then cut her steering yoke to the left so that the Sulewesan command vehicle didn't slam them from behind as it rolled off the last of its inertia. Flares were the only way to signal the remainder of the column, and Jonas wasn't willing to target *Hula Girl* that way. The other vehicles, local and Zaporoskiye alike, stopped anyway without command. Their crews didn't know how close the laager was, and they didn't want to be leading a trek through the desert. Both sides had troops scattered throughout the region.

Sergeant Jonas deployed the mast. Panchin stared at the desert, switching his faceshield repeatedly from thermal viewing to light amplification and back again. He thought one enhancement technique might disclose something that he'd missed using the other. Rebels could be lurking just outside the laager, their electromagnetic signatures hidden by those of the friendly vehicles; waiting to ambush late-comers like *Hula Girl* and the column she was shepherding in.

There was nothing but sand and bushes bending in the night wind. In the false-color thermal display, dew-gathering tendrils were a cool blue against the warmer orange of the branches from which they hung.

Major Lebusan talked animatedly on the communicator, waving his arms. Jonas watched the night ahead, his hands on his tribarrel's grip. The line troopers knew even better than a clerk like Panchin that this was a dangerous location.

Troops on the other halted vehicles called questions. When that brought no response, an officer in a less-or-nate version of Lebusan's uniform jumped from the nearest APC and ran over to *Hula Girl*. He spoke in quick Malay beside the combat car. The skirts and bulkhead were so high that the small man close to the vehicle couldn't see the major in the fighting compartment.

Frosty Ericssen looked down from his gun. "We're talking to the laager, buddy," he said to the local in Standard. "Do you understand? Your friends are right over the hill there."

"Ah!" said the local. He ran back to the APC, chattering loudly.

Lebusan turned from the microphone fixed at the base of the mast. "Yes, yes, we're clear to enter," he said angrily to Jonas. "Where was I? they ask! They abandon me in the desert and they claim *I'm* at fault?"

Jonas telescoped the mast. Moving stresses would break the raised wand. Panchin helped the sergeant coil the braces as he had before.

An engine roared. The nearer APC started forward, spraying gravel from all six wheels. The remainder of the column followed a moment later. It was like watching the starting grid of a race. Two routes over the low ridge merged beyond a grove of shrubs with intertwined branches. Panchin expected to see a collision, but the recovery vehicle gave way at the last moment to the tank towing an APC.

Jonas shook his head in disgust as he locked the mast in place. "Take us in, Rita," he said. "I guess we eat dust for the last half klick."

Hula Girl accelerated slowly: a quick jerk against the inertia of the command vehicle would snap the tow cables. Dust from the rest of the column was almost a wall rather than a cloud. Panchin breathed through his helmet filters. An electrostatic charge was supposed to keep his faceshield clear, but some of the grit was too large to be repelled. Lebusan covered his face with his bandanna again.

This ridge was a slightly lower step of Knoll 45/13. When *Hula Girl* topped it, the laager was in view just ahead. APCs and Zaporoskiye tanks faced out from a circle so that their thicker bow armor and main weapons were toward a potential enemy.

There were many more vehicles than Panchin had expected to see.

"Via, sarge!" Ericssen said. "That's the firebase, not an outpost. Did they give us the wrong coordinates?"

So quietly that his crew could barely hear him over the intercom, Sergeant Jonas said, "Those are Brazilian free-launch artillery vehicles. They aren't ours."

Major Lebusan bobbed his head enthusiastically. "I used to complain because the Council spent so much money on you Brazilians but didn't pay its own officers properly," he shouted through the bandanna. "Now I know you're worth the expense!"

Panchin looked over his shoulder. The locals still aboard the command vehicle were inside with the hatches closed; dust turned all the surfaces white, armor and vision blocks alike. Nobody could see what was happening aboard *Hula Girl*.

He smiled at Major Lebusan and kneed him in the groin.

The rebel officer doubled up with a squeal. His hat fell off. Ericssen chopped Lebusan on the back of the head with the butt of a grenade launcher.

Panchin felt cold and sick to his stomach. He had to consciously force his lips to straighten out of the frozen smile.

Ericssen tossed the rebel major over the side. Lebusan was a small man, but it was still an impressive one-handed lift by the gunner. Hysterical strength, very likely.

"Awaiting instructions!" Cortezar said urgently.

"Keep going," Sergeant Jonas said. He sounded calm. "We'll never get away if we turn around a hundred meters from them. We'll proceed till they notice us, then bull straight in and raise so much hell that maybe we'll be able to get out the other side."

"I make it four Brazilian launchers and a calliope," Cortezar said. Her voice was an octave higher than normal, but she didn't speak any faster than usual. "The rest of the hardware's local or Zaporoskiye like the folks in the column. That what you've got too, sarge?"

"There ought to be a second calliope with a battery of artillery," Jonas said. "Maybe it's deadlined, but don't count on that."

The Slammers depended on the 2-cm tribarrels of their tanks and combat cars to sweep incoming shells and missiles from the sky. Most other high-end mercenary units used specialized equipment to protect themselves from artillery. Calliopes, eight or nine-tube fixed powergun arrays, could blast incoming even if one or more of the individual guns jammed.

They could also shred a combat car the way a shark tears a man.

"Brigadier Vijanta's going to be pleased to know where to find the rebel main body," Ericssen said sourly. "If we get to Scepter Base to tell him, that is."

Panchin was suddenly thankful for the dust. His sweaty hands wouldn't slip from the grips of his tribarrel.

"Rita, when I give the word, break the tow lines," Jonas said. "We won't have time to do it any other way. Wing guns shoot at everything on your side. Try to get the launchers and any reload vehicles. Remember, we need to confuse them for long enough to get away."

The Slammers' own rocket howitzers fired individual rounds from a tube with a closed breech. The Brazilians launched from open troughs, a less efficient technique. In exchange for needing more fuel to reach a given range, the Brazilians were able to mount their artillery on much lighter chassis than the Slammers' massive Hogs.

Ericssen turned his head. "You okay with this, Panchin?" he asked.

Panchin nodded. "I'm okay," he said. His mouth was dry and his soul was already trying to squeeze free. He knew in a moment his body would be ripped and burned.

The rebels hadn't raised a dirt berm around the encampment for protection, but the air-cushion artillery vehicles were dug in hull deep. Soldiers were filling sandbags under artificial light. The layout was at least as professional as that of a government firebase.

A pair of female soldiers lounged against a sandbag bunker near the entrance, drinking from a bottle they passed back and forth. They wore chameleon-weave uniforms whose fabric adjusted to match the background patterns.

One of the soldiers straightened and spoke to her companion. They both stared at *Hula Girl*, now only forty meters away.

"Hit it!" Sergeant Jonas shouted as his tribarrel lashed the night. His cyan bolts missed the Brazilian women, but he blew the side of the bunker in. The metal-plank roof buried the gun position.

Hula Girl lurched forward on the full thrust of her fans. The right tow cable parted. The combat car and the command vehicle whipsawed on the remaining cable. *Hula Girl* sideswiped the Zaporoskiye tank being towed by its fellow ahead of them. The impact helped Cortezar fight her controls straight. She continued to accelerate, pulling the command vehicle into the pair of tanks in a crash that finally broke the cable.

Panchin pressed his trigger with both thumbs, blinking reflexively. The barrel group spun at 500 rpm. Each stubby iridium tube fired with a *hissCRACK* when it rotated into the top position, then ejected the spent matrix from the port in a spurt of liquid nitrogen before loading a fresh round in the third station on the receiver.

He aimed at a parked APC but shot high, raking the roof of a tent in the center of the encampment. The sidewalls were heavily sandbagged, but the centerpole shattered and dropped blazing canvas into the interior.

Frosty Ericssen's bolts glanced crazily from the turtle-backed hull of a Zaporoskiye tank. When the ceramic armor finally failed, the tank exploded in a mushroom of flame—fuel for the turbine and the main gun's MHD generator.

Hula Girl drove into the crowded firebase at 40 kph and still accelerating. Panchin squeezed the butterfly trigger, remembering to fire short bursts. His faceshield blanked the bolts' intense blue-green glare to save his vision. He didn't hit what he aimed at—he was constantly behind his targets even though he tried to allow for the combat car's acceleration. He'd lowered his muzzles, and there were too many targets to miss everything.

When he shot at the three crew members running for a Zaporoskiye tank, his bolts slapped the flank of their vehicle instead. The cyan reflection threw the men down anyway, their clothing afire.

Hula Girl skidded. Panchin aimed at the open rear hatch of an APC close enough to spit into but punched the side of a carrier twenty meters away. The steel armor burned white in the heat of the plasma; then the whole vehicle erupted. The commander's cupola spun out of the fireball.

Cortezar was dodging obstacles as best she could, but *Hula Girl* repeatedly brushed a vehicle or a sandbag wall. The skirts were sturdy, but they weren't a bulldozer blade. If the plenum chamber was too damaged to hold high-pressure air, the car became a sitting duck for everything a regimental firebase could throw at her.

An explosion with three distinct pulses hammered the camp. *Hula Girl* spun ninety degrees before Cortezar got her under control again. The quivering yellow flare threw the shadows of men and equipment a kilometer across the desert. Jonas or Ericssen had hit an artillery vehicle, detonating some of the ready ammo.

Metal clanged discordantly. Pink tracers clipped one of the stakes holding *Hula Girl's* overhead screen and kicked smoldering dimples in the baggage.

Panchin tried to swing his tribarrel onto the Zaporoskiye tank firing at them with the automatic weapon in its cupola. Sergeant Jonas was faster, pounding the tank's mid-hull with a long burst that crumbled the ceramic. The tank didn't explode violently, but a red flash lifted all the hatches. The machine gun stopped firing.

Panchin shot at a supply truck and for once hit his target. Greasy flames enveloped the crates stacked on the bed. Men jumped off the other side of the vehicle and ran unharmed into the night.

Panchin's iridium barrels glowed so brightly that his faceshield had to gray out their glare. The long burst Sergeant Jonas fired to destroy the tank had jammed his tribarrel. He tilted his weapon up to chip with a knifeblade at the matrix material gumming his ejection port.

Cortezar swung *Hula Girl* hard left on the track within the outer ring of vehicles. Half a dozen rebel soldiers squatted behind their APC and the sandbag wall they'd started for a sleeping bunker. They fired at *Hula Girl* with automatic rifles. Panchin slewed his gun toward them. A bullet whanged Jonas' weapon. The impact spun the tribarrel on its pintle. Like a white-hot baseball bat, the lower muzzle knocked the sergeant down.

A second artillery vehicle blew up. This time at least four rounds detonated simultaneously. The blast threw *Hula Girl* ten meters sideways into a heavy tractor with an earthmoving blade. The combat car rotated a half turn and stalled because Cortezar had dropped the controls when her helmet bounced off the side of her compartment.

Panchin screamed in fear and clamped his trigger. There was a sound like water dropped into an ocean of hot grease, and the center of his faceshield became a shadow with cyan edges. The protective spot collapsed to show the ruin of an air-cushion vehicle, still glowing but no longer so bright that it could etch retinas.

"Drive!" Sergeant Jonas said. "Drive!"

Hula Girl shuddered, rose minusculy, and turned to lurch off the northern edge of knoll between a pair of Sulewesan APCs. One burned sluggishly; the other was as still as a grave though apparently undamaged.

More Brazilian rockets exploded. *Hula Girl* pogoed twice even though this time high ground shielded them from the shockwave. Debris from a previous explosion must have set this one off because Frosty wasn't shooting and Panchin's tribarrel had jammed.

Hula Girl tore through the night. Tracers arched across the sky, but the rebel laager was out of direct sight. There was a risk that the car might hit a large boulder, but Cortezar was driving with a touch as deft as a brain surgeon's.

Panchin knelt with his hands clasped over the chestplate of his armor. He knew he ought to clear his tribarrel, but his whole body was shaking.

Ericssen worked on Sergeant Jonas' forearm. "It's just a bruise!" the sergeant said. His voice was tight with pain.

"So the medics at Scepter Base take the splint off," Ericssen said equably. "Where's the harm in that? Now, you just relax until the blue tab—" The analgesic injector built into Slammers body armor, beside the red tab which injected stimulant. "—kicks in."

The night behind them belched yellow again. The shockwave was a dull thump instead of a world-devouring roar when it reached *Hula Girl* several seconds later.

"I never thought it'd work," Panchin whispered.

"Hey snake?" Ericssen said. "You did good to nail that second calliope before it waxed us. I didn't even see it till you lit the spics up."

"I'm glad," Panchin said. He closed his eyes, then opened them again very quickly. He'd throw up if he closed them.

"Blood and martyrs!" Cortezar said. "I don't get it. We were shaking *hands* with those bastards and we didn't even know they were the other side. And them too! It don't make sense that if everybody's the same they're all trying to kill each other."

The overhead net sagged. The bullet-damaged stake had bent and might break at any moment.

"Maybe in some universe there's got to be a difference before people kill each other," Panchin said to his clasped hands. "That's never been a requirement in the universe humans live in, though."

Code-Name Feirefitz

"LORD, WE GOT ONE!" cried the trooper whose detector wand pointed toward the table that held the small altar. "That's a powergun for sure, Captain, nothing else'd read so much iridium!"

The three other khaki-clad soldiers in the room with Captain Esa Mboya tensed and cleared guns they had not expected to need. The villagers of Ain Chelia knew that to be found with a weapon meant death. The ones who were willing to face that were in the Bordj, waiting with their households and their guns for the Slammers to rip them out. Waiting to die fighting.

The houses of Ain Chelia were decorated externally by screens and colored tiles; but the tiles were set in concrete walls and the screens themselves were cast concrete. Narrow cul-de-sacs lined by blank, gated courtyard walls tied the residential areas of the village into knots of strongpoints. The rebels had elected to make their stand in Ain Chelia proper only because the fortress they had cut into the walls of the open pit mine was an even tougher objective.

"Stand easy, troopers," said Mboya. The householder

279

gave him a tight smile; he and Mboya were the only blacks in the room—or the village. "I'll handle this one," Captain Mboya continued. "The rest of you get on with the search under Sergeant Scratchard. Sergeant—" calling toward the outside door—"come in here for a moment."

Besides the householder and the trooper, a narrow-faced civilian named Youssef ben Khedda stood in the room. On his face was dawning a sudden and terrible hope. He had been Assistant Superintendent of the ilmenite mine before Kabyles all over the planet rose against their Arabized central government in al-Madinah. The Superintendent was executed, but ben Khedda had joined the rebels to be spared. It was a common enough story to men who had sorted through the ruck of as many rebellions as the Slammers had. But now ben Khedda was a loyal citizen again. Openly he guided G Company from house to house; secretly he whispered to Captain Mboya the names of those who had carried their guns and families to the mine. "Father," said ben Khedda to the householder, lowering his eyes in a mockery of contribution, "I never dreamed that there would be contraband *here*, I swear it."

Juma al-Habashi smiled back at the small man who saw the chance to become undisputed leader of as much of Chelia as the Slammers left standing and alive. "I'm sure you didn't dream it, Youssef," he said more gently than he himself expected. "Why should you, when I'd forgotten the gun myself?"

Sergeant Scratchard stepped inside with a last glance back at the courtyard and the other three men of Headquarters Squad waiting there as security. Within, the first sergeant's eyes touched the civilians and the tense enlisted men; but Captain Mboya was calm, so Scratchard kept his own voice calm as he said, "Sir?"

"Sergeant," Mboya said quietly, "you're in charge of the search. If you need me, I'll be in here."

"Sir," Scratchard agreed with a nod. "Well, get the

lead out daisies!" he snarled to the troopers, gesturing them to the street. "We got forty copping houses to run yet!"

As ben Khedda passed him, the captain saw the villager's control slip to uncover his glee. The sergeant was the last man out of the room; Mboya latched the street door after him. Only then did he meet the householder's eyes again. "Hello, Juma" he said in the Kabyle he had sleep-learned rather than the Kikuyu they had both probably forgotten by now. "Brothers shouldn't have to meet this way, should we?"

Juma smiled in mad irony rather than humor. Then his mouth slumped out of that bitter rictus and he said sadly, "No, we shouldn't, that's right." Looking at his altar and not the soldier, he added, "I knew there'd be a—unit sent around, of course. But I didn't expect you'd be leading the one that came here, where I was."

"Look, I didn't volunteer for Operation Feirefitz," Esa blazed, "And Via, how was I supposed to know where you were anyway? We didn't exactly part kissing each other's cheeks ten years ago, did we? And here you've gone and changed your name even—how was I supposed to keep from stumbling over you?"

Juma's face softened. He stepped to his brother, taking the other's wrists in his hands. "I'm sorry," he said. "Of course that was unfair. The—what's going to happen disturbs me." He managed a genuine smile. "I didn't really change my name, you know. 'Al-Habashi' just means 'the Black', and it's what everybody on this planet was going to call me whatever I wanted. We aren't very common on Dar al-B'heed, you know. Any more than we were in the Slammers."

"Well, there's one fewer black in the Slammers than before *you* opted out," Esa said bitterly; but he took the civilian's wrists in turn and squeezed them. As the men stood linked, the clerical collar that Juma wore beneath an ordinary jellaba caught the soldier's eye. Without the harshness of a moment before, Esa asked, "Do they all call you 'Father'?"

The civilian laughed and stepped away. "No, only the hypocrites like Youssef," he said. "Oh, Ain Chelia is just as Islamic as the capital, as al-madinah, never doubt. I have a small congregation here . . . and I have the respect of the rest of the community, I think. I'm head of equipment maintenance at the mine, which doesn't mean assigning work to other people, not here." He spread his hands, palms down. The fingernails were short and the grit beneath their ends a true black and no mere skin tone. "But I think I'd want to do that anyway, even if I didn't need to eat to live. I've guided more folk to the Way by showing them how to balance a turbine than I do when I mumble about peace."

Captain Mboya walked to the table on top of which stood an altar triptych, now closed. Two drawers were set between the table legs. He opened the top one. In it were the altar vessels, chased brasswork of local manufacture. They were beautiful both in sum and in detail, but they had not tripped a detector set to locate tool steel and iridium.

The lower drawer held a powergun.

Juma watched without expression as his brother raised the weapon, checked the full magazine, and ran a fingertip over the manufacturer's stampings. "Heuvelmans of Friesland," Esa said conversationally. "Past couple contracts have been let on Terra, good products . . . but I always preferred the one I was issued when they assigned me to a tribarrel and I rated a sidearm." he drew his own pistol from its flap holster and compared it to the weapon from the drawer. "Right, consecutive serial numbers," the soldier said. He laid Juma's pistol back where it came from. "Not the sort of souvenir we're supposed to take with us when we resign from the Slammers, of course."

Very carefully, and with his eyes on the wall as if

searching for flaws in its thick plastered concrete, Juma said, "I hadn't really . . . thought of it being here. I suppose that's grounds for carrying me back to a Re-education Camp in al-Madinah, isn't it?"

His brother's fist slammed the table. The triptych jumped and the vessels in the upper drawer rang like Poe's brazen bells. "Re-education? It's grounds for being burned at the *stake* if I say so! Listen, the reporters are back in the capital, not here. My orders from the District Governor are to *pacify* this region, not coddle it!" Esa's face melted from anger to grief as suddenly as he had swung his fist a moment before. "Via, elder brother, why'd you have to leave? There wasn't a man in the Regiment could handle a tribarrel the way you could."

"That was a long time ago," said Juma, facing the soldier again.

"I remember at Sphakteria," continued Esa as if Juma had not spoken, "when they popped the ambush and killed your gunner the first shot. You cut'em apart like they weren't shooting at you too. And then you led the whole platoon clear, driving the jeep with the wick all the way up and working the gun yourself with your right hand. Nobody else could've done it."

"Do you remember," said Juma, his voice dropping into a dreamy caress as had his brother's by the time he finished speaking, "the night we left Nairobi? You led the Service of Farewell yourself, there in the starport, with everyone in the terminal joining in. The faith we'd been raised in was just words to me before then, but you made the Way as real as the tiles I was standing on. And I thought 'Why is he going off to be a soldier? If ever a man was born to lead other men to peace, it was Esa.' And in time, you did lead me to peace, little brother."

Esa shook himself, standing like a centipede in his body armor. "I got that out of my system," he said.

Juma walked over to the altar. "As I got the Slammers

out of my system," he said, and he closed the drawer over the powergun within.

Neither man spoke for moments that seemed longer. At last Juma said, "Will you have a beer?"

"What?" said the soldier in surprise. "That's permitted on Dar al-B'heed?"

Juma chuckled as he walked into his kitchen. "Oh yes," he said as he opened a trapdoor in the floor, "though of course not everyone drinks it." He raised two corked bottles from their cool recess and walked back to the central room. "There are some Arab notions that never sat very well with Kabyles, you know. Many of the notions about women, veils and the like. Youssef ben Khedda's wife wore a veil until the revolt . . . then she took it off and walked around the streets like the other women of Ain Chelia. I suspect that since your troops swept in, she has her veil on again."

"*That* one," said the Captain with a snort that threatened to spray beer. "I can't imagine why nobody had the sense to throttle him—at least before they went off to their damned fortress."

Juma gestured his brother to one of the room's simple chairs and took another for himself. "Not everyone has seen as many traitors as we have, little brother," he said. "Besides, his own father was one of the martyrs whose death ignited the revolt. He was caught in al-Madinah with hypnocubes of Kabyle language instruction. The government called that treason and executed him."

Esa snorted again, "And didn't anybody here wonder who shopped the old man to the security police? Via! But I shouldn't complain—he makes my job easier." He swallowed the last of his beer, paused a moment, and then pointed the mouth of the bottle at Juma as if it would shoot. "What about you?" the soldier demanded harshly. "Where do you stand?"

"For peace," said Juma simply, "for the Way. As I always have since I left the Regiment. But . . . my closest friends in the village are dug into the sides of the mine pit now, waiting for you. Or they're dead already outside al-Madinah."

The soldier's hand tightened on the bottle, his fingers darker than the clear brown glass. With a conscious effort of will he set the container down on the terrazzo floor beside his chair. "They're dead either way," he said as he stood up. He put his hand on the door latch before he added, pausing but not turning around, "Listen, elder brother. I told you I didn't ask to be assigned to this mop-up operation; and if I'd known I'd find you here, I'd have taken leave or a transfer. But I'm here now, and I'll do my duty, do you hear?"

"As the Lord wills," said Juma from behind him.

The walls of Juma's house, like those of all the houses in Ain Chelia, were cast fifty centimeters thick to resist the heat of the sun. The front door was on a scale with the walls, close-fitting and too massive to slam. To Captain Mboya, it was the last frustration of the interview that he could elicit no more than a satisfied thump from the door as he stamped into the street.

The ballistic crack of the bullet was all the louder for the stillness of the plateau an instant before. Captain Mboya ducked beneath the lip of the headquarters dugout. The report of the sniper's weapon was lost in the fire of the powerguns and mortars that answered it. "Via, Captain!" snarled Sergeant Scratchard from the parked commo jeep. "Trying to get yourself killed?"

"Via!" Esa wheezed. He had bruised his chin and was thankful for it, the way a child is thankful for any punishment less than the one imagined. He accepted Scratchard's silent offer of a fiber-obtics periscope. Carefully, the captain raised it to scan what had been the Chelia Mine and was now the Bordj—the Fortress—holding approximately one hundred and forty Kabyle rebels with enough supplies to last a year.

Satellite photographs showed the mine as a series of neatly-stepped terraces in the center of a plateau. From the plateau's surface, nothing of significance could be seen until a flash discovered the position of a sniper the moment before he dodged to fire again.

"It'd be easy," Sergeant Scratchard said, "if they'd just tried to use the pit as a big foxhole . . . Have Central pop a couple antipersonnel overhead and then we go in and count bodies. But they've got tunnels and spider holes—and command-detonated mines—laced out from the pit like a giant worm-farm. This one's going to cost, Esa."

"Blood and martyrs," the captain said under his breath. When he had received the Ain Chelia assignment, Mboya had first studied reconnaissance coverage of the village and the mine three kilometers away. It was now a month and a half since the rebel disaster at al-Madinah. The Slammers had raised the siege of the capital in a pitched battle that no one in the human universe was better equipped to fight. Surviving rebels had scattered to their homes to make what preparations they could against the white terror they knew would sweep in the wake of the government's victory. At Ain Chelia, the preparations had been damned effective. The recce showed clearly that several thousand cubic meters of rubble had been dumped into the central pit of the mine, the waste of burrowings from all around its five kilometer circumference.

"We can drop penetrators all year," Mboya said, aloud but more to himself than to the non-com beside him. "Blow the budget for the whole operation, and even then I wouldn't bet they couldn't tunnel ahead of the shelling faster than we broke rock on top of them."

"If we storm the place," said Sergeant Scratchard, "and then go down the tunnels after the hold-outs, we'll have thirty per cent casualties if we lose a man."

A rifle flashed from the pit-edge. Almost simultaneously, one of the company's three-barreled automatic weapons slashed the edge of the rebel gunpit. The trooper must have sighted in his weapon earlier when a sniper had popped from the pit, knowing the site would be re-used eventually. Now the air shook as the powergun detonated a bandolier of grenades charged with industrial explosives. The sniper's rifle glittered as it spun into the air; her head was by contrast a ragged blur, its long hair uncoiling and snapping outward with the thrust of the explosion.

"Get that gunner's name," Mboya snapped to his first sergeant. "He's earned a week's leave as soon as we stand down. But to get all the rest of them . . ." and the officer's voice was the more stark for the fact that it was so controlled, "we're going to need something better. I think we're going to have to talk them out."

"Via, Captain," said Scratchard in real surprise, "Why would they want to come out? They saw at al-Madinah what happens when they faced us in the field. And nobody surrenders when they know all prisoners're going to be shot."

"Don't say nobody," said Esa Mboya in a voice as crisp as the gunfire bursting anew from the Bordj. "Because that's just what you're going to see this lot do."

The dead end of Juma's street had been blocked and turned into the company maintenance park between the time Esa left to observe the Bordj and his return to his brother's house. Skimmers, trucks, and a gun-jeep with an intermittent short in its front fan had been pulled into the cul-de-sac. They were walled on three sides by the courtyards of the houses beyond Juma's.

Sergeant Scratchard halted the jeep with the bulky commo equipment in the open street, but Mboya swung his own skimmer around the supply truck that formed a makeshift fourth wall for the park. A guard saluted. "Muller!" Esa shouted, even before the skirts of his one-man vehicle touched the pavement. "What in the name of heaven d'ye think you're about! I told you to set up in the main square!"

Bog Muller stood up beside a skimmer raised on edge. He was a bulky Technician with twenty years service in the Slammers. A good administrator, but his khakis were clean. Operation Feirefitz had required the company to move fast and long, and there was no way Muller's three half-trained subordinates could have coped with the consequent rash of equipment failures. "Ah, well, Captain," Muller temporized, his eyes apparently focused on the row of wall spikes over Esa's head, "we ran into Juma and he said—"

"He *what!*" Mboya shouted.

"I said," said Juma, rising from behind the skimmer himself, "that security in the middle of the village would be more of a problem than anyone needed. We've got some hot heads; I don't want any of them to get the notion of stealing a gun-jeep, for instance. The two households there—" he pointed to the entrances now blocked by vehicles, using the grease gun in his right hand for the gesture—"have both been evacuated to the Bordj." The half-smile he gave his brother could have been meant for either what he had just said or for the words he added, raising both the grease gun and the wire brush he held in his left hand: "Besides, what with the mine closed, I'd get rusty myself with no equipment to work on."

"After all," said Muller in what was more explanation than defense, "I knew Juma back when."

Esa took in his brother's smile, took in as well the admiring glances of the three Tech I's who had been watching the civilian work. "All right," he said to Muller, "but the next time clear it with me. And you," he said, pointing to Juma, "come on inside for now. We need to talk."

"Yes, little brother," the civilian said with a bow as submissive as his tone.

In the surprising cool of his house, Juma stripped off the gritty jellaba he had worn while working. He began washing with a waterless cleaner, rubbing it on with smooth strokes of his palms. On a chain around his neck glittered a tiny silver crucifix, normally hidden by his clothing.

"You didn't do much of a job persuading your friends to your Way of Peace," Esa said with an anger he had not intended to display.

"No, I'm afraid I didn't," the civilian answered mildly. "They were polite enough, even the Kaid, Ali ben Cheriff. But they pointed out that the Arabizers in al-Madinah intended to stamp out all traces of Kabyle culture as soon as possible . . . which of course was true. And we did have our own martyr here in Ain Chelia, as you know. I couldn't—" Juma looked up at his brother, his dark skin glistening beneath the lather—"argue with their *military* estimate, after all, either. The Way doesn't require that its followers lie about reality in order to change it—but I don't have to tell you that."

"Go on," said the captain. His hand touched the catches of his body armor. He did not release them, however, even though the hard-suit was not at the moment protection against any physical threat.

"Well, the National Army was outnumbered ten to one by the troops we could field from the backlands," Juma continued as he stepped into the shower. "That's without defections, too. And weapons aren't much of a problem. Out there, any jack-leg mechanic can turn out a truck piston in his back room. The tolerances aren't any closer on a machine gun. But what we didn't expect—" he raised his deep voice only enough to override the hiss of the shower—was that all six of the other planets of the al-Ittihad al Arabi—" for Arab Union Juma used the Arabic words, and they rasped in his throat like a file on bars—"would club together and help the sanctimonious butchers in al-Madinah hire the Slammers."

He stepped shining from the stall, no longer pretending detachment or that he and his brother were merely chatting. "I visited the siege lines then," Juma rumbled, wholly a preacher and wholly a man, "and I begged the men from Ain Chelia to come home while there was time. To make peace, or if they would not choose peace then at least to choose life—to lie low in the hills till the money ran out and the Slammers were off on somebody else's contract, killing somebody else's enemies. But my friends would stand with their brothers . . . and so they did, and they died with their brothers, too many of them, when the tanks came through their encirclement like knives through a goat-skin." His smile crooked and his voice dropped. "And the rest came home and told me they should have listened before."

"They'll listen to you now," said Esa, "if you tell them to come out of the Bordj without their weapons and surrender."

Juma began drying himself on a towel of coarse local cotton. "Will they?" he replied without looking up.

Squeezing his fingers against the bands of porcelain armor over his stomach, Esa said, "The Re-education Camps outside al-Madinah aren't a rest cure, but there's too many journalists in the city to let them be too bad. Even if the hold-outs are willing to die, they surely don't want their whole families wiped out. And if we have to clear the Bordj ourselves—well, there won't be any prisoners, you know that. . . . There wouldn't be even if we wanted them, not after we blast and gas the tunnels, one by one."

"Yes, I gathered the Re-education Camps aren't too bad," the civilian agreed, walking past his brother to don a light jellaba of softer weave than his work garment. "I gather they're not very full, either. A—a cynic, say, might guess that most of the trouble-makers don't make it to al-Madinah where journalists can see them. That they die in the desert after they've surrendered. Or they don't surrender, of course. I don't think Ali ben Cheriff and the others in the Bordj are going to surrender, for instance."

"Damn you!" the soldier shouted, "The choice is *certain* death, isn't it? *Any* chance is better than that!"

"Well, you see," said Juma, watching the knuckles of his right hand twist against the palm of his left, "they know as well as I do that the only transport you arrived with was the minimum to haul your own supplies. There's no way you could carry over a hundred prisoners back to the capital. No way in . . . Hell."

Esa slammed the wall with his fist. Neither the concrete nor his raging expression showed any reaction to the loud impact. "I could be planning to put them in commandeered ore haulers, couldn't I?" he said. "Some of them must be operable!"

Juma stepped to the younger man and took him by the wrists as gently as a shepherd touching a newborn lamb. "Little brother," he said, "swear to me that you'll turn anyone who surrenders over to the authorities in al-Madinah, and I'll do whatever I can to get them to surrender."

The soldier snatched his hands away. He said, "Do you think I wouldn't lie to you because we're brothers? Then you're a fool!"

"What I think, what anyone thinks, is between him and the Lord," Juma said. He started to move toward his brother again but caught the motion and turned it into a swaying only. "If you will swear to me to deliver them unharmed, I'll carry your message into the Bordj."

Esa swung open the massive door. On the threshold he paused and turned to his brother. "Every one of my boys who doesn't make it," he said in a venomous whisper. "His blood's on your head."

Captain Mboya did not try to slam the door this time. He left it standing open as he strode through the courtyard. "Scratchard!" he roared to the sergeant with an anger not meant for the man on whom it fell. "Round up ben Khedda!" Mboya threw himself down on his skimmer and flicked the fans to life. Over their whine he added, "Get him up to me at the command dugout, Now!"

With the skill of long experience, the captain spun his one-man vehicle past the truck and the jeep parked behind it. Sergeant Scratchard gloomily watched his commander shriek up the street. The captain shouldn't have been going anywhere without the jeep, his commo link to Central, in tow. No point in worrying about that, though. The non-com sighed and lifted the jeep off the pavement. Ben Khedda would be at his house or in the cafe across the street from it. Scratchard hoped he had a vehicle of his own and wouldn't have to ride the jump seat of the jeep. He didn't like to sit that close to a slimy traitor.

But Jack Scratchard knew he'd done worse things than sit with a traitor during his years with the Slammers; and, needs must, he would again.

The mortar shell burst with a white flash. Seconds later came a distant *chunk!* as if a rock had been dropped into a trash can. Even after the report had died away, fragments continued ricocheting from rock with tiny gnat-songs. Ben Khedda flinched beneath the clear night sky.

"It's just our harassing fire," said Captain Mboya. "You rag-heads don't have high-angle weapons, thank the Lord. Of course, all our shells do is keep them down in their tunnels."

The civilian swallowed. "Your sergeant," he said, "told me you needed me at once." Scratchard stirred in the darkness at the other end of the dugout, but he made no comment of his own.

"Yeah," said Mboya, "but when I cooled off I decided to take a turn around the perimeter. Took a while. It's a bloody long perimeter for one cursed infantry company to hold."

"Well, I," ben Khedda said, "I came at once, sir. I recognize the duty all good citizens owe to our liberators." Firing broke out, a burst from a projectile weapon answered promiscuously by powerguns. Ben Khedda winced again. Cyan bolts from across the pit snapped overhead, miniature lightning following miniature thunder.

Without looking up, Captain Mboya keyed his commo helmet and said, "Thrasher Four to Thrasher Four-Three." Anybody shoots beyond his sector again and it's ten days in the glass house when we're out of this cop." The main unit in Scratchard's jeep purred as it relayed the amplified signal. All the firing ceased.

"Will ben Cheriff and the others in the Bordj listen to you, do you think?" the captain continued.

For a moment, ben Khedda did not realize the officer was speaking to him. He swallowed again, "Well, I . . . I can't say," he blurted. He began to curl in his upper lip as if to chew a moustache, though he was clean shaven. "They aren't good friends of mine, of course, but if God wills and it would help you if I addressed them over a loudspeaker as to their true duties as citizens of Dar al-B'heed—"

"We hear you were second in command of the Chelia contingent at Madinah," Mboya said inflexibly. "Besides, there won't be a loudspeaker, you'll be going in person."

Horror at past and future implications warred in ben Khedda's mind and froze his tongue. At last he stammered, "Oh no, C-captain, before G-god, they've lied to you! That accurst al-Habashi wishes to lie away my life! I did no more than any man would do to stay alive!"

Mboya waved the other to silence. The pale skin of his palm winked as another shell detonated above the Bordj. When the echoes died away, the captain went on in a voice as soft as a leopard's paw, "You will tell them that if they all surrender, their lives will be spared and they will not be turned over to the government until they are actually in al-Madinah. You will say that I swore that on my honor and on the soul of my house."

Ben Khedda raised a hand to interrupt, but the soldier's voice rolled on implacably,, "They must deposit all their arms in the Bordj and come out to be shackled. The tunnels will be searched. If there are any holdouts, three of those who surrendered will be shot for each hold-out. If there are any boobytraps, ten of those who surrendered will be shot for every man of mine who is injured."

Mboya drew a breath, long and deep as that of a power lifter. The civilian, tight as a house-jack, strangled his own words as he waited for the captain to conclude. "You will say that after they have done as I have said, all of them will be loaded on ore carriers with sunscreens. You will explain that there will be food and water brought from the village to support them. And you will tell them that if some of them are wounded or are infirm, they may ride within an ambulance which will be air-conditioned."

"Do you understand?"

For a moment, ben Khedda struggled with an inability to phrase his thoughts in neutral terms. He was unwilling to meet the captain's eyes, even with the darkness as a cushion. Finally he said, "Captain—I, I trust your word as I would trust that of no man since the Prophet, on whom be peace. When you say the lives of the traitors will be spared, there can be no doubt, may it please God."

"Trust has nothing to do with it," said Captain Mboya without expression. "I have told you what you will say, and you will say it."

"Captain, Captain," whimpered the civilian, "I understand. The trip is a long one and surely some of the most troublesome will die of heat stroke. They will know that themselves. But there will be no . . . general tragedy? I must live here in Ain Chelia with the friends of the, the traitors. You see my position?"

"Cheer up, citizen," Sergeant Scratchard said. "You're getting a great chance to pick one side and stick with it. The change'll do you good."

Ben Khedda gave a despairing cry and stood, his dun jellaba flapping as a lesser shadow. He stared over the rim of the dugout into a night now brightened only by stars and a random powergun bolt, harassment like that of the mortars. He turned and shouted at the motionless captain, "It's easy for you—you go where your colonel sends you, you kill who he tells you to kill. And then you come all high and moral over the rest of us, who have to make our own decisions! You despise me? At least I'm a man and not somebody's dog!"

Mboya laughed harshly. "You think Colonel Hammer told us how to clear the back country? Don't be a fool. My official orders are to co-operate with the District Governor and to send all prisoners back to al-Madinah for internment. The colonel can honestly deny ordering anything else—and letting him do that is as much a part of my job as co-operating with a governor who knows that anybody really sent to a Re-education Camp will be back in his hair in a year."

There was a silence in the dug-out. At last the sergeant said, "He can't go out now, sir." The moan of a ricochet underscored the words.

"No, no, we'll have to wait till dawn," the captain agreed tiredly. As if ben Khedda were an unpleasant machine, he added, "Get him the hell out of my sight, though. Stick him in the bunker with the Headquarters Squad and tell them to hold him till called for. Via! but I wish this operation was over."

The guns spat at one another all through the night. It was not the fire that kept Esa Mboya awake, however, but rather the dreams that plagued him with gentle words whenever he did manage to nod off.

"Well," said Juma, scowling judiciously at the gun-jeep

on the rack before him, "I'd say we pull the wiring harness first. Half the time that's the whole problem—grit gets into the conduits and when the fans vibrate, it saws through the insulation. Even if we're wrong, we haven't done anything that another few months of running on Dar al-B'heed wouldn't have required anyway."

"You should have seen him handle one a' these when I first knew him," said Bog Muller proudly to his subordinates. "Beat it to hell, he would, Via—bring her in with rock scrapes on both sides that he'd put on at the same time!"

The Kikuyu civilian touched a valve and lowered the rack. His hand caressed the sand-burnished skirt of the jeep as it sank past him. The joy-stick controls were in front of the left-hand seat. Finesse was a matter of touch and judgment, not sophisticated instrumentation. He waggled the stick gently, remembering. In front of the other seat was the powergun, its three iridium barrels poised to rotate and hose out destruction in a nearly-continuos stream.

"You won't believe it," continued the Technician, "but I saw it with my own eyes—" that was a lie—"this boy here steering with one hand and working the gun with the other. Bloody miracle that was—even if he did give Maintenance more trouble than any three other troopers."

You learn a lot about a machine when you push it, when you stress it." said Juma. His fingers reached for but did not quite touch the spade grips of the tribarrel. "About men, too," he added and lowered his hand. He looked Muller in the face and said, "What I learned about myself was that I didn't want to live in a universe that had no better use for me than to gun other people down. I won't claim to be saving souls . . . because that's in the Lord's hands and he uses what instruments he desires. But at least I'm not taking lives."

One of the younger Techs coughed, Muller nodded heavily and said, "I know what you mean, Juma. I've never regretted getting into Maintenance right off the way I did. Especially times like today. . . . But Via, if we stand here fanning our lips, we won't get a curst bit of work done, will we?"

The civilian chuckled without asking for an explanation of 'especially times like today.' "Sure, Bog," he said, latching open the left-side access ports one after another.

"Somebody dig out a 239B harness and we'll see if I remember as much as I think I do about changing one of these beggars." He glanced up at the truncated mass of the plateau, wiping his face with a bandanna. "Things have quieted down since the sun came up," he remarked. "Even if I weren't—dedicated to the Way—I know too many people on both sides to like to hear the shooting at the mine."

None of the other men responded. At the time it did not occur to Juma that there might be something about his words that embarrassed them.

"There's a flag," said Scratchard, his eyes pressed tight to the lenses of the periscope. "Blood and martyrs, Cap—there's a flag!"

"No shooting!" Mboya ordered over his commo as he moved. "Four to all Thrasher units, stand to but no shooting!"

All around the mine crater, men watched a white rag flapping on the end of a long wooden pole. Some looked through periscopes like those in the command dugout, others over the sights of their guns in hope that something would give them an excuse to fire. "Well, what are they waiting for?" the captain muttered.

"It's ben Khedda," guessed Scratchard without looking away from the flag. "He was just scared green to go out there. Now he's just as scared to come back."

The flag staggered suddenly. Troopers tensed, but a moment later an unarmed man climbed full height from the Bordj. The high sun threw his shadow at his feet like a pit. Standing as erect as his age permitted him, Ali ben Cheriff took a step toward the Slammers' lines. Wind plucked at his jellaba and white beard; the rebel leader was a patriarch in appearance as well as in simple fact. On his head was the green turban that marked him as a pilgrim to al-Meccah on Terra. He was as devotedly Moslem as he was Kabyle, and he—like most of the villagers—saw no inconsistencies in the facts. To ben Cheriff it was no more necessary to become an Arab in order to accept Islam than it had seemed necessary to Saint Paul that converts to Christ first become Jews.

"We've won," the captain said as he watched the figure through the foreshortened lenses. "That's the Kaid, ben Cheriff. If he comes, they all do."

Up from the hidden tunnel clambered an old woman wearing the stark black of a matron. The Kaid paused and stretched back his hand, but the woman straightened without help. Together the old couple began to walk toward the waiting guns.

The flagstaff flapped erect again. Gripping it like a talisman, Youssef ben Khedda stepped from the tunnel mouth where the Kaid had shouldered aside his hesitation. He picked his way across the ground at increasing speed. Where ben Khedda passed the Kaid and his wife, he skirted them widely as if he were afraid of being struck. More rebels were leaving the Bordj in single file. None of them carried visible weapons. Most, men and women alike, had their eyes cast down; but a red-haired girl leading a child barely old enough to walk glared around with the haughty rage of a lioness.

"Well, no rest for the wicked," grunted Sergeant Scratchard. Settling his submachinegun on its sling, he climbed out of the dugout. "Headquarters Squad to me," he ordered. Bent over against the possible shock of a fanatic's bullets, experienced enough to know the reality of his fear and brave enough to face it none the less, Scratchard began to walk to the open area between pit and siege lines where the prisoners would be immobilized. The seven men of HQ Squad followed; their corporal drove the jeep loaded with leg irons.

One of the troopers raised his powergun to bar ben Khedda. Scratchard waved and called an order; the trooper shrugged and let the Kabyle pass. The sergeant gazed after him for a moment, then spat in the dust and went on about the business of searching and securing the prisoners.

Youssef ben Khedda was painting with tension and effort as he approached the dugout, but there was a hard glint of triumph in his eyes as well. He knew he was despised, by those he led no less than by those who had driven him; but he had dug the rebels from their fortress when all the men and guns of the Slammers might have been unable to do so without him. Now he saw a way to ride the bloody crest to permanent power in Ain Chelia. He tried to set his flag in the ground. It scratched into the rocky soil, then fell with a clatter. "I have brought them to you," ben Khedda said in a haughty voice.

"Some of them, at least," said Mboya, his face neutral. Rebels continued to straggle from the Bordj, their faces sallow from more than the day they had spent in their tunnels. The Kaid had submitted to the shackles with a stony indifference. His wife was weeping beside him, not for herself but for her husband. Two of the nervous troopers were fanning the prisoners with detector wands set for steel and iridium. Anything the size of a razor blade would register. A lead bludgeon or a brass-barreled pistol would be ignored, but there were some chances you took in the service of practicality.

"As God wills, they are all coming, you know that," ben Khedda said, assertive with dreamed-of lordship. "If they were each in his separate den, many of them would fight till you blew them out or buried them. All are willing to die, but most would not willingly kill their fellows, their families." His face worked. "A fine joke, is it not? A fine joke, is it not?" If what had crossed ben Khedda's lips had been a smile, then it transmuted to a sneer. "They would have been glad to kill me first, I think, but they were afraid that you would have been angry."

"More fools them," said the captain.

"Yes . . . ," said the civilian, drawing back his face like a rat confronting a terrier, "more fools them. And now you will pay me."

"Captain," said the helmet speaker in the first sergeant's voice, "this one says he's the last."

Mboya climbed the four steps to surface level. Scratchard waved and pointed to the Kabyle who was just joining the scores of his fellows. The number of those being shackled in a continuous chain at least approximated the one hundred and forty who were believed to have holed up in the Bordj. Through the clear air rang hammer strokes as a pair of troopers, stapled the chain to the ground at intervals, locking the prisoners even more securely into the killing ground. The captain nodded. "We'll give it a minute to let anybody still inside have second thoughts," he said over the radio. "Then the search teams go in." He looked at ben Khedda. "All right," he said, "you've got your life and whatever you think you can do with it. Now, get out of here before I change my mind."

Mboya gazed again at the long line of prisoners. He was unable not to imagine them as they would look in an hour's time, after the Bordj had been searched and their existence was no longer a tool against potential holdouts. He could not have broken with the Way of his childhood, however, had he not replaced it with a sense of duty as uncompromising. Esa Mboya, Captain, G Company, Hammer's Regiment, would do whatever was required to accomplish the task set him. They had been hired to pacify the district, not just to quiet it down for six months or a year.

Youssef ben Khedda had not left. He was still facing Mboya, as unexpected and unpleasant as a rat on the pantry shelf. He was saying, "No, there is one more thing you must do, as God wills, before you leave Ain Chelia. I do not compel it—" the soldier's face went blank with fury at the suggestion—"your duty that you talk of compels you. There is one more traitor in the village, a man who did not enter the Bordj because he thought his false god would preserve him."

"Little man," said the captain in shock and a genuine attempt to stop the words he knew were about to be said, "don't—"

"Add the traitor Juma al-Habashi to these," the civilian cried, pointing to the fluttering jellabas of the prisoners. "Put him there or his whines of justice and other words and his false god will poison the village again like a dead rat stinking in a pool. Take him!"

The two men stood with their feet on a level. The soldier's helmet and armor increased his advantage in bulk, however, and his wrath lighted his face like a cleansing flame. "Shall I slay my brother for thee, lower-than-a-dog?" he snarled.

Ben Khedda's face jerked at the verbal slap, but with a wave of his arm he retorted, "Will you now claim to follow the Way yourself? There stand one hundred and thirty-four of your brothers. Make it one more, as your duty commands!"

The absurdity was so complete that the captain trembled between laughter and the feeling that he had gone insane. Carefully, his tone touched more with wonder than with rage until the world should return to focus, the Kikuyu said, "Shall I, Esa Mboya, order the death of Juma Mboya? My brother, flesh of my father and of my mother . . . who held my hand when I toddled my first steps upright?"

Now at last ben Khedda's confidence squirted out like blood from a slashed carotid. "The name—" he said. "I didn't *know!*"

Mboya's world snapped into place again, its realities clear and neatly dove-tailed. "Get out, filth," he said harshly, "and wonder what I plan for you when I come down from this hill."

The civilian stumbled back toward his car as if his body and not his spirit had received the mortal wound. The soldier considered him dispassionately. If ben Khedda stayed in Ain Chelia, he wouldn't last long. The Slammers would be out among the stars, and the central government a thousand kilometers away in Al-Madinah would be no better able to protect a traitor. Youssef ben Khedda would be a reminder of friends and relatives torn by blasts of cyan fire with every step he took on the streets of the village. Those steps would be few enough, one way or the other.

And if in the last fury of his well-earned fear ben Khedda tried to kill Juma—well, Juma had made his bed, his Way . . . he could tread it himself. Esa laughed. Not that the traitor would attempt murder personally. Even in the final corner, rats of ben Khedda's stripe tried to persuade other rats to bite for them.

"Captain," murmured Scratchard's voice over the command channel, "think we've waited long enough?"

Instead of answering over the radio, Mboya nodded and began walking the hundred meters to where his sergeant stood near the prisoners. The rebels' eyes followed him, some with anger, most in only a dull appreciation of the fact that he was the nearest moving object on a static landscape. Troopers had climbed out of their gun pits all around the Bordj. Their dusty khaki blended with the soil, but the sun woke bright reflections from the barrels of their weapons.

The search teams are ready to go in, sir," Scratchard said, speaking in Dutch but stepping a pace further from the shackled Kaid besides.

"Right," the captain agreed. "I'll lead the team from Third Platoon."

"Captain—"

"Where are the trucks, unbeliever?" demanded Ali ben

Cheriff. His voice started on a quaver but lashed at the
end.

"—there's plenty cursed things for you to do besides
crawling down a hole with five pongoes. Leave it to the
folks whose job it is."

"There's nothing left of this operation that Mendoza
can't wrap up," Mboya said. "Believe me, he won't like
doing it any less, either."

"Where are the trucks to carry away our children, dog
and son of dogs?" cried the Kaid. Beneath the green
turban, the rebel's face was as savage and unyielding as
that of a trapped wolf.

"It's not for fun," Mboya went on. "There'll be times
I'll have to send boys out to be killed while I stay back,
safe as a staff officer, and run things. But if I lead from
the front when I can, when it won't compromise the
mission if I do stop a load—then they'll do what they're
told a little sharper when it's me that says it the next time."

The Kaid spat. Lofted by his anger and the breeze,
the gobbet slapped the side of Mboya's helmet and
dribbled down onto his porcelain-sheathed shoulder.

Scratchard turned. Ignoring the automatic weapon
slung ready to fire under his arm, he drew a long knife
from his boot sheath instead. Three strides separated the
non-com from the line of prisoners. He had taken two
of them before Mboya caught his shoulder and stopped
him. "Easy, Jack," the captain said.

Ben Cheriff's gaze was focused on the knife-point. Fear
of death could not make the old man yield, but neither
was he unmoved by the approach of its steel-winking eye.
Scratchard's own face had no more expression than did the
knife itself. The Kaid's wife lunged at the soldier to the
limit of her chain, but the look Scratchard gave her husband dried her throat around the curses within it.

Mboya pulled his man back. "Easy," he repeated. "I
think he's earned that, don't you?" He turned Scratchard
gently. He did not point out, nor did he need to do so,

the three gun-jeeps which had swung down the fifty meters in front of the line of captives. Their crews were tense and still with the weight of their orders. They met Mboya's eyes comprehending but without enthusiasm.

"Right," said Scratchard mildly. "Well, the quicker we get down that hole, the quicker we get the rest of the job done. Let's go."

The five tunnel rats from Third Platoon were already squatting at the entrance from which the rebels had surrendered. Captain Mboya began walking toward them. "You stay on top, Sergeant," he said. "You don't need to prove anything."

Scratchard cursed without heat. "I'll wait at the tunnel mouth unless something pops. You'll be out of radio contact and I'll be curst if I trust anybody else to carry you a message."

The tunnel rats were rising to their feet, silent men whose faces were in constant, tiny motion. They carried detector wands and sidearms; two had even taken off their body armor and stood in the open air looking paler than shelled shrimp. Mboya cast a glance back over his shoulder at the prisoners and the gun-jeeps beyond. "Do you believe in sin, Sergeant?" he asked.

Scratchard glanced sidelong at his superior. "Don't know, sir. Not really my field."

"My brother believes in it," said the captain "but I guess he left the Slammers before you transferred out of combat cars. And he isn't here now, Jack, I am, so I guess we'll have to dispense with sin today."

"Team Three ready, sir," said the black-haired man who probably would have had sergeant's pips had he not been stripped to the waist.

"Right," said Mboya. Keying his helmet he went on, "Thrasher to Club one, Club two. Let's see what they left us, boys." And as he stepped toward the tunnel's mouth, without really thinking about the words until he spoke them, he added, "And the Lord be with us all."

❖   ❖   ❖

The bed of the turbine driving Youssef ben Khedda's car was enough out of true that the vehicle announced its own approach unmistakably. Juma wondered in the back of his mind what brought the little man, but his main concentration was on the plug connector he was trying to reeve through a channel made for something a size smaller. At last the connector shifted the last two millimeters necessary for Juma to slip a button-hook deftly above it. The three subordinate Techs gave a collective sigh, and Bog Muller beamed in reflected glory.

"Father!" ben Khedda wheezed, oblivious to the guard frowning over his powergun a pace behind, "Father! You've got to . . . I've got to talk to you. You must!"

"All right, Youssef," the Kikuyu said. "In a moment." He tugged the connector gently through its channel and rotated it to mate with the gun leads.

Ben Khedda reached for Juma's arm in a fury of impatience. One of the watching Techs caught with the kabyle's wrist. "Touch him, rag-head," the trooper said, "and you better be able to grow a new hand." He thrust ben Khedda back with more force than the resistance demanded.

Juma straightened from the gun-jeep and put an arm about the shoulders of the angry trooper. "Worse job than replacing all the fans," he said in Dutch, "but it gives you a good feeling to finish it. Run the static test, if you would, and I'll be back in a few minutes." He squeezed the trooper, released him, and added in Kabyle to his fellow villager, "Come into my house, then, Youssef. What is it you need of me?"

Ben Khedda's haste and nervousness were obvious from the way his car lay parked with its skirt folded under the front from an over-hasty stop. Juma paused with a frown for more than the mechanical problem. He bent to lift the car and let the skirt spring away from the fan it was probably touching at the moment.

"Don't *worry* about that," ben Khedda cried, plucking at the bigger man's sleeve. "We've *got* to talk in private."

Juma had left his courtyard gate unlatched since he was working only a few meters away. Before ben Khedda had reached the door of the house, he was spilling the words that tormented him. "Before God, you have to talk to your brother or he'll kill me, Father, he'll kill *me!*"

"Youssef," said the Kikuyu as he swung his door open and gestured the other man toward the cool interior, "I pray—I have been praying—that at worst, none of our villagers save those in the Bordj are in danger." He smiled too sadly to be bitter. "You would know better than I, I think, who may have been marked out to Esa as an enemy of the government. But he's not a cruel man, my brother, only a very—determined one. He won't add you to whatever list he has out of mere dislike."

The Kabyle's lips worked silently. His face was tortured by the explanation that he needed to give but could not. "Father," he pleaded, "You *must* believe me, he'll have me killed. Before God, you must beg him for my life, you *must!*"

Ben Khedda was gripping the Kikuyu by both sleeves. Juma detached himself carefully and said, "Youssef, why would my brother want you killed—of all the men in Ain Chelia? Did something happen?"

The smaller man jerked himself back with a dawning horror in his eyes. "You planned this with him, didn't you?" he cried. His arm thrust at the altar as if to sweep away the closed triptych. "This is all a lie, your prayers, your *Way*—you and your butcher brother trapped me to bleed like a sheep on Id al-Fitr! Traitor! Liar! Murderer!" He threw his hands over his face and flung himself down and across a stool. The Kabyle's sobs held the torment of a man without hope.

Juma stared at the weeping man. There was something unclean about ben Khedda. His back rose and fell beneath the jellaba like the distended neck of a python bolting a young child. "Youssef," the Kikuyu said as gently as he could, "you may stay here or leave, as you please. I promise you that I will speak to Esa this evening, on your behalf as well as that of . . . others, all the others. Is there anything you need to tell me?"

Only the tears responded.

The dazzling sun could not sear away Juma's disquiet as he walked past the guard and the barricading truck. Something was wrong with the day, with the very silence. Though all things were with the Lord.

The jeep's inspection ports had been latched shut. The Techs had set a pair of skimmers up on their sides as the next project. The civilian smiled. "Think she'll float now?" he asked the trooper who had grabbed ben Khedda. "Let's see if I remember how to put one of these through her paces. You can't trust a fix, you see, till you've run her under full load."

There was a silence broken by the whine of ben Khedda's turbine firing. Juma managed a brief prayer that the Kabyle would find a Way open to him—knowing as he prayed that the impulse to do so was from his mind and not at all from his heart.

"Juma, ah," Bog Muller was trying to say. "Ah, look, this isn't—isn't our idea, it's the job, you know. But the captain—" none of the four Techs were looking anywhere near the civilian—"he ordered that you not go anywhere today until, until . . . it was clear."

The silence from the Bordj was a cloak that smothered Juma and squeezed all the blood from his face. "Not that you're a prisoner, but, ah, your brother thought it'd be better for both of you if you didn't see him or call him till—after."

"I see," said the civilian, listening to his own voice as if a third party were speaking. "Until after he's killed my friends, I suppose . . . yes." He began walking back to his house, his sandaled feet moving without being consciously directed. "Juma—" called Muller, but the Tech thought better of the words or found he had none to say.

Ben Khedda had left the door ajar. It was only by habit that Juma himself closed it behind him. The dim coolness within was no balm to the fire that skipped across the surface of his mind. Kneeling, the Kikuyu unlatched and opened wide the panels of his altar piece. It was his one conscious affectation, a copy of a triptych painted over a millennium before by the Master of Hell, Hieronymous Bosch. Atop a haywain rode a couple. Their innocence was beset by every form of temptation in the world, the World. Where would their Way take them? No doubt where it took all Mankind, saving the Lord's grace, to Hell and the grave—good intentions be damned, hope be damned, innocence be damned. . . . Obscurely glad of the harshness of the tiles on which he knelt, Juma prayed for his brother and for the souls of those who would shortly die in flames as like to those of Hell as man could create. He prayed for himself as well, for he was damned to endure what had not changed. They were all travelers together on the Way.

After a time, Juma sighed and raised his head. A demon faced him on the triptych; it capered and piped through its own blue snout. Not for the first time, Juma thought of how pleasant it would be to personify his own weakness and urgings. Then he could pretend that they were somehow apart from the true Juma Mboya, who remained whole and incorruptible.

The lower of the two drawers beneath the altar was not fully closed.

Even as he drew it open, Juma knew from the lack of resistance that the drawer was empty. The heavy-barreled powergun had rested within when ben Khedda had accompanied the search team. It was there no longer.

Striding swiftly and with the dignity of a leopard,

Mboya al-Habashi crossed the room and his courtyard. He appeared around the end of the truck barricade so suddenly that Bog Muller jumped. The Kikuyu pointed his index finger with the deliberation of a pistol barrel. "Bog," he said very clearly, "I need to call my brother at once or something terrible will happen."

"Via man," said the Technician, looking away, "You know how I feel about it, but it's not my option. You don't leave here, and you don't call, Juma—or it's my ass."

"Lord blast you for a fool!" the Kikuyu shouted, taking a step forward. All four Technicians backed away with their hands lifting. "Will you—" But though there was confusion on the faces watching him, there was nothing of assent, and there was no time to argue. As if he had planned it from the start, Juma slipped into the left saddle of the jeep he had just rewired and gunned the fans.

With an oath, Bog Muller grappled with the civilian. The muscles beneath Juma's loose jellaba had shifted driving fans beneath ore carriers in lieu of a hydraulic jack. He shrugged the Technician away with a motion as slight and as masterful as that of an earth tremor. Juma waggled the stick, using the vehicle's skirts to butt aside two of the younger men who belatedly tried to support their chief. Then he had the jeep clear of the repair rack and spinning on its own axis.

Muller scrambled to his feet again and waited for Juma to realize there was not enough room between truck and wall for the jeep to pass. If the driver himself had any doubt, it was not evident in the way he dialed on throttle and leaned to bring the right-hand skirt up an instant before it scraped the courtyard wall. Using the wall as a running surface and the force of his turn to hold him there, Juma sent the gun-jeep howling sideways around the barricade and up the street.

"Hey!" shouted the startled guard, rising from the shady side of the truck. "Hey!" and he shouldered his weapon.

A Technician grabbed him, wrestling the muzzle of the gun skyward. It was the same lanky man who had caught ben Khedda when he would have plucked at Juma's sleeve. "Via!" cried the guard, watching the vehicle corner and disappear up the main rode to the mine. "We weren't supposed to let him by!"

"We're better off explaining that," said the Tech, "than we are telling the captain how we just killed his brother. Right?"

The street was empty again. All five troopers stared at it for some moments before any of them moved to the radio.

Despite his haste, Youssef ben Khedda stopped his car short of the waiting gun-jeeps and began walking toward the prisoners. His back crept with awareness of the guns and the hard-eyed men behind them; but, as God willed, he had chosen and there could be no returning now.

The captain—his treacherous soul was as black as his skin—was not visible. No doubt he had entered the Bordj as he had announced he would. Against expectation, and as further proof that God favored his cause, ben Khedda saw no sign of that damnable first sergeant either. If God willed it, might they both be blasted to atoms somewhere in a tunnel!

The soldiers watching the prisoners from a few meters away were the ones whom ben Khedda had let on their search of the village. The corporal frowned, but he knew ben Khedda for a confidant of his superiors. "Go with God, brother," said the civilian in Arabic, praying the other would have been taught that tongue or Kabyle. "Your captain wished me to talk once more with that dog—" he pointed to ben Cheriff. "There are documents of which he knows," he concluded vaguely.

The non-com's lip quirked nervously. "Look, can it wait—" he began, but even as he spoke he was glancing at the leveled tribarrels forty meters distant. "Blood," he muttered, a curse and a prophecy. "Well, go talk then. But watch it—the bastard's mean as a snake and his woman's worse."

The Kaid watched ben Khedda approach with the fascination of a mongoose awaiting a cobra. The traitor threw himself to the ground and tried to kiss the Kaid's feet. "Brother in God," the unshackled men whispered, "we have been betrayed by the unbelievers. Their dog of a captain will have you all murdered on his return, despite his oaths to me."

"Are we to believe, brother Youssef," the Kaid said with a sneer, "that you intend to die here with the patriots to cleanse your soul of the lies you carried?"

Others along the line of prisoners were peering at the scene to the extent their irons permitted, but the two men spoke in voices too low for any but the Kaid's wife to follow the words. "Brother," ben Khedda continued, "preservation is better than expiation. The captain has confessed his wicked plan to no one but me. If he dies, it dies with him—and our people live. Now, raise me by the hands."

"Shall I touch your bloody hands, then?" ben Cheriff said, but he spoke as much in question as in scorn.

"Raise me by the hands," ben Khedda repeated, "and take from my right sleeve what you find there to hide in yours. Then wait the time."

"As God wills," the Kaid said and raised up ben Khedda. Their bodies were momentarily so close that their jellabas flowered together.

"And what in the blaze of Hell is *this*, Corporal!" roared Sergeant Scratchard. "Blood and martyrs, who told you to let anybody in with the prisoners?"

"Via, Sarge," the corporal sputtered, "he said—I mean, it was the captain, he tells me."

Ben Khedda had begun to sidle away from the time of prisoners. "Where the hell do you think *you're* going?" Scratchard snapped in Arabic. "Corporal, get another set of leg irons and clamp him onto his buddy there. If he's so copping hot to be here, he can stay till the captain says otherwise."

The sergeant paused, looking around the circle of eyes focused nervously on him. More calmly he continued, "The Bordj is clear. The captain's up from the tunnel, but it'll be a while before he gets here—they came up somewhere in West Bumfuck and he's borrowing a skimmer from First Platoon to get back. We'll wait to see what he says." The first sergeant started at Ali ben Cheriff, impassive as the wailing traitor was shackled to his right leg. "We'll wait till then," the soldier repeated.

Mboya lifted the nose of his skimmer and grounded it behind the first of the waiting gun-jeeps. Sergeant Scratchard trotted towards him from the direction of the prisoners. The non-com was painting with the heat and his armor; he raised his hand when he reached the captain in order to gain a moment's breathing space.

"Well?" Mboya prompted.

"Sir, Maintenance called," said Scratchard jerkily. "Your brother, sir. They think he's coming to see you."

The captain swore. "All right," he said, "if Juma thinks he has to watch this, he can watch it. He's a cursed fool if he expects to do anything *but* watch."

Scratchard nodded deeply, finding he inhaled more easily with his torso cocked forward. "Right, sir, I just— didn't want to rebroadcast on the Command channel in case Central was monitoring. Right. And then there's that rag-head, ben Khedda—I caught him talking to green-hat over there and thought he maybe ought to stay. For good."

Captain Mboya glanced at the prisoners. The men of Headquarters Squad still sat a few meters away because nobody had told them to withdraw. "Get them clear," the captain said with a scowl. He began walking toward the line, the first sergeant's voice turning his direction into a tersely-radioed order. "Somewhere down the plateau, an aircar was being revved with no concern for what pebbles would do to the fans. Juma, very likely. He was the man you wanted driving your car when it had all dropped in the pot and Devil took the hindmost.

"Jack," the captain said, "I understand how you feel about ben Khedda; but we're here to do a job, not to kill sons of bitches. If we were doing that, we'd have to start in al-Madinah, wouldn't we?"

Mboya and his sergeant were twenty meters from the prisoners. The Kaid watched their approach with his hands folded within the sleeves of his jellaba and his eyes as still as iron. Youssef ben Khedda was crouched beside him, a study in terror. He retained only enough composure that he did not try to run—and that because the pressure of the leg iron binding him to ben Cheriff was just sharp enough to penetrate the fear.

A gun-jeep howled up onto the top of the plateau so fast that it bounced and dragged its skirts, still under full throttle. Scratchard turned with muttered surprise. Captain Mboya did not look around. He reached into the thigh pocket of his coveralls where he kept a magnetic key that would release ben Khedda's shackles. "We can't just kill—" he repeated.

"Now, God, *now!*" ben Khedda shrieked. "He's going to *kill* me!"

The Kaid's hands appeared, the right one extending a pistol. It's muzzle was a gray circle no more placable than the eye that aimed it.

Mboya dropped the key. His hand clawed for his own weapon, but he was no gunman, no quick-draw expert. He was a company commander carrying ten extra kilos, with his pistol in a flap holster that would keep his hand out at least as well as it did the wind-blown sand. Esa's very armor slowed him, though it would not save his face or his femoral arteries when the shots came.

Behind the captain, in a jeep still skidding on the edge

of control, his brother triggered a one-handed burst as accurate as if parallax were a myth. The tribarrel was locked on its column; Juma let the vehicle's own side-slip saw the five rounds toward the man with the gun. A single two-centimeter bolt missed everything. Beyond, at the lip of the Bordj, a white flower bloomed from a cyan center as ionic calcium recombined with the oxygen from which it had been freed a moment before. Closer, everything was hidden by an instant glare. The pistol detonated in the Kaid's hand under the impact of a round from the tribarrel. That was chance—or something else, for only the Lord could be so precise with certainty. The last shot of the burst hurled the Kaid back with a hole in his chest and his jellaba aflame. Ali ben Cheriff's eyes were free of fear and his mouth still wore a tight smile. Ben Khedda's face would have been less of a study in virtue and manhood, no doubt, but the two bolts that flicked across it took the traitor's head into oblivion with his memory. Juma had walked his burst on target, like any good man with an automatic weapon; and if there was something standing where the bolts walked—so much the worse for it.

There were shouts, but they were sucked lifeless by the wind. No one else had fired, for a wonder. Troops all around the Bordj were rolling back into dug-outs they had thought it safe to leave.

Juma brought the jeep to a half a few meters from his brother. He doubled over the joy-stick as if he had been shot himself. Dust and sand puffed from beneath the skirts while the fans wound down; then the plume settled back on the breeze. Esa touched his brother's shoulder, feeling the dry sobs that wracked the jellaba. Very quietly the soldier said in the Kikuyu he had not, after all, forgotten. "I bring you a souvenir, elder brother. To replace the one you have lost." From his holster, now unsnapped, he drew his pistol and laid it carefully down on the empty gunner's seat of the jeep.

Juma looked up at his brother with a terrible dignity. "To remind me of the day I slew two men in the Lord's despite?" he asked formally. "Oh no, my brother I need no trinket to remind me of that forever."

"If you do not wish to remember the ones you killed," said Esa, "then perhaps it will remind you of the hundred and thirty-three whose lives you saved this day. And my life, of course."

Juma stared at his brother with a fixity by which alone he admitted his hope. He tugged the silver crucifix out of his jellaba and lifted it over his head. "Here," he said, "little brother. I offer you this in return for your gift. To remind you that wherever you go, the Way runs there as well."

Esa took the chain. With clumsy fingers he slipped it over his helmet. "All right, Thrasher, everybody stand easy," the captain roared into his commo link. "Two-six, I want food for a hundred and thirty-three people for three days. You've got my authority to take what you need from the village. Three-six, you're responsible for the transport. I want six ore carriers up here and I want them fast. If the first truck isn't here loading in twenty, that's two-zero mikes, I'll burn somebody a new asshole. Four-six, there's drinking water in drums down in those tunnels. Get it up here. Now, *move!*"

Juma stepped out of the gun-jeep, his left hand gripping Esa's right. Skimmers were already lifting from positions all around the Bordj. G Company was surprised but now one had forgotten that Captain Mboya meant his orders to be obeyed.

"Oh, one other thing," Esa said, then tripped his commo and added, "Thrasher Four to all Thrasher units—you get any argument from villagers while you're shopping, boys . . . just refer them to my brother."

It was past midday now. The sun had enough westering to wink from the crucifix against the soldier's armor—and from the pistol in the civilian's right hand.

The Tank Lords

They were the tank lords.

The Baron had drawn up his soldiers in the courtyard, the twenty men who were not detached to his estates on the border between the Kingdom of Ganz and the Kingdom of Marshall—keeping the uneasy truce and ready to break it if the Baron so willed.

I think the King sent mercenaries in four tanks to our place so that the Baron's will would be what the King wished it to be . . . though of course we were told they were protection against Ganz and the mercenaries of the Lightning Division whom Ganz employed.

The tanks and the eight men in them were from Hammer's Slammers, and they were magnificent.

Lady Miriam and her entourage rushed back from the barred windows of the woman's apartments on the second floor, squealing for effect. The tanks were so huge that the mirror-helmeted men watching from the turret hatches were nearly on a level with the upper story of the palace.

I jumped clear, but Lady Miriam bumped the chair I had dragged closer to stand upon and watch the arrival over the heads of the women I served.

"Leesh!" cried the Lady, false fear of the tanks replaced by real anger at me. She slapped with her fan of painted ox-horn, cutting me across the knuckles because I had thrown a hand in front of my eyes.

I ducked low over the chair, wrestling it out of the way and protecting myself with its cushioned bulk. Sarah, the Chief Maid, rapped my shoulder with the silver-mounted brush she carried for last-minute touches to the Lady's hair. "A monkey would make a better page than you, Elisha," she said. "A gelded monkey."

But the blow was a light one, a reflexive copy of her mistress' act. Sarah was more interested in reclaiming her place among the others at the windows now that modesty and feminine sensibilities had been satisfied by the brief charade. I didn't dare slide the chair back to where I had first placed it; but by balancing on tiptoes on the carven arms, I could look down into the courtyard again.

The Baron's soldiers were mostly off-worlders themselves. They had boasted that they were better men than the mercenaries if it ever came down to cases. The fear that the women had mimed from behind stone walls seemed real enough now to the soldiers whose bluster and assault rifles were insignificant against the iridium titans which entered the courtyard at a slow walk, barely clearing the posts of gates which would have passed six men marching abreast.

Even at idle speed, the tanks roared as their fans maintained the cushions of air that slid them over the ground. Three of the Baron's men dodged back through the palace doorway, their curses inaudible over the intake whine of the approaching vehicles.

The Baron squared his powerful shoulders with his dress cloak of scarlet, purple, and gold. I could not see his face, but the back of his neck flushed red and his left hand tugged his drooping moustache in a gesture as meaningful as the angry curses that would have accompanied it another time.

Beside him stood Wolfitz, his chamberlain; the tall-
est man in the courtyard; the oldest; and, despite the
weapons the others carried, the most dangerous.

When I was first gelded and sold to the Baron as his
Lady's page, Wolfitz had helped me continue the studies
I began when I was training for the Church. Out of his
kindness, I thought, or even for his amusement . . . but
the Chamberlain wanted a spy, or another spy, in the
women's apartments. Even when I was ten years old, I
knew that death lay on that path—and life itself was all
that remained to me.

I kept the secrets of all. If they thought me a fool
and beat me for amusement, then that was better than
the impalement which awaited a boy who was found
meddling in the affairs of his betters.

The tanks sighed and lowered themselves the last
finger's breadth to the ground. The courtyard, clay and
gravel compacted over generations to the density of stone,
crunched as the plenum-chamber skirts settled visibly into
it.

The man in the turret of the nearest tank ignored the
Baron and his soldiers. Instead, the reflective faceshield
of the tanker's helmet turned and made a slow, arrogant
survey of the barred windows and the women behind
them. Maids tittered; but the Lady Miriam did not, and
then the taker's face shield suddenly lifted, the
mercenary's eyes and broad smile were toward the
Baron's wife.

The tanks whispered and pinged as they came into
balance with the surroundings which they dominated.
Over those muted sounds, the man in the turret of the
second tank to enter the courtyard called, "Baron
Hetziman, I'm Lieutenant Kiley and this is my number
two—Sergeant Commander Grant. Our tanks have been
assigned to you as a Protective Reaction. Force until the
peace treaty's signed."

"You do us honor," said the Baron curtly. "We trust

your stay with us will be pleasant as well as short. A banquet—"

The Baron paused, and his head turned to find the object of the other tanker's attention.

The lieutenant snapped something in a language that was not ours, but the name "Grant" was distinctive in the sharp phrase.

The man in the nearest turret lifted himself out gracefully by resting his palms on the hatch coaming and swinging up his long, powerful legs without pausing for footholds until he stood atop the iridium turret. The hatch slid shut between his booted feet. His crisp moustache was sandy blond, and the eyes which he finally turned on the Baron and the formal welcoming committee were blue. "Rudy Grant at your service, Baron," he said, with even less respect in his tone than in his words.

They did not need to respect us. They were the tank lords.

"We will go down and greet our guests," said the Lady Miriam, suiting her actions to her words. Even as she turned, I was off the chair, dragging it toward the inner wall of imported polychrome plastic.

"But, Lady . . . ," said Sarah nervously. She let her voice trail off, unwillingness to oppose a course on which her mistress was determined.

With coos and fluttering skirts, the women swept out the door from which the usual guard had been removed for the sake of the show in the courtyard. Lady Miriam's voice carried back: "We were to meet them at the banquet tonight. We'll just do so a little earlier."

If I had followed the women, one of them would have ordered me to stay and watch the suite—though, everyone, even the tenants who farmed the plots of the home estate here, was outside watching the arrival of the tanks. Instead, I waited for the sounds to die away down the stair tower—and I slipped out the window.

Because I was in a hurry. I lost one of the brass buttons from my jacket—my everyday livery of buff; I'd be wearing the black plush jacket when I waited in attendance at the banquet tonight, so the loss didn't matter. The vertical bars were set close enough to prohibit most adults, and few of the children who could slip between them would have had enough strength to then climb the bracing strut of the roof antenna, the only safe path since the base of the West Wing was a thicket of spikes and razor ribbon.

I was on the roof coping in a matter of seconds, three quick hand-over-hand surges. The women were only beginning to file out through the doorway. Lady Miriam led them, and her hauteur and lifted chin showed she would brook no interface with her plans.

Most of the tankers had, like Grant, stepped out of their hatches, but they did not wander far. Lieutenant Kiley stood on the sloping bow of his vehicle, offering a hand which the Baron angrily refused as he mounted the steps recessed into the tank's armor.

"Do you think I'm a child?" rumbled the Baron, but only his pride forced him to touch the tank when the mercenary made a hospitable offer. None of the Baron's soldiers showed signs of wanting to look into the other vehicles. Even the Chamberlain, aloof if not afraid, stood at arm's length from the huge tank which even now trembled enough to make the setting sun quiver across the iridium hull.

Because of the Chamberlain's studied unconcern about the vehicle beside him, he was the first of the welcoming party to notice Lady Miriam striding toward Grant's tank, holding her skirts clear of the ground with dainty, bejeweled hands. Wolfitz turned to the Baron, now leaning gingerly against the curve of the turret so that he could look through the hatch while the lieutenant gestured from the other side. The Chamberlain's mouth opened to speak, then closed again deliberately.

There were matters in which he too knew better than to become involved.

One of the soldiers yelped when Lady Miriam began to mount the nearer tank. She loosed her dress in order to take the hand which Grant extended to her. The Baron glanced around and snarled an inarticulate syllable. His wife gave him a look as composed as his was suffused with rage. "After all, my dear," said the Lady Miriam coolly, "our lives are in the hands of these brave men and their amazing vehicles. Of *course* I must see how they are arranged."

She was the King's third daughter, and she spoke now as if she were herself the monarch.

"That's right, milady," said Sergeant Grant. Instead of pointing through the hatch, he slid back into the interior of his vehicle with a murmur to the Lady.

I think Lady Miriam and I, alone of those on the estate, were not nervous about the tanks for their size and power. I loved them as shimmering beasts, whom no one could strike in safety. The Lady's love was saved for other objects.

"Grant, that won't be necessary," the lieutenant called sharply—but he spoke in our language, not his own, so he must have known the words would have little effect on his subordinate.

The Baron bellowed, "*Mir*—" before his voice caught. he was not an ungovernable man, only one whose usual companions were men and women who lived or died as the Baron willed. The Lady squeezed flat the flounces of her skirt and swung her legs within the hatch ring.

"Murphy," called the Baron to his chief of soldiers. "Get up there with her." The Baron roared more often than he spoke quietly. This time his voice was not loud, but he would have shot Murphy where he stood if the soldier had hesitated before Clambering up the bow of the tank.

"Vision blocks in both the turret and the driver's

compartment," said Lieutenant Kiley, pointing within his tank, "give a three-sixty-degree view at any wavelength you want to punch in."

Murphy, a grizzled man who had been with the Baron a dozen years, leaned against the turret and looked down into the hatch. Past him, I could see the combs and lace of Lady Miriam's elaborate coiffure. I would have given everything I owned to be there within the tank myself—and I owned nothing but my life.

The hatch slid shut. Murphy yelped and snatched his fingers clear.

Atop the second tank, the Baron froze and his flushed cheeks turned slatey. The mercenary lieutenant touched a switch on his helmet and spoke too softly for anything but the integral microphone to hear the words.

The order must have been effective, because the hatch opened as abruptly as it had closed—startling Murphy again.

Lady Miriam rose from the turret on what must have been a power lift. Her posture was in awkward contrast to the smooth ascent, but her face was composed. The tank and its apparatus were new to the Lady, but anything that could have gone on within the shelter of the turret was a familiar experience to her.

"We have seen enough of your equipment," said the Baron to Lieutenant Kiley in the same controlled voice with which he had directed Murphy. "Rooms have been prepared for you—the guest apartments alongside mine in the East Wing, not the barracks below. Dinner will be announced—" he glanced at the sky. The sun was low enough that only the height of the tank's deck permitted the Baron to see the orb above the courtyard wall "—in two hours. Make yourselves welcome."

Lady Miriam turned and backed her way to the ground again. Only then did Sergeant Grant follow her out of the turret. The two of them were as powerful as they were arrogant—but neither a king's daughter nor a tank lord is immortal.

"Baron Hetziman," said the mercenary lieutenant. "Sir—" the modest honorific for the tension, for the rage which the Baron might be unable to control even at risk of his estates and his life. "That building, the gatehouse, appears disused. We'll doss down there, if you don't mind."

The Baron's face clouded, but that was his normal reaction to disagreement. The squat tower to the left of the gate had been used only for storage for a generation. A rusted barrow, upended to fit farther within the doorway, almost blocked access now.

The Baron squinted for a moment at the structure, craning his short neck to look past the tank from which he had just climbed down. Then he snorted and said, "Sleep in a hog byre if you choose, Lieutenant. It might be cleaner than that."

"I realize," explained Lieutenant Kiley as he slid to the ground instead of using the steps, "that the request sounds odd, but Colonel Hammer is concerned that commandos from Ganz or the Lightning Division might launch an attack. The gatehouse is separated from everything but the outer wall—so if we have to defend it, we can do so without endangering any of your people."

The lie was a transparent one; but the mercenaries did not have to lie at all if they wished to keep us away from their sleeping quarters. So considered, the statement was almost generous, and the Baron chose to take it that way. "Wolfitz," he said offhandedly as he stamped toward the entrance. "Organize a party of tenants—" he gestured sharply toward the pattern of drab garments and drab faces lining the walls of the courtyard "—and clear the place, will you?"

The Chamberlain nodded obsequiously, but he continued to stride along at his master's heel.

The Baron turned, paused, and snarled, *"Now,"* in a voice as grim as the fist he clenched at his side.

"My Lord," said Wolfitz with a bow that danced the line between brusque and dilatory. He stepped hastily toward the soldiers who had broken their rank in lieu of orders—a few of them toward the tanks and their haughty crews but most back to the stone shelter of the palace.

"You men," the Chamberlain said, making circling motions with his hands. "Fifty of the peasants, *quickly.* Everything is to be turned out of the gatehouse, thrown beyond the wall for the time being. *Now. Move* them."

The women followed the Baron into the palace. Several of the maids glanced over their shoulders, at the tanks—at the tankers. Some of the women would have drifted closer to meet the men in the khaki uniforms, but Lady Miriam strode head high and without hesitation.

She had accomplished her purposes; the purposes of her entourage could wait.

I leaned from the roof ledge for almost a minute further, staring at the vehicles which were so smooth-skinned that I could see my amorphous reflection in the nearest. When the sound of women's voices echoed through the window, I squirmed back only instants before the Lady reentered her apartment.

They would have beaten me because of my own excitement had they not themselves been agog with the banquet to come—and the night which would follow it.

The high-arched banquet hall was so rarely used that it was almost as unfamiliar to the Baron and his household as it was to his guests. Strings of small lights had been led up the cast-concrete beams, but nothing could really illuminate the vaulting waste of groins and coffers that formed the ceiling.

The shadows and lights trembling on flexible fastenings

had the look of the night sky on the edge of an electrical storm. I gazed up at the ceiling occasionally while I waited at the wall behind Lady Miriam. I had no duties at the banquet—that was for house servants, not body servants like myself—but my presence was required for show and against the chance that the Lady would send me off with a message.

That chance was very slight. Any messages Lady Miriam had were for the second-ranking tank lord, seated to her left by custom: Sergeant-Commander Grant.

Only seven of the mercenaries were present at the moment. I saw mostly their backs as they sat at the high table, interspersed with the Lady's maids. Lieutenant Kiley was in animated conversation with the Baron to his left, but I thought the officer wished primarily to distract his host from the way Lady Miriam flirted on the other side.

A second keg of beer—estate stock; not the stuff brewed for export in huge vats—had been broached by the time the beef course followed the pork. The serving girls had been kept busy with the mugs—in large part, the molded-glass tankards of the Baron's soldiers, glowering at the lower tables, but the metal-chased crystal of the tank lords were refilled often as well.

Two of the mercenaries—drivers, separated by the oldest of Lady Miriam's maids—began arguing with increasing heat while a tall, black-haired server watched in amusement. I could hear the words, but the language was not ours. One of the men got up, struggling a little because the arms of his chair were too tight against those to either side. He walked toward his commander, rolling slightly.

Lieutenant Kiley, gesturing with his mug toward the roof peak, was saying to the Baron, "Has a certain splendor, you know. Proper lighting and it'd look like a cross between a prison and a barracks, but the way you've tricked it out is—"

The standing mercenary grumbled a short, forceful paragraph, a question or a demand, to the lieutenant who broke off his own sentence to listen.

"Ah, Baron," Kiley said, turning again to his host. "Question is, what, ah, sort of regulations would there be on my boys dating local women. That one there—" his tankard nodded toward the black-haired servant. The driver who had remained seated was caressing her thigh "—for instance?"

"Regulations?" responded the Baron in genuine surprise. "On *servants*? None, of course. Would you like me to assign a group of them for your use?"

The lieutenant grinned, giving an ironic tinge to the courteous shake of his head. "I don't think that'll be necessary, Baron," he said.

Kiley stood up to attract his men's attention. "Open season on the servants, boys," he said, speaking clearly and in our language, so that everyone at or near the upper table would understand him. "Make your own arrangements. Nothing rough. And no less than two men together."

He sat down again and explained what the Baron already understood: "Things can happen when a fellow wanders off alone in a strange place. He can fall and knock his head in, for instance."

The two drivers were already shuffling out of the dining hall with the black-haired servant between them. One of the men gestured toward another buxom server with a pitcher of beer. She was not particularly well-favored, as men describe such things; but she was close, and she was willing—as any of the women in the hall would have been to go with the tank lords. I wondered whether the four of them would get any farther than the corridor outside.

I could not see the eyes of the maid who watched the departure of the mercenaries who had been seated beside her.

Lady Miriam watched the drivers leave also. Then she turned back to Sergeant Grant and resumed the conversation they held in voices as quiet as honey flowing from a ruptured comb.

In the bustle and shadows of the hall, I disappeared from the notice of those around me. Small and silent, wearing my best jacket of black velvet, I could have been but another patch of darkness. The two mercenaries left the hall by a side exit. I slipped through the end door behind me, unnoticed save as a momentary obstacle to the servants bringing in compotes of fruits grown locally and imported from across the stars.

My place was not here. My place was with the tanks, now that there was no one to watch me dreaming as I caressed their iridium flanks.

The sole guard at the door to the women's apartments glowered at me, but he did not question my reason for returning to what were, after all, my living quarters. The guard at the main entrance would probably have stopped me for spite: he was on duty while others of the household feasted and drank the best quality beer.

I did not need a door to reach the courtyard and the tanks parked there.

Unshuttering the same window I had used in the morning, I squeezed between the bars and clambered to the roof along the antenna mount. I was fairly certain that I could clear the barrier of points and edges at the base of the wall beneath the women's suite, but there was no need to take that risk.

Starlight guided me along the stone gutter, jumping the pipes feeding the cistern under the palace cellars. Buildings formed three sides of the courtyard, but the north was closed by a wall and the gatehouse. There was no spiked barrier beneath the wall, so I stepped to the battlements and jumped to the ground safely.

Then I walked to the nearest tank, silently from

reverence rather than in fear of being heard by someone in the palace. I circled the huge vehicle slowly, letting
the tip of my left index finger slide over the metal. The
iridium skin was smooth, but there were many bumps
and irregularities set into the armor: sensors, lights, and
strips of close-range defense projectors to meet an enemy
or his missile with a blast of pellets.

The tank was sleeping but not dead. Though I could
hear no sound from it, the armor quivered with inner
life like that of a great tree when the wind touches its
highest branches.

I touched a recessed step, the spring-loaded fairing
that should have covered it was missing, torn away or
shot off—perhaps on a distant planet. I climbed the bow
slope, my feet finding each higher step as if they knew
the way.

It was as if I were a god.

I might have attempted no more than that, than to
stand on the hull with my hand touching the stubby
barrel of the main gun—raised at a sixty-degree angle
so that it did not threaten the palace. But the turret hatch
was open and, half-convinced that I was living in a hope-
induced dream, I lifted myself to look in.

"Freeze," said the man looking up at me past his pistol
barrel. His voice was calm. "And then we'll talk about
what you think you're doing here."

The interior of the tank was coated with sulfurous
light. It was too dim to shine from the hatch, but it
provided enough illumination for me to see the little man
in the khaki coveralls of the tank lords. The bore of the
powergun in his hand shrank from the devouring cavity it had first seemed. Even the 1 cm bore of reality
would release enough energy to splash the brains from
my skull, I knew.

"I wanted to see the tanks," I said, amazed that I was
not afraid. All men die, even kings; what better time than
this would there be for me? "They would never let me,

so I sneaked away from the banquet. I—it was worth it. Whatever happens now."

"Via," said the tank lord, lowering his pistol. "You're just a kid, ain'tcha?"

I could see my image foreshortened in the vision screen behind the mercenary, my empty hands shown in daylit vividness at an angle which meant the camera must be in another of the parked tanks.

"My Lord," I said—straightening momentarily but overriding the reflex so that I could meet the mercenary's eyes. "I am sixteen."

"Right," he said, "and I'm Colonel Hammer. Now—"

"Oh Lord!" I cried, forgetting in my joy and embarrassment that someone else might hear me. My vision blurred and I rapped my knees on the iridium as I tried to genuflect. "Oh, Lord Hammer, forgive me for disturbing you!"

"Blood and *martyrs*, boy!" snapped the tank lord. A pump whirred and the seat from which, cross-legged, he questioned me rose. "Don't be an idiot! Me name's Curran and I drive this beast, is all."

The mercenary was now head and shoulders out of the hatch now, watching me with a concerned expression. I blinked and straightened. When I knelt, I had almost slipped from the tank; and in a few moments, my bruises might be more painful than my present embarrassment.

"I'm sorry, Lord Curran," I said, thankful for once that I had practice in keeping my expression calm after a beating. "I have studied, I have dreamed about your tanks ever since I was placed in my present status six years ago. When you came I—I'm afraid I lost control."

"You're a little shrimp, even alongside me, ain'tcha?" said Curran reflectively.

A burst of laughter drifted across the courtyard from a window in the corridor flanking the dining hall.

"Aw, Via," the tank lord said. "Come take a look, seein's yer here anyhow."

It was not a dream. My grip on the hatch coaming made the iridium bite my fingers as I stepped into the tank at Curran's direction; and besides, I would never have dared to dream this paradise.

The tank's fighting compartment was not meant for two, but Curran was as small as he had implied and I— I had grown very little since a surgeon had fitted me to become the page of a high-born lady. There were screens, gauges, and armored conduits across all the surfaces I could see.

"Drivers'll tell ye," said Curran, "the guy back here, he's just along for the ride 'cause the tank does it all for 'em. Been known t' say that myself, but it ain't really true. Still—"

He touched the lower left corner of a screen. It had been black. Now it became gray unmarked save by eight short orange lines radiating from the edge of a two centimeter circle in the middle of the screen.

"Fire control," Curran said. A hemispherical switch was set into the bulkhead beneath the screen. He touched the control with an index finger, rotating it slightly. "That what the Slammer's all about, ain't we? Firepower and movement, and the tricky part—movement—the driver handles from up front. Got it?"

"Yes, My Lord," I said, trying to absorb everything around me without taking my eyes from what Curran was doing. The West Wing of the palace, guest and baronial quarters above the ground-floor barracks, slid up the screen as brightly illuminated as if it were daylight.

"Now *don't* touch nothin'!" the tank lord said, the first time he had spoken harshly to me. "Got it?"

"Yes, My Lord."

"Right," said Curran, softly again. "Sorry, kid. Lieutenant'll have my ass if he sees me twiddlin' with the gun, and if we blow a hole in Central Prison here—" he gestured at the screen, though I did not understand the reference "—the Colonel'll likely shoot me hisself."

"I won't touch anything, My Lord," I reiterated.

"Yeah, well," said the mercenary. He touched a four-position toggle switch beside the hemisphere. "We just lowered the main gun, right? I won't spin the turret, 'cause they'd hear that likely inside. Matter of fact—"

Instead of demonstrating the toggle, Curran fingered the sphere again. The palace dropped off the screen and, now that I knew to expect it, I recognized the faint whine that must have been the gun itself gimbaling back up to a safe angle. Nothing within the fighting compartment moved except for the image on the screen.

"So," the tanker continued, slipping the toggle to one side. An orange numeral 2 appeared in the upper left corner of the screen. "There's a selector there too—" he pointed to the pistol grip by my head, attached to the power seat which had folded up as soon as it lowered me into the tank at Curran's direction.

His finger clicked the switch to the other side—1 appeared in place of 2 on the screen—and then straight up—3. "Main gun," he said, "co-ax—that's the tribarrel mounted just in front of the hatch. You musta seen it?"

I nodded, but my agreement was a lie. I had been too excited and too overloaded with wonder to notice the automatic weapon on which I might have set my hand.

"And 3," Currant went on, nodding also, "straight up— that's both guns together. Not so hard, was it? You're ready to be a tank commander now—and—" he grinned, "—with six months and a little luck, I could teach ye t' drive the little darlin' besides."

"Oh, My Lord," I whispered, uncertain whether I was speaking to God or to the man beside me. I spread my feet slightly in order to keep from falling in a fit of weakness.

"*Watch* it!" the tank lord said sharply, sliding his booted foot to block me. More gently, he added, "Don't be touching, *nothing*, remember? That—" he pointed to a pedal on the floor which I had not noticed "—that's the foot trip. Touch it and we give a little fireworks demonstration that nobody's gonna be very happy about."

He snapped the toggle down to its original position; the numeral disappeared from the screen. "Shouldn't have it live nohow," he added.

"But—all this," I said, gesturing with my arm close to my chest so that I would not bump any of the close-packed apparatus. "If shooting is so easy, then why is— *everything*—here?"

Curran smiled. "Up," he said, pointing to the hatch. As I hesitated, he added, "I'll give you a leg-up, don't worry about the power lift."

Flushing, sure that I was being exiled from Paradise because I had overstepped myself—somehow—with the last question, I jumped for the hatch coaming and scrambled through with no need of the tanker's help. I suppose I was crying, but I could not tell because my eyes burned so.

"Hey, slow down, kid," called Curran as he lifted himself with great strength but less agility. "It's just Whichard's about due t' take over guard, and we don't need him t' find you inside. Right?"

"Oh," I said, hunched already on the edge of the tank's deck. I did not dare turn around for a moment. "Of course, My Lord."

"The thing about shootin'," explained the tank lord to my back, "ain't *how* so much's when and what. You got all this commo and sensors that'll handle any wavelength or take remote feeds. But *still* somebody's gotta decide which data t' call up—and decide what it means. And decide t' pop it er not—" I turned just as Curran leaned over to slap the iridium barrel of the main gun for emphasis. "Which is a mother-huge decision for whatever's down-range, ye know."

He grinned broadly. He had a short beard, rather sparse, which partly covered the pockmarks left by some childhood disease. "Maybe even puts tank commander up on a level with driver for tricky, right?"

His words opened a window in my mind, the frames branching and spreading into a spidery, infinite structure: responsibility, the choices that came with the power of a tank.

"Yes, My Lord," I whispered.

"Now, you better get back t' whatever civvies do," Curran said, a suggestion that would be snarled out as an order if I hesitated. "And *don't* be shootin' off yer mouth about t'night, right?"

"No, My Lord," I said as I jumped to the ground. Tie-beams between the wall and the masonry gatehouse would let me climb back to the path I had followed to get here.

"And thank you," I added, but varied emotions choked the words into a mumble.

I thought the women might already have returned, but I listened for a moment, clinging to the bars, and heard nothing. Even so I climbed in the end window. It was more difficult to scramble down without the aid of the antenna brace, but a free-standing wardrobe put that window in a sort of alcove.

I didn't know what would happen if the women saw me slipping in and out through the bars. There would be a beating—there was a beating whenever an occasion offered. That didn't matter, but it was possible that Lady Miriam would also have the openings cross-barred too straitly for even my slight form to pass.

I would have returned to the banquet hall, but female voices were already greeting the guard outside the door. I only had enough time to smooth the plush of my jacket with Sarah's hairbrush before they swept in, all of them together and their mistress in the lead as usual.

By standing against a color-washed wall panel, I was able to pass unnoticed for some minutes of the excited babble without being guilty of "hiding" with the severe flogging that would surely entail. By the time Lady Miriam called, "Leesh? *Elisha!*" in a querulous voice, no one else could have sworn that I hadn't entered the apartment with the rest of the entourage.

"Yes, My Lady" I said, stepping forward?

Several of the women were drifting off in pairs to help one another out of their formal costumes and coiffures. There would be a banquet every night that the tank lords remained—providing occupation to fill the otherwise featureless lives of the maids and their mistress.

That was time consuming, even if they did not become more involved than public occasion required.

"Leesh," said Lady Miriam, moderating her voice unexpectedly. I was prepared for a blow, ready to accept it unflinchingly unless it were aimed at my eyes and even then to dodge as little as possible so as not to stir up a worse beating.

"Elisha," the Lady continued in a honeyed tone—then, switching back to acid sharpness and looking at her Chief Maid, she said, "Sarah, what *are* all these women doing here? Don't they have rooms of their own?"

Women who still dallied in the suite's common room— several of the lower-ranking stored their garments here in chests and clothes presses—scurried for their sleeping quarters while Sarah hectored them, arms akimbo.

"I need you to carry a message for me, Leesh," explained Lady Miriam softly. "To one of our guests. You—you do know, don't you, boy, which suite was cleared for use by our guests?"

"Yes, My Lady," I said, keeping my face blank. "The end suite of the East Wing, where the King slept last year. But I thought—"

"Don't think," said Sarah, rapping me with the brush which she carried on all but formal occasions. "And don't interrupt milady."

"Yes, My Lady," I said, bowing and rising.

"I don't want you to *go* there, boy," said the Lady with an edge of irritation. "If Sergeant Grant has any questions, I want you to point the rooms out to him—from the courtyard."

She paused and touched her full lips with her tongue while her fingers played with the fan. "Yes," she said at last, then continued, "I want you to tell Sergeant Grant oh-four hundred and to answer any questions he may have."

Lady Miriam looked up again, and though her voice remained mild, her eyes were hard as knife points. "Oh. And Leesh? This is business which the Baron does not wish to be known. Speak to Sergeant Grant in private. And never speak to anyone else about it—even to the Baron if he tries to trick you into an admission."

"Yes, My Lady," I said bowing.

I understood what the Baron would do to a page who brought him the news—and how he would send a message back to his wife, to the king's daughter whom he dared not impale in person.

Sarah's shrieked order carried me past the guard at the women's apartment, while Lady Miriam's signet was my pass into the courtyard after normal hours. The soldier there on guard was muzzy with drink. I might have been able to slip unnoticed by the hall alcove in which he sheltered.

I skipped across the gravel-in-clay surface of the courtyard, afraid to pause to touch the tanks again when I knew Lady Miriam would be peering from her window. Perhaps on the way back . . . but no, she would be as intent on hearing how the message was received as she was anxious to know that it had been delivered. I would ignore the tanks—

"*Freeze*, buddy!" snarled someone from the turret of the tank I had just run past.

I stumbled with shock and my will to obey. Catching my balance, I turned slowly—to the triple muzzles oft he weapon mounted on the cupola, not a pistol as Lord Curran had pointed. The man who spoke wore a shielded helmet, but there would not have been enough light to recognize him anyway.

"Please, My Lord," I said, "I have a message for Sergeant-Commander Grant?"

"From who?" the mercenary demanded. I knew now that Lieutenant Kiley had been serious about protecting from intrusion the quarters allotted to his men.

"My Lord, I . . ." I said and found no way to proceed.

"Yeah, Via," the tank lord agreed in a relaxed tone. "None a' my affair." He touched the side of his helmet and spoke softly.

The gatehouse door opened with a spill of light and the tall, broad-shouldered silhouette of Sergeant Grant. Like the mercenary on guard in the tank, he wore a communications helmet.

Grant slipped his face shield down, and for a moment my own exposed skin tingled—or my mind *thought* it perceived a tingle—as the tank lord's equipment scanned me.

"C'mon, then," he grunted, gesturing me toward the recessed angle of the building and the gate leaves. "We'll step around the corner and talk."

There was a trill of feminine laughter from the upper story of the gatehouse: a servant named Maria, whose hoots of joy were unmistakable. Lieutenant Kiley leaned his head and torso from the window above us and shouted to Grant, his voice and his anger recognizable even though the words themselves were not.

The sergeant paused, clenching his left fist and reaching for me with his right because I happened to be closest to him. I poised to run—survive this first, then worry about what Lady Miriam would say—but the tank lord caught himself, raised his shield, and called to his superior in a tone on the safe side of the insolent, "All right, all right. I'll stay right here where Cermak can see me from the tank."

Apparently Grant had remembered Lady Miriam also, for he spoke in our language so that I—and the principal for whom I acted—would understand the situation.

Lieutenant Kiley banged his shutters closed.

Grant stared for a moment at Cermak until the guard understood and dropped back into the interior of his vehicle. We could still be observed through the marvelous vision blocks, but we had the minimal privacy needed for me to deliver my message.

"Lady Miriam," I said softly, "says oh-four hundred."

I waited for the tank lord to ask me for directions. His breath and sweat exuded sour echoes of the strong estate ale.

"Won't go," the tank lord replied unexpectedly. "I'll be clear at oh-three *to* oh-four." He paused before adding, "You tell her, kid, she better not be playin' games. Nobody plays prick-tease with *this* boy and likes what they get for it."

"Yes, My Lord," I said, skipping backward because I had the feeling that this man would grab me and shake me to emphasize the point.

I would not deliver his threat. My best small hope for safety at the end of this affair required that Lady Miriam believe I was ignorant of what was going on, and a small hope it was.

That *was* a slim hope anyway.

"Well, go on, then," the tank lord said.

He strode back within the gatehouse, catlike in his grace and lethality, while I ran to tell my mistress of the revised time.

An hour's pleasure seemed a little thing against the risk of two lives—and my own.

✧   ✧   ✧

My "room" was what had been the back staircase before it was blocked to convert the second floor of the West Wing into the women's apartment. The dark cylinder was furnished only with the original stone stair treads and whatever my mistress and her maids had chosen to store there over the years. I normally slept on a chair in the common room, creeping back to my designated space before dawn.

Tonight I slept *beneath* one of the large chairs in a corner; not hidden, exactly, but not visible without a search.

The two women were quiet enough to have slipped past someone who was not poised to hear them as I was, and the tiny flashlight the leader carried threw a beam so tight that it could scarcely have helped them see their way. But the perfume they wore, imported, expensive, and overpowering—was more startling than a shout.

They paused at the door. The latch rattled like a tocsin though the hinges did not squeal.

The soldier on guard, warned and perhaps awakened by the latch, stopped them before they could leave the apartment. The glowlamp in the sconce beside the door emphasized the ruddy anger on his face.

Sarah's voice, low but cutting, said, "Keep silent, my man, or it will be the worse for you." She thrust a glean of gold toward the guard, not payment but a richly-chased signet ring, and went on, "Lady Miriam knows and approves. Keep still and you'll have no cause to regret this night. Otherwise . . ."

The guard's face was not blank, but emotions chased themselves across it too quickly for his mood to be read. Suddenly he reached out and harshly squeezed the Chief Maid's breast. Sarah gasped, and the man snarled, "What've they got that *I* don't, tell me, huh? You're *all* whores, that's all you are!"

The second woman was almost hidden from the soldier by the Chief Maid and the panel on the half-opened door. I could see a shimmer of light as her hand rose, though I could not tell whether it was a blade or a gun barrel.

The guard flung his hand down from Sarah and turned away from Sarah and turned away. "Go on, then," he grumbled. "What do I care? Go *on*, sluts."

The weapon disappeared, unused and unseen, into the folds of an ample skirt, and the two women left the suite with only the whisper of felt slippers. They were heavily veiled and wore garments coarser than any I had seen on the Chief Maid before—but Lady Miriam was as recognizable in the grace of her walk as Sarah was for her voice.

The women left the door ajar to keep the latch from rattling again, and the guard did not at first pull it to. I listened for further moments against the chance that another maid would come from her room or that the Lady would rush back, driven by fear or conscience— thought I hadn't seen either state control her in the past.

I was poised to squeeze before the window-bars again, barefoot for secrecy and a better grip, when I heard the hum of static as the guard switched his belt radio live. There was silence as he keyed it, then his low voice saying, "They've left, sir. They're on their way toward the banquet hall."

There was another pause and a radio voice too thin for me to hear more than the fact of it. The guard said, "Yes, Chamberlain," and clicked off the radio.

He latched the door.

I was out through the bars in one movement and well up the antenna brace before any of the maids could have entered the common room to investigate the noise.

I knew where the women were going, but not whether the Chamberlain would stop them on the way past the banquet hall or the Baron's personal suite at the head of East Wing. The fastest, safest way for me to cross the roof of the banquet hall was twenty feet up the side, where the builder's forms had left a flat, thirty-centimeter path in the otherwise sloping concrete.

Instead, I decided to pick my way along the trash-filled stone gutter just above the windows of the corridor on the courtyard side. I could say that my life—my chance of life—depended on knowing what was going on . . . and it did depend on that. But crawling through the starlit darkness, spying on my betters, was also the only way I had of asserting myself. The need to assert myself had become unexpectedly pressing since Lord Curran had showed me the tank, and since I had experienced what a man *could* be.

There was movement across the courtyard as I reached the vertical extension of the load-bearing wall that separated the West Wing from the banquet hall. I ducked beneath the stone coping, but the activity had nothing to do with me. The gatehouse door had opened and, as I peered through dark-adapted eyes, the mercenary on guard in a tank exchanged with the man who had just stepped out of the building.

The tank lords talked briefly. Then the gatehouse door shut behind the guard who had been relieved while his replacement climbed into the turret of the vehicle parked near the West Wing—Sergeant Grant's tank. I clambered over the wall extension and stepped carefully along the gutter, regretting now that I had not worn shoes for protection. I heard nothing from the corridor below, although the casements were pivoted outward to catch any breeze that would relieve the summer stillness.

Gravel crunched in the courtyard as the tank lord on guard slid from his vehicle and began to stride toward the end of the East Wing.

He was across the courtyard from me—faceless behind the shield of his commo helmet and at best only a shadow against the stone of the wall behind him. But the man was Sergeant Grant beyond question, abandoning his post for the most personal of reasons.

I continued, reaching the East Wing as the tank lord disappeared among the stone finials of the outside staircase at the wing's far end. The guest suites had their own entrance, more formally ornamented than the doorways serving the estate's own needs. The portal was guarded only when the suites were in use—and then most often by a mixed force of the Baron's soldiers and those of the guests.

That was not a formality. The guest who would entrust his life solely to the Baron's good will was a fool.

A corridor much like that flanking the banquet hall ran along the courtyard side of the guest suites. It was closed by a cross-wall and door, separating the guests from the Baron's private apartment, but the door was locked and not guarded.

Lady Miriam kept a copy of the door's microchip key under the plush lining of her jewel box. I had found it but left it there, needless to me so long as I could slip through the window grates.

The individual guest suites were locked also, but as I lowered myself from the gutter to a window ledge I heard a door snick closed. The sound was minuscule, but it had a crispness that echoed in the lightless hall.

Skirts rustled softly against the stone, and Sarah gave a gentle, troubled sigh as she settled herself to await her mistress.

I waited on the ledge, wondering if I should climb back to the roof—or even return to my own room. The Chamberlain had not blocked the assignation, and there was no sign of an alarm. The soldiers, barracked on the ground floor of this wing, would have been clearly audible had they been aroused.

Then I did hear something—or feel it. There had been motion, the ghost of motion, on the other side of the door closing the corridor. Someone had entered or left the Baron's apartment, and I had heard them through the open windows.

It could have been one of the Baron's current favorites—girls from the estate, the younger and more vulnerable, the better. They generally used the little door and staircase on the outer perimeter of the palace—where a guard *was* stationed against the possibility that an axe-wielding relative would follow the lucky child.

I lifted myself back to the roof with particular care, so that I would not disturb the Chief Maid waiting in the hallway. Then I followed the gutter back to the portion of roof over the Baron's apartments.

I knew the wait would be less than an hour, the length of Sergeant Grant's guard duty, but it did not occur to me that the interval would be as brief as it actually was. I had scarcely settled myself again to wait when I thought I heard a door unlatch in the guest suites. That could have been imagination or Sarah, deciding to wait in a room instead of the corridor; but moments later the helmeted tank lord paused on the outside staircase.

By taking the risk of leaning over the roof coping, I could see Lord Grant and a woman embracing on the landing before the big mercenary strode back across the courtyard toward the tank where he was supposed to be on guard. Desire had not waited on its accomplishment, and mutual fear had prevented the sort of dalliance after the event that the women dwelt on so lovingly in the privacy of their apartment . . . while Leesh, the Lady's page and no man, listened of necessity.

The women's slippers made no sound in the corridor, but their dresses brushed one another to the door which clicked and sighed as it let them out of the guest apartments and into the portion of the East Wing reserved to the Baron.

I expected shouts, then; screams, even gunfire as the Baron and Wolfitz confronted Lady Miriam. There was no sound except for skirts continuing to whisper their way up the hall, returning to the women's apartment. I stood up to follow, disappointed despite the fact that bloody chaos in the palace would endanger everyone—and me, the usual scapegoat for frustrations, most of all.

The Baron said in a tight voice at the window directly beneath me, "Give me the goggles, Wolfitz," and surprise almost made me fall.

The strap of a pair of night-vision goggles rustled over the Baron's grizzled head. Their frames clucked against the stone sash as my master bent forward with the unfamiliar headgear.

For a moment, I was too frightened to breathe. If he leaned out and turned his head, he would see me poised like a terrified gargoyle above him. Any move I made—even flattening myself behind the wall coping—risked a sound and disaster.

"You're right," said the Baron in a voice that would have been normal if it had any emotion behind it. There was another sound of something hard against the sash, a metallic clink this time.

"*No*, my lord!" said the Chamberlain in a voice more forceful than I dreamed any underling would use to the Baron. Wolfitz must have been seizing the nettle firmly, certain that hesitation or uncertainty meant the end of more than his plans. "If you shoot him now, the others will blast everything around them to glowing slag."

"Wolfitz," said the Baron, breathing hard. They had been struggling. The flare-mouthed mob gun from the Baron's nightstand—scarcely a threat to Sergeant Grant across the courtyard—extended from the window opening, but the Chamberlain's bony hand was on the Baron's wrist. "If you tell me I must let those arrogant outworlders pleasure *my* wife in *my* palace, I will kill you."

He sounded like an architect discussing a possible staircase curve.

"There's a better way, My Lord," said the Chamberlain. His voice was breathy also, but I thought exertions was less to account for that than was the risk he took. "We'll be ready the next time the—outworlder gives us the opportunity. We'll take him in, in the crime; but quietly so that the others aren't aroused."

"Idiot!" snarled the Baron, himself again in all his arrogant certainty. Their hands and the gun disappeared from the window ledge. The tableau was the vestige of an event the men needed each other too much to remember. "No matter what we do with the body, the others will blame us. Blame *me*."

His voice took a dangerous coloration as he added, "Is that what you had in mind, Chamberlain?"

Wolfitz said calmly, "The remainder of the platoon here will be captured—or killed, it doesn't matter—by the mercenaries of the Lightning Division, who will also protect us from reaction by King Adrian and Colonel Hammer."

"But . . ." said the Baron, the word a placeholder for the connected thought which did not form in his mind after all.

"The King of Ganz won't hesitate an instant if you offer him your fealty," the Chamberlain continued, letting the words display their own strength instead of speaking loudly in a fashion his master might take as badgering.

The Baron still held the mob gun, and his temper was doubtful at the best of times.

"The mercenaries of the Lightning Division," continued Wolfitz with his quiet voice and persuasive ideas, "will accept any risk in order to capture four tanks undamaged. The value of that equipment is beyond any profit the Lightning Division dreamed of earning when they were hired by Ganz."

"But . . ." the Baron repeated in an awestruck voice. "The truce?"

"A matter for the kings to dispute," said the Chamberlain offhandedly. "But Adrian will find little support among his remaining barons if you were forced into your change of allegiance. When the troops he billeted on you raped and murdered Lady Miriam, that is."

"How quickly can you make the arrangements?" asked the Baron. I had difficulty in following the words: not because they were soft, but because he growled them like a beast.

"The delay," Wolfitz replied judiciously, and I could imagine him lacing his long fingers together and staring at them, "will be for the next opportunity your—Lady Miriam and her lover give us. I shouldn't imagine that will be longer than tomorrow night."

The Baron's teeth grated like nutshells being ground against stone.

"We'll have to use couriers, of course," Wolfitz added. "The likelihood of the Slammers intercepting any other form of communication is too high . . . But all Ganz and its mercenaries have to do is ready a force to dash here and defend the palace before Hammer can react. Since these tanks *are* the forward picket, and they'll be unmanned while Sergeant Grant is—otherwise occupied—the Lightning Division will have almost an hour before an alarm can be given. Ample time, I'm sure."

"Chamberlain," the Baron said in a voice from which amazement had washed all the anger. "You think of everything. See to it."

"Yes, My Lord," said Wolfitz humbly.

The tall Chamberlain *did* think of everything, or very nearly; but he'd had much longer to plan than the Baron thought. I wondered how long Wolfitz had waited for an opportunity like this one; and what payment he had arranged to receive from the King of Ganz if he changed the Baron's allegiance?

A door slammed closed, the Baron returning to his suite and his current child-mistress. Chamberlain Wolfitz's rooms adjoined his master's, but my ears followed his footsteps to the staircase at the head of the wing.

By the time I had returned to the West Wing and was starting down the antenna brace, a pair of the Baron's soldiers had climbed into a truck and gone rattling off into the night. It was an unusual event but not especially remarkable: the road they took led off to one of the Baron's outlying estates.

But the road led to the border with Ganz, also; and I had no doubt as to where the couriers' message would be received.

The tank lords spent most of the next day busy with their vehicles. A squad of the Baron's soldiers kept at a distance the tenants and house servants who gawked while the khaki-clad tankers crawled through access plates and handed fan motors to their fellows. The bustle racks welded to the back of each turret held replacement parts as well as the crew's personal belongings.

It was hard to imagine that objects as huge and powerful as the tanks would need repair. I had to remember they were not ingots of iridium but vastly complicated assemblages of parts—each of which could break, and eight of which were human.

I glanced occasionally at the tanks and the lordly men who ruled and serviced them. I had no excuse to take me beyond the women's apartment during daylight.

Excitement roused the women early, but there was little pretense of getting on with their lacemaking. They dressed, changed, primped—argued over rights to one bit of clothing or another—and primarily, they talked.

Lady Miriam was less a part of the gossip than usual, but she was the most fastidious of all about the way she would look at the night's banquet.

The tank lords bathed at the wellhead in the courtyard like so many herdsmen. The women watched hungrily, edging forward despite the scandalized demands of one of the older maids that they at least stand back in the room where their attention would be less blatant.

Curran's muscles were knotted, his skin swarthy.
Sergeant Grant could have passed for a god—or at least
a man of half his real age. When he looked up at the
women's apartments, he smiled.

The truck returned in late afternoon, carrying the two
soldiers and a third man in civilian clothes who could
have been—but was not—the manager of one of the
outlying estates. The civilian was closeted with the Baron
for half an hour before he climbed back into the truck.
He, Wolfitz, and the Baron gripped one another's forearms in leave-taking; then the vehicle returned the way
it had come.

The tank lord on guard paid less attention to the truck
than he had to the column of steam-driven produce vans,
chuffing toward the nearest rail terminus.

The banquet was less hectic than that of the first night,
but the glitter had been replaced by a fog of hostility
now that the newness had worn off. The Baron's soldiers
were more openly angry that Hammer's men picked and
chose—food at the high table and women in the corridor or the servant's quarters below.

The Slammers, for their part, had seen enough of the
estate to be contemptuous of its isolation, of its low
technology—and of the folk who lived on it. And yet—
I had talked with Lord Curran and listened to the others as well. The tank lords were men like those of the
barony. They had walked on far worlds and had been
placed in charge on instruments as sophisticated as any
in the human galaxy—but they were not sophisticated
men, only powerful ones.

Sergeant-Commander Grant, for instance, made the
child's mistake of thinking his power to destroy conferred
on him a sort of personal immortality.

The Baron ate and drank in a sullen reverie, deaf to
the lieutenant's attempts at conversation and as blind to
Lady Miriam on his left as she was to him. The Chamberlain was seated among the soldiers because there were

more guests than maids of honor. He watched the activities at the high table unobtrusively, keeping his own counsel and betraying his nervousness only by the fact that none of the food he picked at seemed to go down his throat.

I was tempted to slip out to the tanks, because Lord Curran was on duty again during the banquet. His absence must have been his own choice; a dislike for the food or the society perhaps . . . but more probably, from what I had seen in the little man when we talked, a fear of large, formal gatherings.

It would have been nice to talk to Lord Curran again, and blissful to have the controls of the huge tank again within my hands. But if I were caught then, I might not be able to slip free later in the night—and I would rather have died than missed that chance.

The Baron hunched over his ale when Lieutenant Kiley gathered his men to return to the gatehouse. They did not march well in unison, not even by comparison with the Baron's soldiers when they drilled in the courtyard.

The skills and the purpose of the tank lords lay elsewhere.

Lady Miriam rose when the tankers fell in. She swept from the banquet hall regally as befit her birth, dressed in amber silk from Terra and topazes of ancient cut from our own world. She did not look behind her to see that her maids followed and I brought up the rear . . . but she did glance aside once at the formation of the tank lords.

She would be dressed no better than a servant later that night, and she wanted to be sure that Sergeant Grant had a view of her full splendor to keep in mind when next they met in darkness.

The soldier who had guarded the women's apartments the night before was on duty when the Chief Maid led her mistress out again. There was no repetition of the previous night's dangerous by-play this time. The guard was subdued, or frightened; or, just possibly, biding his time because he was aware of what was going to come.

I followed, more familiar with my route this time and too pumped with excitement to show the greater care I knew was necessary tonight, when there would be many besides myself to watch, to listen.

But I was alone on the roof, and the others, so certain of what *they* knew and expected, paid no attention to the part of the world which lay beyond their immediate interest.

Sergeant Grant sauntered as he left the vehicle where he was supposed to stay on guard. As he neared the staircase to the guest suites, his stride lengthened and his pace picked up. There was nothing of nervousness in his manner; only the anticipation of a man focused on sex to the extinction of all other considerations.

I was afraid that Wolfitz would spring his trap before I was close enough to follow what occurred. A more reasonable fear would have been that I would stumble into the middle of the event.

Neither danger came about. I reached the gutter over the guest corridor and waited, breathing through my mouth alone so that I wouldn't make any noise.

The blood that pounded through my ears deafened me for a moment, but there was nothing to fear. Voices murmured, Sarah and Sergeant Grant, and the door that had waited ajar for the tank lord clicked to shut the suite.

Four of the Baron's soldiers mounted the outside steps, as quietly as their boots permitted. There were faint sounds, clothing and one muted clink of metal, from the corridor on the Baron's side of the door.

All day I'd been telling myself that there was no safe way I could climb down and watch the events through a window. I climbed down, finding enough purchase for my fingers and toes where weathering had rounded the corners of stone blocks. Getting back to the roof would be more difficult, unless I risked gripping an out-swung casement for support.

Unless I dropped, bullet-riddled, to the ground.

I rested a toe on a window ledge and peeked around the stone toward the door of the suite the lovers had used on their first assignation. I could see nothing—

Until the corridor blazed with silent light.

Sarah's face was white, dazzling with direct reflection of the high-intensity floods at either end of the hallway. Her mouth opened and froze, a statue of a scream but without the sound that fear or self preservation choked in her throat.

Feet, softly but many of them, shuffled over the stone flags toward the Chief Maid. Her head jerked from one side to the other, but her body did not move. The illumination was pinning her to the door where she kept watch.

The lights spilled through the corridor windows, but their effect was surprisingly slight in the open air: highlights on the parked tanks; a faint wash of outline, not color, over the stones of the wall and gatehouse; and a distorted shadowplay on the ground itself, men and weapons twisting as they advanced toward the trapped maid from both sides.

There was no sign of interest from the gatehouse. Even if the tank lords were awake to notice the lights, what happened at night in the palace was no affair of theirs.

Three of perhaps a dozen of the Baron's soldiers stepped within my angle of vision. Two carried rifles; the third was Murphy with a chip recorder, the spidery wands of its audio and video pickups retracted because of the press of men standing nearby.

Sarah swallowed. She closed her mouth, but her eyes stared toward the infinite distance beyond this world. The gold signet she clutched was a drop from the sun's heart in the floodlights.

The Baron stepped close to the woman. He took the ring with his left hand, looked at it, and passed it to the stooped, stone-faced figure of the Chamberlain.

"Move her out of the way," said the Baron in a husky whisper.

One of the soldiers struck the muzzle of his assault rifle under the chin of the Chief Maid, pointing upward. With his other hand, the man gripped Sarah's shoulder and guided her away from the door panel.

Wolfitz looked at his master, nodded and set a magnetic key on the lock. Then he too stepped clear.

The Baron stood at the door with his back to me. He wore body armor, but he can't have thought it would protect him against the Slammer's powergun. Murphy was at the Baron's side, the recorder's central light glaring back from the door panel, and another soldier poised with his hand on the latch.

The Baron slammed the door inward with his foot. I do not think I have ever seen a man move as fast as Sergeant Grant did then.

The door opened on a servants' alcove, not the guest rooms themselves, but the furnishings there were sufficient to the lovers' need. Lady Miriam had lifted her skirts. She was standing, leaning slightly backwards, with her buttocks braced against the bedframe. She screamed, her eyes blank reflections of the sudden light.

Sergeant-Commander Grant still wore his helmet. He had slung his belt and holstered pistol over the bedpost when he unsealed the lower flap of his uniform coveralls, but he was turning with the pistol in his hand before the Baron got off the first round with his mob gun.

Aerofoils, spread from the flaring muzzle by asymmetric thrust, spattered the lovers and a two-meter circle on the wall beyond them.

The tank lord's chest was in bloody tatters and there was a brain-deep gash between his eyebrows, but his body and the powergun followed through with the motion reflex had begun.

The Baron's weapon clunked twice more. Lady Miriam flopped over the footboard and lay thrashing on the bare springs, spurting blood from narrow wounds that her clothing did not cover. Individual projectiles from the mob gun had little stopping power, but they bled out a victim's life like so many knife blades.

When the Baron shot the third time, his gun was within a meter of what had been the tank lord's face. Sergeant Grant's body staggered backward and fell, the powergun unfired but still gripped in the mercenary's right hand.

"Call the Lightning Division," said the Baron harshly as he turned. His face, except where it was freckled by fresh blood, was as pale as I had ever seen it. "It's time."

Wolfitz lifted a communicator, short range but keyed to the main transmitter, and spoke briefly. There was no need for communications security now. The man who should have intercepted and evaluated the short message was dead in a smear of his own wastes and bodily fluids.

The smell of the mob gun's propellant clunk chokingly to the back of my throat, among the more familiar slaughterhouse odors. Lady Miriam's breath whistled, and the bedsprings squeaked beneath her uncontrolled motions.

"Shut that off," said the Baron to Murphy. The recorder's pool of light shrank into shadow within the alcove.

The Baron turned and fired once more, into the tank lord's groin.

"Make sure the others don't leave the gatehouse till Ganz's mercenaries are here to deal with them," said the Baron negligently. He looked at the gun in his hand. Strong lights turned the heat and propellant residues rising from its barrel into shadows on the wall beyond.

"Marksmen are ready, My Lord," said the Chamberlain.

The Baron skittered his mob gun down the hall. He strode toward the rooms of his own apartment.

It must have been easier to climb back to the roof than I had feared. I have no memory of I, of the stress on fingertips and toes or the pain in my muscles as they lifted the body which they had supported for what seemed (after the fact) to have been hours. Minutes only, of course; but instead of serial memory of what had happened, my brain was filled with too many frozen pictures of details for all of them to fit within the real timeframe.

The plan that I had made for this moment lay so deep that I executed it by reflex, though my brain roiled.

Executed it by instinct, perhaps; the instinct of flight, the instinct to power.

In the corridor, Wolfitz and Murphy were arguing in low voices about what should be done about the mess.

Soldiers had taken up positions in the windowed corridor flanking the banquet hall. More of the Baron's men, released from trapping Lady Miriam and her lover, were joining their fellows with words too soft for me to understand. I crossed the steeply-pitched roof on the higher catwalk, for speed and from fear that the men at the windows might hear me.

There were no soldiers on the roof itself. The wall coping might hide even a full-sized man if he lay flat, but the narrow gutter between wall and roof was an impossible position from which to shoot at targets across the courtyard.

The corridor windows on the courtyard side were not true firing slits like those of all the palace's outer walls. Nonetheless, men shooting from corners of the windows could shelter their bodies behind stone thick enough to stop bolts from the Slammers' personal weapons. The sleet of bullets from twenty assault rifles would turn anyone sprinting from the gatehouse door or the pair of second-floor windows into offal like that which had been Sergeant Grant.

The tank lords were not immortal.

There was commotion in the woman's apartments when I crossed them. Momentarily a light fanned the shadow of the window bars across the courtyard and the gray curves of Sergeant Grant's tank. A male voice cursed harshly. A lamp casing crunched, and from the returned darkness came a blow and a woman's cry.

Some of the Baron's soldiers were taking positions in the West Wing. Unless the surviving tank lords cloud blow a gap in the thick outer wall of the gatehouse, they had no exit until the Lightning Division arrived with enough firepower to sweep them up at will.

But I could get in, with a warning that would come in time for them to summon aid from Colonel Hammer himself. They would be in debt for my warning, owing me their lives, their tanks, and their honor.

Surely the tank lords could find a place for a servant willing to go with them anywhere?

The battlements of the wall closing the north side of the courtyard formed my pathway to the roof of the gatehouse. Grass and brush grew there in ragged clumps. Cracks between stones had trapped dust, seeds, and moisture during a generation of neglect. I crawled along, on my belly, tearing my black velvet jacket.

Eyes focused on the gatehouse door and windows were certain to wander: to the sky; to fellows slouching over their weapons; to the wall connecting the gatehouse to the West Wing. If I stayed flat, I merged with the stone . . . but shrubs could quiver in the wrong pattern, and the Baron's light-amplifying goggles might be worn by one of the watching soldiers.

It had seemed simpler when I planned it; but it was necessary in any event, even if I died in a burst of gunfire.

The roof of the gatehouse was reinforced concrete, slightly domed, and as proof against indirect fire as the stone walls were against small arms. There was no roof entrance, but there was a capped flue for the stove that had once heated the guard quarters. I'd squirmed my way through that hole once before.

Four years before.

The roof of the gatehouse was a meter higher than the wall on which I lay, an easy jump but one which put me in silhouette against the stars. I reached up, feeling along the concrete edge less for a grip than for reassurance. I was afraid to leave the wall because my body was telling itself that the stone it pressed was safety.

It the Baron's men shot me now, it would warn the tank lords in time to save them. I owed them that, for the glimpses of freedom Curran had showed me in the turret of a tank.

I vaulted onto the smooth concrete and rolled, a shadow in the night to any of the watchers who might have seen me. Once I was *on* the gatehouse, I was safe because of the flat dome that shrugged off rain and projectiles. The flue was near the north edge of the structure, hidden from the eyes and guns waiting elsewhere in the palace.

I'd grown up only slightly since I was twelve and beginning to explore the palace in which I expected to die. The flue hadn't offered much margin, but my need wasn't as great then, either.

I'd never need *anything* as much as I needed to get into the gatehouse now.

The metal smoke pipe had rusted and blocked down decades before. The wooden cap, fashioned to close the hole to rain, hadn't been maintained. It crumbled in my hands when I lifted it away, soggy wood with only flecks remaining of the stucco which had been applied to seal the cap in place.

The flue was as narrow as the gap between window bars, and because it was round, I didn't have the luxury of turning sideways. So be it.

If my shoulders fit, my hips would follow. I extended my right arm and reached down through the hole as far as I could. The flue was as empty as it was dark. Flakes of rust made mouselike pattering as my touch dislodged them. The passageway curved smoothly, but it had no sharp-angled shot trap as far down as I could feel from outside.

I couldn't reach the lower opening. The roof was built thick enough to stop heavy shells. At least the slimy surface of the concrete tube would make the job easier.

I lowered my head into the flue with the pit of my extended right arm pressed as firmly as I could against the lip of the opening. The cast concrete brought an electric chill through the sweat-soaked velvet of my jerkin, reminding me—now that it was too late—that I could have stripped off the garment to gain another millimeter's tolerance.

It was too late, even though all but my head and one arm were outside. If I stopped now, I would never have the courage to go on again.

The air in the flue was dank, because even now in late Summer the concrete sweated and the cap prevented condensate from evaporating. The sound of my fear-lengthened breaths did not echo from the end of a closed tube, and not even panic could convince me that the air was stale and would suffocate me. I slid farther down; down to the *real* point of no return.

By leading with my head and one arm, I was able to tip my collarbone endwise for what would have been a relatively easy fit within the flue if my ribs and spine did not have to follow after. The concrete caught the tip of my left shoulder and the ribs beneath my right armpit—let me flex forward minutely on the play in my skin and the velvet—and held me.

I would have screamed, but the constriction of my ribs was too tight. My legs kicked in the air above the gatehouse, unable to thrust me down for lack of purchase. My right arm flopped in the tube, battering my knuckles and fingertips against unyielding concrete.

I could die here, and no one would know.

Memory of the tank and the windows of choice expanding infinitely above even Leesh, the Lady's page, flashed before me and cooled my body like rain on a stove. My muscles relaxed and I could breathe again—though carefully, and though the veins of my head were distending with blood trapped by my present posture.

Instead of flapping vainly, my right palm and elbow locked on opposite sides of the curving passage. I breathed as deeply as I could, then let it out as I kicked my legs up where gravity, at least, could help.

My right arm pulled while my left tried to clamp itself within my rib cage. Cloth tore, skin tore, and my torso slipped fully within the flue, lubricated by blood as well as condensate.

If I had been upright, I might have blacked out momentarily with the release of tension. Inverted, I could only gasp and feel my face and scalp burn with the flush that darkened them. The length of a hand farther and my pelvis scraped. My fingers had a grip on the lower edge of the flue, and I pulled like a cork extracting itself from a wine bottle. My being, body and mind, was so focused on its task that I was equally unmoved by losing my trousers—dragged off on the lip of the flue—and the fact that my hand was free.

The concrete burned my left ear when my right arm thrust my torso down with real handhold for the first time. My shoulders slid free and the rest of my body tumbled out of the tube which had seemed to grip it tightly until that instant.

The light that blazed in my face was meant to blind me, but I was already stunned—more by the effort than the floor which I'd hit an instant before. Someone laid the muzzle of a powergun against my left ear. The dense iridium felt cool and good on my damaged skin.

"Where's Sergeant Grant?" said Lieutenant Kiley, a meter to the side of the light source.

I squinted away from the beam. There was an open bedroll beneath me, but I think I was too limp when I dropped from the flue to be injured by bare stone. Three of the tank lords were in the room with me. The bulbous commo helmets they wore explained how the lieutenant already knew something had happened to the guard. The others would be on the ground floor, poised.

The guns pointed at me were no surprise.

"He slipped into the palace to see Lady Miriam," I said, amazed that my voice did not break in a throat so dry. "The Baron killed them, both, and he's summoned the Lightning Division to capture you and your tanks. You have to call for help at once or they'll be here."

"Blood and martyrs," said the man with the gun at my ear, Lord Curran, and he stepped between me and the dazzling light. "Douse that, Sparky. The kid's alright."

The tank lord with the light dimmed it to a glow and said, "Which *we* bloody well ain't."

Lieutenant Kiley moved to a window and peeked through a crack in the shutter, down into the courtyard.

"But . . ." I said. I would have gotten up but Curran's hand kept me below the possible line of fire. I'd tripped the mercenaries' alarms during my approach, awakened them—enough to save them, surely. "You have your helmets?" I went on. "You can call your Colonel?"

"That bastard Grant," the lieutenant said in the same emotionless, diamond-hard voice he had used in questioning me. "He salved all the vehicle transceivers to his own helmet so Command Central wouldn't wake *me* if they called while he was—out fucking around."

"Via," said Lord Curran, holstering his pistol and grimacing at his hands as he flexed them together. "I'll go. Get a couple more guns up these windows—" he gestured with jerks of his forehead "—for cover."

"It's my platoon," Kiley said, stepping away from the window but keeping his back to the others of us in the room. "Via, *Via!*"

"Look, sir," Curran insisted with his voice rising and wobbling like that of a dog fighting a choke collar. "I was his bloody driver, I'll—"

"*You* weren't the fuck-up!" Lieutenant Kiley snarled as he turned. "This one comes with the rank, trooper, so shut your—"

"I'll go, My Lords," I said, the squeal of my voice lifting it through the hoarse anger of grown men arguing over a chance to die.

They paused and the third lord, Sparky, thumbed the light up and back by reflex. I pointed to the flue. "That way. But you'll have to tell me what to do then."

Lord Curran handed me a disk the size of a thumbnail. He must have taken it from his pocket when he planned to sprint for the tanks himself. "Lay it on the hatch—anywhere on the metal. Inside, t' the right a' the main screen—"

"Curran, *knot* it, will you?" the lieutenant demanded in peevish amazement. "We can't—"

"*I* don't want my ass blown away, Lieutenant," said the trooper with the light—which pointed toward the officer suddenly, though the pistol in Sparky's other hand was lifted idly toward the ceiling. "Anyhow, kid's got a better chance'n you do. Or me."

Lieutenant Kiley looked from one of his men to the other, then stared at me with eyes that could have melted rock. "The main screen is on the forward wall of the fighting compartment," he said flatly. "That is—"

"He's used it, Lieutenant," said Lord Curran. "He knows where it is." The little mercenary had drawn his pistol again and was checking the loads for the second time since I fell into the midst of these angry, nervous men.

Kiley looked at his subordinate, then continued to me, "The commo screen is the small one to the immediate right of the main screen, and it has an alphanumeric keypad beneath it. The screen will have a numeral two or a numeral three on it when you enter, depending whether it's set to feed another tank or to Grant's helmet."

He paused, wet his lips. His voice was bare of affect, but in his fear he was unable to sort out the minimum data that my task required. The mercenary officer realized that he was wandering, but that only added to the pressure which already ground him from all sides.

"Push numeral one on the keypad," Lieutenant Kiley went on, articulating very carefully. "The numeral on the visor should change to one. That's all you need to do—the transceiver will be cleared for normal operation, and we'll do the rest from here." He touched his helmet with the barrel of his powergun, a gesture so controlled that the iridium did not clink on the thermoplastic.

"I'll need," I said, looking up at the flue, "a platform—tables or boxes."

"We'll lift you," said Lieutenant Kiley, "and we'll cover you as best we can. Better take that shirt off now and make the squeeze easier."

"No, My Lord," I said, rising against the back wall—out of sight, though within a possible line of fire. I stretched my muscles, wincing as tags of skin broke loose from the fabric to which blood had glued them. "It's dark-colored, so I'll need it to get to the tank. I, I'll use—"

I shuddered and almost fell; as I spoke, I visualized what I had just offered to do—and it terrified me.

"Kid—" said Lord Curran, catching me; though I was all right again, just a brief fit.

"I'll use my trousers also," I said. They're at the other—

"Via!" snapped Lord Sparky, pointing with the light which he had dimmed to a yellow glow that was scarcely a beam. "What *happened* t' you?"

"I was a servant in the women's apartments," I said. "I'll go now, if you'll help me. I must hurry."

Lord Curran and Lieutenant Kiley lifted me. Their

hands were moist by contrast with the pebbled finish of their helmet, brushing my bare thighs. I could think only of how my nakedness had just humiliated me before the tank lords.

It was good to think of that, because my body eased itself into the flue without conscious direction and my mind was too full of old anger to freeze me with coming fears.

Going up was initially simpler than worming my way down the tube had been. With the firm fulcrum of Lieutenant Kiley's shoulders beneath me, my legs levered my ribs and shoulder past the point at which they caught on the concrete.

Someone started to shove me farther with his hands.

"No!" I shouted, the distorted echo unintelligible even to me and barely heard in the room below. Someone understood, though, and the hands locked instead into a platform against which my feet could push in the cautious increments which the narrow passage required.

Sliding up the tube, the concrete hurt everywhere it rubbed me. The rush of blood to my head must have dulled the pain when I crawled downward. My right arm had not strength and my legs, as the knees cramped themselves within the flue, could no longer thrust with any strength.

For a moment, the touch of the tank lord's lifted hands left my soles. I was wedged too tightly to slip back, but I could no more have climbed higher in the flue than I could have shattered the concrete that trapped me. Above, partly blocked by my loosely-waving arm, was a dim circle of the sky.

Hands gripped my feet and shoved upward with a firm, inexorable pressure that was now my only chance of success. Lord Curran, standing on his leader's shoulders, lifted me until my hand reached the outer lip. With a burst of hysterical strength, I dragged the rest of my body free.

It took me almost a minute to put my trousers on. The time was not wasted. If I had tried to jump down to the wall without resting, my muscles would have let me tumble all the way into the courtyard—probably with enough noise to bring an immediate storm of gunfire from the Baron's soldiers.

The light within the gatehouse must have been visible as glimmers through the same cracks in the shutters which the tank lords used to desperately survey their position. That meant the Baron's men would be even more alert . . . but also, that their attention would be focused even more firmly on the second-floor windows— rather than on the wall adjacent to the gatehouse.

No one shot at me as I crawled backwards from the roof, pressing myself against the concrete and then stone hard enough to scrape skin that had not been touched by the flue.

The key to the tank hatches was in my mouth, the only place from which I could not lose it—while I lived.

My knees and elbows were bloody from the flue already, but the open sky was a relief as I wormed my way across the top of the wall. The moments I had been stuck in a concrete tube more strait than a coffin convinced me that there were worse deaths than a bullet.

Or even than by torture, unless the Baron decided to bury me alive.

I paused on my belly where the wall mated with the corner of the West Wing. I knew there were gunmen waiting at the windows a few meters away. They could not see me, but they might well hear the thump of my feet on the courtyard's compacted surface.

There was no better place to descend. Climbing up to the roofs of the palace would only delay my danger, while the greater danger rushed forward on the air cushion vehicles of the Lightning Division.

Taking a deep breath, I rolled over the rim of the wall. I dangled a moment before my strained arms let me fall

the remaining two meters earlier than I had intended
to. The sound my feet, then fingertips, made on the
ground were not loud even to my fearful senses. There
was no response from the windows above me—and no
shots from the East Wing or the banquet hall, from which
I was an easy target for any soldier who chanced to stare
at the shadowed corner in which I poised.

I was six meters from the nearest tank—Lord Curran's
tank, the tank from which Sergeant Grant had surveyed
the women's apartments. Crawling was pointless—the
gunmen were above me. I considered sprinting, but the
sudden movement would have tripped the peripheral
vision of eyes turned toward the gatehouse.

I strolled out of the corner, so frightened that I could
not be sure my joints would not spill me to the ground
because they had become rubbery.

One step, two steps, three steps, four—

"Hey!" someone shouted behind me, and seven
powerguns raked the women's apartments with cyan
lightning.

Because I was now so close to the tank, only soldiers
in the West Wing could see me. The covering fire sent
them ducking while glass shattered, fabrics burned, and
flakes spalled away from the face of the stone itself. I
heard screams from within, and not all of the throats
were female.

A dozen or more automatic rifles—the soldiers elsewhere in the palace—opened fire on the gatehouse with
a sound like wasps in a steel drum. I jumped to the bow
slope of the tank, trusting my bare feet to grip the metal
without delay for the steps set into the iridium.

A bolt from the powergun struck the turret a centimeter from where my hand slapped it. I screamed with
dazzled surprise at the glowing dimple in the metal and
the droplets that spattered my bare skin.

Only the tank lords' first volley had been aimed. When
they ducked away from the inevitable return fire, they

continued to shoot with only their gun muzzles lifted above the protecting stone. The bolts which scattered across the courtyard at random did a good job of frightening the Barn's men away from accurate shooting, but that randomness had almost killed me.

As it was, the shock of being fired at by a friend made me drop the hatch key. The circular field-induction chip clicked twice on its way to disappear in the dark courtyard.

The hatch opened. The key had bounced the first time on the cover.

I went through the opening head first, too frightened by the shots to swing my feet over the coaming in normal fashion. At least one soldier saw what was happening, because his bullets raked the air around my legs for the moment they waved. His tracers were green sparks; and when I fell safely within, more bullets disintegrated against the dense armor around me.

The seat, though folded, gashed my forehead with a corner and came near enough to stunning me with pain that I screamed in panic when I saw there was no commo screen where the lieutenant had said it would be. The saffron glow of instruments was cold mockery.

I spun. The main screen was behind me, just where it should have been, and the small common screen—reading 3—was beside it. I had turned around when I tumbled through the hatch.

My finger stabbed at the keypad, hit 1 and 2 together. A slash replaced the 3—and then 1, as I got control of my hand again and touched the correct key. Electronics whirred softly in the belly of the great tank.

The West Wing slid up the main screen as I palmed the control. There was a 1 in the corner of the main screen also.

My world was the whole universe in the hush of my mind. I pressed the firing pedal as my hand rotated the turret counterclockwise.

The tribarrel's mechanism whined as it cycled and the bolts thumped, expanding the air on their way to their target; but when the blue-green flickers of released energy struck stone, the night and the facade of the women's apartments shattered. Stones the size of a man's head were blasted from the wall, striking my tank and the other palace buildings with the violence of the impacts.

My tank.

I touched the selector toggle. The numeral 2 shone orange in the upper corner of the screen which the lofty mass of the banquet hall slid to fill.

"Kid!" shouted speakers somewhere in the tank with me. *"Kid!"*

My bare toes rocked the firing pedal forward and the world burst away from the axis of the main gun.

The turret hatch was open because I didn't know how to close it. The tribarrel whipped the air of the courtyard, spinning hot vortices smoky from fires the guns had set and poisoned by ozone and gases from the cartridge matrices.

The 20 cm main gun sucked all the lesser whorls along the path of its bolt, then exploded them in a cataclysm that lifted the end of the banquet hall ten meters before dropping it back as rubble.

My screen blacked out the discharge, but even the multiple reflections that flashed through the turret hatch were blinding. There was a gout of burning stone. Torque had shattered the arched concrete roof when it lifted, but many of the reinforcing rods still held so that slabs danced together as they tumbled inward.

Riflemen had continued to fire while the tribarrel raked toward them. The 20 cm bolt silenced everything but its own echoes. Servants would have broken down the outside doors minutes before. The surviving soldiers followed them now, throwing away weapons unless they forgot them in their hands.

The screen to my left was a panorama through the

vision blocks while the orange pips on the main screen provided the targeting array. Men, tank lords in khaki, jumped aboard the other tanks. Two of them ran toward me in the vehicle farthest from the gatehouse.

Only the west gable of the banquet hall had collapsed. The powergun had no penetration, so the roof panel of the palace's outer side had been damaged only by stresses transmitted by the panel that took the bolt. Even on the courtyard side, the reinforced concrete still held its shape five meters from where the bolt struck, though fractured and askew.

The tiny figure of the Baron was running toward me from the entrance.

I couldn't see him on the main screen because it was centered on the guns' point of impact. I shouted in surprise, frightened back into slavery by that man even when shrunken to a doll in a panorama.

My left hand dialed the main screen down and across so that the center of the Baron's broad chest was ringed with sighting pips. He raised his mob gun as he ran, and his mouth bellowed a curse or a challenge.

The Baron was not afraid of me or anything else. But he had been *born* to the options that power gives.

My foot stroked the firing pedal.

One of the mercenaries who had just leaped to the tank's back deck gave a shout as the world became ozone and a cyan flash. Part of the servant's quarters beneath the banquet hall caught fire around the three-meter cavity blasted by the gun.

The Baron's disembodied right leg thrashed once on the ground. Other than that, he had vanished from the vision blocks.

Lieutenant Kiley came through the hatch, feet first but otherwise with as little ceremony as I had shown. He shoved me hard against the turret wall while he rocked the gun switch down to safe. The orange numeral blanked from the screen.

"In the *Lord's* name, kid!" the big officer demanded while his left hand still pressed me back. "Who told you to do *that?*"

"Lieutenant," said Lord Curran, leaning over the hatch opening but continuing to scan the courtyard. His pistol was in his hand, muzzle lifted, while air trembled away from the hot metal. "We'd best get a move on unless you figure t' fight a reinforced battalion alone till the supports get here."

"Well, get in and *drive*, curse you!" the lieutenant shouted. The words relaxed his body and he released me. "*No*, I don't want to wait around here alone for the Lightning Division!"

"Lieutenant," said the driver, unaffected by his superior's anger, "we're down a man. You ride your blower. Kid'll be all right alone with me till we join up with the colonel and come back t' kick ass."

Lieutenant Kiley's face became very still. "Yeah, get in and drive," he said mildly, gripping the hatch coaming to lift himself out without bothering to use the power seat.

The driver vanished but his boots scuffed on the armor as he scurried for his own hatch. "Gimme your bloody key," he shouted back.

Instead of replying at once, the lieutenant looked down at me. "Sorry I got a little shook, kid," he said. "You did pretty good for a new recruit." Then he muscled himself up and out into the night.

The drive fans of other tanks were already roaring when ours began to whine up to speed. The great vehicle shifted greasily around me, then began to turn slowly on its axis. Fourth in line, we maneuvered through the courtyard gate while the draft from our fans lifted flames out of the palace windows.

We are the tank lords.

Appendix

Supertanks

Tanks were born in the muck and wire of World War One. Less than sixty years later, there were many who believed the technology had made the behemoths as obsolete as horse cavalry. Individual Infantrymen of 1970 carried missiles whose warheads burned through the armor of any tank. Slightly larger missiles ranged kilometers to blast with pinpoint accuracy vehicles costing a thousand times as much. Similar weaponry was mounted on helicopters which skimmed battlefields in the nape of the earth, protected by terrain irregularities. At the last instant the birds could pop up to rip tanks with their missiles. The future of armored vehicles looked bleak and brief.

Technology had dragged the tank to the brink of abandonment. Not surprisingly, it was technology again which brought the panzers back. The primary breakthrough was the development of portable fusion power plants. Just as the gasoline engine with its high horsepower-to-weight ratio had been necessary before the first tanks could take the field, so the fusion unit's almost limitless output was

required to move the mass which made the new
supertanks viable. Fusion units were bulky and moder-
ately heavy themselves, but loads could be increased on
a fusion-powered chassis with almost no degradation of
performance. Armor became thick—and thicker. With the
whole galaxy available as a source of ores, iridium replaced the less effective steels and ceramics without
regard for weight.

Armor alone is not adequate protection. Stationary for-
tresses can always be battered down—as the French
learned in 1940, having forgotten the lesson Caesar taught
their ancestors at Alexia two millennia before. Caterpillar
treads have given the first tanks cross-country ability; but
at the cost of slow speed, frequent breakage, and great
vulnerability to attack. Now that power was no longer
a factor, even the armored bulk of a tank could be
mounted on an air cushion.

The air cushion principle is a very simple one. Fans
fill the plenum chamber, a solid-skirted box under a
vehicle, with air under pressure. To escape, the air must
lift the edges of the skirts off the ground—and with the
skirts, the whole vehicle rises. Fans tilt with the velocity and angle of attack of the blades determine the
amount and direction of thrust. The vehicle skims over
surfaces it does not touch.

On tanks and combat cars, the lift was provided by
batteries of fans mounted on the roof of the plenum
chamber. Each fan had its own armored nacelle. Mines
could still do considerable damage; but while a single
broken track block would deadline a tracked vehicle,
a wrecked fan only made a blower a little more sluggish.

Successful protection for the supertanks went beyond
armor and speed. Wire-guided missiles are still faster,
and their sharp-charge warheads can burn holes in any
practical thickness of any conceivable material—if they
are allowed to hit. Reconnaissance satellites, computer

fire control, and powerguns combined to claw missiles out of the air before they were dangerous. The satellites spotted missile launchers usually before they fired and never later than the moment of ignition. Fire control computers, using data from the satellites, locked defensive weaponry on the missiles in microseconds. And a single light-swift tribarrel could hose any missile with enough fire in its seconds of flight to disintegrate it.

Hand-launched, unguided rockets—buzzbombs—were another problem, and in some ways a more dangerous one despite their short range and small bursting charges. Individual infantrymen fired them from such short ranges that not even a computer had time enough to lay a gun on the little rockets. But even here there was an answer—beyond the impossible one of killing every enemy before he came within two hundred meters.

Many armored vehicles were already fitted with a band of anti-personnel directional mines just above the skirts. Radar detonated the mines when an object came within a set distance. Their blast of shrapnel was designed to stop infantry at close quarters. With only slight modification, the system could be adapted against buzzbombs. It was not perfect, since the pellets were far less destructive than powergun bolts, and the mines could not be used in close terrain which would itself set them off. Still, buzzbombs were apt to be ill-aimed in the chaos of battle, and a tank's armor could shrug off all but a direct hit by the small warheads.

So tanks roamed again as lords of battle, gray-gleaming phoenixes on air cushions. Their guns could defeat the thickest armor, their armor could blunt all but the most powerful attacks. They were fast enough to range continents in days, big enough to carry a battery of sensors and weaponry which made them impossible to escape when they hunted. The only real drawback to the supertanks was their price.

A tank's fire control, its precisely metered lift fans,

the huge iridium casting that formed its turret—all were constructs of the highest sophistication. In all the human galaxy there were probably no more than a dozen worlds capable of manufacturing war tools as perfect as the panzers of Hammer's tank companies.

But Hammer paid for the best, man and tank alike; and out of them he forged the cutting edge of a weapon no enemy seemed able to stop.

The Church of the Lord's Universe

Perhaps the most surprising thing about the faith that men took to the stars—and vice versa—was that it appeared to differ so little from the liturgical protestantism of the Nineteenth and Twentieth Centuries. Indeed, services of the Church of the Lord's Universe—almost always, except by Unitarians, corrupted to "Universal Church"—so resembled those of a high-flying Anglican parish of 1920 that a visitor from the past would have been hard put to believe that he was watching a sect as extreme in its own way as the Society for Krishna Consciousness was in its.

The Church of the Lord's Universe was officially launched in 1985 in Minneapolis, Minnesota, by the merger of 230 existing protestant congregations—Methodist, Presbyterian, Episcopalian, and Lutheran. In part the new church was a revolt against the extreme fundamentalism peaking at that time. The Universalists sought converts vigorously from the start. Their liturgy obviously attempted to recapture the traditional beauty of Christianity's greatest age, but there is reason to believe that the extensive use of Latin in the service was part of a design to avoid giving doctrinal offense as well. Anyone who has attended both Presbyterian and Methodist services has felt uneasiness at the line, "Forgive us our debts/trespasses . . . " St. Jerome's Latin version of the Lord's Prayer flows smoothly and unnoticed from the tongue of one raised in either sect.

But the Church of the Lord's Universe had a mission beyond the entertainment of its congregations for an hour every Sunday. The priests and laity alike preached the salvation of Mankind through His works. To Universalists, however, the means and the end were both secular. The Church taught that Man must reach the stars and there, among infinite expanses, find room to live in peace. This temporal paradise was one which could be grasped by all men. It did not detract from spiritual hopes; but heaven is in the hands of the Lord, while the stars were not beyond Man's own strivings.

The Doctrine of Salvation through the Stars—it was never labeled so bluntly in Universalist writings, but the peevish epithet bestowed by a Baptist theologian was not inaccurate—gave the Church of the Lord's Universe a dynamism unknown to the Christian center since the days of Archbishop Laud. It was a naive doctrine, of course. Neither the stars nor anything else brought peace to Man; but realists did not bring men to the stars, either, while the hopeful romantics of the Universal Church certainly helped.

The Universalist credo was expressed most clearly in the BOOK OF THE WAY, a slim volume commissioned at the First Consensus and adopted after numerous emendations by the Tenth. The BOOK OF THE WAY never officially replaced the Bible, but the committee of laymen which framed it struck a chord in the hearts of all Universalists. Despite its heavily Eastern leanings (including suggestions of reincarnation), the BOOK spoke in an idiom ineligible and profoundly moving to men and women who in another milieu would have been Technocrats.

While the new faith appealed to men and women everywhere, it by no means appealed to every man and woman. By their uncompromising refusal to abandon future dreams to cope with present disasters—the famines, pollution, and pogroms of every day—the Universalists faced frequent hatred. During the Food Riots of 2039, three hundred Universalists were ceremonially murdered and eaten in a packed amphitheater in Dakkah, and there were other martyrs as well. But the survivors and their faith drove on. Their ranks swelled every time catastrophe proved Man was incapable of solving his problems on Earth alone.

Thus, when Man did reach the stars, the ships were crewed in large measure by Universalists. Those who had prayed for, worked for, and even sworn by the Way of the Stars, *Via Stellarum*, were certain to be among the first treading it. On Earth, the Church of the Lord's Universe had been a vocal minority; in the colonies spreading like a bacterial culture through the galaxy, Universalists were frequently in the majority.

There were changes. Inevitably, fragmentation followed success as centuries and the high cost of interstellar communication made each congregation a separate entity. But the basic thrust of the Church, present peace and safety for Mankind, remained even when reality diluted it to lip service or less. Mercenaries were recruited mostly from rural cultures which were used to privation—and steeped in religion as well. Occasionally a trooper might feel uneasy as he swore, "Via!" for the Way had been a way of peace.

But mercs swore by blood and the martyrs as well; and few had better knowledge of either blood or innocent victims than the gunmen of the mercenary companies.

Powerguns

By the 21st Century, missile-firing small arms appeared to have reached the pinnacle of their development, and there was nothing on hand to replace them. The mass and velocity of projectiles could be juggled but they could not be increased in sum without a corresponding increase in recoil or backblast. Explosive bullets were very destructive on impact, but they had no penetration beyond the immediate blast radius. An explosive bullet might vaporize a leaf it hit near the muzzle as easily as the intended target down-range, and using explosives in heavy brush was worse than useless because it endangered the shooter.

Lasers, though they had air-defense applications, were not the infantryman's answer either. The problem with lasers was the power source. Guns store energy in the powder charge. A machinegun with one cartridge—once—as it is with a thousand round belt, so the ammunition load can be tailored to circumstances. Man-killing lasers required a four hundred-kilo fusion unit to drive them. Hooking a laser on line with any less bulky energy source was of zero military effectiveness rather than lesser effectiveness.

Science lent Death a hand in this impasse—as Science has always done, since the day the first wedge became the first knife. Thirty thousand residents of St. Pierre, Martinique, had been killed on May 8, 1902. The agent of their destruction was a "burning cloud" released during an eruption of Mt. Pelee. Popular myth had attributed the deaths to normal volcanic phenomena, hot gases or ash like that which buried Pompeii; but even the most cursory examination of the evidence indicated that direct energy release had done the lethal damage. In 2073, Dr. Marie Weygand, heading a team under contract to Olin-America, managed to duplicate the phenomenon.

The key had come from spectroscopic examination of pre-1902 lavas from Pelee's crater. The older rocks had shown inexplicable gaps among the metallic elements expected there. A year and a half of empirical research followed, guided more by Dr. Weygand's intuition than by the battery of scientific instrumentation her employers had rushed out at the first signs of success. The principle ultimately discovered was of little utility as a general power source—but then, Olin-America had not been looking for a way to heat homes.

Weygand determined that metallic atoms of a fixed magnetic orientation could be converted directly into energy by the proper combination of heat, pressure, and intersecting magnetic fields. Old lava locks its rich metallic burden in a pattern dictated by the magnetic ambiance at the time the flow cools. At Pelee in 1902, the heavy Gauss loads of the new eruption made a chance alignment with the restressed lava of the crater's rim. Matter flashed into energy in a line dictated by the intersection, ripping other atoms free of the basalt matrix and converting them in turn. Below in St. Pierre, humans burned.

When the principle had been discovered, it remained only to refine its destructiveness. Experiments were held with different fuel elements and matrix materials. A copper-cobalt charge in a wafer of microporous polyurethane became the standard, since it appeared to give maximum energy release with the least tendency to scatter. Because the discharge was linear, there was no need of a tube to channel the force as a rifle's barrel does; but some immediate protection from air-induced scatter was necessary for a hand-held weapon. The best barrel material was iridium. Tungsten and osmium were even more refractory, but those elements absorbed a large component of the discharge instead of reflecting it as the iridium did.

To function in service, the new weapons needed to be cooled. Even if a white-hot barrel did not melt, the next charge certainly would vaporize before it could be fired. Liquified gas, generally nitrogen or one of the noble gases which would not themselves erode the metal, was therefore released into the bore after every shot. Multiple barrels, either rotating like those of a Gatling gun or fixed like those of the mitrailleuse, the Gatling's French contemporary, were used to achieve high rates of fire or to fire very high intensity charges. Personal weapons were generally semi-automatic to keep weight and bulk within manageable limits. Submachineguns with large gas reservoirs to fire pistol charges had their uses and advocates, as their bullet-firing predecessors had.

Powerguns—the first usage of the term is as uncertain as that of "gun" itself, though the derivation is obvious—greatly increased the range and destructiveness of the individual soldier. The weapons were so destructive, in fact, that even on most frontier planets their use was limited to homicide. Despite that limited usefulness, factories for the manufacture of powerguns and their ammunition would probably have been early priority items on most worlds—had not that manufacture been utterly beyond the capacity of all but the most highly industrialized planets.

Precision forming of metal as hard as iridium is an incredible task. Gas reservoirs required a nul-conductive sheath if they were not to bleed empty before they even reached the field. If ammunition wafers were rolled out in a fluctuating electronic field, they were as likely to blow out the breech of a weapon or gang-fire in the loading tube as they were to injure a foe. All of the planetary pride in the cosmos would not change laws of physics.

Of course, some human cultures preferred alternate weaponry. The seven world of the Gorgon Cluster equipped their armies—and a number of mercenary units—with flechette guns for instance. Their hypervelocity osmium projectiles had better short-range penetration than 2 cm powerguns, and they cycled at a very high rate. But the barrels of flechette guns were of synthetic diamond, making them at least as difficult to manufacture as the more common energy weapons.

Because of the expense of modern weapons, would be combatants on rural worlds often delayed purchasing guns until fighting was inevitable. Then it became natural to consider buying not only the guns but men who were used to them—for powerguns were no luxury to the mercenaries whose lives and pay depended on their skill with the best possible equipment. The gap between a citizen-soldier holding a powergun he had been issued a week before, and the professional who had trained daily for years with the weapon, was a wide one.

Thus if only one side on a poor world hired mercenaries, its victory was assured—numbers and ideology be damned. That meant, of course, that both sides had to make the investment even if it meant mortgaging the planetary income for a decade. Poverty was preferable to what came with defeat.

All over the galaxy, men with the best gifts of Science and no skills but those of murder looked for patrons who would hire them to bring down civilization. Business was good.

Backdrop to Chaos

The mercenary companies of the late Third Millennium were both a result of and a response to a spurt of empire-building among the new industrial giants of the human galaxy. Earth's first flash of colonization had been explosive. Transit was an expensive proposition for trade or tourism; but on a national scale, a star colony was just as possible as the high-rise Palace of Government which even most of the underdeveloped countries had built for the sake of prestige.

And colonies were definitely a matter of prestige. The major powers had them. So, just as Third World countries had squandered their resources on jet fighters in the Twentieth Century (and on ironclads in the Nineteenth), they bought or leased or even built starships in the Twenty-first. These colonies were almost invariably mono-national, under-capitalized, and stratified by class even more rigidly than were their mother countries. All of those factors affected later galactic history. There was a plethora of suitable words on which to plant colonies, however, so that even the most ineptly-handled groups of settlers generally managed to survive. Theirs was a hand-to-mouth survival of farming and barter, though, not of spaceports shipping vast quantities of minerals and protein back to Earth.

A few of the better-backed colonies did become very successful. Most of them had been spawned by the larger nations, though a few were private ventures (including that of the Dutch consortium which founded Friesland). Success left their backers in the same situation of those whose colonies were barely surviving, however, since the first result of planetary self-sufficiency was invariably to cut ties and find the best prices available for manufactures on the open market.

There is followed a spate of secondary colonization from the successful colony worlds. These new colonies were planted with a specific product in mind: a mineral; a drug; sometimes simply agriculture, freeing more valuable real estate on the homeworlds. Even a planet could be filled in a few centuries by the asymotic population growth which empty spaces seem to engender in human beings. Secondary colonies were frequently joint efforts, combining settlers and capital from several worlds. They were a business proposition, after all, not matters of national honor.

Unfortunately for the concept, the newly-mixed national and racial groups got along just as badly as their ancestors had a few centuries earlier on Earth. The planetary governments of Hiroseke and Stewart, for instance, conferred placidly with each other, but in the iridium-mining colony they had founded together on Kalan, Japanese and Scotsmen were shooting at each other within five years.

The new colonizers had thought they would be able to control their colonies without military force. Their own experience had taught them to control space transport to the new colonies. Without the ability to sell its produce in markets of its own choice, a colony could not strike off on its own—as the homeworlds had themselves done.

But a colony could be forced into a pattern of logical subservience only if its populace were willing to be logical. If instead the settlers decided to eat their own guts out through internal warfare, the colony would become as commercially valueless as Germany in 1648. Inevitably, homeworlds attempted through military force to control and unify their colonies; also inevitably, they increased the disruption by their activities.

And even if some sort of a military solution *was* imposed, there remained the question of how to deal with the defeated troublemakers—however they were defined—to avoid a new outbreak of fighting. Ideally, they could be used as expendables in battles elsewhere. It was a course which had been followed with success often in the past—Germans in French Indo-China in 1948, and Scots borderers in Ulster in 1605, for two examples. The course required that there be other battles to fight—but there were other unruly colonies as well as backwater worlds whose produce would be useful if it could be controlled at acceptable cost. Perhaps the first case of this occurred in 2414 when Monument equipped four thousand Sikh rebels from Ramadan and shipped them to Portales to take over that planet's tobacco trade, but there were many other examples later.

And in any case, there was always someone willing to hire soldiers, somewhere. World after world armored its misfits and sent them off to someone else's backyard, to attack or defend, to kill or die—so long as they were not doing it at home. Because of the pattern of colonization, there were only a few planets that were not so tense that they might snap into bloody war if mercenaries from across the galaxy were available.

Even for the stable elite of worlds, Friesland and Kronstad, Ssu-ma and Wylie, the system was a losing proposition. Wars and the warriors they spawned were short-term solutions, binding the industrial worlds into a fabric of short-term solutions. In the long run, off-world markets were destroyed, internal investment was channeled into what were basically non-productive uses, and the civil populace became restive in the omnipresence of violence and a foreign policy directed toward its continuance.

On rural worlds, the result was nothing so subtle as decay. It was life and society shattered forever by the sledge of war.

The Bonding Authority

Wars result when one side either misjudges its chances or wishes to commit suicide; and not even Masade *began* as a suicide attempt. In general, both warring parties expect to win. In the event, they are wrong more than half the time.

Employing mercenaries adds new levels of uncertainty to the already risky business of war. Too often in history a mercenary force has disappeared a moment before the battle; switched sides for a well-timed bribe; or even conquered its employer and brought about the very disasters it was hired to prevent.

Mercenaries, for their part, face the chances common to every soldier of being killed by the enemy. In addition, however, they must reckon with the possibility of being bilked of their pay or massacred to avoid its payment; of being used as cannon fodder by an employer whose distaste for "money-grubbing aliens" may exceed the enemy's; or of being abandoned far from home when defeat or political change erases their employer or his good will. As Xenophon and the Ten Thousand learned, in such circumstances the road home may be long—or as short as a shallow grave.

A solution to both sets of special problems was made possible by the complexity of galactic commerce. The recorded beginnings came early in the Twenty-seventh

Century when several planets caught up in the Confederation Wars used the Terra firm of Felchow und Sohn as an escrow agent for their mercenary's pay. Felchow was a commercial banking house which had retained its preeminence even after Terran industry had been in some measure supplanted by that of newer worlds. Neither Felchow nor Terra herself had any personal stake in the chaotic rise and fall of the Barnard Confederation; thus the house was the perfect neutral to hold the pay of the condottieri being hired by all parties. Payment was scrupulously made to mercenaries who performed according to their contracts. This included the survivors of the Dalhousie debacle who were able to buy passage off that ravaged world, despite the fact that less than ten percent of the populace which had hired them was still alive. Conversely, the pay of Wrangel's Legion, which had refused to assault the Confederation drop zone on Montauk, was forfeited to the Montauk government. The Third Armistice intervened and Wrangel's troops were hunted across the face of the planet by both sides, too faithless to use and too dangerous to ignore.

Felchow und Sohn had performed to the satisfaction of all honest parties when first used as an intermediary. Over the next three decades the house was similarly involved in other conflicts, a passive escrow agent and paymaster. It was only after the Ariete Incident of 2662 that the concept coalesced into the one stable feature of a galaxy at war.

The Ariete, a division recruited mostly from among the militias of the Aldoni System, was hired by the rebels on Paley. Their pay was banked with Felchow, since the rebels very reasonably doubted that anyone would take on the well-trained troops of the Republic of Paley if they had already been handed the carrot. But the Ariete fought very well indeed, losing an estimated thirty percent of its effective before surrendering in the final collapse of the rebellion. The combat losses have to best estimated because the Republican forces, in defiance of the "Laws of War" and their own promises before the surrender, butchered all their fifteen or so thousand mercenary prisoners.

Felchow und Sohn, seeing an excuse for an action which would raise it to incredible power, reduced Paley to Stone Age savagery.

An industrialized world (as Paley was) is an interlocking whole. Off-planet trade may amount to no more than five percent of its GNP; but when that trade is suddenly cut off, the remainder of the economy resembles a car lacking two pistons. It may make whirring sounds for a time, but it isn't going anywhere.

Huge as Felchow was, a single banking house could not have cut Paley off from the rest of the galaxy. When Felchow, however, offered other commercial banks membership in a cartel and a share of the lucrative escrow business, the others joined gladly and without exception. No one would underwrite cargoes to or from Paley; and Paley, already wracked by a war and its aftermath, shuddered down into the slag heap of history.

Lucrative was indeed a mild word for the mercenary business. The escrowed money itself could be put to work, and the escrowing bank was an obvious agent for the other commercial transactions needed to run a war. Mercenaries replaced equipment, recruited men, and shipped themselves by the thousands across the galaxy. The new banking cartel served those needs smoothly— and maximized its own profits.

With the banks' new power came a new organization. The expanded escrow operations were made the responsibility of a Bonding Authority, still based in Bremen but managed independently of the cartel itself. The Authority's fees were high. In return, its Contracts Department was expert in preventing expensive misunderstandings from arising, and its investigative staff could neither be bribed nor deluded by a violator. Under the Authority's ruthless nurture, the business of war became as regular as any other commercial endeavor, and more profitable than most.

Table of Organization and Equipment, Hammer's Regiment

Sec I: Headquarters battalion

Except for Artillery and Replacement, all the support elements were grouped for administrative convenience in HQ Battalion. In practice, a large percentage of the strength of these units was parceled out to line companies according to need.

a) Headquarters Company—Colonel Hammer and his personal staff, including battalion officers; satellite launch and maintenance personnel; finance; and a security element. Total: 153 effectives.

b) Maintenance—Capable of handling anything short of full hull rebuilds and internal work on fusion units. Company included three tank and six combat car transporters, stretched-chassis vehicles with fans at either end; ACVs cannot, of course, be towed. Total: 212 effectives.

c) Communications—Included not only the staff of Command Central, but the staffs of local headquarters with area responsibilities. Total: 143 effectives.

d) Medical—Twenty-four first line medics with medicomps linked to Central, and a field hospital with full-life support capability. Total: 60 effectives.

e) Supply—Included Mess and Quartermaster functions. Total: 143 effectives.

f) Intelligence—Order of Battle was performed mostly by computer. Imagery Interpretation, study of satellite recce, was in large measure still a human function. There were three mechanical interrogation (i.e., mind probe) teams. Total: 84 effectives.

g) Transport—312 men (heavily supplemented from Replacement Battalion) and 288 air cushion trucks for local unit supply from spaceport or planetary logistics centers. True aircraft, flying above the nape of the earth, would have been suicidally vulnerable to powerguns.

h) Combat Engineers—Carried out bridging, clearing, mine-sweeping, and very frequently fighting tasks. Formed in three 16-man platoons, each mounted on a pair of tank-chassis Engineer Vehicles. Total: 50 effectives.

I) Recreation—Field brothels. The strength and composition of this unit varied from world to world. Generally, teams of 3-6 were put under the direct control of company supply personnel.

Sec II: Combat Cars

Eight combat car companies, each of a command section (one car) and four line platoons. Each platoon contained a command car and five combat cars, or six combat cars. Company total: 100 effectives.

Sec III: Tanks

Four tank companies, each of a command tank and four line platoons. Each line platoon contained four tanks. Company total: 36 effectives.

Sec IV: Infantry

Four companies, each of four platoons. Each platoon contained four 10-man line squads; two 2-man tribarrel teams (jeep-mounted); one 2-man 100 mm mortar team (jeep-mounted); and a command element. All but Heavy Weapons were on 1-man skimmers. Buzzbombs could be issued for special purposes; but in general, support from the armored vehicles allowed the Slammers' infantry to travel lighter than most pongoes. Company total: 202 effectives.

Sec V: Artillery

Three batteries of self-propelled 200 mm rocket howitzers. Each battery contained six tubes; one command car; and two munitions haulers. Battery total: 37 effectives.

Sec VI: Replacement

The training and reserve component of the Slammers, normally totaling 1500 men (including cadre) with about ten tanks, twenty-five combat cars, and a hundred trucks. because Hammer had no permanent base world, training had to be performed wherever the Regiment was located. Because men were more vulnerable than the armored vehicles they rode, and the vehicles were too valuable to run undercrewed or held out of service while replacements were trained, a pool of trained men had to be on hand to fill gaps immediately. Until they were needed in combat slots, they acted as extra drivers, loading crews, camp police, and firebase security.

Note: as personal weapons line infantry were issued 2 cm shoulder powerguns and grenades. Vehicle and Heavy Weapons crewmen carried 1 cm pistols (unless they had picked up shoulder arms on their own). Officers carried pistols or 1 cm submachineguns as they desired.

Afterword: We Happy Few

We few, we happy few, we band of brothers,
For he today that sheds his blood with me
Shall be my brother; be he ne'er so vile,
This day shall gentle his condition.
And gentlemen in England now abed
Shall think themselves accursed they were not
  here,
And hold their manhoods cheap whiles any
  speaks
That fought with us upon Saint Crispin's day.
                              —Shakespeare

I wouldn't have—and couldn't have—written these stories without being a Nam vet. Because of that and because I'm sometimes accused of believing things that I certainly don't believe, I've decided to state clearly what I think about Viet-Nam and about war in general. I don't insist that I'm right, but this is where I stand.

The speech Shakespeare creates for Henry V to deliver on the morning of Agincourt (the Speech on St. Crispin's Day) is one of his most moving and effective. The degree to which the sentiments therein are true in any absolute sense, though—that's another matter.

My own suspicion is that most soldiers (and maybe the real Henry among them, a soldier to the core) would have agreed with the opinion put in the mouth of the Earl of Warwick earlier in the scene. Warwick, noting the odds were six to one against them, wishes that a few of the men having a holiday in England were here with the army in France. One of the leader's jobs is to encourage his troops, though. If Henry'd had a good enough speechwriter, he might have said exactly what Shakespeare claims he did.

A soldier in a combat unit may see the world, but he or she isn't likely to "meet exotic people" in the sense implied by the recruiting posters. (Mind you, one's fellow soldiers may turn out to be exotic people, and one may turn into a regrettably exotic person oneself.) I travelled through a fair chunk of Viet-Nam and a corner of Cambodia. My only contact with the locals as people came on a couple MedCAPs in which a platoon with the company medics and the Civil Affairs Officer entered a village to provide minor medical help and gather intelligence.

My other contacts involved riding an armored vehicle past silent locals; searching a village whose inhabitants had fled (for good reason; the village was a staging post for the North Vietnamese just over the Cambodian border, and we burned it that afternoon); the Coke girls, hooch maids and boom-boom girls who were really a part of the U.S. involvement, not of Viet-Nam itself.

And of course there's also the chance that some unseen Vietnamese or Cambodian was downrange when I was shooting out into the darkness. That doesn't count as meeting people either.

I was in an armored unit: the 11th Armored Cavalry, the Blackhorse Regiment. Infantrymen probably saw more of the real local people, but not a lot more. The tens of thousands of U.S. personnel working out of air-conditioned buildings in Saigon, Long Binh, and other centers saw merely a large-scale version of the Coke girls, hooch maids and boom-boom girls whom combat units met. The relative handful of advisors and Special Forces were the only American citizens actually living among the Vietnamese as opposed to being geographically within Viet-Nam.

I very much doubt that things were significantly different for soldiers fighting foreign wars at any other period of history. Sensible civilians need strong economic motives to get close to groups of heavily-armed foreigners, and the needs of troops in a war zone tend to be more basic than a desire to imbibe foreign culture.

Soldiers aren't any more apt to like all their fellows than members of any other interest group are. In school you were friends with some of your classmates, had no particular feelings about most of the rest, and strongly disliked one or two. The same is true of units, even quite small units, in a war zone. The stress of possible external attack makes it harder, not easier, to get along with the people with whom you're isolated.

And isolated is the key word. We changed base frequently in the field. One day we shifted an unusually long distance, over fifty miles. The tank I was riding on was part of a group that got separated from the remainder of the squadron. We had three tanks, four armored personnel carriers modified into fighting vehicles (ACAVs), an APC with added headroom and radios (a command track), and a light recovery vehicle that we called a cherrypicker though it had just a crane, not a bucket. We ran out of daylight.

By this point three ACAVs and the command track had broken down and were being towed. The remaining ACAV and one of the tanks were going to blow their engines at any moment. All the *vehicles* were badly overloaded with additional weapons and armor, and the need to pack all the squadron's gear for the move had exacerbated an already bad situation.

We shut down, trying by radio to raise the new base camp which *had* to be somewhere nearby. The night was pitch dark, a darkness that you can't imagine unless you've seen rural areas in a poor part of the Third World. We were hot, tired, and dizzy from of twelve hours' hammering by tracked vehicles with half of the torsion bars in their suspensions broken.

And we were very much alone. So far as I could tell, nobody in the group would have described himself as happy, but we were certainly a few. Personally, I felt like a chunk of raw meat in shark waters.

The squadron commander's helicopter lifted from the new base, located our flares, and guided us in. No enemy contact, no harm done. But I'll never forget the way I felt that night, and the incident can stand as an unusually striking example of what the whole tour felt like: I was alone and an alien in an environment that might at any instant explode in violence against me.

Don't mistake what I'm saying: the environment and particularly the people of Viet-Nam and Cambodia were in much greater danger from our violence than we were from theirs. I saw plenty of examples of that, and I was a part of some of them. I'm just telling you what it felt like at the time.

So Shakespeare was right about "few" and wrong about "happy." The jury (in my head) is still out about folks who missed the war counting their manhoods cheap.

I'd like to think people had better sense than that. The one thing that ought to be obvious to a civilian is that war zones are an experience to avoid. Nonetheless, I know a couple men who've moaned that they missed "Nam," the great test of manhood of our generation. They're idiots if they believe that, and twits if they were just mouthing words that had become the in thing for their social circles.

I haven't tested my manhood by having my leg amputated without anesthetic; I don't feel less of a man for lack of the experience. And believe me, I don't feel more of a man for anything I saw or did in Southeast Asia.

The people I served with in 1970 (the enlisted men) were almost entirely draftees. At that time nobody I knew in-country:

- thought the war could be won;
- thought our government was even trying to win;
- thought the brutal, corrupt Saigon government was worth saving;
- thought our presence was doing the least bit of good to anybody, particularly ourselves.

But you know, I'm still proud of my unit and the men I served with. They weren't exactly my brothers, but they were the folks who were alone with me. Given the remarkably high percentage of those eligible who've joined the association of war-service Blackhorse veterans, my feelings are normal for the 11th Cav.

Nobody who missed the Viet-Nam War should regret the fact. It was a waste of blood and time and treasure. It did no good of which I'm aware, and did a great deal of evil of which I'm far too aware. But having said that . . .

I rode with the Blackhorse.

Dave Drake
Chatham County, NC